Teaching Science Fiction

Teaching the New English
Published in association with the English Subject Centre
Director: Ben Knights

Teaching the New English is an innovative series concerned with the teaching of the English degree in universities in the UK and elsewhere. The series addresses new and developing areas of the curriculum as well as more traditional areas that are reforming in new contexts. Although the series is grounded in intellectual and theoretical concepts of the curriculum, it is concerned with the practicalities of classroom teaching. The volumes will be invaluable for new and more experienced teachers alike.

Titles include:

Gail Ashton and Louise Sylvester (*editors*)
TEACHING CHAUCER

Richard Bradford (*editor*)
TEACHING THEORY

Charles Butler (*editor*)
TEACHING CHILDREN'S FICTION

Robert Eaglestone and Barry Langford (*editors*)
TEACHING HOLOCAUST LITERATURE AND FILM

Michael Hanrahan and Deborah L. Madsen (*editors*)
TEACHING, TECHNOLOGY, TEXTUALITY
Approaches to New Media and the New English

David Higgins and Sharon Ruston
TEACHING ROMANTICISM

Andrew Hiscock and Lisa Hopkins (*editors*)
TEACHING SHAKESPEARE AND EARLY MODERN DRAMATISTS

Peter Middleton and Nicky Marsh (*editors*)
TEACHING MODERNIST POETRY

Andrew Maunder and Jennifer Phegley (*editors*)
TEACHING NINETEENTH-CENTURY FICTION

Anna Powell and Andrew Smith (*editors*)
TEACHING THE GOTHIC

Andy Sawyer and Peter Wright (*editors*)
TEACHING SCIENCE FICTION

Gina Wisker (*editor*)
TEACHING AFRICAN AMERICAN WOMEN'S WRITING

Teaching the New English
Series Standing Order ISBN 978-1-4039-4441-2
Hardback 978-1-4039-4442-9 Paperback
(*outside North America only*)

You can receive future titles in this series as they are published by placing a standing order. Please contact your bookseller or, in case of difficulty, write to us at the address below with your name and address, the title of the series and the ISBN quoted above.

Customer Services Department, Macmillan Distribution Ltd, Houndmills, Basingstoke, Hampshire RG21 6XS, England

Teaching Science Fiction

Edited by

Andy Sawyer

and

Peter Wright

Introduction, selection and editorial matter © Andy Sawyer and Peter Wright 2011
Individual chapters © contributors 2011

All rights reserved. No reproduction, copy or transmission of this publication may be made without written permission.

No portion of this publication may be reproduced, copied or transmitted save with written permission or in accordance with the provisions of the Copyright, Designs and Patents Act 1988, or under the terms of any licence permitting limited copying issued by the Copyright Licensing Agency, Saffron House, 6–10 Kirby Street, London EC1N 8TS.

Any person who does any unauthorized act in relation to this publication may be liable to criminal prosecution and civil claims for damages.

The authors have asserted their rights to be identified as the authors of this work in accordance with the Copyright, Designs and Patents Act 1988.

First published 2011 by
PALGRAVE MACMILLAN

Palgrave Macmillan in the UK is an imprint of Macmillan Publishers Limited, registered in England, company number 785998, of Houndmills, Basingstoke, Hampshire RG21 6XS.

Palgrave Macmillan in the US is a division of St Martin's Press LLC, 175 Fifth Avenue, New York, NY 10010.

Palgrave Macmillan is the global academic imprint of the above companies and has companies and representatives throughout the world.

Palgrave® and Macmillan® are registered trademarks in the United States, the United Kingdom, Europe and other countries.

ISBN 978–0–230–22850–4   hardback
ISBN 978–0–230–22851–1   paperback

This book is printed on paper suitable for recycling and made from fully managed and sustained forest sources. Logging, pulping and manufacturing processes are expected to conform to the environmental regulations of the country of origin.

A catalogue record for this book is available from the British Library.

Library of Congress Cataloging-in-Publication Data

Teaching science fiction / edited by Andy Sawyer and Peter Wright.
    p. cm. — (Teaching the new English)
  Includes bibliographical references and index.
  ISBN 978–0–230–22851–1 (pbk.) — ISBN 978–0–230–22850–4 (hdbk.)
 1. Science fiction—Study and teaching.   2. Science fiction, English—Study and teaching.   3. Science fiction, American—Study and teaching.
  I. Sawyer, Andy.   II. Wright, Peter (Peter Ronald)   III. Title. IV. Series.
 PN3433.7.T39 2011
 809.3'8762071—dc22   2011006098

10 9 8 7 6 5 4 3 2 1
20 19 18 17 16 15 14 13 12 11

Printed and bound in Great Britain by
CPI Antony Rowe, Chippenham and Eastbourne

To James E. Gunn, writer, teacher, scholar and inspiration and
To the memory of Thomas D. Clareson, who lit the way.

Contents

List of Tables ix
Series Preface x
Acknowledgements xii
Notes on Contributors xiii
A Chronology of Significant Works xvii

Introduction 1
Andy Sawyer and Peter Wright

1. Through Time and Space: A Brief History of Science Fiction 21
Paul Kincaid
2. Theorizing Science Fiction: The Question of Terminology 38
Gary K. Wolfe
3. Utopia, Anti-Utopia and Science Fiction 55
Chris Ferns
4. Teaching the Scientific Romance 72
Adam Roberts
5. Teaching Pulp Science Fiction 86
Gary Westfahl
6. Good SF: Teaching the Golden Age as Cultural History 102
Lisa Yaszek
7. Teaching the New Wave 116
Rob Latham
8. Postmodernism, Postmodernity and the Postmodern: Telling Local Stories at the End of Time 129
Andrew M. Butler
9. Teaching Gender and Science Fiction 146
Brian Attebery
10. Teaching Postcolonial Science Fiction 162
Uppinder Mehan
11. Teaching Latin American Science Fiction and Fantasy in English: A Case Study 179
M. Elizabeth Ginway

| 12 | Teaching Science and Science Fiction: A Case Study
Mark Brake and Neil Hook | 202 |
| 13 | Design, Delivery and Evaluation
Andy Sawyer and Peter Wright | 219 |

References, Resources and Further Reading   247

Index   256

List of Tables

12.1 Award structure and cognate strands 210
13.1 Proposal for a 12-week semester sf course 224
13.2 Contrasting 'mainstream' and science fiction 234

Series Preface

One of many exciting achievements of the early years of the English Subject Centre was the agreement with Palgrave Macmillan to initiate the series 'Teaching the New English'. The intention of the then Director, Professor Philip Martin, was to create a series of short and accessible books which would take widely-taught curriculum fields (or, as in the case of learning technologies, approaches to the whole curriculum) and articulate the connections between scholarly knowledge and the demands of teaching.

Since its inception, 'English' has been committed to what we know by the portmanteau phrase 'learning and teaching'. Yet, by and large, university teachers of English – in Britain at all events – find it hard to make their tacit pedagogic knowledge conscious, or to raise it to a level where it might be critiqued, shared or developed. In the experience of the English Subject Centre, colleagues find it relatively easy to talk about curriculum and resources, but far harder to talk about the success or failure of seminars, how to vary forms of assessment, or to make imaginative use of virtual learning environments. Too often this reticence means falling back on received assumptions about student learning, about teaching, or about forms of assessment. At the same time, colleagues are often suspicious of the insights and methods arising from generic educational research. The challenge for the English group of disciplines is therefore to articulate ways in which our own subject knowledge and ways of talking might themselves refresh debates about pedagogy. The implicit invitation of this series is to take fields of knowledge and survey them through a pedagogic lens. Research and scholarship, and teaching and learning are part of the same process, not two separate domains.

'Teachers', people used to say, 'are born not made'. There may, after all, be some tenuous truth in this: there may be generosities of spirit (or, alternatively, drives for didactic control) laid down in earliest childhood. But why should we assume that even 'born' teachers (or novelists, or nurses, or veterinary surgeons) do not need to learn the skills of their trade? Amateurishness about teaching has far more to do with university claims to status than with evidence about how people learn. There is a craft to shaping and promoting learning. This series of books is dedicated to the development of the craft of teaching within English Studies.

Ben Knights
Teaching the New English *Series Editor*
Director, English Subject Centre
Higher Education Academy

The English Subject Centre

Founded in 2000, the English Subject Centre (which is based at Royal Holloway University of London) is part of the subject network of the Higher Education Academy. Its purpose is to develop learning and teaching across the English disciplines in UK Higher Education. To this end it engages in research and publication (web and print), hosts events and conferences, sponsors projects, and engages in day-to-day dialogue with its subject communities.
http://www.english.heacademy.ac.uk

Acknowledgements

We would like to thank Professor Ben Knights and Jane Gawthrope at the English Subject Centre for their encouragement and support of this project. We would also like to thank Paula Kennedy, Steven Hall and Benjamin Doyle at Palgrave Macmillan for their commitment to *Teaching Science Fiction*. Our thanks also go to our contributors for their enthusiasm and professionalism in shaping this book. Finally, we would like to thank Mary Sawyer and Jenni Woodward for their patience and support.

Notes on Contributors

Brian Attebery, editor of the *Journal of the Fantastic in the Arts*, is the author of *Decoding Gender in Science Fiction* (2002) and co-editor with Ursula K. Le Guin of *The Norton Book of Science Fiction* (1998). His award-winning book *Strategies of Fantasy* (1992) has recently come back into print from Indiana University Press. He is both Professor of English and Instructor in Cello at Idaho State University, which is located somewhere between Western Civilization and the Mythic West. His current projects include a study of family stories as a genre, forthcoming in *Children's Literature*, and an examination of fantasy's ways of confronting traditional religious narratives.

Mark Brake is an author, broadcaster and professor in the communication of science, who has engaged the public with science on five continents. The UK's first chair in science communication, he has been professor in the subject at the University of Glamorgan since 2002. He is a Fellow of the Institute of Physics and Director of the Science Communication Research Unit at the University of Glamorgan. He was a founding member of the NASA Astrobiology Institute science communication group between 2003 and 2006, and is perhaps best known for his work in popularizing the relationship between space, science and culture, much of which he has done with his good friend and colleague, Neil Hook.

Andrew M. Butler is the author of *Pocket Essentials* on Philip K. Dick (2007), Cyberpunk (2000), Terry Pratchett (2001), Film Studies (2005) and (with Bob Ford) Postmodernism (2003). With Mark Bould, Adam Roberts and Sherryl Vint he is the co-editor of *The Routledge Companion to Science Fiction* (2009) and *Fifty Key Figures in Science Fiction* (2009). His article for *Science Fiction Studies*, 'Thirteen Ways of Looking at the British Boom' (2003), won the Pioneer Award. He is an editor of *Extrapolation* and is currently working on *Solar Flares: A Cultural History of Science Fiction in the 1970s*.

Chris Ferns is a Professor of English at Mount Saint Vincent University in Halifax, Nova Scotia. He is the author of *Narrating Utopia: Ideology, Gender, Form in Utopian Literature* (1999) and *Aldous Huxley: Novelist* (1980) as well as numerous articles on utopian literature and the historical novel.

M. Elizabeth Ginway is Associate Professor of Portuguese in the Department of Spanish and Portuguese at the University of Florida, where she teaches Portuguese language and Brazilian literature and culture. Her 2004 *Brazilian Science Fiction: Cultural Myths and Nationhood in the Land of the Future* was placed on the 'Recommended Reading List for Non-Fiction' by *Locus: Magazine of the Science Fiction and Fantasy World* in 2005, and was also nominated for MLA Katherine Singer Kovacs Prize by Bucknell University Press. In July 2005 she travelled to Brazil to launch the book in Portuguese translation. She organized and hosted the symposium 'Latin America Writes Back: Science Fiction in the Global Era' at the University of Florida in October 2005. Her other research interests include nineteenth and twentieth-century Brazilian literature. She is currently working on organizing a collection of critical essays on Latin American SF with J. Andrew Brown of Washington University, St Louis.

Neil Hook is a priest, scholar and author who divides his time between his parochial duties and his work as a senior lecturer in science communication at the University of Glamorgan. A member of the university's pioneering Science Communication Research Unit his particular field of interest is in the use of science fiction as a tool for science communication.

Paul Kincaid is a winner of the Thomas Clareson Award and is the author of the Hugo nominated book *What It Is We Do When We Read Science Fiction* (2008). He is a former administrator of the Arthur C. Clarke Award and is currently on the jury for the John W. Campbell Memorial Award. He reviews for a wide range of journals and has contributed to numerous books on science fiction.

Rob Latham is Associate Professor of English at the University of California, Riverside. A co-editor of *Science Fiction Studies* since 1997, he is the author of *Consuming Youth: Vampires, Cyborgs, and the Culture of Consumption* (2002). He is currently working on a book on New Wave science fiction.

Uppinder Mehan teaches at the University of Houston-Victoria in Victoria, Texas where he also serves as Associate Director of the Society for Critical Exchange. His articles on science fiction and postcolonial literature have appeared in *Foundation, Comparative Literature, American Book Review* and the *Journal of Comparative Literature and Aesthetics* among others. He is the co-editor with Nalo Hopkinson of *So Long Been Dreaming: Postcolonial Science Fiction and Fantasy*. He is currently at work on a book-length introduction to postcolonial science fiction and fantasy.

Adam Roberts is Professor of Nineteenth-Century Literature at Royal Holloway University of London. He has published widely on nineteenth-century topics, and is also the author of *The History of Science Fiction* (2006). His novels (all science fiction) include: *Gradisil* (2006), *Land of the Headless* (2007), *Swiftly* (2008) and *Yellow Blue Tibia* (2009).

Andy Sawyer is librarian of the Science Fiction Foundation Collection at the University of Liverpool Library, Course Director of the MA in Science Fiction Studies offered by the School of English, and a widely-published critic and reviewer. Recent essays include work on Gwyneth Jones, Terry Pratchett, Ramsey Campbell, Christopher Priest and Ursula K. Le Guin. He is Reviews Editor of *Foundation: The International Review of Science Fiction*. He recently co-edited (with David Ketterer) *Plan for Chaos*, a previously-unpublished novel by John Wyndham. He is the 2008 recipient of the Science Fiction Research Association's Clareson Award for services to science fiction.

Gary Westfahl, who teaches at the University of California, Riverside, is the author, editor, or co-editor of twenty-two books on science fiction and fantasy, including the Hugo Award-nominated *Science Fiction Quotations: From the Inner Mind to the Outer Limits* (2005) and *The Greenwood Encyclopedia of Science Fiction and Fantasy* (2005). He has also published over three hundred articles and reviews in various journals, magazines, scholarly anthologies, reference works and on websites. His contributions to other media include two radio interviews, appearances on the nationally televised documentaries *New Visions of the Future: Prophecies III* (1996) and *Visions from the Edge: The Art of Science Fiction* (2005), and voiceover commentary for the DVD release of the film *Jerome Bixby's The Man from Earth* (2007). In 2003, he received the Science Fiction Research Association's Pilgrim Award for lifetime contributions to science fiction and fantasy scholarship.

Gary K. Wolfe, Professor of Humanities and English at Roosevelt University and contributing editor and lead reviewer for *Locus: The Magazine of the Science Fiction and Fantasy Field*, is the author of critical studies *The Known and the Unknown: The Iconography of Science Fiction* (1979), *David Lindsay* (2007), *Critical Terms for Science Fiction and Fantasy* (1986) and *Harlan Ellison: The Edge of Forever* (with Ellen R. Weil) (2002). His most recent book, *Soundings: Reviews 1992–1996* (2005), received the British Science Fiction Association Award for best nonfiction, and was nominated for a Hugo Award by the World Science Fiction Convention. Wolfe has received the Eaton Award, the Pilgrim Award from the Science Fiction Research Association, the Distinguished Scholarship Award from the International Association for the Fantastic in the Arts and, in 2007, a World Fantasy Award for criticism. A collection of essays, *Evaporating Genres: Essays on Fantastic Literature*, is forthcoming.

Peter Wright is Reader in Speculative Fictions at Edge Hill University in the North West of England. He is author of *Attending Daedalus: Gene Wolfe, Artifice and the Reader* (2003). He has written numerous articles and has contributed to Blackwell's *A Companion to Science Fiction* (2005), *The Routledge Companion to Science Fiction* (2009) and *Fifty Key Figures in Science Fiction* (2009). In 2005, he co-edited *British Science Fiction Television* with John Cook. His *Shadows of the New Sun: Wolfe on Writing/Writers on Wolfe* (2007) was a finalist for the Locus Award for non-fiction in 2008. He is currently working on *When Worlds Collide: The Critical Companion to Science Fiction Film Adaptations* and a collection of essays on the *Star Wars* 'Expanded Universe'.

Lisa Yaszek is Associate Professor in the School of Literature, Communication and Culture at the Georgia Institute of Technology, where she also curates the Bud Foote Science Fiction Collection. Her research interests include science fiction, gender studies, technoscience studies and cultural history. She was the 2005 recipient of the Pioneer Award for Outstanding Science Fiction Scholarship and is current President of the Science Fiction Research Association. Yaszek's essays on science, society, and science fiction appear in diverse journals including *Extrapolation*, *NWSA Journal*, *Socialism & Democracy*, *electronic book review*, and *Rethinking History*. Her most recent book is *Galactic Suburbia: Recovering Women's Science Fiction* (2008).

A Chronology of Significant Works

Events are in bold type. All given dates for novels indicate first publication in book form unless otherwise stated.

1516	Thomas More, *Utopia*
1543	**Copernicus publishes his theory that the Earth revolves around the Sun**
1609	**Galileo builds telescope**
1634	Kepler, *Somnium*
1668	Margaret Cavendish, *The Blazing World*
1640	John Wilkins, Bishop of Chester, *The Discovery of a New World* (3rd edn) in which he speculates about travel to the moon
1667	Milton, after Giordano Bruno, speculates about life on other worlds (*Paradise Lost, Book VIII*, 140–78)
1726	Jonathan Swift, *Travels into Several Remote Nations of the World... by Lemuel Gulliver* (aka *Gulliver's Travels*) published
1752	Voltaire, *Micromegas* in which an alien from a planet orbiting Sirius visits Earth
1763	Anon., *The Reign of George VI* (the earliest future-war story)
1818	Mary Shelley, *Frankenstein*
1826	Mary Shelley, *The Last Man* (rev. 1831)
1827	Jane C. Louden, *The Mummy! A Tale of the Twenty-Second Century*
1831	Mary Shelley, revised edition of *Frankenstein*
1859	**Charles Darwin and Alfred Russel Wallace propose the theory of evolution by natural selection**
1864	Jules Verne, *Journey to the Centre of the Earth*
1865	**Gregor Mendel's laws of inheritance, which form the basis of the science of genetics**

1865	Jules Verne *From the Earth to the Moon*
1869	**Dmitri Mendeleev formulates the first widely used periodic table**
	Jules Verne, *Twenty Thousand Leagues Under the Sea*
1871	George Chesney, *The Battle of Dorking* in *Blackwood's Magazine*
	Edward Bulwer-Lytton, *The Coming Race*
1873	**James Clerk Maxwell's theory of electromagnetism**
1888	Edward Bellamy, *Looking Backward*
1889	Mark Twain, *A Connecticut Yankee at King Arthur's Court*
1890	William Morris, *News from Nowhere*
1893	Camille Flammarion, *La Fin du Monde*
1895	**Wilhelm Conrad Roentgen discovers x-rays**
	H.G. Wells, *The Time Machine*
1896	**Henri Becquerel discovers radioactivity**
	H.G. Wells, *The Island of Doctor Moreau*
1897	**J. J. Thompson discovers the electron in cathode rays**
	H.G. Wells, *The Invisible Man*
1898	H.G. Wells, *The War of the Worlds*
1899–1902	**Boer War**
1899	H.G. Wells, *The Sleeper Wakes*
1900	**Max Planck publishes his quantum theory**
1901	M.P. Shiel, *The Purple Cloud*
	H.G. Wells, *The First Men in the Moon*
1903	**The Wright brothers first heavier than air flight**
1905	**Albert Einstein's special theory of relativity**
	Edwin Lester Arnold, *Lt. Gulliver Jones: His Vacation*
	Rudyard Kipling, 'With the Night Mail'
1907	Jack London, *The Iron Heel*
1908	H.G. Wells, *The War in the Air*
1909	E.M. Forster, 'The Machine Stops'
1911	April 1911–March 1912: Hugo Gernsback, *Ralph 124C 41+* serialized in *Modern Electrics*
1912	Feb–July: Edgar Rice Burroughs's 'Under the Moons of Mars' serialized in *All-Story*

A Chronology of Significant Works xix

	Arthur Conan Doyle, *The Lost World* Rudyard Kipling, 'As Easy as A.B.C.'
1913	Niels Bohr's model of the atom
1914–18	First World War
1915	Albert Einstein publishes the general theory of relativity Karl Schwarzchild identifies the 'Schwarzchild radius' which leads to the discovery of black holes
1917	Russian Revolution Edgar Rice Burroughs, *A Princess of Mars* (originally published as 'Under the Moons of Mars' [1912]. See above)
1920	Karel Capek, *R.U.R.* David Lindsay, *Voyage to Arcturus*
1922	Edgar Rice Burroughs, *At the Earth's Core*
1923	J.J. Connington, *Nordenholt's Million* H.G. Wells, *Men Like Gods*
1924	Yevgeny Zemyatin, *We*
1925	Erwin Schrödinger formulates Schrödinger's equation (quantum mechanics) Hugo Gernsback, *Ralph 124C 41+*
1926	Hugo Gernsback founds *Amazing Stories* Fritz Lang (dir.), *Metropolis*
1927	Werner Heisenberg's Uncertainty Principle (quantum mechanics) Georges Lemaître's theory of the Big Bang First public demonstration of television Sidney Fowler Wright, *Deluge*
1928	E.E. 'Doc' Smith, *The Skylark of Space*
1929	Edwin Hubble's law of the expanding universe Stock market crash
1930	Olaf Stapledon, *The Last and First Men*
1932	Aldous Huxley, *Brave New World*
1933	Roosevelt's New Deal Edwin Balmer and Philip Wylie, *When Worlds Collide* C.L. Moore, *Shambleau* H.G. Wells, *The Shape of Things to Come*

xx A Chronology of Significant Works

1934	E.E. 'Doc' Smith, *Triplanetary* Jack Williamson, *The Legion of Space*
1935	Olaf Stapledon, *Odd John*
1936	Karel Capek, *War with the Newts*
1937	Murray Constantine (Kathryn Burdekin), *Swastika Night* John W. Campbell Jr. assumes editorship of *Astounding Science Fiction* Olaf Stapledon, *Star Maker*
1938	C.S. Lewis, *Out of the Silent Planet*
1939–45	**Second World War**
1940	Olaf Stapledon, *Sirius*
1942	A.E. Van Vogt, 'The Weapon Shop'
1943	**Oswald Avery establishes that DNA is the genetic component of the chromosome** C.S. Lewis, *Perelandra*
1944	C.L. Moore, 'No Woman Born' Clifford Simak, *City*
1945	**US drops the atomic bombs on Hiroshima and Nagasaki** C.S. Lewis, *That Hideous Strength*
1946	**First meeting of UN General Assembly** A.E. Van Vogt, *Slan*
1947	Robert Heinlein, *Rocketship Galileo*
1948	John W. Campbell Jr, *Who Goes There?* (coll.) Judith Merril, 'That Only a Mother'
1949	**Soviets test their first atom bomb** George Orwell, *Nineteen Eighty-Four* George R. Stewart, *Earth Abides*
1950–53	**Korean War**
1950	Isaac Asimov, *I, Robot* (coll.) Ray Bradbury, *The Martian Chronicles* (coll.) Judith Merril, *Shadow on the Hearth*
1951	Isaac Asimov, *Foundation* Alfred Bester, *The Demolished Man* John Wyndham, *The Day of the Triffids*

A Chronology of Significant Works xxi

1952	Isaac Asimov, *Foundation and Empire* Judith Merril, *Beyond Human Ken* (anth.) Kurt Vonnegut Jr, *Player Piano* Bernard Wolfe, *Limbo*
1953	**John Watson and Francis Crick discover the double helical structure of DNA** Isaac Asimov, *Second Foundation* Ray Bradbury, *Fahrenheit 451* Arthur C. Clarke, *Childhood's End* Ward Moore, *Bring the Jubilee* Frederick Pohl and C.M. Kornbluth, *The Space Merchants* John Wyndham, *The Kraken Wakes*
1954	**First kidney transplant** Isaac Asimov, *The Caves of Steel* Hal Clement, *Mission of Gravity* Richard Matheson, *I Am Legend*
1955	Leigh Brackett, *The Long Tomorrow* Jack Finney, *The Body Snatchers* John Wyndham, *The Chrysalids*
1956	**First transatlantic telephone cable** Isaac Asimov, *The Naked Sun* Alfred Bester, *The Stars My Destination* John Christopher, *The Death of Grass* Arthur C. Clarke, *The City and the Stars*
1957	**The first satellite, Sputnik, is launched by the Soviet Union; start of the Space Age** Fred Hoyle, *The Black Cloud* Fritz Leiber, *The Big Time* Nevil Shute, *On the Beach*
1959	William Burroughs, *The Naked Lunch* Robert Henlein, *Starship Troopers* Walter Miller Jr, *A Canticle for Leibowitz* Mordecai Roshwald, *Level 7* Kurt Vonnegut Jr, *The Sirens of Titan*
1960	Kingsley Amis, *New Maps of Hell* Theodore Sturgeon, *Venus Plus X*
1961	Robert Heinlein, *Stranger in a Strange Land* Zenna Henderson, *Pilgrimage: The Book of the People* Stanislaw Lem, *Solaris*

xxii A Chronology of Significant Works

1962	Cuban Missile Crisis J.G. Ballard, *The Drowned World* Anthony Burgess, *A Clockwork Orange* Philip K. Dick, *The Man in the High Castle* Naomi Mitchison, *Memoirs of a Spacewoman* H. Beam Piper, *Little Fuzzy*
1963	Kurt Vonnegut Jr, *Cat's Cradle*
1964	China explodes first atom bomb International Business Machines (IBM) introduces the 360 computer J.G. Ballard, *The Drought* Philip K. Dick, *Martian Time-Slip* Michael Moorcock assumes editorship of *New Worlds*
1965–73	Vietnam War
1965	Philip K. Dick, *The Three Stigmata of Palmer Eldritch* Thomas Disch, *The Genocides* Frank Herbert, *Dune*
1966	J.G. Ballard, *The Crystal World* Samuel R. Delany, *Babel-17* Robert Heinlein, *The Moon is a Harsh Mistress* Daniel Keyes, *Flowers for Algernon*
1967	Jocelyn Bell Burnell and Anthony Hewish discover the first pulsar First heart transplant performed by Christiaan Barnard Samuel Delany, *The Einstein Intersection* Harlan Ellison (ed.), *Dangerous Visions* Roger Zelazny, *Lord of Light* Pamela Zoline, 'The Heat Death of the Universe'
1968	John Brunner, *Stand on Zanzibar* Samuel R. Delany, *Nova* Philip K. Dick, *Do Androids Dream of Electric Sheep?* Keith Roberts, *Pavane* Joanna Russ, *Picnic on Paradise* Stanley Kubrick (dir.), *2001: A Space Odyssey*
1969	Apollo 11 launched; Neil Armstrong is the first man on the Moon Prototype Concorde makes its maiden flight (it enters commercial service in 1975)

A Chronology of Significant Works xxiii

	John Brunner, *The Jagged Orbit* Michael Moorcock, *Behold the Man* Ursula K. Le Guin, *The Left Hand of Darkness* Norman Spinrad, *Bug Jack Barron* Kurt Vonnegt Jr, *Slaughterhouse Five*
1970	Poul Anderson, *Tau Zero* Larry Niven, *Ringworld*
1971	Ursula K. Le Guin, *The Lathe of Heaven*
1972	John Brunner, *The Sheep Look Up* Harlan Ellison, *Again, Dangerous Visions* (anth.) Christopher Priest, *Fugue for a Darkening Island* Norman Spinrad, *The Iron Dream* Gene Wolfe, *The Fifth Head of Cerberus: Three Novellas*
1973	Arthur C. Clarke, *Rendezous with Rama* Thomas Pynchon, *Gravity's Rainbow*
1974	**India explodes nuclear device** Suzy McKee Charnas, *Walk to the End of the World* Philip K. Dick, *Flow My Tears, the Policeman Said* Thomas Disch, *334* Joe Haldeman, *The Forever War* Ursula K. Le Guin, *The Dispossessed* Christopher Priest, *Inverted World*
1975	John Crowley, *The Deep* Samuel Delany, *Dhalgren* Ursula K. Le Guin, *The Wind's Twelve Quarters* (coll.) Joanna Russ, *The Female Man*
1976	Marge Piercy, *Woman on the Edge of Time* Christopher Priest, *The Space Machine: A Scientific Romance* Kate Wilhelm, *Where Late the Sweet Birds Sang*
1977	Philip K. Dick, *A Scanner Darkly*
1978	Suzy McKee Charnas, *Motherlines* C.J. Cherryh, *The Faded Sun: Kesrith* Sally Miller Gearhart, *The Wanderground: Tales of the Hill Women* Vonda MacIntyre, *Dreamsnake* James Tiptree Jr (Alice Sheldon), *Up the Walls of the World* Chelsea Quinn Yarbro, *False Dawn*

xxiv A Chronology of Significant Works

1979	**Three Mile Island nuclear accident** Zoë Ann Fairbairns, *Benefits* Doris Lessing, *Shikasta*
1980	Gregory Benford, *Timescape* Doris Lessing, *The Marriages Between Zones 3, 4, and 5* Joan Vinge, *The Snow Queen* Gene Wolfe, *The Shadow of the Torturer*
1981	Philip K. Dick, *VALIS* Russell Hoban, *Ridley Walker* Nancy Kress, *Beggars in Spain* Doris Lessing, *The Sirian Experiments* (1981) Gene Wolfe, *The Claw of the Conciliator*
1982	C.J. Cherryh, *Downbelow Station* Doris Lessing, *The Making of the Representative for Planet 8*
1983	Mary Gentle, *Golden Witchbreed* Doris Lessing, *Documents Relating to the Sentimental Agents in the Volyen Empire*
1984	**AIDS virus reported isolated by French scientists** William Gibson, *Neuromancer* Suzette Haden Elgin, *Native Tongue*
1986	**Chernobyl nuclear disaster** Margaret Atwood, *The Handmaid's Tale* Lois McMaster Bujold, *Shards of Honor* Orson Scott Card, *Ender's Game* Josephine Saxton, *Queen of the States* Pamela Sargent, *The Shore of Women*
1987	Iain M. Banks, *Consider Phlebas* Octavia Butler, *Dawn* Pat Cadigan, *Mindplayers* Storm Constantine, *The Enchantments of Flesh and Spirit* Lucius Shepard, *Life During War Time*
1988	Storm Constantine, *The Bewitchments of Love and Hate* Candas Jane Dorsey, *Machine Sex and Other Stories* Sheri Tepper, *The Gate to Women's Country* Octavia Butler, *Adulthood Rites*
1989	**Fall of the Berlin Wall** Octavia Butler, *Imago*

A Chronology of Significant Works xxv

Storm Constantine, *The Fulfilments of Fate and Desire* (1989)
Dan Simmons, *Hyperion*

1990 Ian M. Banks, *The Player of Games*
William Gibson and Bruce Sterling, *The Difference Engine*
Kim Stanley Robinson, *Pacific Edge*
Dan Simmons, *The Fall of Hyperion*

1991 **The USSR comes formally to an end**
Gwyneth Jones, *White Queen*
Vernor Vinge, *A Fire upon the Deep*

1992 Kim Stanley Robinson, *Red Mars*

1993 Octavia Butler, *Parable of the Sower*
Kim Stanley Robinson, *Green Mars*

1994 Pat Cadigan, *Fools*
John Clute and Peter Nicholls, *The Encyclopedia of Science Fiction*, 2nd edn (non-fiction)
Greg Egan, *Permutation City*
Nicola Griffith, *Slow River*
Gwyneth Jones, *North Wind*
Michael Marshall Smith, *Only Forward*

1995 **Michel Mayor and Didier Queloz observe the first planet orbiting around a main sequence star**
Stephen Baxter, *The Time Ships*
Ken MacLeod, *The Star Fraction*
Kim Stanley Robinson, *Blue Mars*
Tricia Sullivan, *Lethe*

1996 Peter F. Hamilton, *The Reality Dysfunction*
Gwyneth Jones, *Kairos*
Elizabeth Moon, *Remnant Population*
Mary Doria Russell, *The Sparrow*
Michael Marshall Smith, *Spares*

1997 **Mars Pathfinder lands**
Greg Egan, *Diaspora*
Peter F. Hamilton, *The Neutronium Alchemist*
Tricia Sullivan, *Someone to Watch Over Me*

1998	Octavia Butler, *Parable of the Talents*
	Nicola Griffith and Stephen Pagels (eds), *Bending the Landscape: Science Fiction* (anth.)
	Gwyneth Jones, *Phoenix Café*
	Nalo Hopkinson, *Brown Girl in the Ring*
1999	Greg Bear, *Darwin's Radio*
	Peter F. Hamilton, *The Naked God*
	Vernor Vinge, *A Deepness in the Sky*
2000	Nalo Hopkinson, *Midnight Robber*
	China Miéville, *Perdido Street Station*
	Alastair Reynolds, *Revelation Space*
	Sheree R. Thomas (ed.), *Dark Matters: A Century of Speculative Fiction from the African Diaspora*
2001	**The first draft of the human genome is completed**
	Terrorist attacks destroy the World Trade Center (9/11)
	Jon Courtenay Grimwood, *Pashazade: The First Arabesk*
	China Miéville, *The Scar*
2002	Steven Barnes, *Lion's Blood*
	Ted Chiang, *Stories of Your Life, and Others*
	William Gibson, *Pattern Recognition*
	Jon Courtenay Grimwood, *Effendi: The Second Arabesk*
	M. John Harrison, *Light*
	Christopher Priest, *The Separation*
2003	Steven Barnes, *Zulu Heart*
	Jon Courtenay Grimwood, *Felaheen: The Third Arabesk*
	Nalo Hopkinson, *The Salt Roads*
	Audrey Niffenegger, *The Time Traveller's Wife*
	Justina Robson, *Natural History*
	Charles Stross, *Singularity Sky*
2004	Uppinder Mehan and Nalo Hopkinson (eds), *So Long Been Dreaming*
	Margo Lanagan, *Black Juice*
	Ian McDonald, *River of Gods*
	China Miéville, *Iron Council*
	Alastair Reynolds, *Century Rain*
	Kim Stanley Robinson, *Forty Signs of Rain*
2005	Andreas Eschbach, *The Carpet Makers*
	Kazuo Ishiguro, *Never let Me Go*
	Ken Macleod, *Learning the World*

	Geoff Ryman, *Air*
	Tricia Sullivan, *Double Vision*
2006	Jon Courtenay Grimwood, *End of the World Blues*
	M. John Harrison, *Nova Swing*
	Jo Walton, *Farthing*
	Liz Williams, *Darkland*
2007	Brian W. Aldiss, *Harm*
	Michael Chabon, *The Yiddish Policeman's Union*
	William Gibson, *Spook Country*
	Ian McDonald, *Brasyl*
	James and Kathryn Morrow (eds), *The SFWA European Hall of Fame*
2008	Stephen Baxter, *Flood*
	Ian M. Banks, *Matter*
	Cory Doctorow, *Little Brother*
	Neal Stephenson, *Anathem*
	Ann and Jeff Vandermeer (eds), *The New Weird*
2009	Paolo Bacigalupi, *The Windup Girl*
	Gwyneth Jones, *Spirit*
	China Miéville, *The City and the City*
	Cherie Priest, *Boneshaker*
	Geoff Ryman (ed.), *When It Changed*
	Lavie Tidhar (ed.), *Apex Book of World sf*
2010	**Dr Craig Venter and his team develop a living cell controlled by synthetic DNA**
	Alastair Reynolds, *Terminal World*

Introduction
Andy Sawyer and Peter Wright

The continuing contemporary growth in science fiction scholarship, the expansion of undergraduate provision, and the interest shown in the genre at postgraduate level firmly situate sf within the provinces of the 'New English'. It is, arguably, one of the most effective literary genres for challenging the perspectives of a student body which, in Great Britain at least, seems detached from social, political and cultural debate and which sees the status quo as immutable. Its speculative nature, its incessant philosophizing on 'what if?', invites a comparative speculative response; it requires engagement with thought-experiments that confront and often overturn passive acceptance of contemporary conditions; it has the capacity to stimulate, to unsettle, to provoke the reader into an intellectual response. Constantly reinventing itself to react imaginatively to transformations in its cultural and ideological milieu, it remains the most vibrant of the popular genres and affords considerable scholarly pleasure to those involved in its teaching and study.

The acceptance of science fiction as a literature worthy of discussion and analysis was not easily won, and resulted from a number of factors arising within the literature and the academy itself. Like many 'popular' forms, it suffered from its association with mass-market modes of production such as pulp magazines and cheap paperbacks, its use of stereotypical characters, melodramatic plots, and prose that often veered between the colourless and the hyperbolic. Equally, it was the victim of the sort of literary snobbery that refused to find value in anything published under the label of 'popular fiction', or denied the label to anything that was deemed to be of value: 'But this looks good. Well, then, it's not sf!' wrote an exasperated Robert Conquest in the epigraph to one of the early 1960s *Spectrum* anthologies.[1] Whilst some of the criticism sf received was justified, many of sf's faults in the first decades of its existence as a 'named' mode were a result of the fact that, apart from the scientific romances of H.G. Wells, confident models for how to engage with the exhilarating or terrifying future transformed by the technological changes of the late nineteenth and early twentieth centuries were comparatively few. Science fiction was seen by its practitioners and readers alike as a 'new' literature, with the naiveties and clumsiness of novelty but with immense potential before it.

Throughout the late 1930s and the 1940s, science fiction's speculations became less concerned with 'superscience' and sensationalism and more interested in sober considerations of possible futures. Similarly, a hesitant but growing literary sensibility amongst genre writers in the 1940s and 1950s began to displace what Patrick Parrinder terms the 'brash, commercial mode of writing' that characterized American pulp writing of the 1930s.[2] This burgeoning stylistic awareness became more self-conscious with the formal, narrative, linguistic and thematic experimentation of the New Waves in Britain and the United States in the mid-1960s. Writers such as Philip K. Dick, J.G. Ballard, Harlan Ellison and Samuel R. Delany demonstrated the radical potential of the genre through widely different though equally innovative means. Equally, the feminist writers of the 1960s and 1970s, who were eager to exploit science fiction's speculative possibilities to challenge the monolithic structures of patriarchy, helped develop the literariness of the genre. The oppositional politics of writers such as Joanna Russ, James Tiptree Jr (Alice Sheldon) and Suzy McKee Charnas demonstrated more eloquently and more powerfully the genre's potential for radical speculation not only about technology and the future but about the social construction of gender roles and gender identities. In the 1980s, the information-saturated futures of cyberpunk writers William Gibson, Bruce Sterling, Pat Cadigan and Rudy Rucker explored the post-human landscapes of biotechnological interfacing and virtual reality with a style and content that chimed with the concerns of postmodernist and cyborg theory.

Although the brevity of such a summary suggests that the literariness of science fiction has continued in one, smooth progressive line from pulp excess to literary respectability, nothing could be further from the truth. As with most popular genres, 'brash, commercial' writing remains available, most obviously in the plethora of tie-in novels relating to *Star Wars* and *Star Trek* and assorted game-related fiction. Again, generalizations are misleading. Not all tie-in novels are ill-conceived or poorly written; their fans can often be discerning readers and their writers accomplished novelists. Nevertheless, such fiction constitutes a new pulp that can display many of the shortcomings of the old.

Historically, however, science fiction's growing literary self-awareness, observable in refinements of style and in an increased attention to plotting, characterization and psychological depth, all developed within the genre's formal speculative framework, meant that sf began to attract attention from the academic community. In 1953, fan, historian and critic Sam Moskowitz taught possibly the first college sf course at City College of New York. Almost ten years later, when he delivered a largely utopian/anti-utopian-based course at Colgate, Mark Hillegas noted that 'the English department was not wildly enthusiastic; but the Administration was happy because the course attracted publicity in the form of newspaper articles across the country, including *The New York Times* and *The National Review*'.[3] Hillegas was not, however, optimistic for the growth of science fiction studies within the academy.

In his reflections on the development of sf courses in the United States, R.D. Mullen recalls:

> When my own course began in 1969 I received a visit from a reporter that resulted in a full-page gee-whiz story in *The Terre Haute Tribune*, and between 1962 and 1969 there had been similar stories in numerous newspapers in various parts of the country. The fanfare arose first from astonishment that colleges would teach pulp fiction and then from the general acceptance of the argument that a number of works in the literary canon (works included in the reading list for the course) could be classified as science fiction and that much present-day science fiction, even though originally published in pulp-paper magazines, was much more serious than the generality of popular fiction. The courses were seen by reporters and their readers as making a kind of breakthrough, as breeching [sic] the walls of the literary establishment so that worthwhile books different from those students had been restricted to could be studied. In sum, this was progress.[4]

The gradual, sometimes begrudging, recognition that 'a number of works in the literary canon ... could be classified as science fiction' (notably Huxley's *Brave New World* [1932] and Orwell's *Nineteen Eighty-Four* [1949]) and that sf 'was much more serious than the generality of popular fiction' led to a proliferation of university and college courses in the following decade. In contrast to Hillegas's pessimism regarding the viability of science fiction studies, by 1976 there were approximately 2000 courses in the United States alone. As Parrinder points out, this equated to 'at least one course for every major college and university in the country' at that time.[5] A comparable progress was not seen in the more conservative halls of British academia, however. In 1993, the journal *Foundation: The International Review of Science Fiction* conducted a survey of sf courses in British higher education, to report a little over twenty modules. In the last fifteen years, this has changed, however, with many new modules actively recruiting year on year, an MA in Science Fiction Studies at the University of Liverpool and a number of students undertaking sf research at doctoral level.

In America, most of the early sf courses were taught by academic pioneers with an interest in science fiction rather than by science fiction specialists. What they achieved – J.O. Bailey, Thomas D. Clareson, Philip Babcock Gove and Marjorie Hope Nicholson among them – was considerable, and certainly contributed to the consolidation of science fiction studies and the development of a community for and of sf academics. Clareson was undeniably instrumental in this, establishing *Extrapolation*, the first academic journal concerned solely with the analysis of sf and fantastic literature, in 1959. Novelist and instructor James Gunn returned to the University of Kansas in 1970 to teach science fiction courses including regular summer schools on the teaching of science fiction, which are still offered by his Center for Science Fiction Studies. In his account of the period, Gunn notes that 'Frank McConnell [at Northwestern University] taught SF courses to classes enrolling hundreds of students' while he himself 'enrolled as many students as the auditorium would hold'.[6]

The 1970s were the key years in the consolidation of sf studies. The Science Fiction Research Association (SFRA) was founded in 1971 and two further journals appeared immediately thereafter: *Foundation* in 1972 and *Science Fiction Studies* in 1973. Collectively, these journals and major theoretical studies, including Alvin Toffler's *Future Shock* (1970), Robert Scholes's *Structural Fabulation: An Essay on the Fiction of the Future* (1975), Darko Suvin's *Metamorphoses of Science Fiction* (1979) and Gary K. Wolfe's *The Known and the Unknown: The Iconography of Science Fiction* (1979) finally helped overcome the Leavisite-derived prejudice that had dismissed science fiction as a ghetto literature unrewarding for academics and students alike.[7] Also published in 1979, *The Encyclopedia of Science Fiction*, edited by Peter Nichols with John Clute and Brian Stableford, marked a major, consolidated effort to address the genre as a whole, and offered highly informative, if necessarily concise, entries on authors, themes, concepts and periods. A second, massively expanded, revised edition edited by Clute and Nichols appeared in 1993 and quickly became the major reference work for scholars and students. The third edition is likely to be so extensive that it will be available exclusively online.

It is, perhaps, a measure of sf's acceptance by the academy, of its movement from marginalized popular literature to being an integral part of many English literature programmes, that the twenty-first century has seen the publication by scholarly publishers of a number of companions to the genre. Both Blackwell's *Companion to Science Fiction*, edited by David Seed, and the *Cambridge Companion to Science Fiction*, edited by Edward James and Farah Mendlesohn appeared in 2003; and *The Routledge Companion to Science Fiction*, edited by Mark Bould, Andrew Butler, Adam Roberts and Sherryl Vint, was published in 2009. All are excellent resources for students and lecturers. Routledge's *Fifty Key...* series was also expanded to include *Fifty Key Figures in Science Fiction*, edited by Bould, Butler, Roberts and Vint. Liverpool University Press commenced its Science Fiction Texts and Studies Series in 1994; to date, it has published thirty-eight volumes by sf writers and academics including Joanna Russ, Gwyneth Jones and Brian Aldiss. Subject matter has ranged from Charlotte Perkins Gilman to the history of science fiction magazines, from queer science fiction to author studies of Ramsey Campbell, Philip K. Dick, H.P. Lovecraft and Gene Wolfe.[8]

The expansion of academic interest in, and support for, the study of science fiction has produced a fertile intellectual context for developing courses and modules in sf, and there are important reasons for doing so. Primarily, sf has engaged – often self-consciously – with the key social and political movements of the twentieth and twenty-first centuries, producing a multiplicity of science fictions that engage with feminism, postcolonialism, postmodernism, queer theory, the interaction between self and other, and the collapsing distinctions between the virtual and the real and the human and the synthetic. Where it has avoided direct engagement with such matters, it has often exaggerated the relationships defining the status quo by accepting them as unalterable. In either instance, it is open to contestation through, and analysis using, the major critical theories available to undergraduates and postgraduates. Indeed, its very amenability to such theoretical approaches, whether through conscious dramatization of their oppositional politics or through a conservative preservation of the status quo in varied fictional futures, allows the lecturer or instructor to deploy critical theory in an applied and invigorating context.

Clearly, the research and pedagogic potential of the genre is considerable. In addition to its usefulness for engaging with the major critical and cultural theories common to humanities teaching, science fiction facilitates close textual analysis (particularly through the work of the New Wave writers and cyberpunks), historical and cultural approaches, linguistics (Peter Stockwell's *The Poetics of Science Fiction* [2000] is an invaluable source text), single author studies (science fiction has its lauded writers, including H.G. Wells, Philip K. Dick, Ursula K. Le Guin, Gene Wolfe, but many remain largely ignored or overlooked), textual and intertextual considerations, and the problematizing of genre theory. Students who take pleasure in science fiction's speculative qualities, its engendering of a sense of wonder or estrangement, its exploitation of language's rich possibilities and inherent tensions, can be introduced to theoretical concepts and reading protocols specific to the genre which will enhance both their learning experiences and their understanding of literature's diverse potential.

Given the contemporary context, the question central to teaching science fiction is not *whether* to teach sf but *what kind of sf to teach*? Science fiction can be considered the story of the twentieth century or, more accurately (and more rewardingly for the student and scholar), *a* story of the twentieth century, a story composed of many stories – a mega-text.[9] John Clute's concept of 'First SF' is proving useful for understanding how these narratives, somewhere between 1926 and the present, began to coalesce into one overarching metanarrative and eventually to collapse.[10] Graham Sleight's essay, 'Last and First SF' in *Polder: A Festschrift for John Clute and Judith Clute* (2006) defines this metanarrative, beyond the technical effects and imagery of the fiction identified by editor Hugo Gernsback in the first issue of *Amazing Stories* (April 1926), as a new kind of literature. As Gernsback puts it in his editorial for *Amazing*: 'the Jules Verne, H.G. Wells and Edgar Allan Poe type of story – a charming romance intermingled with scientific fact and prophetic vision'.[11] First 'SF was a *promise*', Sleight argues. 'The promise was that, some distance off, there was a place called the future, and that SF was both a map for how to get to it and a manual for how to get by once you arrived there.'[12] Gernsback encouraged his readers to engage with the future his magazine celebrated, to revel in the paradox of 'Extravagant Fiction Today – Cold Fact Tomorrow' and to invest emotionally in the way the scientists and inventors of his time were creating a world of wonders. Whether First SF was an identifiable 'promise', or an optical illusion caused by the fact that a fandom enthused by this apparent agenda came together through the niche-marketing examples of Gernsback's magazines, is perhaps the first of our challenges. Either way, it is a useful concept.

Clute's First SF is certainly the story of the twentieth century. With it, we could integrate all those movements and sub-movements that immediately formed it and that reacted against it: the last-gasp achievement of Wells-like 'logical fantasy' from the former pulp-writer John Wyndham; the 'speculative fiction' of the British and American New Waves; the kick-start of the feminist utopias/dystopias by writers such as Le Guin and Russ who had been publishing in, but paying attention to movements outside, the American magazines; the cyberpunks; and the steady but regular use of science fiction tropes by writers such as P.D. James, Doris Lessing, Gore Vidal, Philip Roth, Margaret Atwood, Jeanette Winterson and Kazuo Ishiguro. Clute, however, suggests that the launch of the first Russian sputnik satellite in 1957 – the first step into making *real* the speculations of so many sf writers, which also undermined the sense, encouraged by the sf magazines, that space was an *American* domain – was a crucial turning point. This was the moment when 'the quasi-organic conversation of American SF – for the moment considered as First SF – began to ramble, and to lose the thread of the story; began to give off a sense that for all those years since 1926 it had been *telling the wrong story*'.[13] The 'promise' that the twentieth century would segue into the future envisioned by the First SF mega-text was one that could not be delivered by history. The recognition of this fact provides an important historical perspective on science fiction which can, and possibly should, inform curricula design, particularly when courses are structured historically or thematically.

Sf, though, is more than the twentieth century storied. In his *History of Science Fiction* (2007) Adam Roberts suggests that sf draws upon the sensibilities of the Western Enlightenment and its crystallization of a particularly secular concept of change and futurity, engineered by science and technological developments.[14] Darko Suvin, whose suggestion that sf is the literature of cognitive estrangement was one of the most influential developments of critical thinking in the 1970s, also enabled scholars of sf to consider how the discussion of the modes could move beyond the squabble about 'priority' favouring either the American magazines of the early to mid-twentieth century, or the British scientific romance mode of the late nineteenth century, to explore the ways in which different cultures or time periods experience these effects.[15] In other words, while the mode we know as 'science fiction' has become the natural way (for the Western Anglo-American culture of the twentieth to twenty-first centuries) of dramatizing contemporary hopes and fears centred around change, this may only be a local case of a much more general phenomenon. Here, we may stand accused of attempting to expand the empire of science fiction. However, the recognition that many cultures will respond to technological or social changes, or to new theories about the universe, by speculating about their effects allows us, say, to take a much more nuanced approach to Greek legends involving the marvels of the inventor Daedalus or the god Hephaestus, or the moon voyages of Lucian's *True History*, than either calling them anticipations of Isaac Asimov or Arthur C. Clarke or ignoring them altogether as responses to technology and the physical universe.

Over the last decade or so, scholars have begun to explore the different 'voices' of science fiction in Europe, Latin America and the Asian and African diasporas, and to realize that what these voices are asking us to do is to question our assumptions of Otherness and Futurity, and ask ourselves what happens when these ideas are expressed by those who were the *subjects* of earlier explorations of Otherness in science fiction. We might also consider, as M. Elizabeth Ginway does in Chapter 11, how sf may be increasingly a cultural 'given' which may be adapted to local circumstances. The idea of dramatizing a problem in the 'real world' in the guise of a science fiction B-movie assumes a sophisticated response in film-maker and audience (and film-makers and audience in the diegesis of the film by Jorge Furtado she describes) to what a pulp sf scenario is and what it does. Both *Basic Sanitation: The Movie* (Jorge Furtado, 2007) and the film-within-a-film which is its subject assume a knowledge of science fiction as a cultural form which can be consumed and, what is more important, appropriated outside the Anglo-Saxon milieu with which it is so often associated.

Although Clute notes that we no longer see the future shaped through American sf, he seems to suggest that our position in a world 'shaped by the futures that the sf story *had failed to notice*'[16] is still illuminated by examining our fantasies about it:

> the literatures of the fantastic do model how the world works ... they do address how reality is addressed by us, at this cusp moment for the human species, and for the world we increasingly own ... Even the crappiest SF novel or story has embedded within it the absolutely terrifying knowledge that what we see – through the augmented eyes we now habitually wear in the 21st century ... is what we have ourselves made. Our gaze upon the world is all that counts now. The world is what we make it.[17]

What Clute seems to mean by this is complex, but includes the sense that the theory and practice of sf as shaped by its progenitors in the Gernsback/Campbell magazines ignored many of the possible futures which could have arisen from their present. It is not the naive criticism that science fiction writers 'got the future wrong' by failing to predict our world, but the more nuanced understanding that many sf writers were more influenced by the fictional futures conceived by their predecessors than by the context in which they were living and *its* implications for the future.

As Farah Mendlesohn explains in her editorial to *Foundation 100*, which collected contemporary sf stories rather than the usual critical essays and reviews, the anthology was compiled in response to John Clute's 'argument that First SF was dead: that no one now wrote in the belief that the future they depicted was both possible from where we stand now, and desirable'.[18] For many of the 'default futures' of twentieth century sf, it is increasingly obvious that we can't get there from here.[19] Another point Mendlesohn makes is that these 'default futures' are utterly monochrome; as she sarcastically puts it, 'too much modern SF is clearly descended from a past in which genocide had wiped out most of the non-white population because they were so clearly *not* the futures of the places that so many of us live in'.[20] The challenge for writers of modern science fiction, therefore, is to engage in speculation without falling into the trap of simply imitating established models. For tutors, the challenge is to ensure that historically and thematically structured courses in particular acknowledge the dynamic between the history (or rather, the multiple and often competing 'histories' of sf) and the practice of those who draw upon its techniques and traditions to represent the world in which they live.

Sf, however, offers further challenges. It confronts our conception of modes of reading, for example. The idea of sf as a *vehicle* for ideas suggests that the medium is less important than the message. Sf's ambiguous relationship with what we may consider to be 'the real' is both underlined and undermined by its origins as a form which hybridizes (among others) the popular adventure story, the literary utopia, the naive sense of wonder, and the speculative essay. Its development as a *symbolic* literature which uses 'realistic' techniques to manipulate our readings of time and space, and as a literature in which paratextual contexts such as the means of literary production and the extra-literary discussions surround it, are important to understanding it. The Western print culture of the nineteenth and twentieth centuries is not automatically destined to survive. If it does not, a science fiction response will crystallize in other ways. If it does, the way sf manipulates language may be among its most interesting achievements.[21] By use of neologism and sentences such as 'The door dilated' (doors, in our world, do not usually 'dilate'), science fiction draws our attention to what Suvin calls the *novum* – the 'new thing'[22] – which tells us that we are estranged from the world of mundane fiction and invites us to consider the nature of this estrangement. In science fiction, metaphor becomes, for the purpose of the story, reality: sf *literalizes the metaphor*. Our feeling that the world we live in is in some way 'unreal' or 'inauthentic' is transposed by Philip K. Dick in *Time out of Joint* (1959) into a story in which the world *really is* unreal. The dismissive comment by the male narrator of James Tiptree Jr's story 'The Women Men Don't See' (1973) – 'Mrs Ruth Parsons isn't even living in the same world with me' – is ironized by the author when she reveals that 'Mrs Ruth Parsons' really does not *want* to live in the same world as the narrator, or any other man, and would rather take her chances with a couple of random 'cultural-exchange students' who are *real* aliens. Two sentences after his comment, the narrator, Fenton, uses the word 'alienation'. But it takes the science fiction element of the story to underline just how much this word is a thoroughly accurate description of what Parsons feels.

Sf is celebrated for its neologistic innovation; some of its neologisms, such as 'robot' or 'cyberspace', have entered the language. The word 'robot', for example (from Karel Capek's play, R.U.R. ['Rossum's Universal Robots'], first performed in Prague in 1921), entered the English language in 1923. Almost immediately (the OED cites *The Times* of 9 June and the *Westminster Gazette* of 22 June) it became metaphoric shorthand for the relationship between people and society. It also became one of the icons of science fiction, capable of representing Otherness in numerous contexts from industrial alienation to anxieties about artificial intelligence.

Sf also confronts our ideas of 'canon' and 'the academy'. Mendlesohn's introduction to the *Cambridge Companion to Science Fiction* argues that 'Science fiction is less a genre...than an ongoing discussion.'[23] This discussion is held, as are many such conversations, in the pages of literary journals and monographs. However, the debate also exists in fanzines, at conventions and (increasingly) on the internet through interest groups, e-lists, blogs and so on. Who is holding this conversation? Obviously academics and critics are major voices, but to a greater extent than almost any other literary group, writers, other professionals and fans contribute to the discourse. Until the 1970s, for example, virtually all the serious analysis and bibliographical work was conducted by fans and collectors. As we have noted, the beginnings of American sf – the mode that gave the form its name and shaped its generic tone – were in magazines, and apart from a few mavericks – C.S. Lewis, J.O. Bailey (whose *Pilgrims Through Time and Space* [1947] was possibly the earliest book about sf), Kingsley Amis (whose *New Maps of Hell* [1961] was the first major British assessment of sf), and others – little academic attention was initially given to the field (although British scholarship has always been kinder to that branch of SF that stems clearly from the tradition of H.G. Wells).

Perhaps because of fan-based scholarship, *knowledge* of the field has always been important, and the construction of a 'canon' has been based upon different criteria from those used by formal literary scholars. What does this mean in practice? First, that it is impossible to develop a theory of appreciation of sf upon 'representative' texts. It *may* (the italics are deliberate) be possible to pass oneself off as knowledgeable about Elizabethan/Jacobean literature by considering the plays of Marlowe, Shakespeare or Jonson, rather than those of Dekker, Chettle or Heyward. No serious sf scholar, though, would, or should, admit to an ignorance of Isaac Asimov or Robert A. Heinlein, even though by many literary criteria (and by many of the extra-literary criteria sf fans bring to their reading) Ursula K. Le Guin or John Crowley are better writers. This is why it is possible to consider *Ralph 124C 41+* (first published in book form in 1925 but serialized in 1911–12) by Hugo Gernsback as 'the one essential text for all studies of science fiction'.[24] (Although it is also necessary to take into account Brian Aldiss's comments on Gernsback – 'one of the worst disasters ever to hit the science fiction field' – in *Trillion Year Spree*[25] and the reactions by Aldiss, Stableford and others to the essays in *Foundation* 47 and 48 that later became part of Westfahl's extended study of Gernsback, *The Mechanics of Wonder* [1999]).[26]

Indeed, our very ideas of who reads and writes science fiction need to be examined in the context of this debate. Students may frequently present essays in which the predominantly *masculine* nature of science fiction is stated, sometimes citing authority, but at other times simply assuming that this is something which is obvious. And it is indeed obvious, but it is a stereotype, and stereotypes need examining, because they are often true. It is the nature of that truth – and why other people perceive that 'truth' – which is interesting. Recent scholarship by, for example, Justine Larbalestier, Helen Merrick, Lisa Yaszek and Batya Weinbaum, editor of *Fem-Spec*, not only argues for the existence of women in the sf world but *how* they exist. Larbalestier, for example, notes the female readership of the sf magazines and the arguments within their letter columns. Yaszek, in *Galactic Suburbia* (2008), examines the female presence in the sf magazines of the 1950s and finds it much more concrete than received wisdom assumes. She identifies nearly three hundred women who began publishing in the sf magazines after World War II and notes that the science column *Amazing Stories* ran until 1953 regularly featured female contributors.[27] Weinbaum, in her work on the pulp writer Leslie F. Stone and her fellow-authors ('Leslie F. Stone as a Case of Author-Reader Responding') suggests that there *was* a 'close-down' of female presence but, again, that the early sf magazines were more open to women readers and writers than the stereotype suggests.[28] If science fiction is a mode which offers challenges, the assumptions of its readers, writers and scholars are among those areas which are sometimes in greatest need of questioning.

Cognizant of these factors, the current volume unites an international group of science fiction scholars, who have shaped sf's critical discourse and who have considerable experience in teaching and developing sf or sf-related courses. Most have a reputation for questioning, at one point or another, received wisdom and for taking sf criticism in new directions, for providing new insights into, or exposing counter discourses to, First SF. This book is intended for tutors and scholars who wish to develop their students', or their own, engagement with science fiction as an essentially *speculative* fiction operating at many levels, rather than as a simple example of 'popular literature', an alternative to 'high culture', or a form to which we can easily apply the conventional tools of literary response and analysis.

The collection opens with two contextualizing chapters which present accessibly the fundamental knowledge required by any undergraduate registered for an sf course. Paul Kincaid's 'Through Time and Space: A Brief History of Science Fiction' acknowledges the difficulties of defining the genre whilst providing a concise overview of sf's development and its manifestation in various forms. Echoing Roberts's *History of Science Fiction* (2007), Kincaid situates sf's origins within the Enlightenment and the emergent utopian tradition. In so doing he identifies many of the socio-cultural and rationalist impulses that remain influential: the scientific method, logical speculation, secularism, satire and the sublime. Importantly, Kincaid locates First SF in the broader, richer generic 'prehistory' of the utopian and satiric modes and a wider, global context which is only now beginning to attract critical attention from Anglophone theorists.

In 'Theorizing Science Fiction: The Question of Terminology', Gary K. Wolfe explores some of the difficulties facing the tutor or student confronted by sf's indeterminate origins, its ambiguous status as a genre, and by the wealth of critical terms available. He notes that much of this latter confusion arises from the collision of three 'different traditions of discourse ... the terminology of fandom, the terminology of professional writers and editors, and the terminology of scholars and academics'. As a means of navigating such treacherous semantic waters, Wolfe offers a lucid, concise taxonomy which resolves confusion by differentiating between terms relating to definition, classification, theme, context and technique. For those teaching or studying science fiction for the first time, such distinctions are invaluable both in themselves and as a source of further discussion, additional reading or course development.

Organized historically, the following six chapters explore the practicalities and possibilities of teaching the best-known forms of sf or sf-related literature. In 'Utopia, Anti-Utopia and Science Fiction' Chris Ferns addresses the absorption of the utopian tradition into science fiction, both in terms of teaching and scholarship. This 'englobing', he argues, has had a profound affect on how each form is interpreted and written according to the characteristics of the other. He questions the validity of such a methodology, exposing its assumptions and problematizing arguments related to sf's escapist qualities, its capacity to provoke personal and social transformation, and the criteria by which its 'value' is judged. In this way, he reclaims utopian writing from sf to ask pertinent pedagogical questions about how utopian works can be taught effectively in contexts both outside and within science fiction. Through two case studies, Aldous Huxley's *Brave New World* (1932) and Ursula K. Le Guin's *The Dispossessed* (1974), he offers significant insights into how utopian literature can be taught effectively in two different academic contexts.

Adam Roberts's 'Teaching the Scientific Romance' discusses the pedagogic appeal of engaging with a recognized British tradition in sf separate from the Gernsbackian First SF described by Clute. He not only notes the perennial popularity of a number of its authors, Verne and Wells particularly, but also acknowledges the scientific romance's contemporary re-emergence in 'steampunk' literature, design and graphic art. Here, Roberts emphasizes how teaching the scientific romance enables the tutor and student to consider both sf's founding texts (notably those of Verne and Wells) and the growing interest in contemporary works indebted to those texts (Ronald Wright's *A Scientific Romance* [1998] is an obvious example). In addition, Roberts offers a range of possible literature for study, drawing attention to recent developments in the digitization of hitherto less accessible material. More importantly, perhaps, Roberts identifies opportunities for students to contribute to the 'clamorous critical debate concerning the origins of sf', pointing to the possibility for genuinely original research. He provides a number of considerations regarding how such a course might be structured and the problems inherent in teaching non-Anglophone literature in translation, a factor which continues to oppose a more thorough interrogation of the assumptions of First SF. He concludes with suggestions of how a number of primary texts might be taught with sensitivity to their social and historic contexts and to their abiding contemporary relevance. For those tutors and instructors unable to devote an entire course to the scientific romance, Roberts's chapter provides an invaluable guide to selecting pertinent texts for inclusion in a broader programme of study.

In 'Teaching Pulp Science Fiction', Gary Westfahl looks enthusiastically to the origins of First SF in his consideration of science fiction from the 1920s to the 1940s. Confronted by the wealth of primary material available from the period, Westfahl selects six texts appropriate for understanding pulp sf and includes suggestions for how these could stimulate class discussion and possible student research projects. Importantly, he also discusses pulp sf's audience demographic and the possible implications sf had for America's technological development. Although the texts he proposes for study may be unfamiliar to many students, their themes, narrative structures and ideological assumptions will resonate with undergraduates raised in a post-*Star Wars*, *Star Trek*-informed culture. This in itself points to sf's megatextual nature, allowing for historicized debate regarding the long shadow cast by First SF.

Lisa Yaszek's 'Good SF: Teaching the Golden Age as Cultural History' focuses on the period (roughly between 1937 and 1950) in American sf when critics argue that the worst excesses of Gernsbackian sf were countered by John W. Campbell Jr's appointment as editor of *Astounding Science Fiction*. Yaszek identifies both the formal and cultural aspects of Golden Age sf, noting how its 'authors use the formal characteristics of sf to actively participate in the most pressing cultural debates of their day'. Reflecting on her practice at Georgia Tech, she explores how concepts of 'good sf' can be formulated, interrogated and tested through their application to a range of primary sources both filmic and literary. Yaszek's focus on Campbell's 'rules' for 'good sf' provides the tutor or instructor with a useful methodology for contextualizing and analysing Golden Age sf. This stress on exploring sf's cultural context leads her to emphasize the importance of addressing the issue of gender in sf of this period in order to call student assumptions into question. Accordingly, her chapter, and her earlier *Galactic Suburbia*, significantly enhance the critical understanding of Golden Age sf and provide the tutor or instructor with lively possibilities for study alongside the more usual representative figures of Asimov, Heinlein, Sturgeon and Clarke.

Where Yaszek focuses attention on the critical reclamation and teaching of neglected aspects of Golden Age sf, Rob Latham draws attention to science fiction's self-revisionist period in his treatment of the New Wave sf of the 1960s. Latham's chapter prepares the tutor or instructor and the student for approaching what is hitherto sf's most thematically and stylistically experimental phase. Providing an overview of the individual, historic and cultural forces influencing the New Wave – iconoclastic young writers, wider countercultural and political challenges to hegemonic norms, a growing sensitivity to the possibilities afforded by the literary avant-garde – Latham notes the lack of significant critical material available on the subject itself. Recognizing this as an advantage for creative discussion and assessment, he proposes 'Three Configurations' for approaching the New Wave: as part of an sf survey course, as an element in a survey of postmodern fiction, or as a freestanding course focused entirely on the period. In each case, Latham provides invaluable insights into how differently structured investigations of New Wave sf can richly enhance the student's understanding of science fiction or postmodernism. He concludes with a series of caveats, of 'lessons learned' while teaching New Wave sf, which will undoubtedly assist the tutor or instructor in planning his or her own treatment of the subject matter.

In a wide-ranging essay Andrew M. Butler explores sf's relationship to postmodernism and postmodernity in his assessment of science fiction in the context of the postmodern theories of Lyotard, Baudrillard and Jameson. Although such discussions often restrict themselves to considering cyberpunk, Butler takes this as a starting point for a broader consideration of how theories of the postmodern are found in a wide range of sf. Focusing initially on the pedagogic potential of William Gibson's *Neuromancer* (1984), Butler teases out sf's deep metaphoric resonance before identifying how the novel can be read productively through the opening chapters of Jameson's *Postmodernism, or the Cultural Logic of Late Capitalism* (1991). He then provides a number of additional literary and cinematic texts which would facilitate the student's broader understanding of the subject matter in the context of Jameson's approach. Turning to Lyotard's *The Postmodern Condition* (1984), Butler explores the ways in which postmodern science has been anticipated by, and reflected speculatively in, science fiction's alternate histories and counterfactuals. Lyotard's critiques of rationality and the rational state, he argues, are found in sf's varied critiques of totalitarian authority. Similarly, he notes how Baudrillard's recognition of the collapse of the distinction between the real and the artificial under the influence of the media is dramatized, if not effectively questioned, in sf. As Butler points out, sf 'is not radical enough to solve the problem'. Nevertheless, the works of J.G. Ballard and Philip K. Dick, and Baudrillard's analysis, provide stimulating topics for seminar discussions with students often oblivious to the strategies of capitalist culture. Self-reflexively problematizing the assumptions and implications of postmodern theory, Butler concludes his chapter with several provocative observations which re-emphasize the responsibilities of tutors and instructors everywhere.

In the next four chapters of the current volume, three specific areas of investigation are presented as valuable areas of study in any science fiction course. Brian Attebery's 'Teaching Gender and Science Fiction' traces the emergence of a politically conscious feminist sf in the 1960s and 1970s. He argues that this is a useful pedagogic starting point for students of gender and sf, allowing a free movement back to the Golden Age (where Yazsek's work is of particular interest) and the pulp years. The apparent contrasts and the new insights obtained, he argues, will enhance the student's understanding of gender assumptions, stereotyping and the need for political action, while exposing the value of sf's formal qualities to oppressed groups determined to challenge the patriarchal status quo. Attebery's concept of the term '*parabola* to represent the use of a familiar but flexible scenario' is valuable for tracing the varied, often self-reflexive treatment of gender-related themes through sf's history and varied social context. (Incidentally, it is also useful for introducing students to Clute's idea of First SF.) Attebery points out how the investigation of any particular parabola facilitates the introduction of additional critical concepts pertinent to understanding sf. It thereby provides the tutor or instructor with a coherent concept around which to group key terms and approaches in a potentially supportive and productive manner. The lucidity afforded by such an approach is likely to be appreciated by students who are also familiarizing themselves with the complexities of gender theory and the ways in which sf's speculative potential can dramatize or literalize various theoretical standpoints or models. Attebery concludes with a discussion of various parabolas, including suggested primary texts for each, providing fertile possibilities for the development of gender-based courses or sessions.

Uppinder Mehan's 'Teaching Postcolonial Science Fiction' is an excellent introduction to the topic which establishes a clear context for study before proposing three forms of related science fiction: postcolonial science fiction, colonial science fiction and what Mehan terms 'dissident science fiction'. In his discussion of the former, Mehan focuses on how postcolonial sf writers, including Nalo Hopkinson and Archie Weller, address issues of technology, history and the body. In his treatment of colonial science fiction, a distinct element of First SF, he explores the racist, colonialist and imperialist assumptions underpinning a large proportion of Anglo-American science fiction, with an emphasis on the work of H. Beam Piper. With dissident science fiction, on the other hand, Mehan identifies the ways in which writers from former and current colonial powers, including Kim Stanley Robinson and C.J. Cherryh, have critiqued the processes of imperialism and colonialism. His interpretations of such primary texts are extremely useful to any tutor or instructor intent on developing a course or session exploring science fiction's relationship to colonial and postcolonial discourse or to broader thematically based analysis of sf's conception and representation of the Other.

M. Elizabeth Ginway develops these ideas further in her case study of Latin American science fiction film and literature as she documents her experiences of teaching Spanish-American and Brazilian texts in translation. Like Mehan, she draws attention to the ways in which such courses are highly effective in challenging students' 'underlying assumptions about First-World political and technological hegemony' and, by extension, First SF. Her wide-ranging discussion provides brief, insightful readings of a number of key filmic and literary texts and considers how these represent different South American cultural experiences and conditions, sometimes in relation to wider global contexts. For any instructor or tutor intent on either developing a course on Spanish-American and/or Brazilian sf or incorporating representative material into a broader sf study, Ginway's detailed assessment of Andrea L. Bell and Yolanda Molina-Gavilán's anthology *Cosmos Latinos: An Anthology of Science Fiction from Latin America and Spain* (2003) and her suggestions as to how its contents might be supplemented, are invaluable. As a counterpoint to the stories she analyses, Ginway examines representative Anglo-American sf and fantasy texts set in Brazil to discuss the phenomenon of the 'tropicalization' of Latin America occurring in literature by outsiders. She concludes by recommending Samuel R. Delany's 'Driftglass' (1967), Karen Tei Yamashita's fantasy *Through the Arc of the Rainforest* (1990) and – with some caveats – Ian McDonald's *Brasyl* (2007). Given the wealth of material Ginway identifies as appropriate, these texts are a useful starting point for a course or session preparing students for an instructive juxtaposition of First World and Third World perspectives through science fiction.

In the penultimate chapter, Mark Brake and Neil Hook describe their unique work exploring the teaching of the relationship between science and science fiction in a contemporary British higher education context. They provide a detailed outline of their degree programme and reflect on their experience of a decade teaching such an interdisciplinary study. As they point out, although science fiction was recognized as developing alongside the growth of rationalism and the preponderance of the scientific method in both the hard and soft sciences, the subject had rarely been studied in the context of the sciences it has drawn upon consistently. Indeed, as Brake and Hook indicate, the 'two cultures' dialectic of science versus art has often separated rather than united discussion. Rejecting this antagonistic stance, they describe a degree course which interrogates, in a critical and multidisciplinary manner, the relationship between science and science fiction to 'produce a unique, provocative and compelling account of science fiction as a touchstone of the dialectic of science and progress'. In describing their programme, they assess the characteristics of both science and science fiction and the often complex interaction that exists between them. While the opportunity of teaching an entire degree programme focusing on science and science fiction may not be possible for the majority of universities, their observations regarding the nature of the connections between the two are valuable to anyone planning or teaching a science fiction course as part of a liberal arts or humanities degree.

Andy Sawyer and Peter Wright bring the collection to a close with a chapter that provides practical advice on how a science fiction course might be structured, delivered and assessed productively. Intended largely for tutors and instructors who are considering developing an undergraduate sf course for the first time, it nevertheless draws on the experience of several contributors to offer any sf teacher opportunities for considering possible variations to already well-developed courses, particularly in the area of assessment.

Each of these chapters has been especially commissioned to support scholars and students in developing their knowledge and understanding of science fiction and the ways in which it might be taught, researched and analysed. Sf is a pedagogically exciting, academically rewarding subject that confronts us directly with the possible consequences of universal, planetary, cultural, political, social and personal transformation. Its hybrid nature and the way it emphasizes connections and contrasts between cultures, disciplines and ways of thinking, make it a fitting subject for any syllabus committed to assisting the social and intellectual transformation of its students.

Notes

1. Kingsley Amis and Robert Conquest, eds, *Spectrum 2* (London: Gollancz, 1962) 4. The couplet is often attributed to Kingsley Amis, but is reprinted in Conquest's *The Abomination of Moab* (London: Maurice Temple Smith, 1975).
2. Patrick Parrinder, *Science Fiction: Its Criticism and Teaching* (London: Methuen, 1980) xiv.
3. Mark Hillegas, 'The Course in Science Fiction: A Hope Deferred', *Extrapolation*, 9:18 (1968): 18–21. Throughout his article, Hillegas notes the contemporary antipathy many English departments felt towards the teaching of science fiction.
4. R.D. Mullen, 'Science Fiction in Academe', *Science Fiction Studies*, 23:3 (1996): 371–4 at 372. An electronic copy is available at http://www.depauw.edu/sfs/backissues/70/intro70.htm (accessed 25 June 2009).
5. Parrinder, *Science Fiction*, 131.
6. James Gunn, 'Teaching Science Fiction', *Science Fiction Studies*, 23:3 (1996): 377–84 at 378. An electronic copy is available at http://www.depauw.edu/sfs/backissues/70/gunn70art.htm (accessed 23 July 2009).
7. For an account of early sf scholarship, see Donald M. Hassler, 'The Academic Pioneers of Science Fiction Criticism, 1940–1980', *Science Fiction Studies*, 26:2 (1999): 213–31. An electronic copy is available at http://www.depauw.edu/sfs/backissues/78/hassler78art.htm (accessed 25 June 2009). See also Alvin Toffler, *Future Shock* (New York: Random House, 1970); Darko Suvin, *The Metamorphoses of Science Fiction* (Yale: Yale University Press, 1979).
8. The Liverpool University Press Science Fiction Texts and Studies series can be viewed at http://www.liverpool-unipress.c.uk/html/categories.asp?idCategory=51 (accessed 25 June 2009).
9. Borrowing the term from Christine Brooke-Rose, Damien Broderick explains how science fiction exists as 'a mega-text of imaginary worlds, tropes, tools, lexicons, even grammatical innovations borrowed from other textualities' (*Reading by Starlight* (London: Routledge, 1995) xiii. See 57–63 for a fuller discussion). According to this model, sf texts are built up by means of interaction – deliberate borrowings, unconscious plagiarism, and straightforward assumptions that writing a science fiction story demands certain uses of language, setting and image – with other sf texts. For example, there are similarities in the imagined futures of certain kinds of science fiction: 'galactic empires', faster-than-light travel, dystopian cityscapes. The 'moving roadways' of Wells's *When The Sleeper Wakes* (1899) are seen again in Heinlein's 'The Roads Must Roll' (1940), which mentions Wells, and *The Caves of Steel* (1954) by Isaac Asimov. The success of William Gibson's *Neuromancer* (1984) resulted immediately in a torrent of stories about grimy hi-tech futures in which drugs and artificial intelligences played a large part and words like 'cyberspace', 'the Matrix' and 'The Net' were frequent. *Neuromancer*'s conceptual innovations were so influential that they eventually informed that most British of cultural icons *Doctor Who* in Ben Aaronovich's 'New Adventure', *Transit* (London: Virgin Books, 1992).
10. The vagueness of dating is deliberate: like many overarching narratives, there is no real sense that First SF has vanished, merely that it has outlived its appropriateness.

20 Teaching Science Fiction

11. Hugo Gernsback, 'A New Sort of Magazine', *Amazing Stories*, 1:1 (1926): 3.
12. Graham Sleight, 'Last and First SF', in Farah Mendlesohn, ed., *Polder: A Festschrift for John Clute and Judith Clute* (Baltimore: Old Earth Books, 2006) 258–66 at 258.
13. John Clute, *Look at the Evidence: Essays and Reviews* (Liverpool: Liverpool University Press, 1995) 9.
14. Adam Roberts, *The History of Science Fiction* (Basigstoke: Palgrave, 2007) 64–87.
15. See Suvin, *The Metamorphoses of Science Fiction*.
16. John Clute, *Look at the Evidence*, 9.
17. John Clute interviewed by Nick Gevers, *Interzone*, 166 (April 2000): 29–34 at 30.
18. Farah Mendlesohn, 'Editorial', *Foundation: The International Review of Science Fiction*, 100 (2007): 3–4 at 3.
19. These 'default futures' are a product of sf's mega-textual appropriations and borrowings.
20. Mendlesohn, 'Editorial', 3.
21. See, for example, the works cited by Broderick, Delany, and Stockwell, and the 'Companions' issued by Cambridge University Press, Blackwell and Routledge.
22. Suvin,, *The Metamorphoses of Science Fiction*, 4.
23. Farah Mendlesohn, 'Introduction', in *The Cambridge Companion to Science Fiction* (Cambridge: Cambridge University Press, 2003) 1–12 at 1.
24. Gary Westfahl, *The Mechanics of Wonder* (Liverpool: Liverpool University Press, 1998) 93.
25. Brian Aldiss with David Wingrove, *Trillion Year Spree* (London: Gollancz, 1982) 202.
26. See Gary Westfahl, 'On the True History of Science Fiction', *Foundation* 47 (1989/90): 5–25 and the comments by Brian Aldiss, Brian Stableford and Edwards James: 28–33; and Gary Westfahl, '"An Idea of Scientific Import": Hugo Gernsback's Theory of Science Fiction', *Foundation* 48 (1990): 26–50, and the comments by Andy Sawyer, K.V. Bailey and Steve Carper in *Foundation* 50 (1990): 77–80.
27. Lisa Yaszek, *Galactic Suburbia: Recovering Women's Science Fiction* (Columbus, OH: Ohio State University Press, 2008) 3 and 23.
28. Batya Weinbaum, 'Leslie F. Stone as a Case of Author-Reader Responding', *Foundation* 80 (2000): 40–51.

1
Through Time and Space: A Brief History of Science Fiction
Paul Kincaid

Many undergraduates embarking on a course or module in science fiction have little or no previous knowledge of the genre. Those who have been casual or even habitual readers of the form usually lack historical or theoretical perspectives and often benefit from a historically ordered approach. Chronologically arranged courses provide a structure within which students can more easily locate specific authors and their work, historical events, and the major phases in sf's formal, literary, thematic and conceptual characteristics. Accordingly, this chapter sets out a brief history of the genre which distinguishes a number of areas of potential interest and focus for selection, especially for those tutors or instructors planning courses restricted typically to one semester and intent on providing students with a broad understanding of the subject. In so doing, it identifies a range of relevant authors and texts appropriate for inclusion in both historically-oriented programmes of study and more focused analyses of specific authors, themes or forms.

However, it must be noted that to write a history of science fiction is to attempt to describe the course of something that remains vague and ever shifting. If there is no clear agreement on how to define 'science fiction' how can there be any agreement on where it starts and how it develops? Indeed, most so-called histories of science fiction are little more than genealogies that start with something arbitrary and not-quite genre – 'proto-science fiction' is a popular term – and proceed by a series of biblical begats: Wells begat Stapledon who begat Clarke who begat Baxter.

For the purposes of this history, therefore, I intend to be as loose and eclectic in my definition of the genre as possible. I will take sf as a form of the literary fantastic employing any of a wide variety of commonly recognized themes, techniques, tropes and approaches that have tended to braid together over time into something to which we now give the name science fiction.[1] Some of those themes and tropes can be found in the novels and narrative poems of the Hellenistic period, most notably the voyage to the Moon recounted by Lucian of Samosata in his *True History* (2nd century CE). But although some of the early pioneers of sf were familiar with Lucian's work, it would be wrong to characterize this as anything other than a false start in the history of the genre.

The history of science fiction really begins with the Renaissance, or more specifically with the exploration of the New World and the coincident spread of humanist learning through Europe at the beginning of the sixteenth century. Out of this emerged *Utopia* by Thomas More (1516), which set against the medieval wish-fulfilment fantasia of Cockaigne (or Cokaygne) the notion that man might fashion through rational endeavour his own better world. Utopian ideas were widely and quickly taken up, appearing for instance in *I Mondi* by Anton Francesco Doni (1552) and more famously *The City of the Sun* by Thomas Campanella (1623).

One other outgrowth of humanism and the emphasis on education that followed the Reformation, particularly in Protestant lands, was the development of science based on observation and experiment. The most significant consequences of this were the Copernican revolution, which displaced the Earth from its position at the centre of the universe, and Galileo's observations of other planets, which gave them a landscape not dissimilar to that of Earth. Such ideas were not always welcome: Giordano Bruno was burned at the stake in Rome in 1600 for proposing an infinite universe in which there might be worlds inhabited by races never visited by Christ. Nevertheless, these ideas did begin to creep into the fiction of the day.

In 1620, just ten years after the publication of Galileo's map of the moon, Ben Jonson wrote a masque for the court of James I called *Newes from the New World Discovered in the Moone*, which fancifully imagined moon people riding in clouds. It was perhaps the first British work to imagine beings inhabiting a landscape on the moon. The astronomer Johannes Kepler took this notion further in his posthumously-published *Somnium* (1634), which recounted a dream journey to a moon described according to the best scientific knowledge of the time. Another posthumous work, *The Man in the Moone* (1638) by Francis Godwin, is a picaresque adventure in which the antihero, Domingo Gonsales, visits the moon in a carriage towed by gansas (geese). Incorporating the first description of a technological conveyance to another world, the text (which included a number of other then-radical scientific ideas ranging from the Copernican system to weightlessness between worlds) was highly influential, inspiring, among many other works, a play by Aphra Behn and later fictions by Cyrano de Bergerac. It would later be cited by Jules Verne as one of his major influences. Not only that, but John Wilkins rewrote his treatise, *The Discovery of a World in the Moone* (1638), to add a chapter about ways of travelling to the moon: so the idea of interplanetary travel became a part of scientific thinking. Wilkins would later also be instrumental in founding the Royal Society, inspired by Francis Bacon's scientific utopia, *New Atlantis* (1627).

More's *Utopia* was widely reprinted in Britain in the years before the Civil War, and utopian thought had a potent effect on the incendiary combination of political and religious radicalism that marked the period. Numerous utopias were published as the notion changed from literary/philosophical idea to religio-political aspiration. Among these works was *Nova Solyma* (1648) by ex-parliamentarian Samuel Gott, which, inspired by millenarian ideas, was the first novel explicitly set in the future.

Although religious radicalism still found expression following the Restoration of Charles II in 1660 (John Milton's *Paradise Lost* appeared in 1667, John Bunyan's *Pilgrim's Progress* in 1678), utopian writing as a whole became considerably less radical. The completion of Bacon's *New Atlantis* by 'R.H., Gent' (1660) was more Royalist even than Bacon had been, while works like *The Isle of Pines* by Henry Neville (1668), replaced political liberation with sexual liberality. But there was one notable and curious work, *The Blazing World* (1666) by Margaret Cavendish, which posited another world joined to this one at the pole.

Within a few years, however, writers were beginning to imagine the poles providing access not to an adjoining world but to the interior of the Earth. In works such as *Niels Klim in the Underworld* (1741) by Ludvig Holberg, and the extraordinary *Icosameron* (1788) by Jacques Casanova, this notion enjoyed a curious vogue from the latter years of the seventeenth century through to Jules Verne's *A Journey to the Centre of the Earth* (1864) and Edgar Rice Burroughs's *Pellucidar* novels. Most of the alien races encountered in early sf, such as the flying people in *The Life and Adventures of Peter Wilkins* (1750) by Robert Paltock, were found in such works, though there were still mysteries to be encountered in distant parts of the globe. Jonathan Swift's *Gulliver's Travels* (1727) is a case in point. In keeping with the age of Enlightenment, Swift's novel turned its satiric gaze not on kings and churches but upon political parties and the esoteric disputes of the Royal Society. The most remarkable beings in eighteenth-century fiction, however, were the vast cosmic entities that disputed with Earthly savants in Voltaire's *Micromegas* (1752).

Despite the fact that its emergent secularism would eventually have a profound effect on the character of science fiction, the Enlightenment produced little groundbreaking work in the history of the genre. But as the eighteenth century progressed the political ferment of the American and French revolutions and the philosophical ferment represented by the works of Immanuel Kant and by Edmund Burke's notion of the sublime led to renewed questioning of humanity's position in the world and, as it had been in the mid-seventeenth century, this was fertile ground for science fiction.

The romantic notion of the sublime found perhaps its most extravagant literary expression in the Gothic, that fantastical mode beginning with works such as *The Castle of Otranto* by Horace Walpole (1764) which paid elaborate attention to wild landscapes, raging storms and ruined towers. But it was the Gothic mode that Mary Shelley used for what Brian Aldiss, and a number of later commentators, identified as the first true science fiction novel, *Frankenstein* (1818).[2] Grafting contemporary scientific ideas, notably galvanism or animal electricity, onto an archetypal Gothic landscape, Shelley's tale of man creating life was an immediate success. By 1823 it had been adapted for the stage (the first of a wealth of dramatic adaptations); it entered the popular imagination so thoroughly that even today genetically modified food is commonly referred to as 'Frankenstein food'; and it inspired an endless stream of science fictions that explored in innumerable ways (robots, cyborgs, genetic modification, cloning) the possibilities of artificial life. Mary Shelley heavily revised the text for the third edition of 1831, removing, amongst other things, a suggestion of incest.[3] She continued to write in the Gothic mode, producing, in *The Last Man* (1826), a vision of humankind destroyed by plague which proved almost as influential as *Frankenstein* in the history of science fiction. It inspired such works as *After London* by Richard Jeffries (1885) and *Deluge* by S. Fowler Wright (1927), and through them the whole subgenre of the British catastrophe novel.

The Gothic mode also heavily influenced Edgar Allan Poe, who had a significant impact on the history of sf through works including the hollow earth novel, *The Narrative of Arthur Gordon Pym of Nantucket* (1838). A far greater influence on early American science fiction, however, and one less in thrall to the Gothic, was probably 'Rappaccini's Daughter' by Nathaniel Hawthorne (1846) which established a number of themes, particularly the malevolence of the experimenter and the ambiguousness of the distinction between the real and the fictional, that would re-emerge repeatedly in subsequent fiction. But even as the nineteenth century progressed and the Gothic began to lose its influence, its traces could still be found in relatively late works such as Robert Louis Stevenson's *Strange Case of Dr Jekyll and Mr Hyde* (1886), which recast *Frankenstein* as a tale of personal transformation in the new wild places of the modern city.

The nineteenth century was a time of technological progress in an increasingly urbanized society, and writers began to delight in the wondrous new devices such continued progress might bring. In Russia there were futuristic utopias like *Plausible Fantasies* by F.V. Bulgarin (1824) and *The Year 4338* by V.F. Odoevsky (1840). In America, excitement at technological possibilities inspired a string of amazing stories, generally published as dime novels, built around an inventor-hero. These have been christened 'Edisonades' in honour of Thomas Edison, though the novel generally considered the first of the type, *The Huge Hunter, or the Steam Man of the Prairies* by Edward S. Ellis (1868), pre-dated Edison's fame by a decade. (Not coincidentally, Edison actually appeared as the hero of *Edison's Conquest of Mars* by Garrett P. Serviss, 1898 a sequel of sorts to H.G. Wells's *The War of the Worlds*, 1898.) Such Edisonades would feed directly into the 'scientifictions'[4] that, early in the twentieth century, Hugo Gernsback would begin publishing in his popular magazines (for example, *Modern Electronics*, 1908–13, which serialized his own novel *Ralph 124C 41+* in 1911, and *The Electrical Experimenter*, 1913–20) as a way of promoting science. Meanwhile in France technological progress found its most successful fictional expression in the works of Jules Verne who, in novel after novel, would present spectacular devices such as submarines (*Twenty Thousand Leagues Under the Sea*, 1869), airships (*Robur the Conqueror*, 1886) and spaceships (*From the Earth to the Moon*, 1865).

But if the mid- to late nineteenth century was a time that celebrated the scientific contribution to industrial (and therefore military and political) might, as it did for instance at London's Great Exhibition of 1851, it was also a time when science was beginning to undermine many old certainties. Geologists were pushing back the age of the Earth, physicists were breaking down the very structure of reality, and in 1859 Charles Darwin published *On the Origin of Species*, which profoundly affected the complacency of an age that saw English civilization as the peak of historical development. Although Darwin's ideas, then as now, generated huge controversy, particularly from religious ideologues, they soon began to have an effect on the literature of the day, beginning almost immediately in novels such as *The Water Babies* by Charles Kingsley (1862–63). In sf, their best and most important advocate was

H.G. Wells, who had studied with T.H. Huxley, popularly known as 'Darwin's bulldog', and who continued to promote evolution by natural selection throughout his long career.

Wells's contribution to science fiction is difficult to overstate. Though there had been earlier time travel stories (*A Connecticut Yankee in King Arthur's Court* by Mark Twain, 1889, for example), *The Time Machine* (1895) was the first work to propose a device for travelling through time, turning time itself into a dimension that could be negotiated. A measure of its importance can perhaps be gauged from the number of works that have positioned themselves as sequels to *The Time Machine*, including *The Space Machine* by Christopher Priest (1976), *The Time Ships* by Stephen Baxter (1995) and *A Scientific Romance* by Ronald Wright (1998). In another innovation Wells took the paranoid stories of German invasion that had become popular in the wake of German reunification and the Franco-Prussian War, such as George T. Chesney's *The Battle of Dorking* (1871), and turned them into the first significant novel of alien invasion (*The War of the Worlds*, 1898). In his first six years as a novelist, Wells also produced two variants on the *Frankenstein* model, *The Island of Dr Moreau* (1896) and *The Invisible Man* (1897), the first of his futuristic utopias, *The Sleeper Awakes* (1898), and a journey to the moon, *The First Men in the Moon* (1901). Together, these six novels would provide a vocabulary of images and devices that would set the tone for Anglophone science fiction thereafter. Though Wells would continue to write occasional science fictions throughout the rest of his career, nothing that followed would have quite the impact of these early works.

The First World War marked a change in the course of science fiction. In Europe, after the devastation of four years of fighting, economic collapse exacerbated by the unequal terms at Versailles, and the division of the continent into two powerful dictatorial camps (Communist in Soviet Russia, Fascist in Italy, Germany and, after the Civil War, Spain), a bleak mood fed into the fiction of the day. Following the Soviet Revolution the utopian aspect of Russian sf had become dystopian, most significantly with *We* by Yevgeny Zamiatin (or Zamyatin) (1920). Smuggled to the West, this novel was reviewed by George Orwell who would then use it as the structural and thematic model for the most famous dystopia of the twentieth century, *Nineteen Eighty-Four* (1949). Meanwhile the rise of the Nazi Party in Germany provoked a number of dreadful visions of the future, the most important of which was probably *Swastika Night* by Katherine Burdekin (1937). After the war this mode would transform effortlessly into a string of alternative histories imagining German victory, including *The Sound of his Horn* by Sarban (1952), 'The Fall of

Frenchy Steiner' by Hilary Bailey (1964), 'Weinachtsabend' by Keith Roberts (1972) and, more recently, *The Separation* by Christopher Priest (2002) and *Resistance* by Owen Sheers (2007). But even if they did not address such political issues directly, the common assumption throughout the interwar years that another war was inevitable led to stories of catastrophe (T.H. White's *Earth Stopped*, 1934), of intrusive state control (Aldous Huxley's *Brave New World*, 1932), of time as a circular trap (in J.B. Priestley's time plays such as *I Have Been Here Before*, 1937). Even the most ambitious, far-reaching vision of the future, Olaf Stapledon's *Last and First Men* (1930), carries the message that all civilizations must crumble and be forgotten.

America, by contrast, emerged from the war as the world's leading economic power, even though its optimism was dimmed by the stock market crash of 1929 and the subsequent Depression. Coupled with a resolve to stay out of future foreign wars, there was a sense that America saw itself as shaping the future rather than being shaped by it, a sense that was clear in the American science fiction of the period. In 1926, Hugo Gernsback launched *Amazing Stories*, a magazine specifically devoted to the 'scientifiction' he had already been publishing in his popular science magazines. For most of the next half-century, American sf would be predominantly magazine-based. Although at first Gernsback's magazine mostly published reprints of stories by Wells and Verne, the true model for the new writers he encouraged was his own earlier novel, *Ralph 124C 41+*, a brash, stylistically and structurally crude work in which the astonishments of technology take precedence over any literary qualities. A presumed didactic purpose behind these stories of 'super science' (the term that would soon become popular for stories featuring miraculous future technology) quickly became lost as young writers struggled to make a living churning out as many sensationalized and sensationalist stories as possible for low-paying markets.

The characteristic American science fiction of this period was the space opera (named ironically in reference to the 'horse opera' western stories also then popular). Typified by such works as Edmond Hamilton's Captain Future series (beginning with 'The Space Emperor', 1940), and E.E. 'Doc' Smith's Skylark series (beginning with *The Skylark of Space*, 1928) and Lensman series (beginning with *Galactic Patrol*, 1937–38[5]), these were colourful, fast-paced, simplistic and heavily reliant on scale to evoke wonder. However, they developed a devoted following whose exchanges through the letter columns of the pulp magazines would become the basis of science fiction fandom and from whose numbers many of the leading writers in the genre would emerge.

Gernsback lost control of *Amazing Stories* in 1929, and during the 1930s other magazines vied for dominance in what was proving to be a popular market. The one that became the most powerful, and almost the defining voice of American science fiction for the next decade or more, was *Astounding Stories*. In October 1937 John W. Campbell took over editorship of the magazine and became very nearly as influential a figure in the history of sf as H.G. Wells. Campbell promptly retitled the magazine, *Astounding Science Fiction* (it has had numerous changes of title since then and is published still, now under the title *Analog Science Fiction Science Fact*), and set about changing the character of the magazine and of the stories it published. Already a successful writer of space operas (for example, 'The Black Star Passes', 1930), and of more subtle science fictions under the pen name Don A. Stuart ('Twilight', 1934; 'Night', 1935), Campbell would take a very hands-on approach to editing and revising stories and would often provide story ideas for his writers to develop. Above all he discovered or matured a stable of new young writers, many of whom would go on to become the leading names in what has been called the 'Golden Age' of science fiction, including Isaac Asimov, Robert A. Heinlein, A.E. Van Vogt, Theodore Sturgeon, Lester Del Rey and L. Sprague de Camp.

Campbell demanded of his writers a rigorous logic, to such an extent that Tom Godwin was required to rewrite 'The Cold Equations' (1954) until he stopped trying to find ingenious ways to save the young female stowaway and accepted that she had to die in accordance with the story logic. Campbell expected an adherence to scientific laws, although certain devices such as faster than light travel and (a particular favourite of his) psi powers were acceptable. And he urged far greater character development than had been common in the space operas of the 1930s. Although space operatic plots and settings continued to be used, particularly by Van Vogt in works such as *The Voyage of the Space Beagle* (1950) and *Weapon Shops of Isher* (1951), the result was a new approach to science fiction that came to be known as 'hard sf'. These were works that took the hard sciences, particularly physics and chemistry, as their basis. For example, *Mission of Gravity* by Hal Clement (1954) describes what life may be like on the surface of a planet with exceptionally high gravity.

Isaac Asimov based his widely admired story, 'Nightfall' (1941), on a suggestion by Campbell: a planet with many suns whose complex orbits meant the inhabitants only saw the stars once in a millennium. His most lasting contribution to sf, however, is probably his robot stories (*I, Robot*, the first of several collections, appeared in 1950) in which he promulgated the Three Laws of Robotics. 'Robot', a term coined by Karel Capek in his play *R.U.R.* (*Rossums Universal Robots*, 1921) and based on the Czech word for drudgery, was applied by Capek to an entity closer to what is more commonly called an android, but was very quickly appropriated to refer to what had previously been called automata. With his Three Laws, Asimov brought an ethical dimension to the treatment of robots, and over the course of later stories such as 'Bicentennial Man' (1976) and 'Robot Dreams' (1986) traced the development of his robots from mechanical creatures into humans. The Three Laws were often implied or even cited by later authors.

Late in his career, Asimov began revisiting earlier works, including the robot stories and his future history, *The Foundation Trilogy* (1951–53), in a not altogether successful attempt to link them into a larger, coherent narrative of the future. This was a concept more closely associated with other writers of his generation, including Cordwainer Smith and Robert Heinlein. All of Smith's idiosyncratic and ethically complex stories, such as 'The Dead Lady of Clown Town' (1964) and 'The Ballad of Lost C'Mell' (1962) can be fitted into one timeline. Heinlein, considered by some the most important of all hard sf writers, was more diverse, but a number of his novels and stories, such as those collected in *The Man Who Sold the Moon* (1950) and *Revolt in 2100* (1953) did form a basic future history. A consistent political outlook – libertarianism – underlies practically all of Heinlein's work. It is notable in stories such as 'The Roads Must Roll' (1940) which speculates on a society based around a network of moving walkways in which an individual's material rewards are determined by how much that individual has done for society. Heinlein's work, however, is perhaps even more significant as a representative of one of the defining characteristics of hard sf, the competent man as hero. In several novels, including *The Moon is a Harsh Mistress* (1966), which sees a lunar colony revolting against a dictatorial Earth, his work consistently celebrated the man (always a man) who simply got on with the job, who solved problems rather than entered combat, and who went out to new, otherwordly frontiers in search of opportunity. However, by the time of his most famous novel, *Stranger in a Strange Land* (1961), the competent hero, Valentine Michael Smith, is already starting to give way to the garrulous elder statesman (here Jubal Harshaw but more often Lazarus Long) who would come to dominate Heinlein's increasingly self-indulgent later novels.

By the 1950s, new magazines – *The Magazine of Fantasy and Science Fiction* (launched 1949), *Galaxy* (1950) and *If* (1952) – were encouraging a new generation of writers who maintained much of hard sf's aesthetic but brought to it greater literary sensibility. In the stories collected as *The Martian Chronicles* (1950) Ray Bradbury presented the harsh landscape of Mars as an extension of small-town America to explore and explode frontier myths; Alfred Bester's *Tiger Tiger* (also known as *The Stars My Destination*, 1956), turned *The Count of Monte Cristo* (Alexandre Dumas, 1844–46) into a pyrotechnic novel of revenge set in a future that would become a precursor of cyberpunk (and the Dumas novel would also inspire Gwyneth Jones's space opera, *Spirit, or the Princess of Bois Dormant*, 2009); Frederik Pohl and C.M. Kornbluth's *The Space Merchants* (1953) remains one of the finest satires on consumerism in modern science fiction; Walter M. Miller's ultimately elegiac *A Canticle for Leibowitz* (1959) traced the survival of religious faith in a post-apocalyptic wilderness; and Frank Herbert's *Dune* (1965), together with its numerous sequels, provided a rich, socially and politically complex planetary adventure laced with ecological awareness. These and other writers who emerged in the 1950s, including Daniel Keyes, Algis Budrys, Fritz Leiber, James Blish, Poul Anderson and Kurt Vonnegut, all made a significant contribution to the history of the genre, though the most important writer to appear at this time, perhaps paradoxically, was Philip K. Dick. His spare novels, paranoid, often comic, doubting reality and exploring other states of consciousness, seemed apposite in the counterculture of the 1960s but it would take many years, and then initially only among French critics, before he would be recognized as one of the most important of modern sf writers. In novel after novel, Dick's questioning of all we take for granted – our conception of what constitutes the human, of our perception of the nature of reality, of our relationship to the concept of the Divine – estranges the reader at a level to which sf has often aspired but which it has rarely attained. His many notable works include *The Man in the High Castle* (1962) in which Germany and Japan have partitioned America after victory in World War II; *The Three Stigmata of Palmer Eldritch* (1965) in which people use drugs to enter the virtual reality of Perky Pat dolls; and *Do Androids Dream of Electric Sheep* (1968) in which a bounty hunter chases androids across a despoiled San Francisco as his understanding of what separates the artificial from real becomes increasingly compromised.

If the Second World War had surprisingly little impact on American science fiction, the same could not be said of Britain. Before the war many British writers were starting to emulate the space operatic mode of imported American sf; afterwards, the dominant mood of postwar pessimism was reflected in a growing preoccupation with the Wellsian disaster narrative. Although there were many fine writers of what Brian

Aldiss somewhat dismissively termed the 'cosy catastrophe',[6] the best exemplar – John Wyndham – is also the most popular. In *The Day of the Triffids* (1951) and *The Chrysalids* (1955) he presented a situation in which normality is suddenly and disastrously disrupted and a small group of survivors are forced to find a way of establishing stability in a world unmade by events. These novels caught precisely the mood of a colourless, impoverished and newly powerless Britain.

The other major writer of the period, Arthur C. Clarke, matched his peers, Asimov and Heinlein, in his use of the bright machinery of the future and the exotic settings of other worlds. However, he combined the hard sf mode with the aesthetic of the catastrophe narrative. *Childhood's End* (1953) sees humankind transformed to join an advanced spacefaring civilization, an apotheosis made tonally darker by the fact that the aliens facilitating humanity's 'uplift' appear as the demons of Christian mythology. The climax remains one of the most emotionally unsettling in science fiction. Clarke's later novel, *The City and the Stars* (1956), features an elegiac account of the last city on Earth which anticipates the nature of his most famous work, *2001, A Space Odyssey* (1968), a further narrative of transcendence characterized by themes of loss and loneliness.

The thematic and stylistic stability of Anglo-American sf was under assault from May 1964 when the long-established British magazine *New Worlds* acquired a new editor. Michael Moorcock was still only in his mid-twenties when he accepted the post but he was already an experienced editor and a prolific author. Moreover, he was in tune with the pop culture movement that was then creating 'Swinging London'. Through *New Worlds* he would oversee a new mode of sf as revolutionary in its way as the counterculture of which it became a part. Although presented as a counterblast to the 'cosy catastrophe', the best of the New Wave (so called in reference to the French 'nouvelle vague' cinema) writers continued to employ catastrophe as their central image; it was, rather, a counterattack to the brash certainties and glittering futures of contemporary American science fiction. Embracing contemporary anti-establishment attitudes and the psychedelic possibilities of the emergent drug culture, abandoning outer space for what they called 'inner space',[7] featuring characters more likely to be overwhelmed by events in contrast to Heinlein's 'competent man', and using techniques often lifted wholesale from literary modernism that had, to this moment, been largely ignored by sf, *New Worlds* became a home for experimental fictions. In the way of such things, many, if not most of the experiments failed. But a number of writers responded vigorously to the freer atmosphere thus established, particularly Brian Aldiss and J.G. Ballard. Aldiss's *Greybeard* (1964) is a chill novel set in an emptying, childless future and *Barefoot in the Head* (1969) provides a surreal, stylistically innovative narrative set in the aftermath of a war using hallucinogens (the 'Acid Head War') in which fractured language reflects the fractured reality. In *The Crystal World* (1966), one of a series of physical and psychological disaster novels, and *The Atrocity Exhibition* (1969), another work in which fractured narrative is used to illustrate individual breakdown in the face of a media-dominated world, Ballard began to erode the distinction between sf and mainstream or literary fiction. His complex accounts of psychic disjuncture, alienation and self-destructiveness introduced a modernist interiority rarely seen in subsequent sf.

If Aldiss and Ballard were the most literary writers of the New Wave (and, indeed, they have continued to produce highly respected work, though some of their most acclaimed fiction has been outside the genre), the two works that perhaps best represent this period are John Brunner's *Stand on Zanzibar* (1968), which reproduced the structure and devices of John Dos Passos's high modernist work *USA* (1938) in a story of an overpopulated Earth, and 'The Heat Death of the Universe' by Pamela Zoline (1967) which used entropy as a metaphor for the mental disintegration of a housewife oppressed by the domesticity expected of her under patriarchy. The continuing influence of the New Wave, particularly in more fluent use of literary techniques, is seen in the ongoing fiction of Keith Roberts (*Pavane*, 1968; *The Chalk Giants*, 1974), M. John Harrison (*The Centauri Device*, 1975; *Light*, 2002) and Christopher Priest (*Inverted World*, 1974; *The Affirmation*, 1981).

Two editors, Judith Merril (*England Swings SF*, 1968) and Harlan Ellison (*Dangerous Visions*, 1967) brought the literary ambitions and practices of the New Wave to America. But the American New Wave was distinctly different from that in Britain. Though there was still a sense of literary experiment, the primary impulse seemed to be a breaking of the taboos that had, often unconsciously, operated in American science fiction since the 1920s, in particular concerning the portrayal of sex, politics and religion. Some of the generation of writers who had begun to emerge during the 1950s, such as Robert Silverberg (*Son of Man*, 1971; *Dying Inside*, 1972) and Harlan Ellison ('"Repent, Harlequin!" said the Ticktockman', 1965; 'A Boy and His Dog', 1969), embraced the new freedoms; others reacted strongly against the New Wave. Unlike the situation in Britain, where the New Wave was much less controversial among writers, in the US controversy over the New Wave lasted for much of the late 1960s.

The New Wave writers who made most impact were those who emerged from the movement rather than those who simply adapted to it. These included Samuel R. Delany, who brought poetic sensibilities and the experience of being a black homosexual to novels that had a powerful effect on the field, including *Nova* (1968) which grafted images of the Grail Quest onto a space opera format, and *Dhalgren* (1975) which took his literary experimentation even further in an account of a city cut off from the world by an unknown disaster.

In many ways, however, the most important work to emerge from American sf at this time was by writers who built on the freedoms initiated by the New Wave without really being a part of it. Ursula K. Le Guin, in *The Left Hand of Darkness* (1969), forced her audience to consider gender differences in a way that science fiction had never contemplated before. In *The Dispossessed* (1974), she interrogated notions of utopia in an equally uncompromising fashion. Joanna Russ's *The Female Man* (1975) examined attitudes to sex and the role of women in four parallel worlds. And, in a series of extraordinary stories of which the most notable is probably 'The Women Men Don't See' (1973), James Tiptree Jr (Alice Sheldon) completely overturned science fiction's default masculine perceptions of gender roles. The feminist science fiction that flowed from these origins to exploit sf's potential for social, sexual and political estrangement, has had a lasting effect on the genre, encouraging more and more women to write sf and ensuring that writers as varied as Josephine Saxton (*Queen of the States*, 1986), Karen Joy Fowler (*Sarah Canary*, 1991), Sheri Tepper (*Gibbon's Decline and Fall*, 1996) and Kelly Link (*Stranger Things Happen*, 2001) remain powerful and highly regarded voices in contemporary sf.

Throughout the 1960s and 1970s traditional hard sf and even, to an extent, space opera continued to play a significant part in American science fiction, particularly through writers like Gregory Benford (*In the Ocean of Night*, 1976; *Timescape*, 1980), David Brin (*Sundiver*, 1980) and John Varley (*The Ophiuchi Hotline*, 1977), and through the combination of military sf and romance typified by Lois McMaster Bujold (*The Warrior's Apprentice*, 1986). The popularity of this mode of sf was boosted during the 1970s by the continuing support for *Star Trek* even after it had been cancelled in 1969, and then again by the massive success of *Star Wars* in 1977. It continues to be the basis for much science fiction on film and television, especially when spectacle is privileged over content.

At first, the new form of sf that emerged in the early 1980s seemed like a continuation of hard sf, featuring as it did vivid portrayals of the future and obsessive interest in new technologies. But in fact cyberpunk owed as much to the British tradition of catastrophe story (Ballard and Brunner were cited as influences) and to American noir crime thrillers. This blending of styles, and the fact that certain of the cyberpunks explicitly referenced the work of authors like Thomas Pynchon, who would return the compliment in his own fictions, has helped identify cyberpunk as postmodern science fiction.[8] The archetypal cyberpunk novel, *Neuromancer* by William Gibson (1984), was set in 'the Sprawl', a near-future and rundown super city, a far more real presence than the glittering digital world accessed by its characters through computers. There is a similar sense of the world running down and the virtual and digital realms offering at best not an answer but a means of avoidance in *Synners* by Pat Cadigan (1991), *Snow Crash* by Neal Stephenson (1992) and *Islands in the Net* by Bruce Sterling (1988), the leading ideologue for cyberpunk and editor of the definitive anthology, *Mirrorshades* (1986).

At the time, much was made of a presumed clash between the cyberpunks and the so-called humanists, though this quarrel was largely artificial. In fact, though the humanists tended to eschew the computer and its associations, their views of the future and sense of a world at the end of its tether, politically, socially, morally and ecologically, were remarkably similar. The humanists probably draw their inspiration mostly from the work of Gene Wolfe, whose tetralogy, *The Book of the New Sun* (1980–83), is one of the finest works of postwar science fiction. Linguistically and structurally complex, it is the story of a quest for spiritual renewal in a distant and debased future. The writer most commonly associated with the humanists is Kim Stanley Robinson, whose monumental *Mars Trilogy* (1992–96) describes how humanity brings its foibles and disputes to Mars even as it is remaking the planet into a pristine new home.

Cyberpunk, as a movement, lasted little more than a decade, humanism even less, yet their joint influence on science fiction still informs contemporary sf. In particular, visions of a digital reality have fed into a literature of posthumanity. In novels such as *Diaspora* by Greg Egan (1997) and *Accelerando* by Charles Stross (2005) people are downloaded into digital storage to be revived after death, transformed into other shapes, transported as information across the heavens. Even in works considerably less cavalier than these, contemporary science fiction is full of transformed humanity. In *Air* by Geoff Ryman (2005), one of the most sensitive and humane works of sf in recent years, a woman in a remote central Asian village finds she has a direct mental link to the World Wide Web, and the novel relates how, for good and ill, this intrusion of the modern overturns a traditional way of life.

Egan is Australian, Stross British and Ryman a Canadian resident in the UK: recent years have seen a shift in focus away from America (where sf seemed to undergo an apparent but brief stagnation around the turn of the millennium) and towards Britain, apostrophized as the 'British renaissance'. British sf had undergone its own stagnation during the 1970s (the only writers of note to emerge in this decade were Ian Watson, Robert Holdstock and, belatedly, Christopher Evans). A new British magazine, *Interzone* (launched 1982), initially did little to change this; early issues were too in thrall to the model of *New Worlds* or, after 1984, to the influence of American cyberpunk. But it did provide a market for newer British writers; and a call for 'radical hard sf',[9] though ill-defined, seemed to presage a change of tone in British science fiction. At first this took the form of a reclamation of the genre's past. *Take Back Plenty* by Colin Greenland (1990) reworks the planetary romance with very modern sensibilities; the Culture novels by Iain M. Banks, beginning with *Consider Phlebas* (1987), are space operas set in an energy-rich and essentially left-wing utopian future; and the Fall Revolution quartet by Ken MacLeod, beginning with *The Star Fraction* (1995), are loosely linked near-future novels overlaid with different forms of socialist philosophy.

By the mid-1990s there was clearly a new confidence in British science fiction, often shown by an openness to new approaches. Postcolonial ideas, for instance, have proved fertile ground as shown by the Aleutian Trilogy by Gwyneth Jones, beginning with *White Queen* (1991); the Arabesk Trilogy by Jon Courtenay Grimwood, beginning with *Pashazade* (2001); and *River of Gods* by Ian McDonald (2004). More often, however, this openness has manifested itself as an infusion of other generic styles into sf. Paul McAuley, author of *Fairyland* (1995), an intriguing, vital novel of genetic engineering, later turned to the thriller, eventually combining it with sf to produce *Cowboy Angels* (2007). Stephen Baxter, so clearly the natural heir of Arthur C. Clarke that the two have collaborated on a number of novels, and whose novels have such a cosmic scale that they often include the end of the human race, has also written historical fiction, combining the two in *Coalescent* (2003). More usually it is fantasy and horror that have combined with sf, notably in *Perdido Street Station* by China Miéville (2000), resulting in a hybrid form that has been christened 'New Weird'.

Along with New Weird an unusual number of movements have been started or identified within sf over the last decade, including new hard sf, new space opera, mundane sf (proposed by Geoff Ryman and involving a fusion of mainstream and science fiction sensibilities), interstitial arts (the literature that, supposedly, occupies the interstices between genres), and more. These have tended towards dubious expansions of older forms (the new space opera appears to include a number of works that are clearly not space operas), or fusions of sf with, for instance, postmodernism. It is notable that among the new generation of American writers now starting to emerge, the trend has been to follow established forms, such as military sf (*Old Man's War* by John Scalzi, 2005; *Hammered* by Elizabeth Bear, 2005), space opera (*Ragamuffin* by Tobias Buckell, 2007), or steampunk (*Mainspring* by Jay Lake, 2007). Nevertheless one cannot help feeling that this proliferation of movements, this claimed renewal of the core of the genre, disguises a profound unease and uncertainty about the role and position of science fiction in the new century. Certainly the signs are ambiguous: magazine sales are in free fall but new venues for short fiction, particularly on the internet, are expanding; fantasy now takes up far more shelf space in bookshops than sf, but new specialist small presses are appearing all the time.

If this history has given the impression that science fiction in the twentieth century has been an entirely Anglophone affair, that is far from being the case. Stanislaw Lem from Poland, the Strugatski brothers from Russia, and Pierre Boulle from France have all made significant contributions to the genre, and probably the biggest selling series of all has been that of Perry Rhodan from Germany. But generally sf writers not working in English have been hampered by poor or nonexistent translations. With the new century, however, there has been a revival of interest in non-Anglophone writers, including Johanna Sinisalo from Finland (*Not Before Sundown*, 2000), Stefan Brijs from Holland (*The Angel Maker*, 2005), and others from Russia, France and Japan, so perhaps the twenty-first century will see science fiction recognized as the world literature it always was.

Notes

1. For a more thorough development of this approach to science fiction, see Paul Kincaid, 'On the Origins of Genre', *Extrapolation*, 44:4 (2003): 409–19.
2. Defining science fiction as being characteristically cast in the Gothic or post-Gothic mode, Aldiss argued that 'science fiction was born in the heart and crucible of the English Romantic movement in exile in Switzerland, when the wife of the poet Percy Bysshe Shelley wrote *Frankenstein: or, The Modern Prometheus*' (see Aldiss, *Billion Year Spree* [London: Weidenfeld and Nicolson, 1973] 3). Many later commentators have accepted this proposed origin of science fiction.

3. In the 1818 edition, Elizabeth and Frankenstein are cousins, in the later edition they are strangers. For a discussion of this and other changes, see Timothy Morton, ed., *Mary Shelley's Frankenstein: A Sourcebook* (London: Routledge, 2002).
4. 'Scientifiction' was the term Hugo Gernsback coined for the sort of fiction he published in *Amazing Stories* (1926 onwards), but it never enjoyed wide popularity.
5. Smith later revised the unrelated *Triplanetary* (1934) to open the series.
6. Aldiss remarks, 'It was then that [Wyndham] embarked on the course that was to make him master of the cosy catastrophe' (see *Billion Year Spree*, 335). Privately, Aldiss has since insisted that he meant the term to apply only to *The Day of the Triffids*, though the context of this quotation would imply otherwise.
7. As J.G. Ballard put it, 'The biggest developments of the immediate future will take place, not on the Moon or Mars, but on Earth, and it is *inner* space, not outer, that needs to be explored. The only truly alien planet is Earth' (see Ballard, 'Which Way to Inner Space', *New Worlds*, 118 [1962]: 2–3 and 116–18; reprinted in *A User's Guide to the Millennium* [London: HarperCollins, 1996] 195–8 at 197). Italics in original.
8. See Brian McHale, *Constructing Postmodernism* (London: Routledge, 1992) 225–42.
9. See David Pringle and Colin Greenland 'Editorial', *Interzone*, 7 (1984): 2.

2
Theorizing Science Fiction: The Question of Terminology

Gary K. Wolfe

In a controversial review in the January 1983 *Magazine of Fantasy and Science Fiction*, Algis Budrys, a noted science fiction writer who had become one of the field's most respected reviewers, claimed that 'the formal scholarship of speculative fiction is, taken in the whole, worthless'.[1] Quoting a passage from the distinguished Yale University scholar Harold Bloom in the volume under review, Budrys claimed it was 'not directed at anyone outside a tight circle who all share the same vocabulary and the same library'. The would-be literary scholar, Budrys argued, is forced to read more criticism than actual literature, or would be in danger of losing 'his grip on the nomenclature'. Budrys wasn't the first professional science fiction writer to express scepticism toward the sometimes arcane-sounding language of literary scholarship; such concerns were expressed repeatedly during the 1970s not only by science fiction fans, but by professional writers and editors including Lloyd Biggle Jr, William Tenn, Ben Bova and Lester del Rey.[2] And some of the leading academic scholars of the field also seemed to acknowledge that there was a problem; as early as 1976 R.D. Mullen, in the journal *Science-Fiction Studies*, reviewed a new academic study under the title 'Every Critic His Own Aristotle' – suggesting that nearly every author of a theoretical or critical study of the genre found it necessary to invent terms or assign new definitions to old ones as a means of staking a claim to originality[3] – and in his acceptance address for the 1984 Pilgrim Award from the Science Fiction Research Association (the longest-standing award for scholarship in the field), editor Everett F. Bleiler complained, 'Our terms have become muddled, imprecise, and heretical in the derivational sense of the word.' Even such ubiquitous terms as 'science fiction', 'fantasy', 'Gothic' and 'utopia' lack commonly accepted meanings, he argued, and anyone undertaking extended reading in this area of scholarship would even today find much to support his complaint.[4] In the university classroom this problem may be exacerbated in even more fundamental ways. Students may arrive equipped with the notion that science fiction encompasses an almost incoherent range of any sort of non-realistic fiction, from Huxley's *Brave New World* to Stephenie Meyers's teen vampire novels; or that it is principally a market category for film and television and video games; or that it somehow involves UFOs and pseudoscience; or that (in the case of the occasional serious devotee who shows up) it should properly be limited to a handful of favourite writers in the traditions of Heinlein, Asimov or Clarke. Adding to the confusion is the vocabulary of traditional terminology they may bring with them from earlier literature classes, which may incline them to view all science fiction according to familiar categories such as allegory or satire, or in terms of specific critical methodologies they may have encountered, from structuralism to postcolonialism. Beginning such a class by surveying the students' various notions of what they think it is that they will be reading can be a useful and often enlightening exercise, both by way of introducing a discussion of problems of definition and as preparation for the students' later encounters, in their own research, with the sometimes idiosyncratic critical vocabulary that has evolved in science fiction scholarship.

When one begins to explore how this critical and theoretical vocabulary evolved, it's not surprising that the 1970s and 1980s should have become something of a boiling point. Far from being the 'tight circle' of initiates that Budrys alluded to in his review, the scholarship of the fantastic had by then begun more to resemble an intellectual flea market, with various methodologies, values, definitions and even primary texts competing for the attention of scholars from disparate backgrounds who seemed unable even to agree upon what it is they were talking about. In my own glossary, *Critical Terms for Science Fiction and Fantasy* (1986), I tracked down some thirty-three separate definitions of 'science fiction', often contradictory, often clearly at cross-purposes with one another.[5] In the little more than two decades since, it would almost certainly be easy to track down another two or three dozen definitions, adding to the confusion even further.[6]

Is science fiction a body of works with common characteristics and, if so, what are those characteristics? Almost any we can name will likely be greeted with lists of exceptions from knowledgeable readers. If we say it involves the future, what do we do with the vast number of generally accepted works set in the past, or the present, or in a secret history or alternate reality? If we say it involves scientific inventions or developments, what do we do with the equally large number of texts that make no specific reference to the sciences at all, or with stories not generally accepted as science fiction but that nevertheless deal with science? And if we do claim that it's a body of specific works, when do we begin counting – as far back as Plato (as some anthologists and historians have done), or with eighteenth-century Swiftian satire, or with late Gothic-era novels such as Mary Shelley's *Frankenstein* (famously cited by science fiction novelist Brian Aldiss as the first real work of science fiction[7]), or with Jules Verne and H.G. Wells, or as late as the early twentieth century, when it clearly became a self-aware tradition with its own pulp magazines (as is claimed by science fiction historian Gary Westfahl[8])?

Or do we claim it's not really a specific set of texts at all, but rather an attitude, a way of looking at the world, a set of reading protocols that may have as much to do with *how* we read a text as with what the text contains? The latter argument, advanced by author Samuel R. Delany,[9] has become influential in postmodern discussions of the genre, and in fact implies that science fiction isn't really a genre at all. But other critics have also offered approaches that try to define the field in terms other than the material content of its stories; one of the most influential is Darko Suvin's 'estrangement' and 'cognition', both of which terms could, individually, apply to a wide range of literature, but which joined together serve to focus the discussion on works in which the estranged world presented in the text can be understood or 'explained' through cognitive processes. Suvin's only specific requirement as to a work's content is that its 'main formal device is an imaginative framework alternative to the author's empirical environment'.[10]

Part of the reason for this confusion is that the language we use to discuss modern science fiction and fantasy derives from a number of very different traditions of discourse, and from three in particular: the terminology of fandom, the terminology of professional writers and editors, and the terminology of scholars and academics. Fandom, which may be defined as a very loosely organized subset of science fiction's readership, began critical discussions of science fiction in the letters to the editor columns of the early pulp magazines, and soon moved on to creating its own fanzines and even reference works. While much of its terminology is coyly self-referential (describing the behaviour and attitudes of fans themselves), it also gave us a number of terms which have survived to describe specific traditions or themes within science fiction (such as 'space opera' or 'future war story'). The professional community – which for much of science fiction's history has overlapped the fan community – developed its own shorthand for particular themes and techniques, both within the fiction itself and in various reviews, essays and workshops; many of these terms have also entered the general vocabulary of sf criticism, such as 'speculative fiction' or 'alternate history'. Academia, which also overlaps to some degree with the professional community, came into the discussion fairly late – the first academic journals didn't get underway until the 1960s and 1970s, and the first university press studies of the genre began appearing about the same time – bringing with it entirely new terms of critical discourse, some imported from literary scholarship – 'estrangement', 'fabulation', 'dialectic', 'postmodernism'; some invented in order to describe a literary tradition that couldn't fully be accommodated by a critical vocabulary that had largely evolved to discuss the long-dominant tradition of social realism in fiction; some imported from related fields of the social sciences or from such interdisciplinary domains as myth study, semiotics, popular culture, structuralism, feminism, queer theory, postcolonialism and postmodernism.

This is the situation that had evolved when Budrys wrote his scathing review in 1983; what some welcomed as the 'academic awakening' to science fiction became in the view of others the 'academic invasion'. Scholars complained that terms from fandom, such as 'extrapolation' or 'sense of wonder', were imprecise and faddish, while fans and writers complained that academics wrote only for Budrys's 'tight circle who all share the same vocabulary and the same library'. What was originally a publishing term such as 'pulp' confusingly may refer to a kind of cheap paper stock, the prose printed on it, the assumptions underlying that prose, or any authors (even of the modern era) who partake of those assumptions. A term such as this may also carry widely varying connotations: for a fan writer, 'pulp' may invoke a 'Golden Age' (another rubbery term), while to a traditional scholar, it may refer to one of the genre's worst embarrassments. 'Myth' may mean a specific mechanism of cultural organization to one group of scholars or a primitive story to another; for some fans it might be a buzzword to invoke cultural legitimacy for a favourite genre (as in the once-common claim that science fiction is a kind of contemporary mythology). Each group, of course, claims to be speaking English while the others are hopelessly mired in self-indulgent jargon. Each group, to some extent, uses its language to create and maintain a community of initiates.

Even today, these multiple etymologies are reflected in dictionaries and reference works in the field. Jeff Prucher's *Brave New Words: The*

Oxford Dictionary of Science Fiction (2007) includes words and phrases coined by science fiction writers in their own stories, fannish lingo (some all but obsolescent), publishing terminology and the occasional academic term. John Clute and Peter Nicholls's magisterial *Encyclopedia of Science Fiction* (1993) does the same, but adds many coinages that are either original or were rarely used earlier (such as 'fix-up' or 'conceptual breakthrough'). Neil Barron's library reference work *Anatomy of Wonder* (5th edition, 2004) includes a 'theme index' which conflates terms drawn from general literary scholarship ('Absurdist SF', 'Pastoral') with terms likely known only to science fiction readers ('Steampunk', 'Space Opera'). It quickly begins to seem that anyone wanting to participate in the critical discourse on science fiction must begin by mastering multiple sets of codes and code-words, a problem further exacerbated by the significant number of critical neologisms that emerge as critics and scholars, finding little in the way of consensus terminology, simply concoct their own. Some of these coinages, such as Suvin's 'cognitive estrangement', have gained wide currency, while others, such as 'span fiction' (a term suggested by Peter Brigg for mainstream writers using science fiction devices[11]) or 'fabril' (suggested by Tom Shippey for a broad tradition of non-pastoral literature which includes science fiction[12]) have barely survived beyond their original appearances.

How, then, is a student encountering this complex and sometimes thorny tradition of discourse supposed to learn the lingo? One approach might be to begin by asking which particular aspects of science fiction have, in the minds of critics and scholars, created the need for a more specialized critical vocabulary in addition to that found in more traditional glossaries and handbooks to literary study. We might then be able to identify specific critical issues reflected in these emerging vocabularies. Broadly speaking, we can suggest five such issues or domains: *definition*, or genre theory; *classification*, or taxonomies of the literature and its subgenres; *theme*, or characteristic recurrent motifs and topics treated within the genre; *context*, or the location of the genre within larger historical or methodological approaches; and *technique*, or the manner in which literary devices or mechanisms are used within the genre. (This list does not include terms associated with fannish activity, such as 'filk' or 'gafiate'.)

Terms of definition

Perhaps the most widely cited 'definition' of science fiction is author and critic Damon Knight's 'what we point to when we say it' (1952),[13] and the very tautology implicit in Knight's deceptively offhand wisecrack suggests that even in the early days of science fiction criticism it was already apparent that the game of trying to pin down a universally acceptable set of conditions for the genre was a treacherous one. Any single definition seemed to imply an entire conceptual history of the field, and as a result a number of scholars found themselves trying to parse the term, arguing for example (as Roger Luckhurst and Adam Roberts have recently done[14]) that at least some vaguely contemporary notion of 'science' was a precondition for anything that could be called science fiction. These same critics recognize that 'science fiction' itself is a somewhat arbitrary label, however, and that the phrase evolved as a term of convenience rather than as a manifesto. In fact, when one looks at a great many of the definitions offered through the past century or so, it becomes apparent that the nature of the definition depends almost entirely on its purpose and its audience – some are purely functional, some rhetorical and some theoretical– and that trying to adapt a definition intended for one purpose to the service of another can lead to misprision and confusion.

Functional definitions are entirely practical in nature. When, in 1926, editor Hugo Gernsback described the characteristic story of his pioneering pulp magazine *Amazing Stories* as a 'charming romance intermingled with scientific fact and prophetic vision',[15] he was in all likelihood merely trying to differentiate his magazine from other pulps for the benefit of readers and potential contributors – in other words, he was at least in part staking out his market. When a later editor, John W. Campbell Jr, described the field as 'the literature of speculation as to what changes may come',[16] and argued that a good science fiction story should read like a realistic tale to a hypothetical reader in its implied setting, he was similarly differentiating his magazine, *Astounding Science Fiction*, from earlier adventure-oriented pulps like Gernsback's. Similarly, when editor David Hartwell introduced his first *Year's Best Science Fiction* anthology in 1996 by describing its contents as stories 'a chronic reader would recognize as SF',[17] he was deliberately placing himself in opposition to earlier 'best of' annuals (notably those of Gardner Dozois) which he felt had diluted the definition of the field excessively. In all these cases, definitions served essentially as admissions criteria for books and magazines – what should or should not, for practical purposes, be counted as science fiction. Editors, publishers, booksellers, even film and TV producers have tended to define the term in such a purely functional, market-driven way, seldom pausing to consider if their use of the term implied any sort of theoretical or philosophical consistency. To a great extent, Knight's 'what we point to when we say it' is this sort of definition, as is author Norman Spinrad's later variation, 'Science fiction is anything published as science fiction.'[18]

Rhetorical definitions more often come from practising writers in the field, some with a particular axe to grind, and are meant to be persuasive rather than scholarly. When Theodore Sturgeon, one of the most humanistic of pulp-era science fiction writers, defined science fiction as 'a story built around human beings, with a human problem and a human solution, which would not have happened at all without its scientific content' (1951),[19] he was clearly arguing for the primacy of fiction over science, of humanistic concerns over scientific ideas or pure pulp adventure. (Sturgeon later commented that, although this had been widely quoted as a general definition of the genre, he had intended it as the definition of a *good* science fiction story.) But when Robert Heinlein, more often associated with the 'hard' school of science fiction, described it as 'realistic speculation about possible future events, based solidly on adequate knowledge of the real world, past and present, and on a thorough understanding of the nature and significance of the scientific method' (1957),[20] he was offering a kind of counter-argument to Sturgeon by demanding 'adequate knowledge' and understanding of the scientific method. Both Sturgeon and Heinlein were essentially describing their own fiction, but they were also trying to nudge the field in a certain direction: at the time Sturgeon was writing, the sometimes sloppily written adventure pulps were still dominant in the field, and by the time Heinlein was writing a few years later, one of the most popular 'science fiction' writers to have emerged in the 1950s was Ray Bradbury, who was notorious for his cavalier attitude toward science and the scientific method.

Theoretical definitions are more deliberately formal and academic in nature, and are generally less prescriptive than functional or rhetorical definitions. Even for a professional scholar, however, there is an element of functionality in any such definition, a way of delimiting the texts to be discussed. J.O. Bailey's *Pilgrims through Space and Time* (1947), widely regarded as the first academic study of science fiction (and almost certainly the first to be based on a doctoral dissertation; Bailey's was originally written in 1934), described a science fiction story as 'a narrative of an imaginary invention or discovery in the natural sciences and consequent adventures and experiences'.[21] While this might have seemed unnaturally restrictive even in the 1940s, it served to alert the reader (and presumably Bailey's doctoral committee) to his principle of selecting the particular works to be discussed. Historical studies such as Bailey's (or later studies by such authors as Brian Aldiss, Edward James,

Roger Luckhurst and Adam Roberts) have all faced similar problems, and have thus characteristically evaded the temptation to begin with a formal definition. 'I will certainly not make the mistake of trying to begin, or conclude, with a simple definition', writes Edward James,[22] while Adam Roberts concedes that 'This study has been unable to avoid the often tedious debates concerning "definition"', but goes on to say that 'my aim is to present a historically determined narrative of the genre's evolution rather than offering an apophthegmatic version of the sentence "SF is such-and-such"'.[23]

By the late 1960s, however, science fiction had begun to come to the attention of more formalist theoreticians from both inside and outside the genre, and two of the most enduring such critical models were presented at the same convention of the Modern Language Association in New York in 1968: author Samuel R. Delany's argument that the genre could be defined at the syntactical level and by means of its level of 'subjunctivity', and Darko Suvin's definition as a literature of 'cognitive estrangement' (later developed at book length in his 1979 *Metamorphoses of Science Fiction: On the Poetics and History of a Literary Genre*). There followed decades of spirited debate on the formal characteristics of the genre, drawing the participation of both 'mainstream' theorists like Robert Scholes and Eric Rabkin and of practising writers such as Joanna Russ and Damien Broderick. For the most part, these more formalist definitions fell into two broad camps: those which focused on the interactions between text and reader that were peculiar to science fiction (such as Delany's or Suvin's or Carl Malmgren's narratological approach in his 1991 *Worlds Apart: Narratology of Science Fiction*) – a variation on reader-response criticism – and those which focused on the differences between science fiction and other kinds of texts (such as Rabkin's locating science fiction along a spectrum of works ranging from less to more fantastic, in *The Fantastic in Literature,* 1976; or Brian Attebery's adaptation of the logicians' notion of 'fuzzy sets', with groups of fantastic works defined more by their centres than by rigid perimeters, in his *Strategies of Fantasy,* 1992[24]). Both approaches can generate useful methodologies, even if neither can quite claim to be definitive.

Terms of classification

Even the earliest readers of the pulp magazines quickly recognized that their favourite stories were falling into discernible types – space operas, time travel, marvellous inventions, 'superscience' – and by the time science fiction stories began to be widely anthologized in the late

1940s, such categories proved convenient means of organizing the contents. One of the very first such anthologies, Groff Conklin's *The Best of Science Fiction* (1946), clearly reflected both the dominant concerns of its era and the types of stories which were available: the anthology is divided into sections titled 'The Atom', 'The Wonders of Earth and Man', 'The Superscience of Man', 'Dangerous Inventions', 'Adventures in Dimension' and 'From Outer Space'. Conklin later went on to edit anthologies focused entirely on such common themes – invasions of earth, mutations, different dimensions, 'thinking machines', giants or supermen. Again, these were mostly terms of convenience rather than theoretical constructs, but the work of Conklin and other anthologists represented an early effort toward creating a typology of science fiction stories based on theme and content, and such typologies still show up occasionally in textbook anthologies and teaching guides. This almost folkloristic approach to recurring motifs can be useful in approaching large bodies of mostly undistinguished fiction, such as the early pulps, and one of the most ambitious such motif-indexes appears in Everett F. Bleiler and Richard Bleiler's *Science-Fiction: The Gernsback Years*, which summarizes more than 1800 stories from pulp magazines between 1926 and 1936, offering a detailed theme index of more than 30,000 entries and citations.

But such an approach can be confusing as a critical methodology, since science fiction texts may be classified not only by theme, but by form, by historical period, by specific historical movements, or even by narrative strategy. The theme index to Neil Barron's *Anatomy of Wonder*, mentioned earlier, conflates (but does not define) terms adapted from mainstream literary study (absurdist sf, dystopia, pastoral), terms describing subgenres of science fiction (hard sf, space opera, science fantasy), terms referring to broad universal themes (sex, ecology, coming of age, crime and punishment), terms identifying specific movements within science fiction (feminist sf, cyberpunk, steampunk, New Wave), and themes characteristic of sf in particular (parallel worlds, robots, space flight, clones). While the purpose of this index is merely to enable the reader to track down certain works in the annotated bibliography that constitutes the bulk of the book, and not to serve as a proposed taxonomy of the genre, it nevertheless illustrates the hazards of attempting to create classifications within such a diffuse and evolving field.

Complicating the issue further is that terms often change their meaning or connotation over time. 'Space opera', coined by Wilson Tucker in 1941 to refer to the cliché-ridden 'hacky, grinding, stinking, outworn spaceship yarn',[25] later became a term of nostalgia in anthologies such as Brian W. Aldiss's *Space Opera* (1974), and still later, under the rubric 'new space opera', a term to describe a comparatively sophisticated literary movement in which authors used the basic template of the old form for more complex and literary explorations of the possibilities of science fiction. 'New Wave' originally referred mainly to a group of writers associated with the British *New Worlds* magazine in the 1960s, but was soon expanded to include writers on both sides of the Atlantic interested in literary and thematic experimentation, and now is often used to refer to an entire era in the history of science fiction. Similarly, 'cyberpunk' originally referred to a relatively short-lived movement among a limited group of writers in the mid-1980s, but later expanded beyond science fiction altogether to refer to a collective set of cultural attitudes regarding information theory and biotechnology, and now is sometimes used to refer to almost any reflection of these attitudes in fiction; what was once a movement has become a mode.

Terms of theme

As should be evident from the *Anatomy of Wonder* theme index cited above, terms used to refer to specific recurring themes in science fiction may be closely related to terms of classification, and the resulting confusion raises interesting questions about the nature of subgenres within the field. Is 'military science fiction' an actual subgenre (even though it's often marketed that way), or does it simply refer to any science fiction with military themes? Does 'planetary romance' simply refer to a story's setting, or does it describe a particular set of works with common characteristics? Some themes in science fiction (robots, space travel, genetic engineering, aliens, time travel) are so ubiquitous as to support any variety of story-types, while others (future war, alternate history, dystopia, disaster) may refer to specific traditions, often pre-dating modern science fiction itself and including works not usually regarded as science fiction in the contemporary sense. For example, I.F. Clarke's *Voices Prophesying War* (1966; rev. edn 1992) discusses future war narratives dating back to 1763, while bibliographies of utopian and dystopian literature disaster tales might be traced all the way back to *Gilgamesh* or the biblical story of the flood. The question of when a theme becomes coherent enough, and supports enough recurrent structures or tropes, to become a subgenre, can be a fairly thorny one, and perhaps one more easily recognized by the market than by the theorist.

Computers and artificial intelligence, for obvious examples, have become such a fixture of science fiction that it would be useless to attempt to identify a subgenre of 'computer stories', yet some aspects of computers and information theory have indeed begun to generate identifiable traditions. The concept of virtual reality, with its attendant conceit of the possibility of uploading one's entire personality, has nearly led to a school of novels and stories dealing with a possible posthuman condition, often following a kind of transformative 'singularity' (a term adapted by writer Vernor Vinge from physics); similarly, worlds radically transformed by nanotechnology have become almost common enough to suggest a type. Such concepts may remain highly speculative in the real world, but they have long since become common themes in science fiction. Conversely, some once-common themes, such as 'psionics', telepathy, or mutants, have almost faded into historical curiosities, reflecting the obsessions of the genre at a specific period in its history (in this case, the 1940s and 1950s in particular).

Another theme which has virtually become a subgenre unto itself is alternate history, with authors such as Harry Turtledove, S.M. Stirling and Robert Conroy writing what are essentially historical novels involving key changes in the historical record; to a great extent, such novels have found a readership far beyond, and not entirely congruent with, that of science fiction. At the same time, the theme remains popular within science fiction, with authors frequently presenting multiple alternate timelines within the same narrative (such as Paul McAuley's 2007 *Cowboy Angels*) or positing artificial 'pocket universes', which can have the effect of generating alternate universes. This in turn leads to another tangle of confusing terms – 'alternate history', which is coming increasingly to refer to stories which diverge from our own history at a particular 'jonbar point' (a term borrowed from a 1938 story by Jack Williamson), must be distinguished from 'alternate universe', which refers to the possibility referred to in quantum theory of completely different universes existing alongside ours (including the pocket universes mentioned above) and 'alternate reality', which permits a wide variety of devices, including universes which exist entirely within the mind of a character (as in Philip K. Dick's 1955 novel *Eye in the Sky*) or even within a text. All these, in turn, are different from 'secret history', a phrase sometimes used to describe stories in which fantastic or science fictional events are worked seamlessly (one hopes) into the actual historical record (such as Jack Dann's *The Memory Cathedral*, 1996, dealing with missing years from the life of Leonardo da Vinci). Clearly, such terms continue to evolve, and to spin off yet more specialized subthemes and subgenres.

Terms of context

When, in their literary history *Trillion Year Spree*, Aldiss and Wingrove described science fiction as 'characteristically cast in the Gothic or post-Gothic mode',[26] they were attempting to locate it in the context of an earlier literary movement or genre, much as Sam Moskowitz and Donald Wollheim had when they earlier described it (independently of one another) as a 'branch of fantasy'.[27] Unlike terms that seek to anatomize science fiction based on its internal content or structures, such approaches attempt to find a place for the genre in broader cultural landscapes, though they almost inevitably lead to corollary problems of definition (what is fantasy? What is Gothic?) Generally, such descriptions fall into three categories: those which want to place science fiction in specific traditions of literature (such as the examples above), those which seek to place it in wider historical contexts (such as the argument that it is essentially a post-Enlightenment literature or even a characteristically American form), and those which work largely through analogy or metaphor (such as the argument that it is essentially philosophy, or a quest for transcendence, or a kind of mythology). When, for example, the Science Fiction Research Association sponsored a reading anthology in 1978 titled *Science Fiction: Contemporary Mythology, The SFWA-SFRA Anthology* (edited by Patricia Warrick, Martin Harry Greenberg and Joseph Olander), it's unlikely that any of the editors meant literally to claim the genre as representing a mythology in any sense that a classicist or anthropologist would accept as literal – rather, they sought to associate it with a respected and ancient tradition of storytelling. It is likely, though, that Alexei and Cory Panshin had a more or less literal meaning in mind in describing science fiction as 'a literature of the mythic imagination' in their *The World Beyond the Hill: Science Fiction and the Quest for Transcendence* (1989); here they seemed to view 'mythic' as a general kind of psychological and cultural construct rather than as a received body of tales.[28]

Such associations can be useful in understanding the early and prehistory of science fiction. Brian Stableford's 1985 study *The Scientific Romance in Britain, 1890–1950* not only seeks to delineate a history of the British 'scientific romance' as distinct from the American pulp-adventure tradition, but implicitly contextualizes that genre in terms of the 'romance' rather than the realistic novel, and cites a number of earlier traditions which share some of its characteristics – imaginary voyages, utopias, evolutionary fantasies, future war tales, eschatological and metaphysical fantasies, even the speculative non-fiction of early science writers. Similarly, in his history of early American science fiction *Some Kind of Paradise* (1985), Thomas D. Clareson links elements of the field to earlier Gothic novels, romances of reincarnation, lost-race tales, scientific-detective tales, catastrophe stories, satires and utopias. By the same token, many critics have examined specific aspects or subgenres of science fiction in terms of other popular genres – not only the Gothic, but romances, historical fiction, westerns, detective and mystery stories, horror stories, fantasy, military fiction, technothrillers, juvenile or young adult fiction, even family sagas (John J. Pierce's *Odd Genre: A Study in Imagination and Evolution*, 1994, offers examples of a number of these 'crossovers'). Moving even further afield, a fair proportion of recent scholarship has considered how science fictional ideas are expressed outside the realm of prose fiction altogether – in film and television, graphic novels and comic books, video and computer games, art, theatre, speculative or futurist non-fiction, even photography and architecture. Each of these linkages creates new issues of theory and terminology, and collectively they raise the question of whether even so fundamental a term as 'science fiction' – or even 'fiction' – can properly encompass the broad range of cultural expression that has come to be associated with it.

Terms of technique

In a 1947 essay, Robert A. Heinlein described a science fiction story as one in which 'accepted science and established facts are extrapolated to produce a new situation, a new framework for human action',[29] and by 1955 critic Basil Davenport could report that 'extrapolation' was 'a word that is almost as great a favourite in discussions of science fiction as "space-warp" is in science fiction itself; it may be defined as "plotting the curve"'.[30] The term, borrowed from statistics and mathematics, even became the title of science fiction's first academic journal. What Heinlein likely intended to do, and what has been repeated endlessly by science fiction writers ever since, was to identify the essential technique by which science fiction writers arrived at the conditions of their imaginary society or world. While it can reasonably be argued, as H. Bruce Franklin has done, that 'in fact most science fiction does not extrapolate seriously',[31] or that a rigorous definitional usage of the term would eliminate a great many science fiction works from consideration, the term was nevertheless an influential attempt to characterize a specific fictional mechanism involved in the writing of science fiction, and which was more characteristic of science fiction than of most other types of literature.

The popularity of this term reflects an ongoing effort among science fiction writers, editors and critics to identify techniques that may be peculiar to the genre. While all the conventional terms of literary art – plot, character, conflict, exposition, dramatic arc, style, figures of speech and the like – are as relevant to science fiction as to any other sort of fiction, there has long been a sense that more specialized techniques may be involved in generating a successful science fiction tale. Like 'extrapolation', some of these terms may be borrowed from other fields of study. When Ursula K. Le Guin described her novel *The Left Hand of Darkness* (1969) as a 'thought-experiment',[32] she was borrowing a term from German physicists, but was also identifying another technique for creating imaginary societies, one which she regarded as an alternative to extrapolation ('This book is not extrapolative', she also wrote of her novel). Le Guin also has used the term 'literalized metaphor' (a concept borrowed from Samuel R. Delany and adapted from a conventional literary term) to describes sentences which would be read as purely metaphorical in realistic literature, but might be literally true in the context of a science fiction tale (such as 'her face lit up'). As with extrapolation, though, one wonders how often science fiction writers have actually made conscious use of such a technique.

If such terms seem better suited to describing the nature of science fiction than to dealing with the actual process of composition, there are others which have evolved to reflect specific issues faced by writers in constructing a science fictional text. 'World-building', for example – the detailed description of an imaginary setting – is common to many kinds of fiction, but has sometimes been elevated to a principle of composition by science fiction and fantasy writers, some of whom (Hal Clement is a famous early example) conscientiously map out the history, politics, culture, architecture, geography, geology, and sometimes even the astronomical environment of a story, even though many of the details may not appear in the story itself, or may be revealed only over a series of related tales. For some writers and readers, world-building became as much an aesthetic value in science fiction as characterization or style. In early 2007, the writer M. John Harrison created a year-long debate by suggesting on his blog that world-building had become so pervasive that it distracted from the fundamental business of writing fiction.

Because science fiction often does involve world-building, however, and often takes place in environments unfamiliar to the reader, specific problems of exposition also arise – how is the reader to gain bearings in this alienated environment? Several such techniques have evolved in science fiction workshops over the years, and some workshop terminology has begun to work its way back into critical discussions of the genre. 'Heinleining', for example, refers to the technique pioneered by Robert A. Heinlein of weaving the salient aspects of the setting seamlessly into the narrative, while the more awkward 'infodump' refers to lumps of background exposition which interrupt the flow of the tale. Other workshop terms (such as 'As You Know Bob', in which a character recapitulates back story or setting ostensibly for the benefit of another character) have been compiled by members of the Science Fiction Writers of America in its 'Turkey City Lexicon'; most refer to common errors of beginning writers, but many are of equal relevance in discussing even well-known tales.[33]

All literary terminology, like all language, evolves and changes over time – look at any literary handbook from fifty years ago compared to one published today – but it seems reasonable to claim that few areas of literary study have evolved out of so many active and often contentious communities as has science fiction (or its allied genres of fantasy and horror, sometimes collectively referred to as a 'supergenre'[34]). 'Maintaining a grip on the nomenclature', as Budrys put it so long ago, is no longer a problem faced solely by academics and scholars, but by anthologists, teachers, editors, writers, and to some extent any informed reader of the genre. It also seems reasonable to assert that the language associated with science fiction evolves at a more rapid rate than that associated with more traditional literary terms; words like 'cyberpunk' or 'New Wave', originally meant to refer to revolutionary, cutting-edge fiction, can in the space of a couple of decades become historical terms, almost as period-bound as 'Beat' or *nouvelle roman* are in mainstream literary discourse. The last few years have seen a plethora of new terms coined to describe fiction which evades, slips between, or overlaps various genre categories but which still relates to the supergenre of the fantastic – slipstream, interstitial, New Wave Fabulism, transrealism – and it's almost impossible to tell at this point which of these terms might survive, which might grow quaint with age, and which might disappear altogether. What they all have in common, though, is that they seek to identify a perceived new development in a fluid and dynamic arena of fiction. As long as such new developments continue to arise, they will provide evidence of the genre's ongoing vitality – and while this may create a fair amount of confusion or frustration for the dictionary-makers and teachers among us, it is also a major source of the rewards that serious scholars, students and readers have always found in this literature.

Notes

1. Algis Budrys, 'Books', *The Magazine of Fantasy and Science Fiction*, 64:1 (1983): 19.
2. Lloyd Biggle Jr, 'Science Fiction Goes to College: Groves and Morasses of Academe', *Riverside Quarterly*, 6 (1974): 100–9, and 'The Morasses of Academe Revisited', *Analog*, 98 (1978): 146–63; William Tenn, 'Jazz Then, Musicology Now', *Magazine of Fantasy and Science Fiction*, 42 (1972): 107–10; Ben Bova, 'Teaching Science Fiction', *Analog*, 93 (1974): 5–8; Lester del Rey, 'The Siren Song of Academe', *Galaxy*, 36 (1975): 69–80.
3. R.D. Mullen, 'Every Critic His Own Aristotle', *Science-Fiction Studies*, 3:3 (1976): 311. The book under review was Eric S. Rabkin, *The Fantastic in Literature* (Princeton, NJ: Princeton University Press, 1976).
4. Everett F. Bleiler, 'Pilgrim Award Acceptance Address', *SFRA Newsletter*, 123 (1984): 12.
5. Gary K. Wolfe, *Critical Terms for Science Fiction and Fantasy* (Westport, CT: Greenwood Press, 1986).
6. By 1996, the Turkish fan and scholar Neyir Cenk Gökçe had amassed 52 definitions on his website, http://www.panix.com/~gokce/sf_defn.html.
7. Brian Aldiss and David Wingrove, *Trillion Year Spree: The History of Science Fiction* (New York: Atheneum, 1986) 18.
8. Gary Westfahl, *The Mechanics of Wonder* (Liverpool: Liverpool University Press, 1998) 8.
9. See Samuel R. Delany, 'About Five Thousand One Hundred and Seventy-Five Words', in *The Jewel-Hinged Jaw* (New York: Berkley, 1977), and several later essays.
10. Darko Suvin, *Metamorphoses of Science Fiction: On the Poetics of a Literary Genre* (New Haven, CT and London: Yale University Press, 1979) 8.
11. Peter Brigg, *The Span of Mainstream and Science Fiction* (Jefferson, NC: McFarland, 2002) 13–14.
12. Tom Shippey, 'Introduction', in *The Oxford Book of Science Fiction Stories* (New York: Oxford University Press, 1992) ix.
13. Damon Knight, *In Search of Wonder*, 2nd edn (Chicago: Advent, 1967) 1. The observation first appeared in Knight's review column for the pulp magazine *Science Fiction Adventures*, November 1952.
14. See Roger Luckhurst, *Science Fiction* (Cambridge: Polity Press, 2005) and Adam Roberts, *The History of Science Fiction* (Basingstoke: Palgrave Macmillan, 2006).
15. Hugo Gernsback, 'A New Sort of Magazine', *Amazing Stories*, 1:1 (1926) 3.
16. John W. Campbell Jr, quoted in Reginald Bretnor, *Modern Science Fiction: Its Meaning and Its Future* (New York: Coward-McCann, 1953) 12.
17. David Hartwell, 'Introduction', *The Year's Best Science Fiction* (New York: Harper, 1996) xiii.
18. Norman Spinrad, 'Introduction', *Modern Science Fiction* (Garden City, NY: Anchor, 1974) 1–2.
19. Theodore Sturgeon quoted in James Gunn, *Alternate Worlds: The Illustrated History of Science Fiction* (Englewood Cliffs, NJ: Prentice-Hall, 1975) 31.
20. Robert A. Heinlein, 'Science Fiction: Its Nature, Faults, and Virtues', in *The Science Fiction Novel: Imagination and Social Criticism* (Chicago: Advent, 1959) 16.

54 *Teaching Science Fiction*

21. J.O. Bailey, *Pilgrims through Space and Time* (1947; Westport, CT: Greenwood, 1972) 10.
22. Edward James, *Science Fiction in the Twentieth Century* (Oxford: Oxford University Press, 1994) 1.
23. Roberts, *The History of Science Fiction*, 3.
24. See Rabkin, *The Fantastic in Literature*; Brian Attebery, *Strategies of Fantasy* (Bloomington and Indianapolis: Indiana University Press, 1992).
25. Wilson Tucker quoted in David G. Hartwell and Kathryn Cramer, 'Introduction', in *The Space Opera Renaissance* (New York: Tor, 2006) 9–21 at 10. Hartwell and Cramer's introduction provides an extensive and useful overview of the history of this term.
26. Aldiss and Wingrove, *Trillion Year Spree*, 25.
27. See Sam Moskowitz, *Explorers of the Infinite* (Cleveland: World, 1963) and Donald Wollheim, *The Universe Makers* (New York: Harper, 1971).
28. Alexei and Cory Panshin, *The World beyond the Hill: Science Fiction and the Quest for Transcendence* (Los Angeles: Tarcher, 1989) 1.
29. Robert A. Heinlein, 'On the Writing of Speculative Fiction', in Lloyd Arthur Eshbach, ed., *Of Worlds Beyond* (1947; London: Dobson, 1965) 17.
30. Basil Davenport, *Inquiry into Science Fiction* (New York: Longmans, 1955) 12.
31. H. Bruce Franklin quoted in 'Definitions of Science Fiction', 25 May 1996, http://www.panix.com/~gokce/sf_defn.html (accessed 20 April 2008).
32. Ursula K. Le Guin, 'Introduction to *The Left Hand of Darkness*', in *The Language of the Night: Essays on Fantasy and Science Fiction* (New York: HarperCollins, 1989) 151.
33. Turkey City Lexicon, http://www.sfwa.org/writing/turkeycity.html (accessed 21 September 2010).
34. R.D. Mullen, 'Books in Review: Supernatural, Pseudonatural, and Sociocultural Fantasy', *Science Fiction Studies*, 5:2 (1978): 291–8; Rabkin, *The Fantastic in Literature*.

3
Utopia, Anti-Utopia and Science Fiction

Chris Ferns

The relationship between utopian literature and science fiction is a complex and in some respects problematic one. While the two genres have come to overlap to the extent that some argue they have effectively merged, their origins are nevertheless quite distinct. For the teacher of utopian literature (the fictional representation of a more perfect society, as distinct from utopian political theory, which has an even longer history) the obvious starting point is Thomas More's *Utopia* (1516), whereas in the case of science fiction, although its origins are more open to debate, Mary Shelley's *Frankenstein* (1818) is the most commonly assumed foundational text.[1] By most reckonings, then, utopian literature pre-dates the emergence of what comes to be known as science fiction by over three hundred years. And while some utopias of the intervening period, such as Tomasso Campanella's *The City of the Sun* (1623) and Francis Bacon's *The New Atlantis* (1627), may envisage scientific innovation as an important aspect of their imagined societies, it would be hard to describe the result as science fiction, inasmuch as nothing that actually *happens* in either narrative is in any way affected by the fact.

Yet with the passage of time there is an increasing convergence between what might seem at first sight to be two quite independent genres. As the age of exploration draws to a close, the traditional utopian narrative – in which a traveller visits a geographically separate society and returns to attest to its superiority – begins to seem increasingly outdated; and from the late nineteenth century onward, there is a growing tendency for writers of utopian literature to turn to narrative devices characteristic of science fiction. Edward Bellamy's *Looking Backward* (1888) and William Morris's utopian counterblast, *News From Nowhere* (1890), both locate their more perfect societies in the future (although that is about the only science fictional aspect of Morris's utopia). H.G. Wells, in *A Modern Utopia* (1905), imagines another Earth with an alternative history; his *Men Like Gods* (1923) uses the equally science fictional conceit of parallel universes; while Alexander Bogdanov's *Red Star* (1908) is one of a host of narratives where the site of utopia is another planet. And in the case of utopia's negative counterpart, whether one terms this dystopia or anti-utopia,[2] the convergence is still more marked. Works such as Yevgeny Zamyatin's *We* (1920), Aldous Huxley's *Brave New World* (1932) or Margaret Atwood's *The Handmaid's Tale* (1985) can be and are taught in courses on both utopian literature and science fiction.

Certainly, instances of the old, geographically separate utopia persist well into the twentieth century, notable examples being Charlotte Perkins Gilman's *Herland* (1915), B.F. Skinner's *Walden Two* (1948) and Aldous Huxley's *Island* (1962), but these have proved increasingly exceptions to the rule. Virtually all the major developments in utopian literature since the 1970s – the works of Joanna Russ, Ursula K. Le Guin, Samuel Delany, Marge Piercy and, more recently, Kim Stanley Robinson – utilize science fiction as the most appropriate vehicle for the exploration of utopian possibilities. This being so, there has been an increasing tendency for critics to argue that what has taken place is not simply the convergence of two distinct genres, but their actual merger. As Darko Suvin puts it, what has taken place is in effect an 'englobing of utopia' (itself a suggestively science fictional metaphor) by the younger, broader genre of science fiction, to the extent that utopia has become not so much a genre in its own right as, in Suvin's words, 'the *sociopolitical subgenre of science fiction*'.[3]

Taking this position tends to lead, unsurprisingly, to readings of both utopian literature and science fiction that stress their similarities. While earlier utopias have often been criticized for their static, prescriptive quality – their attempt to impose on the (often resistant) reader the view that a more perfect society not only could, but *should* be as the author imagines it – their science fictional successors are more in the business of suggesting possibilities, providing glimpses (or what Angelika Bammer terms 'partial visions'[4]) of how things might be otherwise. Like science fiction, utopian literature provides alternative scenarios that create an effect of estrangement, defamiliarizing existing reality, and making the reader aware of its provisional quality, its potential to be radically changed. What emerges as a result might almost be seen as a new category, one which Tom Moylan, in his influential study *Demand the Impossible*, refers to as the 'critical utopia' – where 'the imposed totality of the single utopian text gives way to the contradictory and diverse multiplicity of a broad utopian dialogue'.[5] For Bammer and Moylan such utopias also transcend some of the aesthetic limitations of earlier utopian literature – its proneness to ponderous didacticism, or the predictability of the narrative where the visitor to utopia is given what amounts to a guided tour of the imagined world, and is easily persuaded of its preferability to the society from which he (it is most often a he) came. Yet while this might suggest that the 'englobing' of utopia by science fiction has resulted in a radical break with the past, others have argued that even some of the most apparently prescriptive utopias may productively be read as having a similar disruptive effect: that even their limitations, whether aesthetic or political, may be seen as tracing the outer limits of the ideological framework of their period, the boundary beyond which it is impossible to imagine.[6] The tendency that has become apparent in more recent utopian writing, in effect, has always been latent, to the extent that even the earliest utopias may be seen as part of the prehistory of science fiction.

But it is not only readings of utopian literature that are affected by the presumption of its absorption by science fiction. If the alternative worlds envisaged by both utopia and science fiction highlight the extent to which existing reality is only one possibility among many, and as such susceptible to change, then it becomes possible to argue that science fiction as a whole may also be read as conducive to the promotion of such change. To pursue Suvin's metaphor further, it is as though the englobing of utopia has resulted in its infecting its host with some of its own characteristics. Science fiction may then be seen as part of what Moylan refers to as 'the larger process of mobilizing the cultural imagination',[7] its capacity to expose the contingent character of contemporary society being in some respects comparable to that of the historical novel in the nineteenth century.

In its most extreme form, this argument has led to claims for the radicalizing potential of science fiction that border on the messianic. Moylan himself, for example, answers the familiar charge that science fiction is 'escapist' by posing the question whether it may not in fact

> offer a possible escape velocity that can sweep readers out of their spacetime continuum, warping their minds into a cognitive zone from which they might look back at their own social moment, perhaps with anxiety or better with anger, and then discover that such a place might be known for what it is and changed for the better?[8]

And, if science fiction contains that utopian possibility, it might seem only logical to argue not merely that it could have such an effect, but that it *should*. Thus Moylan warns that the reader who treats science fiction as merely escapist, and refuses

> an engaged, cognitive reading process risks committing discursive violence to the text and further risks the perpetuation, or at least acceptance, of that ignorance and violence, injustice and domination, that rages in the world outside the text, in that everyday life to which we all return upon turning the last page and closing the book.[9]

If earlier utopias' description of the more perfect society could be criticized as prescriptive, here what is prescribed is the reading process itself.

Nevertheless, this sanguine view of the radicalizing potential of utopian science fiction is by no means universally shared. Rob Latham, for example, argues that such readings pose 'the interesting empirical question of how many people have actually had their consciousnesses raised in this way through their experience with sf' (very few, he suggests).[10] And, in overestimating the political efficacy of science fiction and utopia, such readings risk conflating 'two aspects of critical evaluation, such that ideological commitment becomes the very criterion of aesthetic worth'.[11] Such readings also tend to de-emphasize one crucial aspect that distinguishes the study of utopian literature from that of science fiction, namely, the extent to which it overlaps with other disciplinary approaches. Utopian studies involves not just the study of utopian literature, but of utopian thought – whether from the perspective of philosophy, political science or sociology – and of the ways in which people have sought to create utopias or influence actual political movements. Seen in this context, utopian literature becomes less a subgenre of science fiction than the literary expression of political ideals, likewise designed to influence reality. H.G. Wells, in fact, went so far as to suggest that 'the creation of Utopias – and their exhaustive criticism – is the proper and distinctive method of sociology'.[12]

To see utopian literature in this light, of course, is to run the risk of minimizing its literary aspects – to see the narrative as merely a vehicle for the expression of political ideas, a sort of literary clothing, where fashions change over time. Yet even where there is acceptance that more recent utopian science fiction has succeeded in resolving the aesthetic problems that bedevil its precursors – that considered as *literature*, works such as Le Guin's *The Dispossessed* (1974) or Delany's *Triton* (1976) are far more successful than, say, Bellamy's *Looking Backward*, this is not always viewed as an unmixed blessing. As Krishan Kumar points out, whatever its literary merits, more recent utopian literature has failed to stimulate anything like as much public debate as did *Looking Backward* or *A Modern Utopia*, and that indeed its more limited appeal is in fact a direct result of its use of a science fictional format, rendering it more difficult for such work 'to break out of its specialized literary ghetto'.[13] Similarly, Ruth Levitas argues that the self-conscious, self-reflexive ambiguity of much recent utopian writing, for all its artistic and intellectual appeal

> is not merely exploratory and open, it is also disillusioned and unconfident... The presentation of alternative futures, multiple possibilities and fragmented images of time reflects a lack of confidence about whether and how a better world can be reached.[14]

Without seeking to adjudicate between these contrasting views, there can be little doubt that, whatever utopian literature may have *become*, the context in which it is taught can have a decisive effect on how it is read. To teach any given work of utopian literature in the context of a course specifically devoted to utopia raises a rather different set of questions to those that arise when it becomes part of a course more broadly focused on science fiction; and this is not least because of one of the features of utopian literature that distinguishes it most markedly not only from science fiction, but from most other genres: namely, the extent to which utopian narrative is explicitly and consciously designed to engage with the tradition established by its precursors. As Fredric Jameson remarks:

> what uniquely characterizes this genre is its explicit intertextuality: few other literary forms have so brazenly affirmed themselves as argument and counterargument. Few others have so openly required cross-reference and debate within each new variant: who can read Morris without Bellamy? [O]r indeed Bellamy without Morris? So it is that the individual text carries with it a whole tradition, reconstructed and modified with each new addition...[15]

One could multiply examples: it might equally be asked who can read *The Dispossessed* without reading *Triton*[16] or vice-versa, or *The Handmaid's Tale* without reading *We* or George Orwell's *Nineteen Eighty-Four* (1949) – for to read in isolation is to lose sight of the extent to which utopian literature is, among other things, designed as an intervention in an ongoing debate. To read any given work outside the context of that debate, or with only passing reference to it, is to miss much of what makes it distinctive – not to mention the ways in which the reading of each work modifies the reading of all.

By way of illustration, let us consider in more detail the case of two works which frequently feature in courses on both utopian literature and science fiction: Huxley's *Brave New World* and Le Guin's *The Dispossessed*. Taught as science fiction, their relation to the utopian tradition cannot be ignored; nevertheless, it may be argued that those aspects of the text that such a context highlights are likely to produce rather different readings than emerge from their consideration as utopian literature per se.

The relationship of *Brave New World* to the utopian tradition is, of course, antagonistic. Described by David Sisk as 'the seminal dystopia of the twentieth century',[17] it is also often referred to as an anti-utopia, posing the question of whether there is any useful distinction to be made between the terms. While they are often treated as synonymous, more recently attempts have been made to distinguish between them – although it is fair to say that general agreement has yet to be reached on what the difference actually is.[18] For some, 'dystopia' constitutes specifically the parodic inversion of utopia (into which category *Brave New World* clearly fits) – a representation of where the utopian impulse would really lead – whereas others use the term to refer more broadly to any depiction of an undesirable society, regardless of its provenance, reserving 'anti-utopia' for those depictions that are actively hostile to utopianism. Jameson, indeed, goes so far as to argue that utopia and dystopia are 'not opposites and in reality have nothing to do with each other'.[19] A dystopia, in other words, need not necessarily exclude the possibility of utopian alternatives.

If one accepts this distinction, it is clear that taught in the context of a course on utopian literature, it is the anti-utopian aspect of *Brave New World* that will be foregrounded. Prefaced by an epigraph from Nicholas Berdiaeff warning against the growing danger that utopia might become a reality, it focuses its satiric attack on the centralized utopian visions of writers such as Bellamy and Wells, and their assumption that strong, centralized authority would in act in the best interests of the citizen. At the same time, however, its line of attack differs quite markedly from that, say, of Zamyatin's *We*, whose representation of utopian ideals is by no means as unambiguously hostile, not to mention Orwell's *Nineteen Eighty-Four*, so that the resultant debate becomes not merely about the limitations of utopia, but also those of Huxley's critique.

Taught as science fiction, by contrast – after the study, say, of *Frankenstein*, or Wells's *The Time Machine* (1895), many of whose gloomy assumptions regarding the potential impact of technological progress on human society it shares – its relation to the utopian tradition, while still important, becomes less central. What emerges instead is as much dystopia in the broader sense: a nightmare future which can as easily be taken as an extrapolation from present trends (by no means all of them utopian), the logical conclusion of where society might end up if things continue going on the way they are now. Read alongside *Frankenstein*, with its frightening prevision of the possible impact of scientific discovery on human relationships, Huxley's depiction of a future where meaningful relationships have been literally engineered out of existence becomes as much an indictment of scientific hubris in general as of utopian imagining in particular. Indeed, there is considerable evidence to suggest that Huxley's satiric attack was directed as much at the actual speculations of contemporary scientists such as J.B.S. Haldane and J.D. Bernal regarding the potential transformation of humanity as at the utopian visions of Wells and others.[20] Wells himself, in *The Time Machine*, likewise envisages the degeneration of humanity once all its problems have been solved – in this case into the effete Eloi and bestial Morlocks – which serves to highlight the extent to which *Brave New World* is also an extrapolation of the class politics of the period. While separated by over thirty years, both can be seen as imaginative responses to contemporary threats to the existing class system, each providing a revealing compensatory fantasy. For Wells, ambitious of success, yet haunted by the fear of downward social mobility, what could be more reassuring than a scenario where a vigorous, middle-class Time Traveller visits the future, secures a descendant of the upper class as a sleeping companion, and is able to take out his aggression by beating to death several descendants of the proletariat? Likewise in *Brave New World*, where the presence of characters such as Bernard Marx, Lenina Crowne and Polly Trotsky clearly indicates what Huxley saw as one of the principal dangers to the 'cultivated classes' who Berdiaeff saw as most threatened by the possibility of utopia, the notion of a world where class distinctions are both biologically and psychologically reinforced to the point where they are immutable may be seen as at one level no less appealing to its upper-middle-class author.[21]

Seen in this context, *Brave New World*'s cast list, which includes not merely the characters cited above, but Benito Hoover, Joanna Diesel, Helmholz Watson and Mustapha Mond, suggests less a critique of utopianism than of modernity – of a world where communism, fascism, capitalism, science are all engaged in the common project of erasing individuality. And while the presiding deity of Huxley's World State, Our Ford, was not without his own utopian aspirations, what *Brave New World* highlights is less those aspirations than the mindless consumerism promoted by the process of self-sustaining economic growth that Ford helped to pioneer – a process some might argue that has served to foreclose rather than realize utopian possibility. In a world where 'utopia' has become a brand name for soft drinks and canned tomatoes, and where advertisements mimic the utopian poster art of the Soviet Union in the 1920s to promote the 'freedom' provided by a cell phone, it is hard to resist the conclusion that Bertrand Russell's prediction that 'it is all too likely to come true'[22] has in large measure been proved correct.

Returned to its utopian context, juxtaposed with *Utopia*, *Looking Backward* and the utopias of Wells, while its prescience is no less evident, it becomes far more clearly part of a debate within the tradition of utopian literature, a debate that renders both its strengths and weaknesses more apparent. While the assumptions underlying the Wellsian world state are certainly a valid target for attack, whether satiric or otherwise, what emerges from setting *Brave New World* in its utopian context is the extent of its hostility even to those elements of the utopian vision with which one might sympathize. Here utopia (or rather, its parodic inversion) is prompted by despair at the chaos arising from the pursuit of competing utopian visions. Exhausted by the destruction, humanity accepts the loss of its freedom as the price to be paid for peace and order – and once that price has been paid, the only ones who bridle at or are even aware of the cost are a few pesky intellectuals who pose so little threat that they can be neutralized relatively humanely, by exile, rather than death.

What is especially striking about *Brave New World*, in its utopian context, is how much of its satire depends on Huxley's representation of what amounts to the *fulfilment* of the utopian programme of earlier writers. His World State provides peace, prosperity, security; there is no crime, no war: it is a world where happiness is almost universal – and if that happiness is the product of brainwashing, mindless consumerism and the consumption of stupefying drugs, it may be argued that its strategies for achieving contentment do not differ that markedly from those of modern consumer societies – or, if there is a difference, it lies mainly in the fact that in *Brave New World* the strategies are more effective, and are available to all, rather than only those wealthy enough to employ them. In addition, Huxley posits a society where the state's use of overt coercive power, which renders the dystopias of Zamyatin and

Orwell more obviously unappealing, is rarely necessary: where its citizens are successfully diverted from ever considering other possibilities, why would force be needed? And in this regard it might also be argued that Huxley correctly intuits one of the mechanisms that has enabled Western societies to manage dissent more successfully than the authoritarian regimes of the former Eastern bloc.

What *Brave New World* misses, however (in a way Zamyatin's *We* does not) is an important part of the *appeal* of utopia – and in doing so it may be argued that it reproduces some of the weaknesses of its satiric targets. While Bellamy and Wells imagine societies which provide peace, security, plenty, and also far greater efficiency than their own, the much greater degree of comfort this affords to its citizens is by no means all utopia is about. Indeed, it was that very aspect of Bellamy's utopia that prompted William Morris to declare that he 'wouldn't care to live in such a cockney paradise'[23] and to provide his own contrasting utopian vision in *News From Nowhere*. Yet, as Morris's utopia makes clear, the dream of a better world is also motivated by a desire to change the one that exists, as well as a preparedness to embrace the challenge (and accompanying dangers) of seeking to do so. While the Marx satirized by Huxley may have promoted the ideal of 'From each according to their ability, to each according to their needs',[24] he was far from imagining the result would be the bourgeois paradise imagined by Bellamy, still less that it could be achieved painlessly and with absolutely no opposition. So too with Huxley's other imagined precursors of utopia. The scientists after whom his characters are named were concerned with more than just the promotion of mindless enjoyment, while even fascism, as Ernst Bloch acknowledges, has its utopian aspect, its appeal to strenuousness and 'the dangerous life'[25] – if Mussolini made the trains run on time, that was hardly the main source of his popular appeal. In Huxley's case, however, those who defy the status quo are no less objects of satire than those who accept it. Bernard Marx and the Savage are merely under a different set of illusions, while Helmholz Watson – perhaps the most sympathetic character in the book– is merely concerned with the possibility of individual fulfilment, rather than promoting the good of others.

Not the least impressive aspect of *We*, by contrast, is the extent to which it conveys not only the horror and cruelty of Zamyatin's future society, but also something of the terrible appeal of the dream underlying it – the appeal of sensing oneself part of a whole far greater than the mere sum of its parts. Moreover, while Huxley satirizes both utopia and those who rebel against it, Zamyatin makes it clear that rebellion is not merely an attempt to return to the supposedly more 'natural' world of our own day, but that it may represent an attempt to realize other, better utopian alternatives. Yet at the same time, a comparison with *Brave New World* does highlight some of *We*'s more problematic aspects. Like *Nineteen Eighty-Four* (which in this respect resembles it closely) *We* makes the central character's defiance of the sexual norms of his society a major aspect of his rebellion. D-503 departs from the regulated sexual practices of the One State both by engaging in sexual activity outside the designated private sexual hours, and refraining from it during them. Yet it would appear that the main appeal of his partner in sexual irregularity, E-330, is not so much her disregard for the state's rules on when sex should take place, as her penchant for wearing clothing associated with the stereotypes of female desirability in Zamyatin's own time:

> She was in a saffron-yellow dress of an ancient cut. This was a thousandfold more wicked than if she had had absolutely nothing on. Two sharp points, glowing roseately through the thin tissue: two embers smouldering among ashes. Two tenderly round knees... [26]

D-503's excitement at the prospect is mirrored by that of Winston Smith in *Nineteen Eighty-Four*, who is rendered just as breathless when his lover, Julia, puts on old-fashioned make-up. What Huxley poses, however, is the question of just how subversive a reversion to the sexual *mores* of one's own age actually *is*. Whereas Winston Smith sees his defiance of the sexual puritanism of Airstrip One as 'a political act' – 'Their embrace had been a battle, the climax a victory. It was a blow struck against the Party'[27] – Huxley shows an awareness that the sexual norms of our society are no less socially constructed than those of the world of the future. While both Bernard Marx and the Savage are repelled by the compulsory promiscuity of the World State, their romantic idealization of the vacuous Lenina is represented not as a contrasting positive, but rather a mere fantasy projection, no less ludicrous than the mindless sexual indulgence to which it is opposed. Although Huxley himself claimed never to have read Zamyatin, the juxtaposition of the two texts becomes part of a larger dialogue concerning the sexual politics of utopia, where the imagination of even the most radical changes to existing society are often accompanied by a reinscription of its sexual norms – a dialogue further extended by consideration of Atwood's *The Handmaid's Tale*, which consciously parodies Zamyatin's and Orwell's fetishization of conventional stereotypes of what constitutes female sexual attraction.

Nor is this the only debate which consideration of *Brave New World* in a specifically utopian context encourages. For all its overtly anti-utopian thrust, Huxley later came to question many of its assumptions, notably in his later preface to the work, published in 1946, in *Brave New World Revisited* (1959), and in his final novel, the utopian *Island* – all of which raises questions concerning both Huxley's analysis of what he saw as *Brave New World*'s shortcomings, and the extent to which his proposed alternatives resolve or reproduce its more problematic aspects.

Brave New World also poses the important question of who utopia is actually *for*. Following Berdiaeff's warning of the danger posed by utopia to the 'cultivated classes', Huxley's imagined future makes it clear his real concern is not so much with the dehumanization of the lower orders – the mass-produced Deltas and Epsilons – but rather the hardships imposed on their intellectual superiors. And here it may be argued that Huxley reproduces, uncritically rather than satirically, precisely those assumptions of *Looking Backward* that so repelled William Morris, namely its almost exclusive concern with the interests of the middle class. What Bellamy imagines is a future where middle-class values are universal, where the cultivated classes are no longer 'surrounded by a population of ignorant, boorish, coarse, wholly uncultivated men and women' – as opposed to the plight of the 'cultured man' in the late nineteenth century, which is described as 'like one up to the neck in a nauseous bog solacing himself with a smelling bottle'.[28] As Morris remarks:

> The only ideal of life which such a man can see is that of the industrious *professional* middle-class men of today purified from their crime of complicity with the monopolist class, and become independent instead of being, as they now are, parasitical.[29]

Utopia becomes a world where the middle class no longer have to feel guilty. And while *Brave New World* satirizes utopias such as Bellamy's, it clearly shares the assumption that the *real* problems are not those of society as a whole, but rather those of the middle class who have to endure their consequences.

Yet if this results in the conclusion that the realization of utopia would be a nightmare, it remains to be asked for whom, and on what basis any given utopia would be unappealing. Clearly for the modern reader, at least if s/he happens to be one of the more prosperous inhabitants of a Western democracy, the prospect of life in More's Utopia, or Campanella's City of the Sun is far from alluring – but there remains the question, in which neither Bellamy nor Huxley seem to be much interested: what about the rest of the world? If a strong, centralized, albeit authoritarian government could actually deliver on the promise of a six- or four-hour working day, peace, security, plenty and the likelihood of a significantly greater life expectancy for everyone, how many might see the sacrifice of some of their freedoms as a price worth paying – especially given that the amount of individual freedom in many utopias, even the authoritarian ones, is considerably greater than that enjoyed by millions of the citizens of our world? Even a dystopian vision such as *Brave New World* prompts the same question: granting the considerable imaginative premise that such a society were possible, would it be more desirable, at least for the Deltas and Epsilons, genetically engineered to perform mindless labour with reasonable hours and adequate pay, than for the millions of child labourers employed in sweatshops to produce luxuries for the citizens of Western democracies? In my own experience an interesting (some might say alarming) aspect of such debates, where they have occurred in class, is the consistency with which the proponents of Brave New World out-argue their opponents.

In the case of Le Guin's *The Dispossessed*, the effect of context is no less pronounced. While forming part of the so-called 'Hainish cycle' – a group of science fiction novels and short stories sharing a common narrative regarding the spread of humanoid races across the galaxy – it too becomes a rather different work when considered first and foremost as utopian literature. Set against earlier, centralized utopian visions from *Utopia* on, an important concern that emerges is clearly the extent of the political challenge it represents. The anarchist society created on the planet of Anarres differs markedly from such visions, yet at the same time its increasing drift towards the stasis and conformity so often seen as characteristic of utopia poses the question whether such characteristics are inescapable. What *The Dispossessed* proposes is that they are not, or at least, not necessarily; rather, stasis and conformity result from the rigid separation between our world and its utopian alternative which so many narratives maintain.

What distinguishes *The Dispossessed* from so many of its utopian precursors, in fact, is its attempt to address problematic features of the genre that are both political and narrative. Le Guin reverses the traditional narrative pattern whereby a visitor from our world travels to utopia and returns, converted. Here the central character, Shevek, is a scientist from Anarres, who travels to its parent world (a clear analogue of our own), and in doing so begins to re-establish the political connections between the two that had been severed. On Urras, the glaring political inequities that gave birth to the anarchist society of Anarres still persist, and renewed contact between the worlds offers at least the prospect that the ossification resulting from Anarres's attempt to maintain its utopian purity may be overcome once it becomes part of a larger political struggle. It is an argument for the necessity for permanent revolution not dissimilar to that advanced by Leon Trotsky.

The device whereby someone comes to our world (or its analogue) bringing with them a radically different set of assumptions is a standard satiric device – in some respects Shevek might be seen as a science fictional variant of the 'noble savage' who comes to Europe and starts asking all kinds of inconvenient questions about why things are done the way they are. Yet while Le Guin takes full advantage of the satiric possibilities (Shevek's puzzlement at the Urrasti exam system is a satiric tour de force with which any student is likely to sympathize), what her 'ambiguous utopia' chiefly highlights is the extent to which utopia and dystopia are inseparable one from the other. Indeed, taken on their own, the chapters devoted to life on Anarres read almost like a classic dystopia, with freedom-seeking rebels defying a conformist society. It is only when they are placed in the context of the corresponding narrative on Urras that it becomes clear that Shevek's strengths, his ability successfully to challenge the assumptions of our world, are the product of his upbringing in utopia, a society with which he is also in conflict.

Yet Le Guin's is only one of a number of attempts to address the political and narrative limitations of the traditional utopia, and its consideration in the context of utopian literature will clearly invite comparison with other 'critical utopias' of the period: works such as *Triton*, Russ's *The Female Man* (1975) or Piercy's *Woman on the Edge of Time* (1976) – the last of which employs a not dissimilar narrative strategy. Set alongside these, a major issue that emerges is the issue of sexual politics, on which grounds *The Dispossessed* has often been criticized, not least for its choice of a heterosexual, monogamous male as its protagonist[30] – a privileging of traditional sex roles and familial structures that is seen as re-inscribing rather than challenging prevailing gender norms.

Here *The Dispossessed* might be seen as only too utopian in the traditional sense, since for most of its history the aspects of existing social relations that utopia has most consistently failed to re-imagine are those to do with gender.[31] Yet while there is some validity to this critique, what is troubling about it is its prescriptive quality. While the sexual politics of the other 'critical utopias' referred to are undoubtedly more progressive, it is also true that Le Guin is interested in a rather different area of utopian inquiry, to which the issue of sexual politics is marginal. Equally, it might be argued that the omissions of works like *The Female Man* or *Triton*, in both of which the focus on sexual politics is enabled by the convenient fiction that virtually all economic problems have been resolved by the application of technology, are no less striking. What emerges from some of the attacks on Le Guin by writers and critics in the field is a new orthodoxy concerning what utopias *ought* to be like – ones where 'the more collective heroes of social transformation are presented off-centre and usually as characters who are not dominant, white heterosexual, chauvinist males but female, gay, non-white, and generally operating collectively'.[32] The prescription as to how utopias are to be read referred to earlier is here accompanied by a prescription as to how they are to be written.

Considered first and foremost as science fiction, *The Dispossessed* presents a rather different aspect. Among the thematic links that such a context is likely to foreground is the whole issue of scientific responsibility, first adumbrated in *Frankenstein* – with Shevek's concern that his discovery be shared with all contrasting with the privatization of discovery by Victor Frankenstein. Its concern with the possibility of transcending time likewise takes on a different resonance when set alongside *The Time Machine*, as opposed to *Looking Backward* or *News From Nowhere*, where the act of imagining the future is far more overtly political. Yet what does stand out in such a context is how far Le Guin's progressivist narrative is in contrast to that proposed by Wells (or indeed Shelley). Ultimately, providing it is made universally available, Shevek's discovery of the principle that will make possible instantaneous communication across the galaxy is seen as a Good Thing – which highlights the anthropocentric premise of the whole Hainish cycle, which imagines a galaxy colonized by humanoid life forms with whom such communication is possible. Yet if one sets *The Dispossessed* alongside, say, Stanislaw Lem's *Solaris* (1961), that optimistic assumption becomes more questionable. What Lem poses is the question of whether such communication is even *possible*, let alone desirable, given that if there are other, non-human life-forms their life-experience and cognitive processes may prove literally untranslatable, while the impulse to such communication may actually reflect an unwillingness to confront some of the more unpalatable aspects of our own inner life – questions which *The Dispossessed* largely ignores.

A comparison with *Solaris* also highlights just how much further Lem goes in challenging the often reactionary sexual politics of a good deal of earlier science fiction (including, it should be said, those of *The Time Machine*). Whereas a debate regarding sexual politics in a utopian context poses the question of whether the 'critical utopia' runs the risk of prescribing a particular *kind* of sexual politics as *de rigueur*, setting Le Guin's novel alongside those of Wells (or William Gibson, or Michael Crichton – one might multiply examples) perhaps poses more forcibly the question of why *The Dispossessed* does not do more to challenge their assumptions.

Equally, in a science fictional context, the narrative aspects of the novel, which constitute such a distinctive resolution of some of the problems inherent in the traditional utopian narrative paradigm, seem less remarkable. While science fiction is by no means free of its own narrative challenges – not least a tendency for the imagination of new scientific possibilities to go hand-in-hand with the deployment of the most hackneyed and conventional plots (George Lucas's *Star Wars* movies being a conspicuous example) – it has always lent itself more readily to narrative experiment. While the 'critical utopia', perhaps by virtue of its merger with science fiction, may have succeeded in escaping from the narrative constraints of the traditional utopia, the contrast between the imaginative freedom of Wells's early 'scientific romances' and the awkwardness of some of his attempts to wrestle with the narrative problems of utopia shows that such an escape is no easy matter.

Yet while the context in which utopian literature is taught may result in significantly different readings of the works in question, the relationship between utopia and science fiction poses an important question. While the study of utopia from the perspective of sociology or political science is likely to foreground the issue of content (how viable and/or desirable is the society proposed?), and its consideration from a literary perspective that of form (how does the work overcome the narrative challenges involved?), there is also the question of function. What is the function of utopian literature? To persuade – as often seems to be the case with utopias written prior to the twentieth century? To make us aware of alternative possibilities – to 'educate desire', as Ernst Bloch puts it?[33] And what is its efficacy in fulfilling its function? Has the effective merger of utopian literature with science fiction in recent years made it possible to overcome utopia's long-standing narrative challenges, but only at the cost of sacrificing some of its political effectiveness? To (very loosely) paraphrase Marx, one might suggest that, while writers of utopias have imagined alternatives to this world in various ways, the point is to change it. The question that needs to be asked is how far, and in what ways, the two tasks are related. That they *are* related is a fundamental premise of utopia and anti-utopia alike; where they differ is in their view of the desirability of such change. Taught in the context of a science fiction course, however, utopias and anti-utopias pose the broader question of how far the debate between them is an integral aspect of science fiction as a whole.

Notes

1. See *Science Fiction Studies* 23.3 (1996) for a representative sample of over 400 syllabi for university courses on science fiction and utopian literature.
2. For a helpful discussion of the ways in which the two terms have been used see Tom Moylan, *Scraps of the Untainted Sky: Science Fiction, Utopia, Dystopia* (Boulder: Westview, 2000) 147–82. See also Lyman Tower Sargent, 'The Three Faces of Utopianism Revisited', *Utopian Studies*, 5:1 (1994): 1–37.
3. Darko Suvin, *Metamorphoses of Science Fiction* (New Haven: Yale University Press, 1979) 61 (emphasis in original).
4. See Angelika Bammer, *Partial Visions: Feminism and Utopianism in the 1970s* (London: Routledge, 1991).
5. Tom Moylan, *Demand the Impossible: Science Fiction and the Utopian Imagination* (London: Methuen, 1986) 210.
6. Philip E. Wegner, *Imaginary Communities: Utopia, the Nation, and the Spatial Histories of Modernity* (Berkeley: University of California Press, 2002) 23.
7. Moylan, *Scraps of the Untainted Sky*, 29.
8. Ibid., 30.
9. Ibid., 25.
10. Rob Latham, 'A Tendentious Tendency in SF Criticism', *Science Fiction Studies*, 29:1 (2002): 100–10.
11. Ibid., 109.
12. H.G. Wells, *An Englishman Looks at the World* (London: Cassell, 1914) 204.
13. Krishan Kumar, *Utopia and Anti-Utopia in Modern Times* (Oxford: Blackwell, 1987) 420.
14. Ruth Levitas, *The Concept of Utopia* (Syracuse: Syracuse University Press, 1990) 196.
15. Fredric Jameson, *Archaeologies of the Future: The Desire Called Utopia and Other Science Fictions* (London: Verso, 2005) 2.
16. While Delany states that he did not write *Triton* as a conscious response to *The Dispossessed*, he makes it clear that his choice of subtitle ('An Ambiguous Heterotopia') was designed to emphasize the dialogue he sees as implicit with Le Guin's 'Ambiguous Utopia'. See Robert M. Philmus, 'On Triton and Other Matters: An Interview with Samuel R. Delany', *Science Fiction Studies*, 17:3 (1990): 295–324.
17. David W. Sisk. *Transformations of Language in Modern Dystopias* (Westport: Greenwood, 1997) 18.
18. See note 2 above.
19. Fredric Jameson, *The Seeds of Time* (New York: Columbia University Press, 1994) 55.
20. For an illuminating discussion of the relation of Wells's utopias to contemporary scientific speculation, see Kumar, *Utopia and Anti-Utopia*, 230–42.
21. Another of Wells's 'scientific romances', *The First Men in the Moon*, provides a further parallel, given that the modification of the physiology of the

22. Bertrand Russell, review of *Brave New World*, in *New Leader*, 11 March 1932 quoted in Donald Watt, ed., *Aldous Huxley: The Critical Heritage* (London: Routledge & Kegan Paul, 1975) 212.
23. William Morris quoted in J. Bruce Glasier, *William Morris and the Early Days of the Socialist Movement* (London: Longmans, 1921) 198.
24. Karl Marx, *Critique of the Gotha Programme*. *Karl Marx: Later Political Writings*, ed. and trans. Terrell Carver (Cambridge: Cambridge University Press, 1996) 215.
25. Ernst Bloch, *The Principle of Hope*, trans. Neville Plaice, Stephen Plaice and Paul Knight (Cambridge, MA: MIT Press, 1986) 935.
26. Yevgeny Zamyatin, *We*, trans. Bernard Guilbert Guerney (Harmondsworth: Penguin, 1983) 65. In a number of other translations the female character's name is transliterated as I-330.
27. George Orwell, *Nineteen Eighty-Four* (Harmondsworth: Penguin, 1970) 112.
28. Edward Bellamy, *Looking Backward 2000–1887* (New York: Bantam, 1983) 122.
29. William Morris, review of *Looking Backward* in *The Commonweal*, 22 June 1889.
30. See for example Sarah Lefanu, *In the Chinks of the World Machine: Feminism and Science Fiction* (London: Women's Press, 1988) 130–46. See also Moylan, *Demand the Impossible*, 91–120.
31. For a more extensive discussion of this aspect of utopian narrative, see Chris Ferns, *Narrating Utopia: Ideology, Gender, Form in Utopian Literature* (Liverpool: Liverpool University Press, 1999).
32. Moylan, *Demand the Impossible*, 45.
33. See E.P. Thompson, *William Morris: Romantic to Revolutionary* (London: Merlin, 1977) 791.

Before item 22:

Selenites to suit them for the industrial tasks they are intended to perform is clearly an inspiration for Huxley's description of a similar process.

4
Teaching the Scientific Romance

Adam Roberts

In his influential study of sf between 1890 and 1950 Brian Stableford defends the 'decision to use the old-fashioned and rather quaint term "scientific romance" as a description' on the grounds that the phrase 'make[s] the point that the British tradition of speculative fiction developed during the period under consideration quite separately from the American tradition of science fiction, and can be contrasted with it in certain important ways'.[1] That is to say, he sets out to trace the ways in which the development of sf was fed by a specifically British tradition of sf writing, led by the 'inspiration and example of H.G. Wells', through the first half of the twentieth century. For Stableford this tradition was separate from but acted antithetically upon the tradition of Gernsbackian, American pulp sf; and the synthesis of these two determined later twentieth-century science fiction. Stableford concentrates his critical attention upon twelve authors, most of them not widely known: George Griffith, Wells, M.P. Shiel, Arthur Conan Doyle, William Hope Hodgson, J.D. Beresford, S. Fowler Wright, Olaf Stapledon, Neil Bell, John Gloag, C.S. Lewis and Gerald Heard.

This is a list of names that, in terms of thinking through how we might want to teach scientific romance, might be described as challenging. Whilst it would, of course, be possible to construct a course that took students through the specifics of Stableford's thesis, pedagogic practicality dictates a more inclusive definition of scientific romance, one that more usefully spreads its net widely enough to encompass a broader spectrum of late nineteenth-century and early twentieth-century science fiction. This means covering works informed by the technical developments associated with the industrial revolution, by the impact of Darwin's ideas and the social and political contexts of imperialism and increasing democratization.

Perhaps more importantly, the decision to teach 'scientific romance' rather than 'science fiction' more generally conceived is a decision to look at sf – a genre widely taken to be future-oriented – precisely as *old-fashioned*. A large part of the appeal of scientific romance involves reading quondam futurity styled as retro-Edwardian baroque. Something along these lines, I think, explains the enduring popularity not only of many of the authors Stableford identifies (Wells most prominently) but also the present-day vigour of 'steampunk' and those other subgenres of sf that continue to trade on 'scientific romantic' tropes. In other words, teaching scientific romance enables a double focus: *both* reading and contextualizing the core and (many would argue) founding texts of the tradition of sf, from Jules Verne and Wells through to the end of the nineteenth and the beginning of the twentieth century, *and* covering the reflorescence of interest in versions of sf styled in homage to those works. Scientific romance is a mode of cultural expression that is of more than merely antiquarian interest. Precisely because it is a form connected with the origins of the modern form of the genre, it continues to hold our attention today.

To take the earlier group of texts first, and to consider which authors a teacher may wish to cover when teaching: no course on scientific romance can afford to ignore Jules Verne and H.G. Wells, the two most influential practitioners of scientific romance. There are a number of other significant Victorian and Edwardian scientific romances: Chesney's *The Battle of Dorking* (1871), Percy Greg's *Across the Zodiac* (1880), Conan Doyle's *The Lost World* (1912) and Stapledon's *Last and First Men* (1930). In addition to this, and depending on the level and length of time available to the teacher, there are a number of much less-well-known titles that can be useful in contextualizing the genre as a whole. Recent technology has come to the aid of pedagogy in this regard; for while Wells and Verne have always been available in a variety of useful student editions it used to be the case that other scientific romances were hard to come by, published if at all only in expensive academic editions. The internet has changed that. Indeed, one of the specific advantages of teaching the literature of the later nineteenth century is that, since most of its authors died more than seventy years ago, they are no longer in copyright (Wells will come out of copyright in 2011). What this means is that it is possible to direct students to scans of hitherto elusive scientific romance on – for instance – project Gutenberg (www.gutenberg.org) or Google Books (www.google/books.com). Pragmatically this permits an unprecedented freedom to the designer of courses on nineteenth-century literature. To revert for a moment to the list of titles Stableford covers in depth in his monograph: most of those twelve authors are now out of print, but all (save only Bell) has at least one significant text, and in most cases several, available to be read for free on either Project Gutenberg or Google Books (in the case of Beresford and Heard this is only short fiction, with 'limited previews' of other work; but certainly enough to give students a flavour of their writing). Sydney Fowler Wright's works have been digitized at http://www.sfw.org/.

Students with access to the varieties of nineteenth-century scientific romance can add their voice to the clamorous critical debate concerning the origins of sf: do the works of Wells and Verne, as many critics have argued, constitute a new sort of literature? Or do they continue older traditions of fantastic writing – the Gothic, for instance (it is a simple matter in the classroom to take students through Brian Aldiss's celebrated argument that sf begins with Mary Shelley's *Frankenstein*, 1818) – or an even older tradition of fantastic tales? A brief classroom survey will establish which examples students have already encountered, from Homer's *Odyssey*, through fairy and folk tales, *Beowulf*, medieval Romance, to early utopian writing, or eighteenth-century satire such as Swift's *Gulliver's Travels* (1726; corrected 1735) or Voltaire's *Contes*. This can then lead to discussion as to which elements of this tradition might be called 'science fiction' and which would not be hospitable to such identification.

It is important, of course, that students have some appropriate historical and cultural context in which to read scientific romances. My experience of teaching the Victorian period at both undergraduate and MA level is of encountering students who *think* they understand what 'Victorianism' means because they have internalized a number of prevailing caricatured stereotypes: empire, sexual repression, industrial revolution, young children sent up chimneys, pea-souper fogs, Jack the Ripper and so on. Addressing the implicit cultural logic of this cartoonish Victorianism can be a fruitful business for students, most of whom are very ready to accept that their readings are better served by a more nuanced and fleshed out sense of period. But it can also be time-consuming. Imperialism, Victorian sexuality, industrialization: these are each large topics in their own right, and although they can all be important for a fuller understanding of what is going on in scientific romance the course leader may of course need to balance the pressures of time.

Courses can be structured around authors, or themes; and teachers may wish to group texts that respond (for instance) to the new discourses of evolution and degeneration of the late nineteenth century, or to the mechanistic innovations of industrialization, or – as many critics do – to the burgeoning actualities of imperial expansion and the way writers of the fantastic reverted this aggressive global expansion back upon Western nations. Alternatively it is possible to teach by author, starting (for instance) with Verne and Wells and moving through whichever selection of other scientific romances is deemed most appropriate to the particular pedagogic situation.

Teaching Jules Verne has its own particular problems – beyond, that is to say, the difficulty of finding space for a Francophone author in what still remains an overwhelmingly Anglophone canon of texts taught in English departments. It is very much worth overcoming this latter awkwardness, for no course on scientific romance will be complete without some sense of his *voyages extraordinaires*, and Verne (by some metrics the most widely translated author the world has seen) is hardly a parochial writer. All his titles were published in English language versions, almost all of them near-simultaneously with the French publication, and his influence on other writers of scientific romance and on literary culture more broadly was pervasive and important. But it is a sorrowful refrain of English-language Verne criticism that he has been, by and large, served very poorly by his translators.

I offer a personal anecdote to illustrate this point: in 2006 I wrote a novel called *Splinter*, a postmodern re-imagining of Verne's 1877 novel *Hector Servadac*. In the original novel a comet collides with the earth and carries away a chunk of North Africa, upon which survive a mixed group of people: they journey on a trajectory away from the sun and then back towards it, eventually returning to the Earth in hot-air balloons. At my publisher's behest I agreed to prepare an edition of Verne's original novel to be issued along with my re-imagining, writing a new introduction and checking the original (anonymous) 1877 English translation for accuracy. (My updated translation is available for free download here: http://www.solarisbooks.com/downloads.asp.) I don't believe that I found a single page in the translation that represented an accurate rendering of the French. Dialogue was half the time condensed into a prose summary, or simply omitted. Sentences, or whole paragraphs, were cut. Verne's lengthy chapter 30 was removed in its entirety. The precise technical, engineering and physical science elements of the novel were often treated in an illogical manner (for instance translating 'metres' as 'yards' and 'centimetres' as 'inches' without altering the numerical measurements). The English translator was evidently much more anti-Semitic than Verne – what are in the original French neutral phrases such as '...said Isaac Hakkabut' were replaced in English with phrases such as '...said the repulsive old

Jew'. Finally, the original title *Hector Servadac* was discarded in favour of the breathless *Off on a Comet* – one might as well retitle *À la recherche du temps perdu* as 'Off on a Teacake'. (An American translation by Edward Roth had the even less appealing title: *To the Sun? Off on a Comet!* I thank providence that this approach to naming the novels didn't catch on, or we might have had *To the Centre of the Earth? Off down a Tunnel!*)

The 'Englishing' of *Hector Servadac* is only one of many examples of the mangling of Verne by nineteenth-century translators. Arthur Evans has traced the extent to which Verne's lucid and effective French has been distorted in translation; from the omission of large chunks of the original, the addition of non-Vernean material, the bowdlerization of sentiments hostile towards or injurious to the dignity of Great Britain (such as might be uttered by Captain Nemo, an Indian nobleman who had dedicated himself to an anti-imperialist cause), and many other things. As Arthur Evans concludes: 'readers who read Verne exclusively in English translation are not reading the *real* Jules Verne. Measured by any standard of completeness, accuracy, and style, these translations have committed to Verne's oeuvre what can only be described as a massacre.'[2]

What this means is that any teacher of Verne needs to ensure that s/he is putting reasonably accurate renderings on the syllabus. Several university presses (Oxford University Press in the UK and Wesleyan in the USA) have issued some of Verne's eighty-title output in clean new translations: William Butcher's 2009 translation of *Twenty Thousand Leagues under the Sea* (1869–70) is especially good. That novel, though fairly long, makes in my experience a good classroom text. Many of the students who have not read it will nonetheless have a sense of what it is about from the innumerable cinematic adaptations: Captain Nemo and his high-tech submarine *The Nautilus*. Reading the source novel in such circumstances (something similar happens with *Frankenstein* and *Dracula*) is inevitably to be struck by how the original emphases and iconography of the text has mutated under the pressure of other media, something that can be explored in class discussion. Much of *Twenty Thousand Leagues under the Sea* is given over to Verne's synthesis of up-to-date (in the 1860s) oceanographic science; and this scientific and technically didactic function is a much larger part of the effectiveness of the whole than its many adaptations imply. One cultural dynamic of scientific romance was precisely as a conduit by which new discoveries in science and new potentials in technology were communicated to a larger public.

For students who assume that the late nineteenth-century logic of imperialism was ideologically monolithic, it can be salutary to read a novel in which the hero is an Indian prince devoted to fighting the forces of Empire through the medium of high technology. Teaching can situate the novel in terms of European self-consciousness about the negative as well as positive consequences of imperial expansion, and the ambiguous relationship to advances in technology. *Twenty Thousand Leagues* is also representative of a key Vernean textual logic: it is about motion, literalized as a machine that moves ceaselessly all about the world carrying the protagonists with it (its motto is Latin: '*mobile in mobilum*', 'mobile in the mobile element'). The self-conscious fluidity of this is part of a larger Vernean textual fascination: his narratives are always kinetic, always on the move, always taking the reader to yet another colourful or interesting location – this is part of the reason for his global success with readers – in ways that mirror a cultural restlessness, but also anticipate the rise in tourism as a cultural phenomenon. *Around the World in Eighty Days* (1873), another work rather over-familiar from multiple cinematic adaptation, sweeps Phileas Fogg breathlessly round the whole globe like a proto gap-year student. Here the apprehension of cultural and racial otherness is more stereotypical: Fogg's passage through India, during which he picks up a beautiful Indian widow called Aouda as love-interest, is an orientalist mishmash of violent thuggee cults, opium and incipient sensuality. But what is new is the implicit logic of the text, namely that all these various and previously far-flung nations and cultures are now directly apprehensible by any westerner with the necessary technology. Verne portrays a shrinking globe.

Given Verne's reputation as a founding figure in sf it sometimes surprises students to discover that of more than eighty published titles only two concern space travel. I have already mentioned one of these (1877's *Hector Servadac*). The other is the two-part *From the Earth to the Moon* (1865) and *Around the Moon* (1870) – but even here, the lunar spacecraft only leaves Earth, fired from a huge cannon, at the very end of the first novel; and the second novel does not land its explorers on the moon, but only sweeps them around and back to Earth. Verne was interested in exploring the known, not in speculating about the unknown, and in this he was closer to the typical scientific romance than the more imaginatively freewheeling Wells, for all that Wells (in Stableford's thesis as in more general usage) is the cornerstone figure for scientific romance.

Wells is in many ways an ideal author, pedagogically speaking. His books are always thought-provoking and readable, and his scientific romances in particular are mercifully short. I don't mean to sound cynical in noting this, although it has been my experience as a teacher that this is a pedagogic salient, in that some if not all students demonstrate a remarkably deep-seated disinclination when it comes to reading longer books. Moreover, in his half-dozen most famous scientific romances from the 1890s Wells touches on all the key topics a course on scientific romance needs to address.

The Time Machine (1895) not only effectively invented 'time travel' as a sub-genre, it is also one of the most lucid late-century engagements with the scientific and sociological discourses of the age. By moving his (unnamed) protagonist first hundreds of thousands of years, and then millions of years into the future, Wells was able literally to dramatize Darwinian theory (Wells briefly studied in London under 'Darwin's bulldog', T.H. Huxley) as well as articulating the then-modish theory of degeneration associated in particular with Max Nordau. Excerpts from both Darwin and Nordau's *Degeneration* can make excellent contexts for classroom readings of the novel, as can a survey of that critique of the dehumanizing facets of industrialization associated with Marx, Engels or William Morris – something satirically extrapolated into the existences of Wells's Morlocks. More to the point, *The Time Machine* remains one of the most eloquent articulations of our new apprehension of the dizzyingly enormous scales of the cosmos. Long time, as here, correlates to the topographical widening of global horizons entailed by imperialism. This produced both a sense of opportunity and a more deeply rooted anxiety; the very particularity and sense of unique purpose (as 'chosen' by Providence, or God) that motivated Western nations to expand across the globe was threatened by the scale of the world into which they expanded. It is, after all, easy for a person to feel important in a village, and very hard to feel significant as one among a crowd of billions. Sf repeatedly returns to representations of the overwhelming, swamping scale of the cosmos, and explores the status of the individual against these new orders of magnitude. It is, perhaps, neither oversight nor coincidence that Wells's time traveller is nameless.

The Island of Doctor Moreau (1896) similarly intervenes in the debates about evolutionary narrative and 'deep time' that occupied thinkers in the later nineteenth century. In common with much of the broader discourse, Wells's fictive meditation reads the scientific in terms of the religious. Wells's scientist Moreau, upon his tropical island, has accelerated the evolution of animals into humanoids. They act as his servants, and have developed their own rudimentary religion, with Moreau himself as a God of combined Mercy and Pain ('*His* is the Hand that wounds', they chant: '*His* is the Hand that heals'). The novel's quasi-scientific Eden also includes a version of the biblical command not to eat from the 'Tree of the Knowledge of Good and Evil' in that Moreau has decreed that his beast-men not taste blood. His command is, of course, transgressed, and the creatures revert to their bestial origins; the impetus towards devolution overwhelming the evolutionary.

One way of teaching *The War of the Worlds* (1896) is to set it as reading alongside Chesney's *Battle of Dorking* (1871) – neither work being lengthy, it is a doubling of reading that most students could manage easily enough. This has the benefit of defamiliarizing what is perhaps an over-familiar story (very often adapted, of course, for the screen) and pinpointing the extent to which Wells was working within a popular contemporary sub-genre rather than inventing a new sort of novel out of whole cloth. Chesney's narrative – in effect a long short-story rather than a novel – relates how very easily an imagined Prussian invasion of Britain might be achieved. It was designed to argue that the country was both militarily and socially unprepared for inevitable conflict. I.F. Clarke notes that *The Battle of Dorking* 'was the beginning of a great flood of future war stories that continued right up to the summer of 1914'.[3] More than sixty titles could be listed as examples of this sub-genre, and Clarke usefully distinguishes between different versions of the core narrative. Those published in the 1870s and early 1880s (which is to say, in the aftermath of the Prussian military success of the 1870 Franco-Prussian War) tended to articulate a sense of national fear and paranoia. By the 1890s and 1900s such stories generally acquired a more triumphalist flavour, which played its part in creating the culture of enthusiasm with which Britons anticipated actual war against Germany in the run-up to 1914.

To read *War of the Worlds* in the light of Chesney's work is to be struck not only by the similarities (it is a particularly liberating touch, imaginatively and ideologically speaking, to replace actual Prussians with notional Martians) but by the much greater sophistication of Wells's treatment over *The Battle of Dorking*. Chesney's slim story is one-dimensional, and even strident, in its ideological thrust; but Wells's novel symbolically distils a more dialectical understanding of the concerns of his age. His Martians establish an interplanetary beachhead near Woking and make war upon humanity from towering mechanical tripods before eventually succumbing to the Earthly bacteria against which they have no natural defence. It is a point made by many critics that the Martians and their mechanized brutalities function as eloquent symbolic articulations of the necessary violence of empire-building and of the anxieties of otherness and the encounter with otherness that Empire imposes on the imperialist. John Rieder makes a good point with respect to this relationship, one that can emerge from, or at least be elaborated within, classroom discussion:

> The antithetical relation of colonial or imperial triumphalism to science-fictional catastrophes is in some instances a straightforward matter of the fiction's reversing the positions of colonizer and colonized, master and slave, core and periphery. This relatively simple procedure yields complex results in the three influential texts with which we will begin: George Chesney's *The Battle of Dorking* (1871), Richard Jefferies' *After London; or, Wild England* (1885) and H G Wells' *The War of the Worlds* (1898) ... fantasies of appropriation and conquest sometimes project a set of internal contradictions onto an exterior where they, or their surrogates, can be violently eliminated ... [a] pattern of purification and violence [that] alludes to the mounting imperial competition of the pre-World War I and interwar decades.[4]

Scientific romance – and science fiction more generally – provide particularly good opportunities for students to read beyond simply the level of 'content', and to explore the formal, cultural and ideological vectors of literary signification. The 'pattern of purification and violence' Rieder identifies here – a symbolic and ideological determinant of a great many narratives from the 1890s to the 1930s – finds emblematic expression in the high-tech 'heat ray' (what a later generation would call 'the white heat of technological revolution') with which the Martians sear southern England. Jefferies's *After London* (available in full on Project Gutenberg) describes a future England purged of most of its technology – and population – by some unspecified catastrophe; survivors have reverted to a medievalized and pastoral existence. In the twenty-third chapter the young hero, Sir Felix Aquila, treks to the foul and poisonous black swamp that lies where London once was: a landscape littered with skeletons and the blackened relics of the age of technology. In the countryside, though, life has achieved a natural balance that if not quite utopian is nevertheless more idyllic than otherwise. In *The War of the Worlds*, mankind is saved not by its technology of warfare, but by Nature herself, whose microbes can destroy the same Martians that human cannon shells have proved incapable of harming. In Jefferies's tale Nature is less discriminating but just as powerful.

This revulsion from the technological and the desire to return to uncorrupted 'nature' is also behind the many 'lost world' adventure stories that followed in the wake of the enormous success of H. Rider Haggard's *King Solomon's Mines* (1885) and *She* (1887). These sorts of

High Imperial romances of exotic travel in Africa and the discovery of mysterious, ancient and forgotten people are, perhaps, only obliquely 'science fictional'; although they and their many imitators are nevertheless amongst the purest forms of global romance in the canon, and they can work very well on a scientific romance syllabus. In such stories, the violence of conflict becomes magnified to encompass battles, the deaths of immortals and the destruction of whole races; and purification is found in a return to the natural state: 'When the heart is stricken,' Haggard's hero Quatermain announces, 'and the head is humbled in the dust, civilization fails us utterly. Back, back we creep, and lay us like children on the great breast of Nature.'[5]

One of the most enduring of these 'lost world' tales is the story that gives the sub-genre its name: Conan Doyle's *The Lost World* (1912). Doyle's imperial traveller is, bullishly enough, called 'Professor Challenger' (a name calculated to imply the ideal balance of the intellectual and the man of action), and he expresses his dilemma laconically at the beginning of the story: 'The big blank spaces in the map are all being filled in, and there's no room for romance anywhere. Wait a bit though!'[6] Challenger and his friends are able to find one as-yet unsullied blank space in amongst the mountains of South America, and here they encounter not only primitive ape-men fighting a constant war, but living dinosaurs. But the 'romance' element in 'scientific romance' was indeed diminished, to the extent that it depended, as Challenger suggests, upon empty spaces on the map in which explorers can encounter adventure, by the continually increasing actual knowledge of the globe.

The pressure to find new places to explore is one of the things that shifts the primary logic of science fiction from the Earth into Space. But this transition was relatively slow. As I mentioned earlier, of all Verne's eighty-odd titles, only two (*Around the Moon*, 1870, and *Hector Servadac*, 1877) are set off our world; and even Wells only very rarely leaves the ground: space travel is obliquely a part of *War of the Worlds*, and is more centrally present in Wells's *The First Men in the Moon* (1901), but barely occurs in his approximately one hundred other titles. But if space travel is not centrally a feature of late nineteenth-century scientific romance, it is present nevertheless; and since it was fated to become, of course, one of the central tropes of twentieth-century science fiction, it is worth covering the subject when teaching the mode.

For example, it can add depth to students' appreciation of scientific romance to have them read Percy Greg's (out of print but, once again, available unabridged on both Google Books and Project Gutenberg)

Across the Zodiac: The Story of a Wrecked Record (1880). A veteran of the American Civil War sees a UFO crash ('it had a very perceptible disc … I came upon fragments of shining pale yellow metal … [and a] remarkably hard impenetrable cement'). From its wreckage he extracts a Latin manuscript which tells how its anonymous human inventor discovered the mysterious power source 'apergy' and used it to power an 1820 expedition to Mars in a spaceship called 'the Astronaut' (the first recorded use of this term). Greg correctly anticipated the weightlessness of space travel, and fills the earlier chapters of his book with carefully recorded scientific data, including detailed linguistic tables and declensions of a Martian language. The middle portion of the tale is occupied by some rather dry and certainly lengthy accounts of the society and Utilitarian morals of the natives of Mars, and the narrator's rather listless love for a Martian maid Eveena. But it ends in more adventurous and exciting mode, with political intrigue and attempted assassination. One of the most interesting features of this book is the way it anticipates precisely the quasi-anthropological focus and spurious exoticism of lost world narratives. Mars becomes another place to be apprehended by determined, technologically inventive Western culture.

More far-reaching cosmic voyages are to be found in the works of British writer Olaf Stapledon (1886–1950), a crucial figure in the non-US traditions by which scientific romance came to influence postwar global sf. One of the things that Stapledon brings to the genre is a hitherto unprecedented chronological scale – unprecedented even by Wells. 'Long time' is the least of it: his novel *Last and First Men* (1930) disposes of the whole future history of *Homo sapiens* in a few pages before replacing us with a new species, whose manner of living on the planet he describes. Indeed, Stapledon traces eighteen distinct varieties of continually evolving humanoids, the last being a solar-system spanning set of telepaths who are nonetheless ultimately to be wiped out by a cosmic collision. The narrative stretches across several billion years; but Stapledon's later *Star Maker* (1937) dwarfs even that timescale in its chronological spread, taking in our whole universe, and then myriad other universes as well, all described with unflagging energy and invention, and ultimately revealed to be the work of a chillily impersonal entity the 'star maker' of the book's title.

I have in my time taught both these Stapledonian titles, and have found it more difficult to do well than teaching other, more conventional sf titles. This is not, of course, to say that it cannot be a rewarding pedagogic experience; but it is worth facing the difficulty – namely that they will probably be quite unlike other novels students have encountered before; and that many students, when faced with something radically new, are as likely to retreat into incomprehension as engagement. The way to address this, I think, is to make the very difference of scale, and novelistic conception, the focus of teaching: to discuss what happens to conventional concepts like 'character' and 'narrative' over such mind-boggling lengths of time and space. Giving students some sense of the conceptual history of 'the sublime' as a category (along with its materialist sf equivalent 'sense of wonder') is one way into this question; and it can broaden into a discussion of the endurance of sf's appeal.

As I mentioned at the start of this chapter, it seems to me worth making space in any course about scientific romance to touch on the continuing presence of the mode in current sf. One way of doing this is to introduce such students to the modern sub-genre known as 'Steampunk'. This was a term formed by analogy with 'Cyberpunk', the sub-genre inaugurated especially by William Gibson's high-tech futuristic-noir *Neuromancer* (1984). The first steampunk novel was *The Difference Engine* (1990) co-authored by Gibson and his friend Bruce Sterling, and based on the alternate-history notion that Charles Babbage's early-model computer was successfully produced instead of remaining only a prototype. The invention of computing a century before it was actually developed (the assumption goes) would have produced a nineteenth century in which rapidly accelerated technological advances went hand-in-hand with sometimes quaintly rendered Victorian mores, manners and dress. The items of technological advance need not be literally steam-powered (although many are), but it is one of the conventions of this rapidly burgeoning form of sf that not only the dress and setting but the fictive form of steampunk novels apes late nineteenth-century originals.

In fact steampunk as a cultural phenomenon pre-dates Gibson and Sterling's book by decades, even though that is the text that has given the sub-genre its name. The phenomenon's roots reach at least to the 1960s, when (as with the Beatles dressing up as multicoloured Edwardian band musicians for the cover of *Sgt Pepper*) a flamboyantly re-imagined late Victorian or Edwardian style became the vogue. Large audiences were drawn to neo-scientific romance time travel adventures on the large or small screen (George Pal's cinematic version of Wells's *The Time Machine*, 1960, or the TV serials *Adam Adamant Lives!* 1966–67, and *Doctor Who*, 1963–89, particularly in its Jon Pertwee phase, 1970–74). Michael Moorcock published a trilogy of pastiche Edwardian adventures: *The Warlord of the Air* (1971), *The Land Leviathan* (1973, tellingly subtitled 'A New Scientific Romance') and *The Steel Tsar*

(1981) – later reissued in one volume as *A Nomad of the Time Streams: A Scientific Romance* (1993). In part this was designed to connect with the success of *The Difference Engine*, but it also acknowledges a longer-standing appeal of the form.

It may not be practical to teach any of these texts in detail (although it would certainly be possible, and potentially interesting, to do so). But in a course that balances actual Victorian and Edwardian examples of scientific romance against late twentieth-century pastiches of the form, it may be worthwhile to canvass students for their experience of examples of this mode. Among the most influential recent examples is Alan Moore's ongoing graphic novel *The League of Extraordinary Gentlemen* (3 vols: 2002; 2003; 2008) (not, however, the risible cinematic adaptation of the same, which Moore himself has disowned). Also noteworthy is so-called New Weird fiction (China Miéville's *Perdido Street Station*, 2000, Ian MacLeod's *The Light Ages*, 2003), works that deftly capture the style and feel of late Victorian worlds and put them at the service of canny, postmodern apprehensions of the fractured social and cultural logic of the contemporary.

Steampunk, in fact, has rapidly become a ubiquitous cultural *style* rather than a category: not only do writers produce many stories and novels that are in effect modern-day scientific romances, but sf fans dress in frock coats and wear kid gloves, and companies produce 'steampunk' artefacts for sale: computer keyboards modelled on 1890s typewriter fascias, CD players gleaming with mahogany, brass, clockwork and valves. The popularity of these sorts of props speaks to a continuing fascination with – precisely – scientific romance; and this in itself can make a good ground for student discussion. Students unfamiliar with steampunk as a literary genre might find it useful to read a collection of short fiction rather than whole novels: two recent edited anthologies of interest are Nick Gevers's *Extraordinary Engines: The Definitive Steampunk Anthology* (2008) and Ann and Jeff VanderMeer's *Steampunk* (2008). To explore the multifarious manifestations of steampunk as a cultural commodity or style, students could do worse than go to the website Boing Boing (www.boingboing.com), which amongst other things logs interesting new examples of these latter (type 'steampunk' in the site's search engine for examples of what I mean).

Part of the appeal, here, is evidently nostalgia, compounded by a sense that though ornate (or perhaps precisely because of such ornateness) this cultural logic is more elegant and attractive than more modern aesthetics of sf. But, to return to the point I was making at the beginning, it can be worthwhile in a teaching situation discussing the extent to which there is something more significant going on. For instance, it is worth interrogating the widespread but inchoate sense that sf is somehow 'about the future'. To what extent is it more accurate to talk about sf's notional futures as ways of parsing the present and the past – a logic contemporary scientific romances make manifest – by way of metaphorically unlocking the key discursive dynamics that inform our lives. This is to speak to the continuing relevance of a mode – sf – sometimes denigrated as merely escapist; but it is also to explore the extent to which such apparently Victorian fascinations (evolution and 'devolution'/degeneration; imperialism; the potentials and dangers of technological innovation; imperialism and the encounter with otherness) are actually core to present-day existence.

Notes

1. Brian Stableford, *Scientific Romance in Britain 1890–1950* (New York: St Martin's Press, 1985) 3.
2. Arthur Evans, 'Jules Verne's English Translators', *Science Fiction Studies*, 33:1 (2005): 80–104.
3. I.F. Clarke, ed., *The Tale of the Next Great War 1871–1914* (Liverpool: Liverpool University Press, 1995) 15.
4. John Rieder, *Colonialism and the Emergence of Science Fiction* (Middletown, CT: Wesleyan University Press, 2008) 124.
5. Haggard quoted in Rieder, *Colonialism*, 39.
6. Arthur Conan Doyle, *The Lost World and Other Thrilling Tales* (Harmondsworth: Penguin Classics, 2001) 15.

5
Teaching Pulp Science Fiction

Gary Westfahl

One might derive a working definition of 'pulp science fiction' from a well-known fact, and a well-known opinion. As a matter of fact, science fiction magazines from the 1920s to the early 1950s (wherein science fiction emerged as a recognized genre) were generally printed on cheap yellow paper, 'pulp', and hence termed pulp magazines. As a matter of opinion, Ursula K. Le Guin and Brian Attebery, assembling *The Norton Book of Science Fiction* (1993), included only stories from the 1960s and thereafter because to them that represented, as stated in Le Guin's introduction, the era of science fiction's 'maturity'.[1] One could define pulp science fiction, then, as genre science fiction which is not 'mature'.

To be sure, this definition's time frame must be adjusted, in part because pulp science fiction magazines (as noted) disappeared in the early 1950s, almost universally supplanted by the now-standard digest format. Furthermore, most commentators, including myself, would say the genre matured in the 1950s, not the 1960s, as shown by the appearance of new magazines, *Galaxy* and *The Magazine of Fantasy and Science Fiction*, which explicitly sought and addressed adult readers, and by the publication of many esteemed stories and novels. After all, several works from this decade – including Ray Bradbury's *The Martian Chronicles* (1950), Arthur C. Clarke's *Childhood's End* (1953), Theodore Sturgeon's *More Than Human* (1953), Robert A. Heinlein's *Starship Troopers* (1959) and Walter M. Miller Jr's *A Canticle for Leibowitz* (1959) – are routinely assigned in college science fiction classes, testifying to their literary quality and, one might say, their maturity. And one naturally recoils, I think, from describing such novels as 'pulp science fiction', even though portions of four of them originally appeared in science fiction magazines.

For that reason, I address as 'pulp science fiction' only works that appeared in the science fiction magazines of the 1920s, 1930s and

1940s, since these are usually excluded from the college curriculum, except for a few stories in retrospective anthologies, and since I argue that these works, even if deemed immature, do merit consideration as texts for science fiction classes. I will focus on six works from this era, including ideas for class discussions and suggestions for research projects.

One must approach the magazine science fiction of the 1920s and 1930s with an awareness of their typical readers: young Anglo males, brighter than their peers, particularly fascinated by science, and socially inept loners. Frustrated by a society that lacked their interests and failed to value them as people, unable to find and bond with like-minded others in their immediate vicinity, these adolescents happily turned to the fabulous world of science fiction magazines, wherein they found stories about men like themselves who made amazing discoveries in the future, conquered the universe, earned humanity's acclaim, and won the hands of beautiful women – heartening affirmations of their own true worth and glorious future. Through letters and announcements in these magazines, they also learned about a growing national network of people devoted to such fiction, which they eagerly connected to, finally able to feel a sense of community. For portraits of these individuals, one might examine memoirs written by science fiction authors who grew up reading pulp science fiction – such as Frederik Pohl's *The Way the Future Was* (1978), Jack Williamson's *Wonder's Child* (1984) or Clarke's *Astounding Days* (1990) – but the best choice might be Isaac Asimov's anthology *Before the Golden Age* (1974), offering both a rich selection of science fiction stories of the 1930s and lengthy commentaries on Asimov's youthful reactions to them, effectively making the book Asimov's first autobiography.

In our enlightened, multicultural age, does a population of largely male, largely white, and largely American people from 1920 to 1950 really deserve special attention? First, one must avoid stereotyping these readers: they were not, for example, virulent sexists who excluded women from their all-male world of science and adventure; rather, they were desperately eager to welcome those occasional women who came to science fiction conventions or wrote science fiction stories, as documented in Eric Leif Davin's *Partners in Wonder* (2006). In addition, many of these young men later became the scientists and engineers who helped to build the atomic bomb and launch the American space programme, meaning that, for better or worse, these were people who, as they once dreamed, eventually had a major impact on their society. (It is a matter of record, for example, that John W. Campbell Jr, editor of

Astounding Science-Fiction in the 1940s, first sensed that some sort of special scientific project was going on when he noticed a huge increase in subscriptions from a small town in New Mexico named Los Alamos; and there are numerous testimonials from participants in the Manhattan Project and America's space programme of their early interest in science fiction. How, one wonders, did the extravagant space operas read by these long-time science fiction readers affect their work?)

As a text to shed light on these readers, I personally cherish Williamson's *After Worlds End* (1938) – a particularly hallucinogenic vision of a present-day man whose identity blurs with that of an identical far-future descendant battling an implacable robot adversary intent upon destroying humanity – but Clarke's *Against the Fall of Night* (1953) is more accessible. Though first published in magazine form in 1948, Clarke began writing the book in the 1930s, and its story reflects the style and concerns of that decade. Alvin is a young man in a fantastic future city, Diaspar, which effectively imprisons its immortal residents while benevolently providing for their every need. While everyone else is content within this protective cocoon, the restlessly curious Alvin seeks to escape and learn about the outside world. With the help of an eccentric mentor, he becomes the first person in eons to leave Diaspar and begins a journey which takes him first to another, very different city on Earth and then into space, where he learns that everything Diaspar's citizens had been taught about their history is incorrect.

What sort of person would find this story appealing? Clearly, it would be a young man who feels he is surrounded by boring people inexplicably unexcited about the prospects of futuristic inventions and space travel; a youth anxious to discover that the dull world around him is not as it seems, or will soon be irreversibly transformed; a youth who enjoys daydreaming about becoming the one special person who awakens the world from complacent slumber and leads it to a new, grander destiny. *Against the Fall of Night* is not a literary masterpiece, or even Clarke's best work, but it exudes undeniable energy as it speeds Alvin from revelation to revelation against the backdrop of a vast, empty universe filled with unanswered questions.

Against the Fall of Night might inspire some stimulating research projects. First, after becoming prominent in the 1950s, Clarke was embarrassed by this piece of juvenilia and extensively revised the novel to add depth and polish, publishing the result in 1956 as *The City and the Stars*. However, while one appreciates that novel's better developed scientific ideas and more thoughtful aura, it proved, overall, a lesser work, as its virtues did not compensate for a conspicuous lack of youthful vigour, and over the years *Against the Fall of Night* has been embraced as the definitive version of the story. Students might also ponder Clarke's novel and film *2001: A Space Odyssey* (1968) to explore similarities between Alvin and two other figures who embark upon lonely quests for cosmic wisdom, the prehistoric Moon-Watcher (better characterized in the novel) and astronaut Dave Bowman. Students might examine Gregory Benford's 1989 sequel to *Against the Fall of Night*, *Beyond the Fall of Night* (originally published in tandem with Clarke's novel as a purported collaboration and later republished in a separate, expanded version, with references to Clarke's novel removed, as *Beyond Infinity*, 2004) to observe how abysmally Benford fails to recapture the magic of Clarke's novel with a tiresome, politically-correct continuation of the story focusing on a hapless female protagonist assisted by several strange beings while stumbling through an incongruously crowded reinvention of Clarke's stark and lonely future, now cluttered with aliens and new inventions – all of which represents a betrayal of Clarke's original vision. (Benford is a productive scientist and talented author, but perhaps he has spent too much time working on a college campus to be comfortable with a tale of a solitary young white man single-handedly conquering the universe, explaining his odd take on Clarke's novel.)

Another novel written in the 1930s provides insight into the psychology of its readers not so much through its protagonist as through the character that is central to his concerns. In Williamson's *The Legion of Time* (1938, 1952),[2] the entire future of the universe hinges upon one action to be taken by a bright youngster in our present: if he picks up a magnet and begins playing with it, he will grow up to become a brilliant scientist whose inventions will lead to a benign future utopia; if he does not pick up the magnet, he never becomes a scientist and the future will be a dark dystopia. Both futures now exist in quasi-real, tentative states, and combatants from each universe travel through time in efforts to ensure that the boy will either pick up or ignore the magnet and thus firmly establish the reality of their own universe and erase its rival. Here, while nerdish readers could identify with Williamson's hero from the utopian future which ultimately triumphs, they were surely more inclined to imagine themselves as the novel's child, viewed by contemporaries as insignificant but actually destined to determine the destiny of the universe. And yes, in the 1930s, magnets were common toys for science-minded youth.

Along with sociological analyses, pulp science fiction of the 1930s invites examination as the origin of the sort of science fiction – most prominently represented by the *Star Wars* and *Star Trek* franchises – now dominating popular culture. One place to begin such a study is E.E. 'Doc' Smith's *Galactic Patrol* (1937–38, 1950), first published as a serial in *Astounding Stories* and originally the first of four novels constituting the Lensman series (though Smith later revised a previously unrelated novel, *Triplanetary,* 1948, to serve as the series' first instalment and wrote *First Lensman,* 1950, to bridge the gap between *Triplanetary* and *Galactic Patrol,* creating the six-novel series now familiar to science fiction readers). This novel introduced Smith's main hero, Kimball Kinnison, who leads an alliance of humans and aliens (backed by a benevolent ancient race called the Arisians) in a galactic war against sinister pirates controlled by an implacable enemy named 'Helmuth, speaking for Boskone'[3] (although, as later novels reveal, he actually works for another ancient, but evil, race, the Eddorians). Relying upon the mysterious Lens given to him and other Lensmen by the Arisians, which provides psychic powers, as well as his own scientific know-how and resourcefulness, Kinnison succeeds in a risky mission to gain information about his foes and eventually kills Helmuth by means of a one-man assault on his hidden base.

Students will have a field day critiquing the clunky prose, egregious sexism and childish heroics of *Galactic Patrol*; but despite its inadequacies, they will also discern in the novel a template for the stories they have grown up watching in cinemas and on television: humans allied with colourful aliens opposing evil empires; space battles involving immense starships assailing each other with amazing rays; fierce, hand-to-hand combat on starship decks and planetary surfaces with adversaries wielding futuristic variations of ancient weapons. A question for social historians would be: why were these fantastic narratives so under-appreciated in the 1930s and so popular in the 1970s and thereafter? It is not simply that advances in special effects technology were needed to make such sagas work on film, since films like *Die Frau im Mond* (Fritz Lang, 1929) and *Things to Come* (William Cameron Menzies, 1936) demonstrate that, even in the 1930s, filmmakers who invested time and resources in their efforts could provide persuasive renderings of space travel. Rather, there must be other reasons why cowboys and detectives have largely been supplanted by space-faring adventurers as our larger-than-life heroes of choice.

One cannot entirely dismiss *Star Trek, Star Wars* and similar works as mere adaptations of the space operas written by Smith and others in the 1930s, since these franchises depart from Smith's pattern in ways worth discussing. First, though he often uses the almost magical powers of the Lens – an arguable anticipation of George Lucas's mystical 'Force' – Kinnison also understands the superscience of his day and employs his knowledge to solve problems; for example, stranded on an alien planet and needing energy to recharge their batteries, Kinnison and a cohort visit an alien power plant and ingeniously use 'pliers, screwdrivers, and other tools of the electrician' to extract its power.[4] In contrast, the original *Star Trek* offered an appealing protagonist without such capabilities, James Kirk, who relied upon subordinates Mr Spock and Mr Scott for technological fixes, while the *Star Wars* series almost entirely dispenses with scientifically knowledgeable characters to focus on heroes who simply make clever use of off-the-shelf technology they may not fully understand. Perhaps any story seeking a mass audience must foreground likeable, ordinary characters instead of scientific geniuses like Kinnison.

Also, while *Star Wars* and its sequels follow Smith more closely in emphasizing armed conflict against irredeemable foes, the *Star Trek* universe prefers diplomatic intrigue and a narrative arc tending toward eventual reconciliation between bitter adversaries; thus, the chief enemies of the first series, the Klingons, later become allies, and episodes often depict efforts to peacefully resolve conflicts with other foes like the Romulans. So, fittingly enough for a series that emerged in the Swinging Sixties, *Star Trek* visibly seeks viewers who prefer to make love, not war. Finally, as further material for comparison-contrast papers, students may watch the Japanese anime adaptation of Smith's series, *Lensman* (1984), and there are plans for an American live-action film.

In the 1940s, Campbell, who officially became editor of *Astounding Science-Fiction* in 1938, attracted and nurtured a new generation of writers who, in some cases, appealed to the readers of science fiction in a new way: instead of presenting incredibly talented heroes who mirrored their juvenile, even nerdish, fantasies, these writers offered more plausible, yet attractive visions of the mature adults their readers might some day become. A key transitional work is Heinlein's 'If This Goes On –' (1940), later revised and published along with two further stories as *Revolt in 2100* (1953). Protagonist and narrator John Lyle is an intelligent young man in a dystopian future America controlled by a religious dictatorship. Initially, he accepts the official religion and its government, but he begins to doubt the benevolence and desirability of the regime when he falls in love with an innocent young woman recruited to become the Prophet's latest mistress, and he soon joins a vast underground movement dedicated to replacing the tyranny with a secular, democratic government. While early chapters give Lyle exciting things to do – nocturnal derring-do in the Prophet's Palace and a cross-country mission to deliver an important message – he settles into the role of a minor functionary in the revolutionary movement and is only an observer of their daring and successful *coup d'état* (though he accidentally plays a key role in a final assault on the Prophet's palace).

To some critics, this represents a flaw in the novel, a sign of Heinlein's immaturity as a writer; wouldn't it have been better, they say, to make the leader of the revolution the story's hero? Yet I would invite students to detect a subtle agenda in Heinlein's approach. Essentially, he takes a typical science fiction protagonist from the 1930s – young, smart and energetic – and argues that such individuals, by themselves, can never achieve significant social change; rather, unlike Kinnison – who single-handedly overcomes a cosmic despot – Lyle must join with many others who share his goals, help them build a large, complex organization, and ultimately serve as one of innumerable compatriots each performing small but significant tasks which have a cumulative impact. Heinlein's readers, along with his protagonist, thus receive an education in the realities of advanced civilization, wherein plucky youngsters, even equipped with great intelligence and amazing inventions, can never conquer the universe unaided. The contrast between *Against the Fall of Night* and 'If This Goes On –' is illuminating: Alvin becomes the sole saviour of humanity, while Lyle becomes a foot soldier in a revolutionary army.

As one research project, students might consider 'If This Goes On –' as a bracing comeuppance to the individualistic heroes of the 1930s by examining another Heinlein novel, *Sixth Column* (1941, 1949), which though written after 'If This Goes On –' actually offers a story constructed well before it. In the 1930s, Campbell wrote a novella, 'All' (which eventually appeared in the 1976 collection *The Space Beyond*), but deemed it unpublishable; however, to make use of his labours, he hired Heinlein to write a novel based on its story. Campbell had crafted a classic 1930s saga of astounding victory against daunting odds achieved by remarkable men: after an Asian nation conquers America, six geniuses hole up in an isolated fortress, whip up some superscience that specifically targets people of Asian descent, and overthrow the invaders essentially all by themselves. It represents, then, how 'If This Goes On –' might have proceeded if Heinlein had implausibly presented Lyle as a brilliant scientist who single-handedly defeats America's dictatorship. In adapting 'All', Heinlein did his best to make this racist, unrealistic story palatable, but the result was unquestionably one of his lesser works. One could both understand and convey to others, then, how science fiction changed from the 1930s to the 1940s with some slightly-out-of-chronological-order reading: first, 'All', to sample the wish-fulfilment fantasies of 1930s science fiction; then, *Sixth Column*, to observe a reasonable man of the 1940s vainly striving to make these fantasies seem sensible; and finally, 'If This Goes On –', to observe that same reasonable man abandoning the fantasies and instead undertaking to describe how a successful revolution might actually be achieved. Students particularly interested in Heinlein – one of the field's seminal figures – might read the original magazine version of 'If This Goes On –' and compare it to the revised, expanded version. Some changes are inconsequential: Heinlein adds a mildly salacious skinny-dipping scene for adult readers and reworks one of Lyle's thrilling escapes to make it more realistic. But one change is telling: in the original version, the rebels decide, after their revolution succeeds, to launch a propaganda campaign to persuade citizens to accept their new government, and no one objects. In the revision, upon hearing of this plan, an elderly man stands up to vociferously complain:

'Free men aren't "conditioned"! Free men are free because they are ornery and cussed and prefer to arrive at their own prejudices in their own way – not have them spoon-fed by a self-appointed mind tinkerer! We haven't fought, our brethren haven't bled and died, just to change bosses, no matter how sweet their motives.'[5]

Shamed by his passionate opposition, rebel leaders abandon their plan. This shift in attitude defined Heinlein's later career: originally committed to the importance of working within groups to achieve social change (and once seeking a career in politics), his stories featured individuals who, while brilliant and capable, were willing to work with others within intricate organizations to accomplish worthwhile goals. As such, he would have no quarrel with benign efforts to convince people to accept a new government. Later, disillusioned with society, Heinlein increasingly insisted that brilliant, capable individuals should rather abandon civilization and its annoying restrictions and instead seek unlimited freedom outside society – the recurring message of *Time Enough for Love* (1973). That speech, then, is an early sign of a burgeoning inclination to reject socialization and embrace individualism – although, unlike the heroes of 1930s science fiction, Heinlein's later protagonists did not leave their communities to conquer the universe but rather only sought to fulfil their own personal desires.

The other two stories in *Revolt in 2100*, however, only reinforce Heinlein's original message: 'Misfit' (1939), identified by Sam Moskowitz as Heinlein's first juvenile story,[6] anticipates the pattern of his juvenile novels by describing a troubled young man, Andrew Jackson Libby, who joins a team turning an asteroid into a space station, reveals and uses his amazing calculating abilities to save the day, and then is contentedly integrated into his society. (The character reappears in later novels *Methuselah's Children*, 1941, 1958, *Time Enough for Love*, and *The Number of the Beast*, 1980.) In 'Coventry' (1940), a man unwilling to comply with the reasonable rules of his enlightened, post-revolutionary society must go where all such people are sent – a special zone where no rules are enforced – and in that lawless realm learns the desirability of abiding by social norms. (Heinlein introduced the concept of 'Coventry' in his long-unpublished first novel, *For Us the Living: A Comedy of Customs*, 2004, which 'If This Goes On –' also borrows from in minor ways.)

If Heinlein in the 1940s was striving to train young readers to function as members of society, other authors, such as Asimov, had embarked upon another sort of training, writing stories that effectively showed young readers how to think like scientists. Like the archetypal Heinlein hero, Asimov's protagonists were more sociable than those of the 1930s; they particularly loved engaging in conversations, leading to stories driven more by dialogue than by derring-do. But rather than seeking power, fame or political change, Asimov's heroes primarily needed to solve puzzles – albeit puzzles linked to broader concerns. Still, in describing thoughtful individuals who carefully gathered information, considered alternatives, reasoned everything out, and finally achieved correct solutions, Asimov (then studying to become a chemist and later employed as a chemistry professor) was arguably presenting the first realistic portrayals of working scientists in genre science fiction, even if that was not always their official profession.

One useful collection displaying Asimov's approach is *I, Robot* (1940–50, 1950), offering nine stories about humanoid robots supposedly rendered harmless by the rigid programming of the Three Laws – which famously prevent robots from harming humans or disobeying their orders while otherwise allowing them to protect themselves. Yet crises invariably arise – usually, robots representing a threat to humans – so their masters must deduce the source of the problems and devise solutions. Some stories feature space explorers Gregory Powell and Mike Donovan, who grapple with malfunctioning robots during missions on the frontiers of the solar system, but others foreground the more memorable Dr Susan Calvin, a robot psychologist who works in laboratories to figure out why certain robots are perilously misbehaving. Asimov revised these stories in minor ways to make them consistent with each other – I have elsewhere explored how, throughout the original stories, Asimov kept rephrasing and tinkering with the Three Laws until achieving a final, definitive text, then incorporated into the revisions[7] – but there is little material here for a textual study. More interesting are the texts which emerged from these stories – not only a trilogy featuring detective Lije Baley and robot partner R. Daneel Olivaw, but a fourth novel, *Robots and Empire* (1985), which linked the robot stories to Asimov's far-future Foundation saga, also launched during the 1940s, creating a vast, multi-volume future history of which *I, Robot* is the first instalment. And in almost every work in the series, the focus of attention is a mystery, and protagonists discuss the puzzle, think things through, and finally reach a satisfactory solution.

Students studying *I, Robot* might compare Asimov's book to its purported film adaptation, *I, Robot* (Proyas, 2004) – although the film's script originally had nothing to do with Asimov; instead, the producers owning the script bought the rights to Asimov's title and added a few Asimovian touches to a final revision. Of course, Asimov's emphasis on thoughtful conversation and deduction could not be replicated in a money-making action film, resulting in a production that seems not only divorced from Asimov's stories but antithetical to them. A revelatory scene, discussed in my review of the film, recalls the *I, Robot* story 'Little Lost Robot' (1947) in that a dangerous robot has concealed himself amidst scores of innocuous duplicates, but story and film immediately diverge dramatically:

> In Asimov's story, as one might expect, the problem sets the stage for a series of ingenious tests devised by Calvin which eventually force the robot to reveal himself. In this film, destroying any hopes for a truly Asimovian story, Spooner [Will Smith] just pulls out his gun and starts blasting robots in the head, figuring that the frightened culprit will soon run away.[8]

An intriguing analysis might also involve comparing Asimov's book to Harlan Ellison's unproduced, and reasonably faithful, adaptation, published as *I, Robot: The Illustrated Screenplay* (1994). One question to ponder: if science fiction in fact matured and improved during the 1940s, why did it also, it seems, become less attractive as material for film adaptations? (Along with *I, Robot*, the sorry history of Heinlein film adaptations might be brought into the discussion.)

Even while Heinlein and Asimov established themselves as different sorts of alternatives to the extravagances of the 1930s, another new writer in Campbell's stable – A.E. van Vogt – carried the youthful exuberance of the 1930s to new extremes. In the manner of the previous decade, van Vogt's stories often featured childlike loners with amazing abilities who travelled great distances, battled daunting foes, and emerged as all-powerful saviours of humanity. What he added to the pattern, first, was an abundance of ideas – one tossed out every eight hundred words, following a formula he learned from a guide to writers – that made his works seem more profound than previous space operas. Second, in keeping with this constant, dizzying assault of new concepts and perspectives, van Vogt transcended the traditional rationality of science fiction to instead generate stories that resisted logical explanation. Esteemed in his day, van Vogt is no longer well known or highly regarded, but the model of science fiction that he created – dynamic, breathless and wildly imaginative – powerfully influenced later writers like Philip K. Dick.

To appreciate van Vogt's unique power, students might read his first novel *Slan* (1940, 1946), featuring young Jommy Cross, persecuted member of the tendrilled, telepathic race of mutants called slans. With mesmerizing energy, van Vogt rushes his hero from one death-trap to another as he grows to adulthood, masters his late father's superscientific discoveries, and constructs weapons to wield against two relentless foes: normal humans, who hunt down and kill slans, and newly discovered 'tendrilless slans', who maintain an undercover society while despising and assailing regular slans as much as, if not more than, the humans. In a final confrontation with Kier Gray, the dictator who postures as a fierce opponent of slans, Cross learns that Gray is actually a disguised slan himself, one of many actually controlling the government.

A talented writer who polished his skills in other pulp genres before tackling science fiction, van Vogt will effortlessly enthral students who were unimpressed by Smith's clumsy prose; but they will understand why van Vogt's kaleidoscopic approach to science fiction faded away while Heinlein's and Asimov's more subdued styles became dominant. For no matter how relentlessly van Vogt maintains his frenetic pace and keeps shocking readers with new ideas, they eventually realize that his stories fundamentally do not make sense. In contrast to Heinlein and Asimov's meticulously planned futures, van Vogt's worlds are chaotic mixtures of mind-boggling scientific advances and anachronistic remnants of present-day life. As enemies become friends and victims become victimizers, these reversals inevitably seem implausible, even as van Vogt shouts out quick explanations before lurching in yet another new direction. There is no aura of reality, no sense of conviction, to van Vogt's visions; instead, they have the atmosphere, and logic, of a dream. A scene in *Slan* is revelatory: Kathleen Layton, the young female slan inexplicably sheltered by the apparently slan-hating Gray, wakes in the middle of the night to witness a startling confrontation between Gray and ten chief lieutenants, whose loyalties (as Layton's telepathy reveals) gradually shift away from Gray and toward a rebellious subordinate until Gray abruptly summons these men's assistants into the room; somehow, he anticipated this development and had previously recruited the assistants to enter at this precise moment and kill their bosses, ending the revolt. The timing of this scene gives the game away: impossible to accept as a reasonable series of events, the sequence seems more like Kathleen's dream, reflecting subconscious fears that Gray's associates will contrive to kill her and faith that Gray will always protect her. Even Dick, who as noted emulated van Vogt in some respects, learned enough from Heinlein and Asimov to make his future worlds passably believable, and his strange narrative twists ostensibly plausible. Van Vogt's imaginings, carefully examined, inexorably fall apart.

Slan also suggests several research projects. First, while van Vogt's multiple revisions of *The World of Null-A* (1945, 1948) are better known, van Vogt also revised *Slan* on two occasions, for book publication in 1946 and for republication in 1951, striving always to improve the narrative's logic while retaining its hypnotic appeal. For efforts to build upon and improve van Vogt's story, one might consider Heinlein's *Methuselah's Children*, which has an opening sequence often said to borrow from *Slan*, as citizens of a future society try to locate and capture a despised minority of unusually long-lived people; but rather than developing more and more scientific powers, Heinlein's heroes, more realistically, escape their adversaries without overcoming them, embarking upon a sedate interstellar journey before returning to rejoin humanity as equals (since their former pursuers discover their own method to achieve comparable longevity). Much later, Kevin J. Anderson employed van Vogt's outline and unfinished draft of a sequel to *Slan* to produce the posthumous collaboration *Slan Hunter* (2007), endeavouring to replicate van Vogt's distinctive style while bringing the saga up to the standards of recent science fiction.

Finally, Heinlein, Asimov and van Vogt were all regarded as Campbell's discoveries and mostly published during the 1940s in his *Astounding Science-Fiction*, universally accepted as the decade's leading magazine. Yet surveys of this era's science fiction cannot focus exclusively on Campbell, since other writers outside his circle were producing significant work and developing their own distinctive approaches. In particular, the magazine *Planet Stories* attracted skilful writers who specialized in the subgenre of planetary romance – stories which took place on alien worlds and featured genre tropes like aliens, robots and amazing inventions, but otherwise had the style and ambience of fantasy. Since Edgar Rice Burroughs's *A Princess of Mars* (1912, 1917) first popularized the form and established its conventions, one good example of planetary romance would be its final sequel *Llana of Gathol* (1941, 1948), first published as four novelettes in *Amazing Stories*, a rousing adventure featuring the series' original hero, John Carter, returning to action one more time to assist his impetuous granddaughter. Yet newer writers in the tradition, like Leigh Brackett, were outdoing Burroughs in their prose and atmosphere, and an anthology of her 1940s works, *Lorelei of the Red Mist* (1943–50, 2007), would introduce students to this unique talent, widely cherished within the genre.

Her stories, one realizes, are animated by an entirely different sensibility than previously discussed works, which focus on the future, with capable protagonists dedicated to further advancing humanity with new scientific and social achievements; even *Against the Fall of Night*, which begins with a decadent far-future civilization, concludes with reawakened ambitions and a renewed drive for progress. Brackett's narratives, like fantasies, primarily look toward the past; their protagonists are usually ordinary people, seeking to survive in alien worlds haunted by the glorious accomplishments of long-vanished civilizations and struggling to unravel their ancient mysteries. Further, rather than savouring the power to shape their own destinies, Brackett's heroes seem governed by a sort of cosmic karma that in the end rewards the virtuous and punishes the wicked. While Clarke, Heinlein and Asimov emphasize explanations, Brackett is primarily devoted to descriptions, ignoring inner workings to illustrate surface wonders in lush, evocative prose. Consider her excellent 'The Jewel of Bas' (1944) – the saga of a husband-and-wife team of thieves who fall into the clutches of aliens and robots brought by an ancient immortal who came to their world long ago but now only longs for endless sleep and pleasant dreams – and contrast her stunning description of a robot to Asimov's more prosaic efforts:

> The eyes in that face were what set Ciaran's guts to knotting like a nest of cold snakes. They were not even remotely human. They were like pools of oil under the lashless lids – black, impenetrable, without heart or soul or warmth. ... It was a voice speaking out of a place where no emotion, as humanity knew the word, had ever existed. It came from a brain as alien and incomprehensible as darkness in a

world of eternal light; a brain no human could ever touch or understand, except to feel the cold weight of its strength and cower as a beast cowers before the terrible mystery of fire.

'Sleep,' said the android. 'Sleep, and listen to my voice.'[9]

This passage also shows that students starved for memorable prose – rarely a hallmark of pulp science fiction – will appreciate having a writer like Brackett in the syllabus.

Lorelei of the Red Mist also usefully illustrates the fact that 1930s and 1940s science fiction had both low points and high points. Few will admire stories like 'The Blue Behemoth' (1943), a farcical tale of a tawdry space circus and its misadventures with a mammoth alien; Brackett's disappointing collaboration with Bradbury, 'Lorelei of the Red Mist' (1946), a fairly lifeless exercise in planetary romance that Brackett wisely abandoned to concentrate on film work and asked young Bradbury to complete; and 'Quest of the Starhope' (1949), the predictable saga of a selfish exploiter of captured aliens who receives his just rewards when he is killed by two beings he mistreated. But other stories powerfully linger in one's mind, such as 'Thralls of the Endless Night' (1943), describing the descendants of a spaceship crew and the pirates that attacked it who uncomprehendingly continue their ancient quarrel on the barren world where their ancestors were marooned; 'The Veil of Astrellar' (1944), featuring a human seduced by promised immortality into helping sinister beings from another dimension lure humans into traps so their life-forces can be drained to sustain the aliens' existence; and 'The Dancing Girl of Ganymede' (1950), Brackett's sensitive exploration of a scenario later treated very differently in Dick's *Do Androids Dream of Electric Sheep?* (1968) – humanlike androids who are despised and hunted down in a future dystopia.

Seeking topics for further research, and noting that Bradbury was a one-time collaborator and admirer of Brackett, students might look for signs of her influence on his fiction. For example, Bradbury's 'Frost and Fire' (1946) – involving mutated descendants of stranded space travellers who aspire to reach a rocket on a mountaintop – is, despite significant differences, clearly reminiscent of 'Thralls of the Endless Night'. A more obvious area for study would be how Brackett's haunting stories about dying, decadent Martian cultures influenced Bradbury's own visions of Mars in *The Martian Chronicles* (1950) and elsewhere. Although there are numerous antecedents for Bradbury's work, ranging back to Percival Lowell and Burroughs, students may justifiably argue that Bradbury's

Mars is largely borrowed from Brackett's Mars. Students may also compare her science fiction stories to her screenplays. Finding evidence of her science fiction background in scripts for crime dramas and westerns like *The Big Sleep* (1946) and *Rio Bravo* (1959) might be challenging, but her early horror film *The Vampire's Ghost* (1946) is unusually creative, and students will be familiar with her final screenplay, for Lucas's *The Empire Strikes Back* (1980), co-written with Lawrence Kasdan. Recalling the striking descriptions in her stories, one is unsurprised that her contributions to Lucas's universe – immense 'walkers' marching across an icy planet, the misty swamp home of the diminutive alien Yoda, the 'cave' Han Solo retreats to that is actually the mouth of a space monster, and the elevated city of Lando Calrissian, delicately perched upon a narrow, floating pillar – make *The Empire Strikes Back* the most *visually* imaginative and impressive of all the *Star Wars* films. One also notes her success in making Lucas's characters more rounded and complex than they were in the first film – another one of her special talents.

In choosing books to represent pulp science fiction, I have limited myself to works now in print and likely to remain in print; but other works from the era would be inspired choices if they become available. To survey the period's short fiction, Asimov's *Before the Golden Age*, representing the 1930s, might be paired with Campbell's *The Astounding Science Fiction Anthology* (1952), providing excellent stories from the 1940s. One might find new retrospective anthologies featuring works by writers such as Campbell, Henry Kuttner and C.L. Moore, and Murray Leinster. Along with other books by writers already discussed, meritorious novels include Edmond Hamilton's space opera *The Star of Life* (1947, 1959); Philip Francis Nowlan's *Armageddon 2419 A.D.* (1928, 1962), which introduced the character of Buck Rogers; Clifford D. Simak's apocalyptic story cycle *City* (1944–51, 1952); John Taine's dreamy time-travel epic, *The Time Stream* (1931, 1946), and Stanley G. Weinbaum's superman saga, *The New Adam* (1939). Also, while technically outside the realm of literature classes, no study of this subject is complete without examining the extravagant artwork that accompanied and influenced the stories in pulp magazines, displayed in compilations like Brian W. Aldiss's *Science Fiction Art* (1975).

Finally, by discussing works of pulp science fiction that one might include in a standard science fiction class, I have also crafted what amounts to an annotated syllabus for a graduate-level class devoted exclusively to pulp science fiction, with ambitious research projects perhaps best assigned to graduate students. And in graduate programmes in science fiction, such a class should definitely be offered. Why take students on a forced march through the collected works of, say, Philip K. Dick when one might better spend a semester acquainting them with some of the works that indelibly influenced Dick and countless other writers of his generation and later generations? Too many of today's publishing science fiction critics are shamefully unfamiliar with this literature, perhaps fearful of sullying their eyes with works that are not 'mature'. But they are missing out on a lot of information, a lot of insight, and a lot of fun.

Notes

1. Ursula K. Le Guin, 'Introduction', in Brian Attebery and Ursula K. Le Guin, eds, *The Norton Book of Science Fiction* (New York and London: W.W. Norton, 1993) 15–42 at 18.
2. Whenever two publication dates for a book are in parentheses, the first is the date of the book's original magazine appearance; the second is the date of its first publication in book form (usually revised).
3. E.E. 'Doc' Smith, *Galactic Patrol* (1950; New York: Pyramid, 1964) 38.
4. Smith, *Galactic Patrol*, 67.
5. Robert A. Heinlein, '"If This Goes On –"', in *Revolt in 2100* (New York: Signet, 1953) 118–19.
6. Sam Moskowitz, *Seekers for Tomorrow* (New York: Ballantine Books, 1967) 197.
7. Gary Westfahl, 'Rules for Robots: Version 1.0', *Interzone*, 185 (2003): 53–5.
8. Gary Westfahl, 'A.I.: Artificial Incompetence, or Robots Just Don't Understand: A Review of *I, Robot*', Locus Online website, posted on 17 July 2004, at http://www.locusmag.com/2004/Reviews/07_Westfahl_IRobot.html.
9. Leigh Brackett, 'The Jewel of Bas', in *Lorelei of the Red Mist* (Royal Oak, MI: Haffner Press, 2007) 90–1.

6
Good SF: Teaching the Golden Age as Cultural History

Lisa Yaszek

I like to begin class units on Golden Age (arguably the period from 1937–50) science fiction at the Georgia Institute of Technology with the whimsical delight that is Fred McLeod Wilcox's film *Forbidden Planet* (1956). Based loosely on Shakespeare's *The Tempest*, and echoing the traditions of sf's literary Golden Age, *Forbidden Planet* follows the adventures of a starship crew sent from Earth to investigate the Altair IV colony, which went silent twenty years earlier. Upon arriving at their destination, Captain John J. Adams (Leslie Nielsen) and his crew discover the remains of a high-tech alien race and just two surviving members of the original expedition: the ship's linguist, Dr Edward Morbius (Walter Pigeon), and his daughter Altaira (Anne Francis), who has been raised by Morbius's creation Robbie the Robot. Threatened with the extinction of his own crew at the hands of an unknown force, Adams must solve a series of interlocking puzzles: what happened to the planet's original inhabitants? Did the same fate befall the Earth colony? How did Morbius and Altaira survive? And finally, how can Adams prevent it all from happening again? Replete with sleek starships, exotic landscapes, mad scientists, heroic star captains and beautiful damsels, *Forbidden Planet* is, as students quickly realize, the epitome of the sf space adventure.

But that is just half the story. Students start out eager to solve the mysteries of Altair IV, but they are quickly sidetracked by other issues: why does Wilcox devote so much screen time to scenes of robotic labour ranging from heavy construction work to delicate floral arranging? How can Robbie be so obviously enslaved to Isaac Asimov's three laws of robotics but then resist the commands of his human owners long enough to go drinking with Adams's crewmembers and finish 'giving [him]self an oil job'? Perhaps not surprisingly, the rather saucy tone of *Forbidden Planet* opens up yet another set of questions as well: why does Morbius hold Altaira more like a lover than a daughter? Would a single year in space really turn an all-male crew who are supposed to be humanity's 'finest specimens' into sex-starved maniacs when they catch a glimpse of Altaira? And how is it that the ostensibly human Altaira has somehow completely failed to learn sex and gender norms, leading to outrageous situations in which she tries to learn biology by snuggling with one crew member and then coolly invites Adams to 'kiss me like everyone else does'?

Because *Forbidden Planet* is an extremely witty film, students initially respond to the situations outlined above with great hilarity. But soon they are eager to debate whether the characters of Robbie and Altaira actually advance the story's main plotline, whether postwar moviegoers could have possibly reacted to Wilcox's film in the same manner as contemporary viewers, and why it is that *Forbidden Planet* feels like it would somehow be less of an sf story without its more eccentric elements. These debates get at the heart of the three main points I want students to learn about Golden Age sf: that it is a discrete mode of storytelling with distinct formal properties; that it is a unique window on the cultural moment in which it was written; and that authors use the formal characteristics of sf to actively participate in the most pressing cultural debates of their day.

While similar claims can be made about any period of sf history, the Golden Age is particularly fruitful to study in this manner because the 1940s and 1950s mark the beginning of the modern era and many of the thematic issues introduced in this period are still very much with us today. This has the advantage of enabling sf instructors and tutors to focus units on Golden Age sf as cultural history in ways that will naturally engage both themselves and their target student populations. For example, I capitalize on the interests of Georgia Tech's overwhelmingly male student population by organizing class discussions of Golden Age sf around two issues: the relations of humans to machines and of men to women in a technology-intensive world. More specifically, we consider how widespread cultural debates over these issues intersect with debates over the definition of 'good sf' as they unfold within the sf community itself.

While it is impossible to separate broad questions of science and society from more specific ones about science, society and gender, I foreground the former over the latter in my introductory sf class. This is an upper-level undergraduate course that students can take to fulfil their humanities graduation requirements – and as one might imagine, many students at a school like Georgia Tech do so. The student population tends toward heterogeneity, comprised equally of science, engineering and liberal arts students ranging from sophomores who have just finished our introductory composition sequence to graduating seniors who are in the process of wrapping up undergraduate theses and design projects. Despite their overt differences, students quickly bond over their shared love of sf and a more general excitement about discussing it in a scholarly environment.

I take advantage of this enthusiasm and intimacy by employing a modified lecture/discussion format in which I provide students with primary sf readings, supplementary critical and cultural texts, and lecture outlines for a series of units designed to familiarize students with sf history. Students read in advance for each unit and then work collaboratively to fill in my lecture outlines; this material, in turn, becomes the basis for subsequent tests and paper assignments. (I strive to head off any tendency toward chaos by actually preparing my own lecture points in advance and then gently steering class conversations in appropriate directions as needed.) While this format works well in my particular situation, it could easily be adapted to a range of other pedagogical situations. For example, instructors teaching larger or younger groups of students might employ a more traditionally lecture-oriented approach to their materials, while those working with smaller or more homogeneous groups might forgo the creation of any lecture outlines whatsoever, instead leaving it to small groups of students to design and run each unit. The key in each case is to teach what cultural historian Catherine Belsey calls 'history at the level of the signifier' by situating individual sf stories within larger constellations of scientific and social texts.[1]

As mentioned at the beginning of this chapter, I typically begin units on Golden Age sf with a screening of *Forbidden Planet*. This provides students with a collective experience of one representative text from this period of sf history. After identifying the major issues raised by Wilcox's film, we consider whether or not it meets our working definition for 'good sf'. We generate this definition in the first week of class after brainstorming our own ideas about this subject and reading Darko Suvin's introduction to *Metamorphoses of Science Fiction*, which defines good sf as a mode of literature characterized by 'the presence and interaction of estrangement and cognition and … an imaginative framework alternative to the author's empirical environment'.[2] By the end of the week students usually decide to adopt a modified version of Suvin's criteria, replacing his narrow requirement that good sf must engender progressive political estrangement in readers with the more general one that it must simply cause them to question their assumptions about the natural relations of science and society in some distinctive way. Applying this definition to *Forbidden Planet* makes for rousing discussion. While the film obviously more than meets our first requirement, it is much more difficult to determine whether or not it meets the second one: does Robbie's surprising humanity or Altaira's smouldering sexuality really challenge our assumptions about how the world might look in the future, based on what we know about it already? Is our laughter at the shock of the new, or the recognition of the familiar? Whether students are training to be scientists or literary critics, they know they must provide evidence to prove their hypotheses about this film, and as it turns out, there is plenty of evidence in both the verbal and visual texts of *Forbidden Planet* to support both points of view.

At this point, we move on to consider how the definitions of good sf generated by Golden Age authors and editors themselves might clarify the situation. A combination of critical histories and primary literary texts guide this conversation. Students draw upon readings from Brian Aldiss's *Billion Year Spree* (1973), Gary Westfahl's *The Mechanics of Wonder: The Creation of the Idea of Science Fiction* (1999) and Edward James's *Science Fiction in the Twentieth Century* (1994) to identify the major sf tastemakers of the era, including H.L. Gold of *Galaxy Magazine*, Anthony Boucher of the *Magazine of Fantasy and Science Fiction*, and John W. Campbell of *Astounding Science-Fiction*. I also provide students with editorial statements from Golden Age magazines, anthologies and novels to help them better identify what mid-century editors most valued in sf writing. Students particularly appreciate what Edward James describes as Campbell's 'rules' for good sf: the conditions of the story must differ from the here and now, the new conditions must drive the plot of the story, the plot must revolve around human problems arising from the new conditions, and finally, no scientific facts may be violated without reasonable explanation.[3] They find it easy to identify the dissemination of similar ideas across our editorial readings and to apply them to *Forbidden Planet*. This helps students answer the question of whether or not Robbie and Altaira are logical characters to include in this tale. Students quickly recognize that the alien technologies of Altair IV plus the human science of Freudian psychology are the driving forces of Wilcox's film and that Robbie and Altaira can be profitably discussed as products of these forces.

Our next task is to test Campbell's rules for good sf against key print sf stories of the 1940s and 1950s. In keeping with the more general set of issues raised by *Forbidden Planet*, we focus on stories about human–machine relations, including Eando Binder's 'I, Robot' (1939), C.L. Moore's 'No Woman Born' (1941) and Isaac Asimov's *I, Robot* (1950) collection. We begin discussion by identifying passages from each text that either support or contradict each of Campbell's conditions for good sf. This often leads to a more nuanced consideration of sf character types and whether or not complex characterization is necessary for an sf story to succeed. All of these tales feature classic sf types including brilliant (but sometimes bordering-on-mad) scientists, noble robots (actually a noble cyborg, in the case of Moore's story) and at least one segment of humanity that is prejudiced against the existence of mechanical women and men. Students are struck by the fact that Binder, Moore and Asimov anticipate Wilcox by creating relatively stereotyped depictions of human characters while infusing their robots and cyborgs with great personality and complex motivations – in other words, by employing the kind of deep characterization that is more typically associated with human characters in mainstream realist literature. This realization prompts students to consider how Golden Age authors fulfilled Campbell's dictates for good sf and brought philosophical questions about human–machine relations to life for readers by imagining futures where the products of technology turn out to be far more interesting than their creators. It also enables them to examine Pamela Sargent's claim that sf is a 'literature of ideas'[4] and to think about how and why authors might use specific character types to express specific ideas.

At this point we examine the specific ideas that Golden Age sf authors might have been grappling with while writing robot stories. We begin this section of the unit by reading excerpts from two critical works that connect images of robots to postwar hopes and fears about automation and the creation of increasingly artificial environments: Patricia S. Warrick's *The Cybernetic Imagination in Science Fiction* (1982) and J.P. Telotte's *Replications: A Robotic History of the Science Fiction Film* (1995). We then consider postwar attitudes to these subjects as they were expressed in popular science treatises such as Norbert Weiner's *The Human Use of Human Beings: Cybernetics and Society* (1950), social critiques such as Vance Packard's *The Hidden Persuaders* (1957) and Herbert Marcuse's *One Dimensional Man* (1964),[5] public education films such as New York University's *Machine: Master or Slave?* (1940), and media advertisements such as General Motor's *Design for Dreaming* (1956) and Jam Handy Organization's *American Thrift* (1962). Students enjoy these primary texts because they dramatize the ways in which mid-century debates over automation unfolded across various cultural arenas.

We conclude our unit on the Golden Age by pulling together everything we have read over the past several weeks, putting our sf stories in dialogue with postwar cultural texts and identifying the specific narrative strategies that sf authors used to participate in debates over the meaning and value of automation. After re-reading Binder, Moore and Asimov and re-watching key scenes from *Forbidden Planet*, we attempt to answer the following questions. How do all these stories dramatize Weiner's ideas about the scientific equivalency between biological and mechanical systems? Where do these stories come down on the 'machine: master or slave' question? How do the social critiques embedded in these stories compare with those levied by Packard and Marcuse? Do sf authors equate mechanization with domestic utopia in the same way as postwar advertising? Students generally find that the answers to these questions are not as easy or obvious as they might first seem, because authors – like all participants in widespread cultural conversations – do not simply repeat or deny what others have said about a subject. Instead, they contribute to this ongoing conversation in unique ways that nuance, complicate and otherwise enrich it. This is, of course, a valuable insight in and of itself that helps students create what Clifford Geertz called 'thick descriptions' of cultural history.[6] Furthermore, by carefully studying postwar debates over automation and its impact on human–machine relations as they unfolded in Golden Age sf, students are better prepared to grapple with these issues as they evolve over time and explode, once again, in the post-utopian and post-human worlds of cyberpunk and post-singularity sf.

If time and interest permits, we also devote part of our concluding discussion to the questions of gender that appear time and again in postwar and Golden Age texts about automation. Some of these questions stem from the students' readings of sf in relation to our primary postwar texts: how do Binder and Asimov respond to Marcuse and Packard's fear that humanity will be dangerously feminized if it abdicates control to machines? Does Moore's depiction of the cyborg Deirdre suggest that advanced technologies will liberate women as promised in *Design for Dreaming* and *American Thrift*? Other questions are more free form, arising from the sf stories themselves: why does Asimov present his nominal heroine, Dr Susan Calvin, as scientifically brilliant but socially and sexually inept? Why is it that Altaira suddenly 'gets' sex and gender norms when she falls in love with Adams? Is Maltzer correct when he claims Deirdre is subhuman because she 'hasn't got any sex'?[7] Or does he try to commit suicide soon after making this comment because Deirdre is superhuman and simulates sex so perfectly that he knows he must be wrong? These are fascinating questions and we rarely get to spend as much time on them as we would like. However, they provide excellent background for our later unit on feminist sf, demonstrating that questions of science, society and gender were part of sf long before the advent of its overtly feminist offshoot.

They are also, of course, questions at the heart of my senior seminar on gender and science in sf. This is a much smaller and more homogeneous course comprised of upperclassmen from Georgia Tech's Science, Technology and Culture undergraduate degree programme. It is an ideal population for a cultural studies approach to an sf course because all these students are trained in textual analysis across media and have at least a passing familiarity with science and technology studies. Many students take this senior seminar because they have previous experience with sf and/or gender studies as well. As such, they are prepared to grapple with the issue that Mark Poster identifies as central to cultural history: how different kinds of texts 'configure what they point to, and ... are configured by it' across discursive arenas.[8] While these students are indeed ready, willing and able to assess sf in relation to other texts from a wide variety of discursive arenas, most have never heard of cultural history. Accordingly, I introduce this critical practice through a series of brief written exercises asking students to analyse Golden Age sf in relation to different histories of the genre. Once students have mastered the fundamentals of cultural history as it pertains to the study of sf, we engage in a series of research and teaching activities that enable students to produce cultural histories of sf on their own.[9]

As in my introductory science fiction class, I open my senior seminar on gender and science in sf with a screening of *Forbidden Planet*. Before we begin the film, I remind students that art is meant to make us see the world from new perspectives and that those aspects of an artwork that seem most confusing usually are, upon analysis, the ones that produce the most new meaning. I then ask that students to help me keep track of all the scenes where Wilcox seems to be making surprising claims about science and/or sex. When we have finished viewing the film, we compile a master list of these scenes, looking for any and all patterns that might emerge from our collaborative efforts. We then begin to discuss what kinds of primary and secondary texts might help us make sense of the surprising moments in *Forbidden Planet*. This seemingly simple preliminary exercise has two benefits: it encourages students to understand themselves as a community of critical thinkers who have already mastered basic analytic skills, and it underscores the usefulness of studying individual artistic texts in larger social, political and aesthetic contexts.

This second point can be very difficult for students to grasp, even when they are used to thinking in interdisciplinary terms. And so this is a key moment for me, as an expert scholar and leader of this course, to step in and introduce the practice of cultural history more formally. I do so by providing students with a mini-lecture on the development of this discipline as it pertains to the study of sf (drawn largely from my entry on this subject in *The Routledge Companion to Science Fiction,* 2009). I conclude my lecture with our first major critical assignment, asking students to read excerpts from three cultural histories of sf: Justine Larbalestier's *Battle of the Sexes in Science Fiction* (2002), Brian Attebery's *Decoding Gender in Science Fiction* (2002) and Bonnie Noonan's *Women Scientists in Fifties Science Fiction Films* (2005). Students complete this unit by writing two brief (3–5 page) essays, which serve as the basis for our next two class discussions. The first essay is a fairly standard critical exercise in which students use the assigned cultural histories to make sense of at least one surprising element in *Forbidden Planet.* The second essay is a meta-critical exercise in which students identify the range of sources that our assigned authors used to create their cultural histories of sf. While the first assignment helps students understand what cultural histories of sf look like (and what they can do for engaged readers), the second exercise encourages them to think more actively about the range of sources needed to create thick descriptions of sf history. This assignment encourages students to think past the secondary sources that they have used to write papers for other classes and to consider how they might also use primary sources including magazine advertisements, political speeches and even sf editorials and fan letters to better understand how debates over the proper relations of science, gender and sf unfolded in the postwar era.[10]

We conclude our unit on Golden Age sf as cultural history by considering how such debates unfold in Golden Age women writers' stories about science, society and gender. I ask students to write one final brief essay in which they assess the veracity of Robin Roberts's claim that 'women cannot control scientific narratives because, although they are frequently its subject, they are largely excluded from the practice of science. Through feminist science fiction, however, women can write narratives about science ... to create feminist fairy tales.'[11] Since this is our last formal class discussion of Golden Age sf, I provide students with just three new short stories that explore what Betty Friedan described as mid-century America's belief in the 'mistaken choice' between family and (scientific) career: Marion Zimmer Bradley's 'The Wind People' (1959), Katherine MacLean's 'And Be Merry...' (1950) and Doris Pitkin

Buck's 'Birth of a Gardener' (1961). While Bradley's story emphasizes the literal insanity engendered by the mistaken choice between family and career, MacLean and Buck's tales more optimistically play with the mid-century ideal of the housewife as technical expert to imagine that women might create new modes of domestic science and even whole new worlds built upon that science. All of these stories revolve around images of women as technoscientific producers who strive to combine family and work in new ways, and so it is instructive for students to consider them synthetically in relation to both *Forbidden Planet* and the cultural histories we have considered in class to date.

After completing our model unit on Golden Age sf, students are ready to begin their own 'sf as cultural history' capstone projects. This assignment requires students to pair off, choose a period of sf history, and then lead their classmates in a week-long exploration of just how representative sf texts from the period in question serve as a windows into widespread debates about the proper relations of science, society and gender. While the capstone teaching project is particularly relevant to students pursuing interdisciplinary educations such as those we offer in the liberal arts at Georgia Tech, it can easily be adapted to any group of upper-level undergraduates because the success of this project depends not so much on the subject matter per se as on the students' ability to employ a wide range of research, writing and presentation skills. Indeed, instructors teaching more traditionally art- or science-oriented senior seminars could easily modify this assignment so students more specifically examined sf as a window into the cultural history of their own discipline. This would allow students to do the work of the cultural historian as described by Poster while keeping the content of individual projects in line with the assessment needs of specific academic programmes.

Because the senior capstone project requires students to approach sf texts as historical artefacts, I begin this unit with a research assignment that requires students to boldly go where very few of them have gone before: into the Georgia Tech science fiction collection, which is housed in our institute's library archives. This is often a surprisingly exciting activity for my students, many of whom have so perfected their basic online research skills that they have never actually set foot in the library except to print out papers or get a cup of coffee. Students are delighted to learn that we have one of the largest science fiction collections of its kind at Georgia Tech and even more delighted to find out that they can actually go into the collection and handle books and magazines dating back to the birth of the genre itself. Indeed, the simple act of handling old texts makes concrete a point we have discussed throughout the first section of our class: that no individual story really stands on its own. Instead, as Brian Attebery points out, all sf stories are 'part of a continuous stream of discourse' and the messages about gender and science that emerge in such stories are replicated and elaborated upon by the advertisements, editorials, prefaces, conclusions and fan letters that frame them.[12]

While students are often quite excited about their field trip to our library archives, they are still novice cultural historians who need something to structure their first research day. Accordingly, I prepare students for the task ahead of them with a brief in-class exercise where they use Georgia Tech's sf search engine to quickly review our archival holdings and identify three items that seem particularly promising for their capstone project. Once students actually get into the sf collection, they must secure the items they found online plus three more items they find on adjacent shelves. Students then skim their findings quickly and write up 2–3 sentences evaluating the potential of each text in terms of their capstone projects. This exercise has two benefits. First, it shows students how they can productively combine the familiar task of online research with its less familiar archival counterpart. Second, it underscores the fact that online databases are only as good as their programmers, and that such databases rarely provide all – or even the best – references that students might need for any given project. Indeed, students quickly realize that such databases are sometimes best for pointing them toward real-time locations where they can explore a range of texts that will help them build truly thick descriptions of the historic periods under consideration in their projects.

Once students recognize that they need to expand their research skill-set to become cultural historians of sf, they are ready to rethink their relation to online research as a whole. My next assignment helps them do just that. On our first electronic research day I ask students to bring their laptops to class or to meet in one of our department's computer labs. We begin class by talking about which electronic resources students use when writing research papers. Perhaps not surprisingly, students are quick to admit that they rely on subscription databases like Project Muse, which provide articles in electronic format for immediate download, and free search engines like Google Scholar, which can be accessed from anywhere. I then provide students with a handout listing all the different electronic resources that professional liberal arts scholars use when doing research, putting special emphasis on the MLA International Bibliography database (which, as I point out, archives articles from 4000 rather than 400 scholarly journals) and the Science Fiction and Fantasy Research Database (SFFRD), which, like Google Scholar, can be accessed from anywhere but specifically indexes sf and fantasy scholarship. I ask students to looks up key words and phrases that are relevant to their chosen capstone projects using all the different resources we have just reviewed. Upon doing so, students quickly realize that MLA and SFFRD typically yield fewer but more relevant items than Project Muse and Google Scholar. At this point, however, they are still wary of these new databases because they do not provide immediate electronic access to all their indexed items. Accordingly, I end class with a tutorial on Georgia Tech's Interlibrary Loan system, asking students to request at least three articles that seem interesting or relevant to them. I find that even the most sceptical students become converts when they receive their requested items by email in (usually) less than a week. Indeed, the sense that they are using the same tools – and receiving the same respect – as their professors seems to help students think of themselves as real members of a scholarly community.

I dedicate our last research day to the promises and perils of web-based research. Once again, we begin class with a general brainstorming session in which we list all the resources that could help us construct cultural histories of sf, including timelines of scientific and social development, repositories of political speeches and advertisements, and even caches of sf stories, films and artwork. I then ask students to go online, find three such resources, and evaluate them based on the credibility of their authors and the reasonableness and accuracy of their evidence (especially as such evidence is supported by reference to other credible authors and can be confirmed by at least two other independent sources). As students identify resources that meet these criteria, they email them to our class listserv and/or post them to a class wiki. Much like our other research exercises, this one has the benefit of enabling students to complete a good deal of work in class while underscoring the fact that scholarship is both an individual and communal activity.

At this point students are ready to prepare their capstone teaching projects. I aim to ensure the success of these projects by requiring all teaching teams to do four things. First, they must prepare an annotated bibliography including all the sf texts that are central to their projects as well as five primary and five secondary sources that provide historical and aesthetic context for those sf texts. Second, they must provide all other students with copies of the sf stories in question as well as their two best primary and two best secondary sources. Third, each team must provide all other students with study questions about these stories and sources. Finally, each team must prepare a brief multimedia presentation that provides the rest of the class with an introduction to the topic at hand and fosters class discussion based on the assigned study questions. Breaking the capstone project into a series of small, manageable tasks enables students to put together more focused teaching presentations and, in the long run, helps them become cultural historians who can communicate the truly rich history of sf to others.

When sf studies took serious root in the college classroom of the early 1970s, sf author and literature professor Jack Williamson encouraged instructors to 'take the critic first' and build courses around those issues that most interested serious scholars of the genre. Of course, as he is quick to note, at that time there was very little coherent sf criticism and 'the mainstream critics have seldom made much sense about science fiction', while 'the amateurs are often in violent disagreement'.[13] But Williamson turns this seeming problem into an opportunity, suggesting that in addition to creating classes that teach students about the main themes of sf, instructors might also create courses that actually produce good sf critics. And he is very clear about the qualities those critics should possess: they should have 'a general cultural background' in literary studies and a good grasp of 'the conventions of science fiction', including a 'sensitivity to social change and a grasp of the scientific method'. In short, then, sf critics 'should not belong entirely to either of Snow's two cultures', but should work interdisciplinarily to understand the unique meaning and value of their chosen genre.[14]

What Williamson seems to be working toward is quite similar to the notion of the sf critic as cultural historian. Cultural historians are dedicated to combining the analytic methodologies of the humanities (including art, literary and media studies) with those of the social sciences (including history, sociology and anthropology) to better understand how various texts function as sites of struggle about the meaning and value of culture. While nearly any kind of text may be of value to the cultural historian, sf is an ideal subject matter for this kind of study because, as proponents of the genre have long argued, it is a body of literature that developed in tandem with modern literary, political and technoscientific systems. As such, the cultural historian of sf necessarily works between methodologies and cultures. This is precisely what I strive to teach students in my sf classes. I do so not just by encouraging them to read key texts about cultural history or even the cultural history of sf, but by becoming cultural historians who make active connections between individual sf texts and other primary scientific and social documents. It is particularly rewarding to teach this critical methodology in relation to Golden Age sf precisely because this body of speculative fiction emerges at the beginning of our own literary, political and techno-scientific era. Not only does this drive home for students the point that sf is a privileged vehicle of cultural expression, but that as cultural historians of sf themselves, they can also become better cultural critics of the world around them today.

Notes

1. Catherine Belsey, 'Reading Cultural History', in Tamsin Spargo, ed., *Reading the Past: Literature and History* (New York: Palgrave Macmillan, 2000) 106.
2. Darko Suvin, *Metamorphoses of Science Fiction* (New Haven, CT: Yale University Press, 1979) 6, 7–8.
3. Edward James, *Science Fiction in the Twentieth Century* (Oxford: Oxford University Press, 1994) 59.
4. Pamela Sargent, 'Introduction', in *More Women of Wonder: Science Fiction Novelettes by Women* (New York: Vintage Paperbacks, 1976) xiii–lxiv at xx.
5. For details see References, Resources and Further Reading. See also Vance Packard, *The Hidden Persuaders* (London: Longmans, 1957); Herbert Marcuse, *One Dimensional Man* (Boston: Beacon, 1964).
6. Clifford Geertz, *The Interpretation of Cultures* (New York: HarperCollins, 1973) 5.
7. C.L. Moore, 'No Woman Born', in Lester del Rey, ed. *The Best of C.L. Moore* (New York: Ballantine Books, 1975) 236–88 at 258.
8. Mark Poster, ed., *Cultural History and Postmodernity: Disciplinary Readings and Challenges* (New York: Columbia University Press, 1997) 9.
9. While it is helpful to work with students who already have experience with literary, gender and science studies, it is not necessary to do so. Indeed, I often have great success using a similar sequence of assignments in my freshman English course. They key is to match content to student interest, introducing appropriate reading, research and communication skills when necessary.
10. If time and class interest permits, I also assign excerpts from more general cultural histories of gender and/or science in postwar America. If my class seems particularly interested in the former, we read selections from Betty Friedan's *The Feminine Mystique* (New York: W.W. Norton, 1963), Elaine Tyler May's *Homeward Bound: American Families in the Cold War* (New York: Basic Books, 1988) and Joanne Meyerowitz's *Not June Cleaver: Women and Gender in Postwar America, 1945–1960* (Philadelphia: Temple University Press, 1994). If they are interested in the latter, we read selections from Margaret Rossiter's *Women Scientists in America before Affirmative Action, 1940–1972* (Baltimore: Johns Hopkins University Press, 1995), Ruth Schwartz Cowan's *More Work for Mother: The Ironies of Household Technology from the Open Hearth to the Microwave* (New York: Basic Books, 1989) and Bettyann Holtzmann Kevles's *Almost Heaven: The Story of Women in Space* (Cambridge, MA: MIT Press, 2003). Either way, I ask students to demonstrate their mastery of these texts by writing two more brief essays much like the ones outlined above. Indeed,

by repeating our first two written assignments in relation to other cultural histories, students gain an even better understanding of just how much work is involved in the creation of truly thick histories.
11. Robin Roberts, *A New Species: Gender and Science in Science Fiction* (Urbana, IL: University of Illinois Press, 1993) 6.
12. Brian Attebery, *Decoding Gender in Science Fiction* (New York and London: Routledge, 2002) 43.
13. Jack Williamson, 'Science Fiction, Teaching and Criticism', in Reginald Bretnor, ed., *Science Fiction Today and Tomorrow* (New York: Harper and Row, 1974) 309–30 at 311.
14. Ibid., 319.

7
Teaching the New Wave
Rob Latham

The history of science fiction, like that of popular literature generally, is made up, in large part, of a series of factional movements, emerging on the margins, contesting for terrain and subsiding as they run out of steam or are incorporated into the central trajectory of the genre. When the appearance of one of these movements coincides with a period of crisis in the field's development, the result can be a seismic conflict over basic definitions and core assumptions. In a discussion of the controversy surrounding the cyberpunk movement during the 1980s, Carol McGuirk refers to this process of 'noisy polarization' as a struggle for consensus: 'Each group seems sure that it represents the "real" science fiction. ... In SF studies, terms shift in meaning whenever the centre of power shifts, and a whole group of concepts may become debased when one generation's avant-garde giant ... is dismissed by a subsequent generation as a mere pygmy-with-a-giant-typewriter.'[1] As I have argued elsewhere, a 'recurring cycle of messianic avant-gardism and old-school intransigence is the very motor of SF as a historical genre',[2] and this reality was nowhere more visible than during the mid- to late 1960s, in the furious ideological combat that swirled around the New Wave movement.

The New Wave in historical context

The basic contours of the struggle are well known. During this period, a rising cohort of mostly younger authors began to question both the format and ideology of the traditional sf story, adopting literary techniques and critical perspectives that broke sharply with pulp conventions. In their extrapolation of fictional futures, these writers abjured the celebration of scientific know-how and commitment to linear storytelling that had marked sf's Golden Age in favour of powerful critiques of technocratic society articulated in offbeat, frequently experimental prose. New Wave polemicists scorned the obsession with space exploration that had marked postwar sf, defending instead an 'inner space' orientation that was 'wholeheartedly speculative ... concerned with the creation of new states of mind, new levels of awareness' (as J.G. Ballard put it in an influential essay).[3] Reflecting trends in society at large, the genre was riven by a generational struggle that pitted the pulp tradition against a rising sf counterculture whose incendiary demands for change provoked concerted resistance from the genre establishment. By the late 1960s, this struggle had taken on all the textures and tones of the encompassing political battles between the youth counterculture and the silent majority.

At issue were not merely radical new modes of expression but disturbing new forms of content. Capitalizing on the greater openness of the 1960s book market to controversial material, New Wave writers began to explore alternative gender and sexual arrangements – not to mention forms of chemical self-enhancement – that flouted prevailing codes of belief and conduct. In concert with the burgeoning feminist and gay liberation movements, as well as with experimental trends in the youth counterculture, New Wave writers launched pointed assaults on the white, 'straight' male subject who had long been the heroic centre of the pulp tradition. Ambitious authors developed multiple techniques of 'sextrapolation' to generate ingenious erotic possibilities, often in pornographic scenarios of a startling and unsettling alterity.[4] At the same time, the New Wave introduced a notable strain of social militancy into the genre, forging substantial links with counterculture discourses, such as the media theories of Marshall McLuhan, the avant-garde fictions of William S. Burroughs and the various 'liberation movements' associated with antiwar activism, second-wave feminism and ecological causes. Major sf works of the late 1960s and early 1970s sent controversial reverberations throughout the field, reaching beyond the borders of genre to unite with the radical traditions that informed and inspired them, making New Wave sf a significant counterculture discourse in its own right.

Though there is disagreement over its precise achievements and legacy, most historians of sf agree that the advent of the New Wave 'changed the course of genre history'.[5] Yet, while the movement was extensively debated at the time within the sf community, it has, surprisingly, generated rather little in the way of sustained critical commentary (outside of the summary chapters contained in genre histories).

Only one book – Colin Greenland's *The Entropy Exhibition* (1983) – has been produced on the subject, and it limits its focus to the cadre of writers surrounding the British magazine *New Worlds* under Michael Moorcock's editorship (1964–71).[6] While this group was undoubtedly central to the debates that rocked the field during the 1960s, it was only one component in a multifaceted set of struggles that were ultimately transatlantic in their manifestations and effects. Though the British New Wave was a somewhat different creature to its American cousin, both participated in a concerted assault on the purported complacency and decadence of the sf pulp tradition. Writers and fans throughout the Anglophone world were unable to escape the spreading controversy, and even subsequent generations, such as the cyberpunks, were compelled to define themselves against the New Wave's momentous claims and accomplishments.

Teaching the New Wave: three configurations

The New Wave, as a political and an aesthetic formation, represents a unique moment in sf history when social-critical and literary-experimental impulses converged. It thus provides rich terrain for classroom investigation. The absence of significant critical analyses of the movement is actually auspicious since it allows the instructor or tutor to place a range of texts and issues on the table and invite students to sift through them in the process of developing their own assessments. Two directions in which inquiry might go would be towards an excavation of the New Wave's roots within the genre itself and an investigation of its connections to contemporaneous trends within the broader culture. One could triangulate selected New Wave texts with competing sf traditions and also, since this was a period when the genre was uniquely open to outside influences, with the social and intellectual discourses of the 1960s.

For my own part, I have taught the New Wave in three different contexts: as a unit in a survey of science fiction, as a unit in a survey of postmodernist fiction and as a freestanding topics course. Each of these options presents specific pedagogical challenges.

In an sf survey class, one has at most a couple of sessions to devote to the subject, and one must thus select texts that at once represent the movement effectively and also offer clear contrasts with earlier types of science fiction. One obvious way to highlight these contrasts is to position the New Wave's inner-space agenda against classic Golden Age treatments of space exploration and interstellar adventure; it is not hard for students to grasp the radical reorientation demanded by such stories as Ballard's 'The Terminal Beach' (1963) or Pamela Zoline's 'The Heat Death of the Universe' (1967) by contrast with the work of Heinlein, Asimov and Clarke. Unfortunately, this juxtaposition can sometimes lead to simplistic judgements – for example, that all Golden Age sf ignores issues of psychology or that all New Wave sf eschews space as a narrative venue. Moreover, this sort of 'epochal' approach to sf history can obscure the fact that traditional stories remained quite popular throughout the New Wave period; students can too readily be led to suppose that, following the promulgation of Ballard and Moorcock's manifestos, writers all dutifully turned away from outer space, abandoned conventional modes of storytelling, and embraced the social ethos of the counterculture.

One way to combat such facile misapprehensions is to frame the entire course in terms of a series of overlapping conflicts between conservative and experimental tendencies. Building on McGuirk's notion of an ongoing struggle for consensus, one might stress that the Golden Age was, in its time, quite revolutionary, bringing a fresh sophistication to a field heretofore dominated by pulp super-science, only to become a reactionary force as the social sf movement of the 1950s and then the New Wave arose to contest its cherished orthodoxies. By the same token, the New Wave itself eventually devolved, during the 1970s, into a fairly predictable set of attitudes and approaches, leading to the cyberpunk rejection of its out-dated humanism and sterile avant-gardism in the 1980s. The essential challenge, in short, is to strike a balance between a focus on continuity and an emphasis on change, making clear the ways in which the New Wave was truly innovative and radical while also keeping sight of its limitations as well as its debts to previous historical forms of sf.

One tactic I have found useful in achieving this balance is to place the ideological battles over the New Wave within a larger genre context – specifically, the commercial matrix of publishing, distribution and consumption, which was significantly transformed during the 1960s. Indeed, the emergence of the New Wave coincided, at least in the United States, with the transition from a magazine culture to a book market, a shift with major implications for the types of stories that could be published. Harlan Ellison's *Dangerous Visions* (1967), for example, explicitly presented itself as a showcase for fiction that would not be welcomed in the magazines because of its controversial content, especially its sexual explicitness and political militancy.[7] Other anthology series, from Damon Knight's *Orbit* to Robert Silverberg's

New Dimensions, pushed the envelope further, providing the sort of platform in the US that Moorcock's *New Worlds* offered in the UK for writers to break with prevailing formats and taboos. By the early 1970s, the magazines were compelled to liberalize their content to keep pace; even Golden Age stalwart *Analog* (formerly *Astounding*), now in the hands of Ben Bova, began to feature work that would probably have shocked John W. Campbell.

The advent and maturation of the New Wave movement was thus inextricably linked with ongoing transformations in the basic institutional framework of the genre. As I put it in another essay, 'The New Wave was ... a creature of the boom years of the mid-1960s, its rise coeval with the consolidation of an SF book market that favoured a greater diversity and spoke to a larger audience than the magazines could ever have hoped to do.'[8] Sf writers did not simply, in the mid-1960s, abruptly leap to the polemicists' calls to abandon pulp styles and thus radically reform the field; rather, the growth of the book market made possible a break with the magazine tradition for a whole new generation of authors and readers. It is important for students to grasp this point because it demonstrates that major shifts such as the New Wave do not occur in a vacuum but rather are dependent on the field's evolving material conditions, which both impose constraints and provide enabling conditions for growth.

Teaching the New Wave in a survey of postmodernist fiction presents a different set of challenges. Here, I do not expect students to be able to place the movement within the context of sf history; instead, I want them to see how the arrival of postmodernism impacted not just mainstream literature but also popular fiction, especially sf. The class that I have taught many times examines a range of narrative forms and experimental techniques that have characterized postmodern writing since the 1960s, including the contrast between metafictional and minimalist styles, the playful and/or conspiratorial revision of historical narratives, the interrogation and incorporation of mass media forms and images, the collapse of distinctions between elite and popular cultures, and the transformation of personal and social identity through technological systems. Key New Wave texts, such as Ballard's *The Atrocity Exhibition* (1970) and Joanna Russ's *The Female Man* (1975), illustrate several of these themes, bringing SF into alignment with the cutting-edge fiction of the day. I draw on prominent critics who have emphasized this connection, such as Brian McHale, who has argued that 'SF, far from being marginal to contemporary "advanced" or "state-of-the-art" writing, may actually be *paradigmatic* of it'; like postmodernist writing, it is 'self-consciously world-building fiction, laying bare the process of world-making itself'.[9]

Of course, the champions of the New Wave had always trumpeted this connection, with Ballard and Moorcock frequently citing William Burroughs as an inspiration. Teaching novels by Russ, Philip K. Dick, Samuel R. Delany or Ballard alongside work by Burroughs, Kurt Vonnegut, Ishmael Reed and Thomas Pynchon effectively displays the cross-pollination of genre SF and the literary avant garde. Moreover, assigning New Wave polemics, such as Ballard's 'Inner Space' essay, alongside similarly combative position statements by postmodernists such as John Barth and Raymond Federman serves to illustrate how broadly popular the manifesto form was to 1960s literary movements. And, finally, I have found that students are consistently amused to discover that Pynchon's *Gravity's Rainbow* (1973) was nominated for a Nebula Award for best novel by the Science Fiction Writers of America – only to lose out to Arthur C. Clarke's *Rendezvous with Rama*![10]

Most tutors or instructors are likely to cover the New Wave in one of the above configurations, as a unit within larger surveys of sf or of contemporary fiction; but I have also been lucky enough to teach a freestanding course devoted exclusively to the subject. The advantage of such a setup is that it allows for greater depth and detail in the treatment of key issues – such as the contrast between the British and American wings of the movement – while also providing a more expansive investigation of relevant themes and authors. The challenges include the need to present, up front, a coherent introduction to 'traditional' sf without reducing it to a mere caricature, while also representing the anti-New Wave contingent within the genre in a way that acknowledges its historical importance. In other words, students require sufficient historical context in order to grasp precisely what the New Wave movement was reacting against and how it was perceived by contemporary critics. Otherwise, one is in danger of fostering a kind of triumphalist view, with the New Wave colonizing a genre vacuum and effortlessly besting its competitors.

Since this was a large course (eighty students) and thus conducted lecture style, I was able to provide essential context in summary form. My first two lectures gave an overview of postwar sf in terms of the typical periodization of the field, emphasizing how the social sf of the 1950s paved the way for the New Wave by shifting from the hard towards the 'soft' sciences, pioneering social-critical forms of sf (such as Frederik Pohl's and Robert Sheckley's 'comic infernos'[11]), and beginning to emphasize literary quality as a prerequisite for successful stories. Our first readings were Cordwainer Smith's 'Alpha Ralpha Boulevard' (1961) and Roger Zelazny's 'A Rose for Ecclesiastes' (1963), two tales published on the cusp of the New Wave that display some of the movement's key attributes. Written by humanistically-trained authors and replete with allusions to classic and modernist literature, both stories deploy traditional sf scenarios (alien contact, post-apocalypse futures) in offbeat and highly stylized ways. These readings set up a pair of lectures on Moorcock's *New Worlds* and the emergence of the New Wave in America, with students reading short fiction by Ballard, Ellison, Pamela Zoline and Thomas M. Disch that gave a sense of the experimental energies unleashed by the movement.

The remainder of the course was divided into three broad thematic units, entitled 'Intimations of Apocalypse', 'Life-Style SF' and 'SF as Social Criticism'. The first unit covered works dealing with global catastrophe, such as Vonnegut's *Cat's Cradle* (1963) and John Brunner's *The Sheep Look Up* (1972), or with apocalyptic transformations of self and community, such as Silverberg's *Son of Man* (1971). The second unit focused on texts that foreground what Brian W. Aldiss has identified as a core feature of New Wave fiction, its exploration of 'experimental modes of living', particularly those deriving from counterculture values of personal transformation and (spiritual and pharmaceutical) consciousness-raising.[12] Students read works dealing with gender identity and sexual expression, such as Samuel R. Delany's *Triton* (1976) and the short fiction of James Tiptree Jr (a.k.a. Alice Sheldon), and with the radical reorientations of experience promoted by the drug culture and the new media landscape – excerpts from Aldiss's *Barefoot in the Head* (1969) and Norman Spinrad's *Bug Jack Barron* (1969) providing paradigmatic treatments. The third unit examined works that display the New Wave's political militancy: the critique of technocratic institutions and values in Disch's *Camp Concentration* (1968), the challenge to militarist norms in Joe Haldeman's *The Forever War* (1974), the exposure of patriarchal assumptions in Russ's *The Female Man* (1975). My overall goal in the course was to give a cohesive overview of the movement's conjoined aesthetic and ethico-political agenda, showing how its best fictions manage to be both structurally rich and critically compelling.

Lessons learned 1: the content of New Wave fiction

In the balance of this chapter, I would like to discuss the lessons I learned while teaching this topics course on the New Wave. As I say, most tutors and instructors will not have the leisure to cover the movement so intensively, but I think analysing my experience with the class could prove helpful to those planning compressed units in more broadly focused courses. I should also acknowledge that the lecture format dictated certain decisions about content and methods that would probably not be relevant with smaller enrolments; I did manage, however, to get the class to engage in modest dialogues over the course of the term – exchanges that were very useful in giving me a sense of how the students were receiving the material, which was entirely unfamiliar to the vast majority of them (save for a handful of hardcore sf fans).

While teaching sf history always require some sketching of relevant sociocultural background, this is nowhere more pressing than when covering New Wave texts, not only because of their unusual permeability to current events but also because of the historical amnesia afflicting recent generations of students, for whom (as I soon discovered) the 1960s counterculture exists merely as cartoonish images of grubby hippies rioting in the streets. Since most of my students had been born during the presidency of Ronald Reagan, their sense of the 1960s came filtered not only through distorted media depictions but also through reactionary ideological retrenchments and 'family values' rhetoric that stigmatized dissent as antisocial and scorned gender and sexual liberation as narcissistic delusions. Moreover, the violently antiauthoritarian ethos of the counterculture made little sense to them since they knew next to nothing about the Vietnam War, the military draft, the baiting of student activists by rightwing provocateurs and so forth.

Teaching Disch's *Camp Concentration*, for example, I had to provide extensive information about militarized forms of research and development, including bioweapons technology and psychological warfare, and the government's tactics of infiltrating and suppressing antiwar protest, such as the FBI's Counter Intelligence Program, about which my students were fundamentally ignorant. They could not grasp why the administration of a 'President McNamara' in 1968 should be such a dire prospect, nor could they hear the echoes of famous martyred dissenters in the name of Disch's protagonist, Louis Sacchetti. While undeniably brilliant and a central text of the movement, *Camp Concentration* is a challenge to teach because of its exegetical demands: one must spend a great deal of time clarifying its contemporary references – not to mention explicating its flights of erudition, its frequent allusions to alchemy, the Faust legend, Modernist poetry and so on.

A somewhat different problem besets the teaching of Russ's *The Female Man*. A monument not only of the New Wave but of 1970s feminist sf, the novel, with its intersecting multilevel plot-lines, is structurally very challenging, but the real difficulty lay in getting the majority of my students, male and female, to take its critique of gender ideology seriously. This is not to say that they were avowedly antifeminist; though they preferred not to use this term, which had been rendered suspect by decades of conservative backlash and demonization, they generally accepted the proposition that women were the intellectual compeers of men and deserving of equal treatment economically and before the law. Most of the women in the class were quite comfortable speaking out against overt misogyny, but they squirmed almost as much as the male students did when faced with Russ's ferocious call to arms. The problem, ultimately, lay in the fact that they seemed to assume the major gender battles of the past had been long since settled and were thus embarrassed by what they perceived as the novel's undue 'stridency' (their term). While willing to acknowledge the subtle subterranean persistence of gender bias, especially when reading Tiptree's devastating 'The Women Men Don't See' (1972), they never warmed to Russ's fictive manifesto.

While my students' ignorance of contemporary history and smug sense of superiority over the counterculture's purportedly naive, overblown radicalism was at times galling, I have to admit that, in other cases, their sceptical reactions to the texts were spot on. The groovy hipster lingo of Spinrad's *Bug Jack Barron*, which they found quite risible, has in fact not aged well, nor has that novel's McLuhanesque depiction of broadcast TV as some sort of cultural watershed. Almost frighteningly media-savvy, comfortable with a communications landscape populated by iPhones and wi-fi, digital cameras and instant-messaging, my students found Spinrad's eponymous programme, where a studio-bound host spars with guests linked by satellite and projected on split screens, about as cutting edge as an episode of *Larry King Live*. When I showed the class, during a lecture, a spreadsheet of one week's prime-time programming for 1968, published on a *single page* of the journal *TV Guide*, there were audible gasps at the media poverty this implied. That said, they did come to see how 1960s television, by bringing images of war and social conflict directly into middle-class homes, impacted popular attitudes towards government and the political process more generally, which is a major theme of Spinrad's novel.

On the other hand, the students were shocked not by *Bug Jack Barron*'s sexual explicitness but by the fact that some anti-New Wave partisans had found it shocking for just this reason. When I read them Donald A. Wollheim's outraged indictment of Spinrad's 'nauseous epic' – 'depraved, cynical, utterly repulsive and thoroughly degenerate and decadent'[13] – they merely laughed. The one aspect of 1960s 'liberation' with which most of them seemed entirely comfortable – indeed, blasé – was its loosening of taboos on sexual expression. I considered it something of a challenge to find a text that would genuinely scandalize them: the android sex-machines in *The Female Man*, the erotic bonding among Haldeman's soldiers, the aggressive gender-bending of Tiptree's 'Houston, Houston, Do You Read?' – all this they took quite in their stride. I finally had to give them something from an earlier decade – Philip José Farmer's proto-New Wave story 'Mother' (1953), with its creepily Freudian alien sex – to elicit a reaction of astonished revulsion. In short, the New Wave's erotic militancy, so controversial at the time, has become, for contemporary students, almost quaint.

Lessons learned 2: the form of New Wave fiction

The aforementioned points all have to do with teaching New Wave texts in relation to social currents and trends of the 1960s; but I also learned some lessons regarding students' views of the stylistic experiments promoted by the movement. I had anticipated resistance to stories like Ballard's 'The Terminal Beach' or Zoline's 'The Heat Death of the Universe' based upon their fragmentary form, their wilful subversion of narrative linearity. In fact, however, the students – most of them English majors, so perhaps primed to appreciate formal innovation – loved these stories, and when I summarized some of the Old Guard diatribes that decried the New Wave's arty pretension, they actually sided with the genre rebels.[14] Just as I had a challenge getting them to respect the counterculture attitudes expressed in some New Wave texts, so, conversely, I had great difficulty bringing them to appreciate the conservative critique of formal experimentation and defence of traditional sf. This was true even of the hardcore sf fans in the class, who couldn't grasp why they should have to choose between their love of Asimov and Heinlein on the one hand and their fascination for Ballard and Disch on the other.

What this suggests is that the New Wave has come to exert a subtle, subterranean influence on sf norms of representation, gradually legitimating artistic experiment and social consciousness so that, today, such qualities are seen as central to successful works of sf rather than a fringe phenomenon. In other words, the movement's concerted focus on structure and style has rendered pulp modes of storytelling archaic and thus transformed the 'taste culture' of sf.[15] While it is certainly true that old-fashioned adventure stories can still be published, they are clearly marked as juvenile by contrast with more ambitious work. Space opera, so reviled by Ballard, has now become a sophisticated subgenre in the hands of writers like Iain M. Banks and M. John Harrison – the latter himself a survivor of the 1960s wars. The New Wave's emphasis on style has, in other words, been absorbed by and disseminated throughout the contemporary genre, expanding its technical repertoire systematically even as the New Wave proper ebbed and died in the late 1970s. The truth of this judgement can be tested in an sf survey class, where the legacy of the New Wave can be tracked through subsequent generations. In my more narrowly focused topics course, it was effectively illustrated by Haldeman's *Forever War*, a work of traditional hard sf in many ways, yet showing clear evidence of New Wave influence in its complex structure – not to mention in its political attitudes and content.

If I teach this class again, I will probably assign a couple of texts from the postmodernist canon, in order to help refine and focus student response to the formal strategies of New Wave fiction. Everything I taught, even the most extreme material, ultimately had a genre provenance: it was published in an sf magazine or anthology, or was marketed as an sf novel. Upon reflection, I think asking students to read, as preparation for one of Ballard's 'condensed novels' or Aldiss's *Report on Probability A* (1968), a Burroughsian cut-up or a 'new novel' by Robbe-Grillet could provide useful fodder for comparative discussions. If one were even more ambitious, one might consider assigning Pynchon's *Gravity's Rainbow*, which was (as noted above) embraced by a sizeable minority of the sf authorial community in the midst of the New Wave wars. Pynchon's short story 'Entropy' had, of course, been published in *New Worlds* in 1969, as that journal did its utmost to shatter the boundaries between sf and the literary avant garde. Asking students to read mainstream and genre-based texts *together* in a course on the New Wave is one way to seriously test the question of how successful Moorcock's strategy was.

Conclusion

Teaching the New Wave poses a number of challenges, as we have seen, but it also offers many rewards. First, it gives students a sense of how important factional movements have been to the history of sf. While the New Wave was perhaps the most visible and voluble such group, its polemical strategies and appetite for controversy provided a model for subsequent cohorts eager to shake the genre up, from the cyberpunks in the 1980s to the so-called 'mundane sf' movement today.[16] Second, having students grapple with the bold innovations in form and content propounded by the movement also offers a way for them to come to grips with the legacy of the 1960s more generally. Indeed, the New Wave, from its aggressive political postures to its often psychedelic prose, is a virtual compendium of counterculture attitudes and styles. Finally, teaching the New Wave in its full complexity allows students to perceive the blossoming and diversification of the genre that followed the paperback revolution of the 1950s and the further expansion of the book market during the 1960s and 1970s. Rather than a 'wave', a better metaphor for the movement, as Colin Greenland has pointed out, 'would be an explosion, starting at a definable centre and dissipating swiftly in all directions'.[17] Tracking the fallout from this detonation in the classroom can be an invigorating process of delight and discovery, for instructor and students alike.

Notes

1. Carol McGuirk, 'The "New" Romancers: Science Fiction Innovators from Gernsback to Gibson', in George Slusser and Tom Shippey, eds, *Fiction 2000: Cyberpunk and the Future of Narrative* (Athens, GA: University of Georgia Press, 1992) 109–29 at 109–10.
2. Rob Latham, 'Cyberpunk and the New Wave: Ruptures and Continuities', *New York Review of Science Fiction*, 19:10 (2007): 8.
3. J.G. Ballard, 'Which Way to Inner Space?' *New Worlds*, 118 (1962): 117.
4. See my essay 'Sextrapolation in New Wave SF', *Science Fiction Studies*, 33:2 (2006): 251–74.
5. Roger Luckhurt, *Science Fiction* (London: Polity, 2005) 143.
6. Colin Greenland, *The Entropy Exhibition: Michael Moorcock and the British 'New Wave' in Science Fiction* (London: Routledge & Kegan Paul, 1983).
7. As Ellison put it in his introduction: 'no one has ever told the speculative writer, "Pull out all the stops. No holds barred, get it said!" Until this book came along', in *Dangerous Visions* (New York: Doubleday, 1967) ix–xxix at xxiv.
8. Latham, 'Cyberpunk and the New Wave', 12.
9. Brian McHale, *Constructing Postmodernism* (New York: Routledge, 1992) 12.
10. When I teach the class again, I may end with Michael Chabon's *The Yiddish Policeman's Union* (2007), which has managed the feat – which *Gravity's Rainbow* could not – of being both a popular postmodernist novel and a successful competitor for the Nebula Award.
11. The term was coined by Kingsley Amis in *New Maps of Hell: A Survey of Science Fiction* (New York: Harcourt, 1960) to refer to such satirical near-future dystopias as Frederik Pohl and C.M. Kornbluth's *The Space Merchants* (1953).
12. Brian W. Aldiss with David Wingrove, *Trillion Year Spree: The History of Science Fiction* (1986; New York: Avon, 1988) 291.
13. Donald A. Wollheim, 'Guest of Honor Speech, Lunacon 1968', in *Niekas*, 20 (1968): 5.
14. See, for example, Lester del Rey's Guest of Honour speech to the 1967 World Science Fiction Convention, published as 'Art or Artiness?' in *Famous Science*

Fiction, 8 (1968): 78–86. I discuss Old Guard assaults on the New Wave by del Rey, Donald A. Wollheim and others in my essays 'The New Wave', in David Seed, ed., *A Companion to Science Fiction* (London: Blackwell, 2005) 202–16, and '*New Worlds* and the New Wave in Fandom: Fan Culture and the Reshaping of Science Fiction in the Sixties', *Extrapolation*, 47:2 (2006): 296–315.
15. For a sociological analysis of 'taste cultures', see Herbert J. Gans, *Popular Culture and High Culture: An Analysis and Evaluation of Taste*, revised and updated edition (1974; New York: Basic Books, 1999).
16. The manifesto of mundane sf is Geoff Ryman's 'Take the Third Star on the Left and on 'til Morning', *New York Review of Science Fiction*, 19:10 (2007): 1, 4–7.
17. Greenland, *The Entropy Exhibition*, 206.

8
Postmodernism, Postmodernity and the Postmodern: Telling Local Stories at the End of Time

Andrew M. Butler

When I was an undergraduate, there was a moment in a seminar when I was asked who the Pre-Raphaelites were. I had probably just about heard of them, but that did not stop me and I thought I could just bluff. I suggested that they were a group of artists who came before the Raphaelites. (Naturally I did not know what a Raphaelite was.) The Pre-Raphaelites turned out to be a group of nineteenth-century artists who wished to return to a style that existed prior to the work of Raphael Sanzio (1483–1520). The exchange left me with a residual distrust of chronologies, of terms such as pre- and post-, and of linear notions of history, even those inferred in reverse (or 'traditions' as we call them). This distrust has informed all of my teaching and writing on postmodernism, postmodernity and the postmodern. Indeed, I would push the phenomenon of postmodernism back to the writings of Heraclitus and the pre-Socratics – some of whom, confusingly, post-dated Socrates and clearly pre-dated modernism.

Whilst noting my suspicion of the prefix 'post-', it is not possible to sidestep the terms 'modernism', 'modernity' and the 'modern'. These concepts are more straightforward to grasp than the same terms modified by 'post-'; while modernism and its related forms are used to mean different things by different theorists, there is nonetheless a broad agreement that there is a suspicion of hierarchies and straightforward binary oppositions. Joining an interdisciplinary reading group that brought together philosophers, economists, historians, sociologists and literary critics to discuss postmodernity, I was very aware that we did not agree even on the meanings of key terms like 'modern' and 'realist'. In retrospect – after the postmodern bubble has shrunk – there is a sense that each critic or theorist has used the term postmodernism to mean whatever they have wanted it to mean. It might be frustrating to students not to have a definition of postmodernism that fits on a T-shirt – but a (not *the*) key notion of postmodernism is the problem of drawing definitional boundaries. A distinction must be made between, say, the architectural practices of Charles Jencks and the political interventions of Jean Baudrillard as being very different endeavours. To do otherwise is to risk falling into a wishy-washy cultural relativism in which there are No Wrong Answers (or, more annoyingly for students, No Right Answers) and It's Just One Point of View. In the book on postmodernism I wrote with Bob Ford, we began by suggesting it is:

> a movement, a set of aesthetics, a cultural logic, an ideology, a Zeitgeist, an age, an ethos, a mood. It's a bandwagon. It's a scam, a con trick, an example of the emperor's new clothes, nihilistic nonsense, dangerously fascist and right wing. It's the only surviving form of Marxism. It's a continuation of modernism. It's a rejection of modernism. It is what you need before you can have modernism. It is nothing to do with modernism. It is the only way to understand now. It's all over now. It never existed.[1]

But this vagueness can get in the way of teaching the topic.

It is only appropriate to address the fear of relativism that postmodernism might evoke. Industrialized education requires the delivery of content, in line with Intended Learning Outcomes, followed by the measurement of the recipients' reception of those ILOs. If anticipating outcomes and measurement is called into question, then percentage grades, SATs, league tables and so forth might suddenly be thought of as being a waste of time. It should not be forgotten that Jean-François Lyotard's *The Postmodern Condition* (1979) was commissioned as a report on the state of knowledge, which would have included universities.

In my own case, I lack the conviction to tell the Big Story, where everything fits in. Of course, as a tutor you are authorized to teach, and it is necessary for the student to learn. There are mechanisms to call upon when obedience is not found. I am sure I have made statements in everyday conversations which have unknowingly used this authority. Consciously I try to keep aware of the narratives, the counternarratives, the exceptions, the paradoxes. Rather than producing what Lyotard refers to as grand narratives or metanarratives – that is, narratives about narratives, narratives which give legitimacy to themselves and other narratives – I try to focus in on local narratives, which may contradict other local narratives. I also tend to teach the ideas of those I see as the three leading figures in the *philosophy* of postmodernism: Lyotard, Baudrillard and

Fredric Jameson. Thomas Docherty's anthology, *Postmodernism: A Reader* (1992), is a very useful gathering together of many theoretical strands, if rather male-dominated in his choice of author. Absent from this selection are Donna Haraway and the French feminists, especially Julia Kristeva and Hélène Cixous.

In literary studies there is an understandable attempt to break the discipline down into digestible chunks; these are frequently defined by period – medieval, Elizabethan, Jacobean, eighteenth-century, Romantic, Victorian, modernist and then nebulous categories such as 'contemporary' or 'postwar'. Modernism is a name given to a range of artistic movements between roughly 1900 and 1930, characterized by an aesthetic of newness and refreshment in form and content – it covered poetry (figures such as T.S. Eliot, Ezra Pound and the Imagists), novels (Virginia Woolf, James Joyce), painting (Wyndham Lewis, Pablo Picasso), music (Igor Stravinsky, Arnold Schoenberg), architecture (Le Corbusier, Mies van der Rohe) and beyond. There was a sense that the world was facing an abyss – a worldview confirmed by the First World War – after a century in which humanity was revealed to be related to an ape (Charles Darwin's theory of evolution) and identity was supposed to be largely unconscious (Sigmund Freud). The new art broke from straightforward representations of a shared notion of reality to a more complex depiction of a fractured and disturbed world. The objects produced might not look like art at all – see Marcel Duchamp's ready-made 'Fountain' (1917), a urinal signed R. Mutt, intended to be shown at the Society of Independent Artists' exhibition in New York.

The science fiction of the period is not interested in technology or the space-time continuum, nor in new forms in the same way as modernist texts are. However, a modernist aesthetic *can* be seen at work in Georges Méliès's *Le voyage dans la Lune* (1902) and Fritz Lang's dystopian *Metropolis* (1927), but H.G. Wells's sf novels of the decade or so after 1895, virtually an overture to the themes of the next century of sf, did not break with the tradition of form in the manner of Woolf's *The Waves* (1931), for example. The genre's prose style tended to be functional, designed to tell a story rather than revivify the nature of language. Even the epic future histories of Olaf Stapledon – most crucially *Last and First Men* (1930) and *Star Maker* (1937) – do not get considered alongside the modernist classics.

In the 1960s science fiction changed a little – a group of largely British writers associated with the magazine *New Worlds* experimented with the *techniques* of modernism for both short- and long-form fiction, in a period in which sf, trailing some five or six years behind mainstream literature 'briefly *becomes modernist*'.[2] Such a late flowering can be seen as a continuation of modernism – as with the paintings of Jackson Pollock and Mark Rothko and the music of Philip Glass and Michael Nyman – which it is convenient to label as postmodernism because of its chronological tardiness. Again, though, this is to invoke a notion of progressive development which will be questioned throughout this chapter.

John Brunner's disaster novels of the 1960s and 1970s – especially *Stand on Zanzibar* (1968) and *The Sheep Look Up* (1972) – drew upon techniques pioneered by John Dos Passos in his *USA Trilogy* (1930–36), which combined traditional narration with news clippings, biography and memoirs. Similarly Michael Moorcock mixed and matched his way through the Jerry Cornelius novels, *The Final Programme* (1968), *A Cure for Cancer* (1971), *The English Assassin* (1972) and *The Condition of Muzak* (1977), a series in which the central character may have also been a version of protagonists from other novels by Moorcock, such as Oswald Bastable, Jherek Carnelian, Elric, Dorian Hawkmoon and Corum Jhaelen Irsei. The characterization is broadly the same, but the adventures occur in different milieus. The sf figure most sympathetic to modernism was J.G. Ballard, who drew on the imagery of Salvador Dalí and Max Ernst in his fiction. His condensed novels, collected in *The Atrocity Exhibition* (1970), are assembled from paragraphs which are entire chapters in themselves, and feature a media saturated landscape that is as much internal as external. The protagonist fragments between sections – becoming variously Talbert, Talbot, Traven and Travis. The book also features assassinated, damaged and sexualized versions of 1960s celebrities, such as Ronald Reagan, John F. and Jacqueline Kennedy and Marilyn Monroe. Less well known is the work of John Sladek, whose work included parodies of other sf writers (collected in *The Steam Driven Boy and Other Strangers*, 1970), explorations of Kafkaesque scenarios and even bureaucratic forms, whose increasingly pedantic and impertinent questions evoke a growing sense of anxiety in the reader (see *Alien Accounts*, 1982).

When reading a story of this period, such as Pamela Zoline's 'Heat Death of the Universe' (1968) in which the laws of thermodynamics act as a counterpoint to an ordinary housewife's preparations for a birthday party, the question is whether it is sf at all. The so-called New Wave of 1960s (and early 1970s) science fiction marks the part emergence from the genre ghetto of some writers, whilst non-genre writers produced works which looked like, but were not necessarily marketed as, sf. Philip Roth, Kurt Vonnegut, Saul Bellow, Norman Mailer, William S. Burroughs and Thomas Pynchon, among others, have been given the label of postmodernism because they form a loose stylistic and thematic movement in a period which post-dates (but might be thought sympathetic to) modernism.

In many cases the writer was the star as much as their writing – and there was often awareness within the narrative that the world being described was fictional. Vonnegut's *Cat's Cradle* (1960) is a good exemplar: the events of the apocalypse are being related to us by someone who invites us to call him Jonah, invoking the opening of *Moby Dick* (1851) and a biblical character who (in popular recollection) was swallowed by a whale. With *Slaughterhouse 5* (1969) and *Breakfast of Champions* (1973) Vonnegut goes further, writing himself as characters within the novels; in the former because he was present during the firebombing of Dresden that is at the heart of the novel, in the latter as he emancipates his stock characters from literary slavery. Tom Robbins celebrates getting to chapter one hundred in *Even Cowgirls Get the Blues* (1971) and in *Still Life with Woodpecker* (1980) intervenes in the story to describe his deteriorating relationship with his new typewriter. In *Options* (1975), Robert Sheckley despairs of getting his characters out of a plot hole and decides to produce a cookery book instead. A (non-sf) novel which could be comfortably read alongside these examples is Laurence Sterne's *The Life and Opinions of Tristram Shandy, Gentleman* (1759–67), where the author struggles to advance his deeply digressive narrative. It was published long before the modernist, let alone the postmodernist period.

These novels draw attention to the status of the writer as the author of the events in each novel, playing with the boundaries between fiction and reality. The terms 'metafiction' or 'metadrama' might be more useful in these cases than the label 'postmodernism'. The period since the Second World War has seen many literary movements alternately being embraced and rejected, each a reaction to all the others. Lyotard has noted how the period of modernism was dominated by such movements, each a more rapid or immediate response to what had gone before: 'In an amazing acceleration, the generations precipitate themselves. A work can become modern only if it is first postmodern. Thus understood, postmodernism is not modernism at its end, but in a nascent state.'[3] The reaction and rejection become so complete and rapid, that time appears to be reversed – this feels like a science-fictional thought as indeed much of postmodernism does on the level of its slogans.

That a postmodern work can be written prior to modern ones should destroy any sense that one 'movement' is an improvement on the other – for Lyotard there is the sense that postmodernism lacks 'good' form, and is perhaps immature in its aesthetics. Nothing is too low brow and nothing is too elitist for postmodernism. It would be worth exploring where your students' boundaries of good form are – is it appropriate to study newspapers, comic books, soap operas, pornography? Even science fiction is a form that some people regard as a guilty pleasure at best, and as trash at worst.

The suspicion of chronologies is both pertinent and problematic when looking at the work of Marxist academic Fredric Jameson, who sees postmodernism – in part – as a period which distrusts notions of history. Marxism argues that an economic base or foundation of a given society – its raw materials, its tools, its workforce and its market – determines the superstructure – including social systems, legal systems, politics, arts, culture, aesthetics, media, family structures, religions, philosophies and ideologies. Marx identified four broad epochs – Asiatic, Classical, Feudal and Capitalist societies – which have been part of the history of humanity. Jameson, following Ernest Mandel, notes that capitalism itself can be periodized into market capitalism (1700–1850), monopoly capitalism (1850–1960) and late capitalism (1960–), wherein corporations shift from national to international to multinational. The three epochs correspond to realism, modernism and postmodernism – although part of the aesthetics of postmodernism is a sense of the end of history and a distrust of historical process, progress and development.

If realism reflects accurate notions of space and time – geography and duration – and modernism is aware of the relativity of space/time (especially post-Einstein), then postmodernism explores a collapse/explosion of space/time. Lyotard notes how an eclecticism ignores national boundaries: 'one listens to reggae, watches a western, eats McDonald's food for lunch and local cuisine for dinner, wears Paris perfume in Tokyo and "retro" clothes in Hong Kong; knowledge is a matter for TV games'.[4] In the postmodern era, the individual is assailed from all sides in 'the world space of multinational capital',[5] and needs to define a new cognitive map to deal with the contemporary world.

Jameson, who contributed an essay on *Dr Bloodmoney* (1965) to the 1975 special Philip K. Dick issue of *Science-Fiction Studies* and wrote *Archaeologies of the Future: The Desire Called Utopia and Other Science Fictions* (2007), has no problem in turning to sf for a venue in which the cognitive mapping can take place. Indeed, he writes that the subgenre of cyberpunk is 'henceforth, for many of us, the supreme *literary* expression if not of postmodernism, then of late capitalism itself'.[6] In one chapter of *Postmodernism, or the Cultural Logic of Late Capitalism* (1991) he analyses Philip K. Dick's *Time Out of Joint* (1959), and he makes a few passing (if misremembered) references to Dick's *Now Wait for Last Year* (1966). Jameson's 1984 article of the same name, reprinted as the first chapter of the 1991 book, offers a shopping list of postmodern aesthetics which can be located in sf: depthlessness, simulation, waning of affect, death of the subject, schizophrenic *écriture*, the sublime, nostalgia and pastiche. Mostly I've turned to films to demonstrate these factors – any of the various cuts of the noirish *Blade Runner* (Scott, 1982), the body-technology blurrings of *Videodrome* (Cronenberg, 1983) or *Tetsuo* (Tsukamoto, 1989) and the rich, but motiveless, pastiche of *Gremlins II* (Dante, 1990).

If there is a need to stay with the written word, William Gibson's seminal *Neuromancer* (1984) is a fruitful choice – if necessary the first page or so could suffice. Jamesonian postmodernism is about surfaces, about things that are cool in themselves but have little significance – it is Warhol's delight in images for their own sake, and Jameson compares Vincent Van Gogh's 'A Pair of Boots' to Andy Warhol's 'Diamond Dust Shoes'. (Having realized that one class had not heard of Warhol, I ruefully noted he must have had his fifteen minutes of fame. More blank faces. Fortunately, they *had* heard of the Velvet Underground, whose album *Velvet Underground and Nico* had a banana design by Warhol on its sleeve.) Certainly *Neuromancer* fetishizes fashion and brand names, and features a metaphor-heavy prose which constantly links technology to the human. Focus in on its opening sentence: 'The sky above the port was the colour of television tuned to a dead channel.' What colour is that? I suspect these days we'd say blue, conditioned by the blank screen which kicks in to replace static or marks an audio-video channel, but I suspect Gibson meant dark grey to black. A port is a commercial harbour, of course, a location in the world, but the word is also used in computing to refer to the conduit between the machine and its printer or an external modem. This is the first of many metaphors used by Gibson in which the world is compared to technology, or technology is seen in terms of nature. I think it's worth spending time getting the students to discuss the meaning of Gibson's metaphors.

According to Jameson, in the era of postmodernism simulations have replaced the authentic – most obviously in the use of virtual reality. Emotions themselves may not be authentic, but assumed, perhaps ironic, or perhaps programmed; in *Neuromancer* various characters describe themselves as being 'wired'. Emotions are but one element of the construction of identity, and the protagonist Case is redefined as an individual in his international capers and his moves in and out of virtual space. Perhaps the most vivid character in the novel is Dixie Flatliner, an identity downloaded into storage, who wants to die. The inauthentic is more solid than the so-called real.

Schizophrenic *écriture* is the notion of an open style, in part where any solid link between word and concept, signifier and signified, is broken. Ask the students to think of the title of the novel – *Neuromancer* – which is most obviously the name of an artificial intelligence within the novel, but also suggests New Romancers, a new kind of desiring (and the New Romantics of post-glam rock, and early 1980s fashions), even 'neuro/romance', a romance of the brain, perhaps something to do with the neurons of the brain, 'neuromancy', divination by the brain (and the word is one letter away from 'necromancer', a magician who communicates with the spirits of the dead). Language is not fixed in the image of its author but is allusive and intertextual, always quoting, breaking the boundaries of where the text begins and ends. The sublime is the sense of the infinite, what Edmund Burke called 'delightful horror' – it might be invoked by a mountain, a volcano, vertigo, by the stargate sequence of *2001: A Space Odyssey* (Kubrick, 1968) – and manifests itself as a pleasurable horror. This again might be located in Gibson's prose style and his representation of the data-landscape of the virtual reality matrix. Nostalgia and pastiche might be seen together, in the ways in which the novel draws upon Hammett's *The Maltese Falcon* (1930) or Chandler's *The Big Sleep* (1939); a protagonist who is barely in charge of his own narrative, a Mr Big calling the shots and pulling the strings, and a beautiful but deadly femme fatale, Molly. It can be debated by students as to whether Molly is a feminist role model, as Buffy was to be hailed a decade later, because of her self-reliance and physical strength. In her form-hugging leather catsuit, however, she risks becoming the male sexual fantasy of the dominatrix.

Jameson's shopping list of postmodernist characteristics may be applied to many sf texts produced since the 1980s, such as *Blade Runner* or Jeff Noon's *Vurt* (1993), but it would also be interesting to apply it to some of the works from the 1960s or 1970s, such as Joanna Russ's *The Female Man* (1975) or Zoline's 'The Heat Death of the Universe'. For Jameson the break between one epoch and the next had come at some point in the late 1950s or early 1960s. In addition to his own work on postmodernism, Jameson also contributed a foreword to the 1984 English translation of Lyotard's *The Postmodern Condition*.

This is a volume more concerned with postmodernity than postmodernism, modernity being a mode of thinking that was initially associated with the Enlightenment. Modernity continues a humanist impulse which begins in the sixteenth-century Reformation and Renaissance, with the rise of Protestantism over Catholicism and the emergence of industrial capitalism. Developments in technology meant that weaving, for example, would move from individual artisans working during daylight hours in their own homes, to the twenty-four hour a day working of machines in factories with two or three shifts of workers. Goods could be mass produced, and transported across the country and exported. Whilst the industrial revolution was built upon the exploitation of the working classes, it also saw a growth in rational thought – the written constitution of the United States of America (1776), followed by the overthrow of the aristocracy in the 1789 French Revolution. Over the next century and a half democracy spread throughout the West, with the vote being increasingly extended from the wealthy to all men, and belatedly to women. As symbolized by the Great Exhibition of 1851 in Hyde Park, whose success funded the construction of the museums in South Kensington and the Royal Albert Hall, the Enlightenment project of modernity was a huge success, promising progress, liberty and freedom.

The spirit of modernity can be observed in science fiction, particularly in the early, Golden Age and hard American varieties. Science fiction is a problem-solving genre – classic stories set up a situation in which characters face a problem that is solved by technology, usually thanks to the skills, wisdom and fortitude of an individual hero. Irrespective of the contingency of events on a multitude of intersecting factors, a great, rational man (less often a woman) saves the day or brings down an entire corrupt or decadent regime.

But sf is not unbridled in its optimism for the possibilities of science or the promises of technology, although this is perhaps clearer outside the American genre tradition. British sf is more pessimistic, whether it is Mary Shelley's depiction of the irresponsible scientist destroyed by his own creation in *Frankenstein, or the Modern Prometheus* (1818; rev. 1831), a dystopia such as E.M. Forster's *The Machine Stops* (1909), or any number of texts from the new wave. Atomic fictions – whether about the threat of radiation or depicting the aftermath of a nuclear explosion – also warn about the dangers of science and the limits of human knowledge.

For Lyotard, the condition of postmodernity is one in which the optimism of modernity is rejected. This does not necessarily mean that he is *against* science, but that he rejects a too-rosy view of the possibilities. There are any number of technology stories in the news which offer a space for student debate on the benefits and downside of scientific advances – genetic modification, gene selection, fluoridation, vaccination, social networking sites, phone masts causing cancer – which might allow for the anxieties to be expressed. (Some of these are real causes for concern, others are media panics. Your own position may vary.) We have moved now from modern to postmodern science – a term that would make many scientists angry.

In *The Postmodern Condition*, Lyotard notes that Nicolaus Copernicus, 'states that the path of the planets is circular'.[7] It does not, for the moment, matter that the orbits are in fact ellipses, because the practice of the scientific community will resolve that uncertainty as part of scientific discourse. Copernicus is telling the truth, in that he can present empirical evidence to back his statement up, and will be called upon to refute anyone who disagrees with him. Individuals who hear the statement are to be treated as his equal, and will, on the one hand, test – prove – his statement by reproducing Copernicus's evidence or producing evidence of their own. On the other hand, they may produce evidence that refutes the hypothesis that Copernicus has issued. The third part of this scientific discourse, the referent – Mercury, Venus, Earth, Mars – may or may not be orbiting a star, but we cannot conclusively say whether it is true. Proof comes from the agreement of Copernicus's audience with Copernicus – from his authority as scientist, and our ability to reproduce his results. The progress of modern science is measured in verification and falsification – the reproduction of experimental results.

But more recent science is less open to this process: first, the cost of resources required to conduct certain experiments is ruinous and second, the nature of science pushes beyond what is entirely measurable or predictable. Lyotard notes as a parallel the Jorge Luis Borges story, 'On Rigor in Science' (1946) in which the energies of an entire country are put into producing an accurate map of the country, at a scale of one-to-one. The Large Hadron Collider, a particle accelerator under the Franco-Swiss border, was designed to trap a theorized elementary particle – the Higgs boson – as part of a project that will cost up to 6.4 million euros. This is not an experiment that many can afford to repeat. Equally the search for any elementary particle bumps up against problems of measuring reality – both in terms of their smallness and in the odd ways in which material reality seems to behave at that level. As Lyotard argues, 'Quantum theory and microphysics require a far more radical revision of a continuous and predictable path.'[8] An electron does not move around the nucleus of an atom like a planet around a star – and it is impossible simultaneously to know the position and momentum of a particle. There is only so much that science can discover and render intelligible in everyday language.

Two competing hypotheses now describe the behaviour of particles. The Copenhagen interpretation of quantum mechanics, advanced by Niels Bohr and Werner Heisenberg in 1927, suggests that the position of an electron at a particular point is a result of it being observed there rather than somewhere else; location is expressed as a series of probabilities. The relative state formulation or many-universes interpretation, advanced first by Hugh Everett in 1957 and later by Bryce Seligman DeWitt, suggests that the particle is at that particular point in that specific observer's universe – it is at another point for an observer in an alternate universe. In the first case truth is a matter of probability, in the second truth holds for the local conditions only.

Science fiction has made much use of such postmodern science. The alternate history might be considered one version of the many-universes interpretation. At some point in history, a key event occurs differently, producing a still recognizable but different world – the south wins the American Civil War (Ward Moore's *Bring the Jubilee*, 1953), Germany and Japan win the Second World War (Philip K. Dick's *The Man in the High Castle*, 1961; Robert Harris's *Fatherland*, 1992) and so on. Sometimes such alternates seem to be little more than parlour games; amusing reflections upon the nature of history – witness the various volumes of 'counterfactuals' edited by historians such as Niall Ferguson. Certainly in the classroom I have asked students to imagine how society could be different as a way into getting them to think through what sf does. (The first counterfactuals were published in the 1700s; again, these pre-date modernism.)

All of this is to leave the quantum level far behind. There is sf which is more centrally about physics, for example Isaac Asimov's *The Gods Themselves* (1973), with traffic between alternate universes. Gregory Benford's *Timescape* (1980) features two communities, separated in time, one a future Earth ravaged by environmental disaster, civil unrest and nuclear terrorism, the other a recognizable version of our past. The scientists in the future try to use elementary particles called tachyons to convey a message back in time, to warn the scientists of the past to avert the disaster. This notion runs into all kinds of causality paradoxes, which require a many-universes theory to resolve; that particular future cannot be saved, but others can. More recently the fiction of Greg Egan invokes quantum and theoretical physics.

Lyotard argues that a whole series of factors mean that our notions of truth and knowledge are no longer certain. Modernity – which includes scientific endeavour, industrial capitalism and democracy – has not led to the liberation of the individual, but to a greater degree of alienation than ever before. For Lyotard it is rationality – especially capitalism's rationality – that led to the colonization of Africa and genocide, and, in due course, to industrialized trench warfare and the gas chambers of the concentration camps. 'The nineteenth and twentieth centuries have given us as much terror as we can take', he writes in 'Answer to the Question', 'We have paid a high enough price for the nostalgia of the whole and the one.'[9] Both Nazism and Stalinism – as totalitarian systems of rule – are products of attempts at the rational state. The postmodern, which Lyotard had defined as 'incredulity toward metanarratives'[10] in its fragmentations, offers a space of resistance to the ongoing development of multinational capitalism, or a relativity which renders notions of value (and thus of exchange) as meaningless.

A number of dystopias might be called upon to show the operation of totalitarianism – although sf is usually too optimistic as to the ease with which the regime is brought down. D.F. Jones's 1966 novel, *Colossus*, especially in its film incarnation, *Colossus: The Forbin Project* (Sargent, 1970), illustrates such misguided faith in rationality. Dr Charles Forbin develops a supercomputer to monitor the world's intelligence and protect the West against nuclear threat from the Eastern bloc. Colossus, the computer, discovers the existence of a Soviet computer, Guardian, and joins forces with it. Jointly, with their control of the nuclear weapons, the computers can demand that the world does whatever they want it to; peace *has* been achieved, as long as humanity obeys, but at a cost to the individuality and freedom of the world's population. The rational solution ends in nightmare.

Lyotard's attacks on rationality, progress and the liberating influence of the Enlightenment project of modernity led to his being smeared as a neo-conservative by the Frankfurt School critical theorist Jürgen Habermas. In part this could be a result of Lyotard's dismissal of Marxism as a metanarrative that insufficiently resists capitalism. A similar rejection of political dogma is at the heart of the work of Jean Baudrillard. Baudrillard had done his doctoral research in sociology at Université de Paris-X Nanterre. When in May 1968 there was a student uprising, Nanterre was at the heart of the protest. Baudrillard witnessed the events, and the failure of the unions and the Communist Party to support the move. His subsequent break with Marxism is thought of as a move to the right, and thus to neo-conservatism – but in fact his problem was that the left was not radical enough.

At the heart of Baudrillard's postmodernism was his distrust of capitalism as a sinister force at work within society. The Marxist critique of the system identifies use value – what an object can be used for – and exchange value – what monetary value an object has. Capitalism emphasizes exchange value, and exploits workers by purchasing their labour to produce objects which can be exchanged for a greater value than is invested in the process. Profits derive from the surplus labour of workers. The Frankfurt School, in their analysis of the massification of society, described how the resistance of the individual is worn down by the onslaught of mass culture and the mass media, in which false needs are created in order to give individuals a false sense of satisfaction in their mass consumption. If anything, Baudrillard thought this a too-optimistic view of the world, and felt that socialism, communism and Marxism merely asserted use value over exchange value. In the inversion of the hierarchy the underlying horror is not lifted. Baudrillard writes of the *'evil genius of advertising'*[11] which intervenes in the space between signifier and signified.

For Baudrillard, Western society has been built upon a distinction between truth and falsehood, and the rational distinguishing of one from the other. The mass media has increasingly undercut this, and political campaigning is entirely based around fakery. The staged has taken over from the authentic to such an extent that truth no longer has any meaning. In particular he singles out the theme park as a dangerous phenomenon:

> Disneyland is there to conceal the fact that it is the 'real' country, all of 'real' America, which is Disneyland ... Disneyland is presented as imaginary in order to make us believe that the rest is real, when in fact all of Los Angeles and the America surrounding it are no longer real, but of the order of the hyperreal and of simulation.[12]

Designating something as obviously fake offers the alibi that the rest of the world is 'real'.

Sf is clearly a genre that can dramatize this fakery; or by acting as a safety valve it can contribute to the conditions which facilitate it. Sf, after all, is obviously not about the real world – thus allowing us to believe that there is a real world. Again, the genre is not radical enough to solve the problem rather than adding to it: 'the "good old" SF imagination is dead, and ... something else is beginning to emerge (and not only in fiction, but also in theory). Both traditional SF and theory are destined to the same fate: flux and imprecision are putting an end to them as specific genres.'[13] But Baudrillard repeatedly turned to sf in his analysis of hyperreality and the simulacrum – the copy with no original.

Baudrillard has written on two areas of sf: J.G. Ballard's *Crash* (1973) and the works of Philip K. Dick.[14] In *Crash*, Ballard makes a pornographic linkage between the contemporary technologies of cars, planes, road networks and celebrity culture and sexual fulfilment – the ultimate desire of the novel's protagonist Vaughan is to die at the point of orgasm crashing his car into Elizabeth Taylor, herself having an orgasm. The naming of the still-living Taylor and the narration of the novel by one James Ballard raises ethical issues that would require class discussion, of course, as the novel deliberately flouts the distinction between the real and fictional. It is perhaps more reassuring to read the novel ironically, in the spirit of Swift's *A Modest Proposal* (1729), rather than actually as a call for us to be eroticized by our relationship to technology. Clearly it requires a strong stomach to teach the novel – and a mature audience. An interesting factor is how it reverses expectations – in traditional terms it is not sf at all, but Ballard in his introduction advances the notion that the world is an sf novel, and thus *Crash* is very much sf. Reality has been replaced by the model of the reality – just as polls, statistics, futures and reality television have infected the real.

Philip K. Dick's entire output is based around the two interrelated questions of 'What is real?' and 'What is human?', and thus almost any of his novels and most of his short stories would be suitable to tease out Baudrillard's ideas. *Time Out of Joint* is perhaps the most significant example. The novel is set in an ersatz 1950s, in which loser Ragle Gumm still lives with his sister and her husband, making a precarious living from entering a Find the Little Green Man competition in the local newspaper. All is not as it seems. Objects disappear into thin air, to be replaced by slips of paper. Gumm hears talk about himself on a radio. Society seems a little too insular. By the end of the novel, we realize that the Earth is fighting the colony on the Moon, and that the 1950s town was manufactured to ensure Gumm's participation in the war effort. Dick's 1990s – imagined from the 1950s – is of course very different from the one we remember, whereas the 1950s, set up to be fake, convinces despite the odd minor detail that later readers will miss. For example, the novel features a Tucker motor car, which never went into mass production. But just as the otherwise authentic seeming 1950s present turns out to be false, so the reader should question the authenticity of their own present day. How do your students know they are not living in a reality show – like Truman Burbank in *The Truman Show* (Weir, 1998)? Baudrillard argues that thanks to capitalism, we are living in a false world.

Baudrillard's later writings, in particular his essays on the first Gulf War and the attacks on the World Trade Center, are also provocative for thinking about virtuality, spectacle and disaster. In *The Gulf War Did Not Take Place*, he writes: 'A simple calculation shows that, of the 500,000 American soldiers involved during the seven months of operations in the Gulf, three times as many would have died from road accidents alone had they stayed in civilian life.'[15] It is perhaps typical of his style that this is an unsourced assertion, but it is convincing because it is counterintuitive. Baudrillard suggests that the lack of dead was an embarrassment – the imbalance between the two sides was such that it would be misleading to call it a war, neither like the two massed world wars, nor like the proxy conflicts of the Cold War: 'After the hot war (the violence of conflict), after the cold war (the balance of terror), here comes the dead war – the unfrozen cold war – which leaves us to grapple with the corpse of war.'[16] The American Air Force ran out of legitimate targets but had to keep bombing anyway. In the end, it was both war as spectacle – I remember Tony Benn complaining about the aestheticization of the war by the media just as a television programme cut to live footage of a firework display of an attack – and war as advertisement, for the new generation of missile technology, for Saddam Hussein as someone finally undefeated by the USA and for CNN as a twenty-four hour news service from which even generals took their intelligence. Baudrillard's rhetoric is deliberately provocative – he makes his point through hyperbole. What are the ethics of his argument? Real people will have died in the war, not just simulacra.

It is postmodern that we cannot determine where Baudrillard is being ironic – and there are moments in Lyotard's work when he is similarly ambiguous. Baudrillard, Jameson and Lyotard all argue that there has been a rupture in postwar history, which has destroyed our old systems of beliefs just as an explosion in technology – the mass media, satellites, the internet – has exposed us to more images, words and concepts than at any other point in history. The question we are left with – and that sf has explored for us already – is how far we can resist the onslaught and change the world for the better, how far we are doomed to put up with what we have and how far we should just reach for a gin and a hamburger, cue up the DVD boxset of 1970s TV classics and then tap dance our way across the abyss in our Nike boots, just having fun.

At the same time, there is the sense that the postmodern moment is over. Post-9/11 the notion that capitalism has beaten all other ideologies is less easy to argue, and is the Bush era there were signs of new battle lines being drawn. As to what critical movement has replaced postmodernism – whatever would be post-postmodernist in the re-entry into history – is still not apparent.

I have taught postmodernism in its own right, and as a critical language for looking at particular genres. The cultural certainties of a Matthew Arnold at the start of a module on cultural studies are thrown into sharp relief when contrasted with the eclecticism of Lyotard. The Leavisite Great Tradition is blown away – to be replaced with *Neuromancer*, *Blade Runner* and, more recently, *The Matrix* (Wachowski brothers, 1999). The first theoretically inclined critics to take written sf seriously were Marxists, the next generation were postmodernists (at the risk of writing feminisms out of critical history).

Even if the ostensible subject is not sf, I would reach for sf texts as the best exemplars. The topic also seems to belong at or toward the end of modules of sf – partly because no major critical approach has superseded it (to use an inappropriate chronological term), but also because the texts that are likely to come late in a historical survey – whether prose, film or television – reward a postmodern approach. Since the mid-1980s Gibson has become the touchstone for marketing the genre – with cyberpunk being followed by post-cyberpunk, and being distinguished from the retrospectively named steampunk (a reimagined Victorian age with more advanced technology).

There are a number of common student reactions to postmodernism. The more instrumental ones, who want to know the six key facts about the topic will be disappointed or frustrated by it, because I honestly think that that is to miss the point of the approach. It is certainly not in its spirit. Some students will be liberated by it – to put a graphic novel like, say, *Watchmen* (1987) on a par with Shakespeare makes literature look a whole lot less stuffy. Any work can be compared to any other. Finally, it might be a means of awakening some political sense in the students, whether that is in seeing the resistance to metanarratives as a means of rejecting capitalism, in becoming aware of the various anti-globalization movements, or in defending Marxist or other ideologies against postmodernism's scepticism. (There may be those who wish to speak up for capitalism, of course; the most depressing class I ever taught included women who wanted to marry into the family of a media mogul so they themselves would be rich.)

Hindsight may also allow the students to question the breaking down of categories of sex, gender, sexuality, ethnicity and so forth; the emphasis that this puts on the individual within society (at the same time as individuals apparently cease to exist) seems in retrospect symptomatic of the 'me' society of the 1980s and 1990s. Whilst individuals can make a difference, albeit infinitesimal, changes in society are more often wrought by collectives and groups who feel solidarity. With the undermining of ideologies in common, it may be less easy for such groupings to come together.

Again the contradictions need to be pointed out rather than dismissed. The scepticism – towards time, truth, being, boundaries, hierarchies and meaning – at the heart of postmodernism is finally a tool to get students to work through ideas, and to question everything. I can remember a final year media student complaining that he could no longer watch the news as it was all a series of constructions; I congratulated him on reaching such a state of being able to question the media landscape. Such a person is harder to turn into a consumer. Postmodernism requires students to think through ideas to their logical if absurd conclusions, to question authority and, ideally, to think for themselves. We can give them no more utopian a gift.

Notes

1. Andrew M. Butler and Bob Ford, *Postmodernism* (Harpenden: Pocket Essentials, 2003) 7.
2. Fred Pfeil, *Another Tale to Tell: Politics and Narrative in Postmodern Culture* (London and New York: Verso, 1990) 85–6.
3. Jean-François Lyotard, *The Postmodern Condition: A Report on Knowledge*, trans. Geoff Bennington and Brian Massumi, introduced by F. Jameson (Manchester: Manchester University Press, 1984) 79.
4. Ibid., 76.
5. Frederic Jameson *Postmodernism or, The Cultural Logic of Late Capitalism* (London and New York: Verso, 1991) 54.
6. Ibid., 419.
7. Lyotard, *The Postmodern Condition*, 23.
8. Ibid., 56.
9. Ibid., 81.
10. Ibid., xxiv.
11. Jean Baudrillard, 'Barbara Kruger', in Gary Genosko, ed., *The Uncollected Baudrillard* (London and Thousand Oaks: Sage, 2001) 134.
12. Jean Baudrillard, *Simulations*, trans. Paul Patton, Paul Foss and Philip Beitchman (New York: Semiotext(e), 1983) 25.
13. Baudrillard, 'Simulacra and Science Fiction', *Science Fiction Studies*, 18:3 (1991): 309–13 at 309.
14. See Baudrillard, 'Ballard's *Crash*', *Science Fiction Studies*, 18:3 (1991): 313–20, and 'Simulacra and Science Fiction'.
15. Baudrillard, *The Gulf War Did Not Take Place*, trans. and ed. Paul Patton (Sydney: Power, 1995) 69.
16. Ibid., 23.

9
Teaching Gender and Science Fiction

Brian Attebery

Gender is a culturally mediated way of expressing or performing sexual difference. It pervades every aspect of human behaviour, from baby clothing to funeral customs. It is deeply implicated in issues of identity, power, communication and desire. With only two traditional options, masculine and feminine, gender tends to turn differences into polarities; to divide up the world as either this or that, with no binary-confounding third terms; and to generate hierarchies, in which one alternative always ranks above the other. As a fundamental feature of most natural languages, it shapes not only the ways we talk about the world, but even the ways we can think. Much of the influence of gender on thought and behaviour is at an unconscious level, so that it can be a challenge to make it part of a classroom discussion: students will often react with scepticism if asked to analyse a story in gendered terms. Nonetheless, science fiction, with its ability to defamiliarize many aspects of culture and biology, can take the 'natural' out of human nature, so that something as fundamental as gender can be brought to awareness and examined critically.[1]

Historically, much science fiction was written and read without conscious attention to issues of gender. Aside from some early experiments with feminist utopias, such as Charlotte Perkins Gilman's *Herland* (1915), it was not until writers of the 1960s and 1970s began to challenge a number of genre conventions (including a general silence on sexual matters) that gender became an overt object of critique. One of the turning points was Ursula K. Le Guin's *The Left Hand of Darkness* (1969), a thought-experiment in gender, or, more precisely, the lack of it. What if there were a world, the novel asks, in which there was no sexual difference? How would every institution be different: religion, marriage, kinship, politics, warfare? Another milestone was Joanna

Russ's *The Female Man* (1975), which represents different possible gender systems as a set of linked alternate worlds. Russ shows how the same woman might become timid Jeannine; violent Jael; or, in a world without males where females assume all social roles, confident Janet, the 'female man' of the title. The novel invites us to rethink both society and language, so that by the end we begin to understand that not only Janet but every woman might actually be a man – that is, man as in *mankind*.

The conscious exploration of gender within science fiction has continued since the 1970s and has been institutionalized in such venues as WisCon, the long-running feminist convention held annually in Madison, Wisconsin, and Gaylaxicon, the more recent convention devoted to science fiction and fantasy that addresses gay, lesbian or transgender issues. Each of these annual gatherings has generated a related award: the James Tiptree Jr Award, founded at WisCon in 1991 by writers Pat Murphy and Karen Joy Fowler, and the Gaylactic Spectrum Award, first awarded in 1999. The Tiptree Award, in particular, has had considerable influence on the field, leading directly to the creation of several anthologies, critical studies and original stories answering the award's call to 'explore and expand our understanding of gender'.[2]

Yet even before there was feminist sf, long before there were awards to celebrate it, there was gender in science fiction. Most sf did not question or even acknowledge society's gender coding, but those codes operate whether acknowledged or not. The first place to look for interesting science fictional takes on sexual difference is in fiction by women. Those most interested in challenging a system are those who are ignored or disadvantaged by it. The traditional hierarchies of gender place white heterosexual males above all other categories, and until recently, both the writers and readers of sf have mostly been white heterosexual men, who are all too often not even aware of the systems that favour them. Yet once gender has been called into question – by those who have incentive to do so – the invisible becomes visible, and earlier works of sf begin to seem powerfully governed by gender assumptions and systems of thought. A useful pedagogical method is to start from more recent works and then move backward, from Russ and Le Guin to Heinlein and Clarke and Asimov and beyond, to see how the earlier works imagine social arrangements and the distribution of desire.

For example, after reading Russ's treatment of a male cyborg sex slave in *The Female Man*, one is likely to notice aspects of Lester del Rey's 'Helen O'Loy' (1938) that escaped attention the first time around, or at least that seemed to escape the attention of early readers of the story.

Del Rey's story invites us to see it in romantic terms, as the story of a perfect (if artificial) woman and her selfless love for her Pygmalion-like creator. Seen through Russ's ironic lens, however, it becomes a parody of existing gender arrangements. Helen is the perfect woman because she can perform femininity perfectly. She is manufactured to masculine specifications, she learns how to 'do' womanhood by listening to soap operas and reading romance magazines, and she has no human soul to get in the way of male gratification. Because she is nothing in herself, her last act is to commit suicide – basically an act of suttee, in which the widow immolates herself on her husband's pyre.

There is no direct evidence that del Rey was aware of the ironies in his story, and it is pretty clear that most early readers either missed or ignored them, but once the invisible assumptions about gender are brought to readers' awareness, they are glaringly obvious. Other classic sf stories can be similarly reconfigured by juxtaposing them with feminist reworkings of their themes. Tom Godwin's 'The Cold Equations' (1954), for instance, involves a male pilot in a small shuttle, a female stowaway, and the implacable logic of orbits and fuel allotments that says he must jettison her or fail in his mission. Godwin's story has been read in many ways and has triggered fictional responses such as Don Sakers's 'The Cold Solution' (1991) and James Patrick Kelly's 'Think Like a Dinosaur' (1995). Most critical readings focus on the pilot's ethical dilemma and whether the story's set-up plays fair with science and engineering. Putting the story together with a novel such as Vonda McIntyre's *Superluminal* (1983), however, brings out other aspects of its emotional construction. McIntyre's main character is a woman pilot who has literally had her heart cut out – the premise is that piloting her kind of starship requires replacing natural body rhythms with a steady mechanical flow of blood. Symbolically, she has chosen science over emotion, achievement over personal attachment. Godwin's pilot does the same, though his choice is not written upon his body in such a powerfully symbolic way. McIntyre revises or reverses the gender associations upon which the earlier story depends: the dichotomy of logical, authoritative male versus vulnerable, dim-witted female, along with the masculine imperative to protect the weaker sex. After reading McIntyre, students are better able to think about the gender implications in Godwin's descriptive language, including his choice of 'girl' rather than 'young woman' to designate the female character, and the wildly inappropriate but alluring clothing she wears. They are ready to try a critical thought-experiment in reversing the genders of the characters: what happens to the emotional charge of the story's ending?

They can ask questions about why the story has always been so popular among male readers. Is it because readers identify with the compassionate pilot's reluctant acquiescence to scientific logic or because the story celebrates male exclusion of the feminine from the imaginative territory of the future? Does the pilot make a tragic choice or a clean getaway from womankind?

Such readings across the boundaries of individual texts and historical periods are justified by the dialogic nature of the genre. Science fiction has always been a collaborative form, in which stories build upon and talk back to other stories. There are various names for this sort of interaction: formula, trope, theme. I have proposed the term *parabola* to represent the use of a familiar but flexible scenario.[3] Like a fictional formula, as defined by John Cawelti in his studies of popular genres,[4] a parabola offers a set of initial situations, characters and settings, but unlike formula it does not dictate how those will evolve through the course of the story. A detective must solve a murder and a romance heroine must get married, but a science fictional hero can either solve a problem or fail to solve it, as Godwin's hero fails to save the girl. A lost colony can revert to barbarism or, just as easily, surpass its home world. The ending is open.

Furthermore, *parabola* is cognate with *parable*. This etymological kinship alerts us to the fact that sf scenarios are not merely narrative structures but also vehicles for thought. If a writer selects a familiar situation such as the creation of an artificial being, for example, a whole cluster of ideas come as part of the package: questions of responsibility and free will; echoes of *Genesis* and *Frankenstein*; and multiple, rather than dual, concepts of gendered identity, as represented in the title of Marge Piercy's cyborg novel *He, She, and It* (1991).

Sf's parabolas evolved partly as a result of the genre's incubation in the pulp magazines of the 1930s through the 1950s.[5] Editors and readers sought out stories that carried on the conversation started by other stories – or, as they might have thought about it, they wanted more of the same, only with a twist. Edmund Hamilton's version of the superman ('The Man Who Evolved', 1931) led to alternatives by Stanley Weinbaum (*The New Adam*, 1939), Henry Kuttner ('The Piper's Son', 1945), and A.E. Van Vogt (*Slan*, 1946). Murray Leinster invented a new story arc about a slow-moving starship on a generations-long journey in 'Proxima Centauri' (1935), and over the next decade writers such as Laurence Manning and Don Wilcox added details to the basic idea. Robert Heinlein offered his version of the same parabola in his story 'Universe' (1941), and Samuel Delany implicitly commented on the whole tradition in *The Ballad of Beta 2* (1965). Both of these parabolas, the superman story and the generation starship story, are still generating interesting new variations.

In these follow-ups, writers exploited logical holes and undeveloped premises offered in their predecessors' work. Each subsequent example used earlier ones as thematic springboards and as shorthand ways to fill in details of setting and back-story. Because of the prominence of parabolas and other shared structures, the genre has been compared to jazz, with writers continually improvising upon one another's melodies and chord patterns. Additionally, as reading contexts change over time, old parabolas can be reinvented to deal with new scientific discoveries, technological breakthroughs and social revolutions. By following the development of a single parabola, we can see the sf community periodically rethinking its views on terraforming, robotics, immortality or gender. The scientific backdrop together with previous stories invoking the same parabola form the cognitive horizon within which a fictional work generates meaning – its *megatext*.[6]

A number of parabolas are particularly well suited to the exploration of sexual identity and difference, and any of these could be the basis for a course in sf and gender. Each represents not only a group of thematically related readings but also a sample history of the genre and its social contexts. Each invites a different set of critical readings to accompany the stories. Depending on the level of the class, from introductory to graduate, theoretical texts can be assigned or encapsulated in lectures and handouts. The study of any parabola requires some exposure to the basic critical terminology of sf study: *megatext*, *extrapolation*, *analogy*, Darko Suvin's *cognitive estrangement*, Gary K. Wolfe's *icon*, Joanna Russ's *subjunctivity*, and so on.[7] For a focus on gender, students will also benefit from grounding in prominent feminist theorists such as Virginia Woolf, Simone de Beauvoir, Sandra Gilbert and Susan Gubar, Hélène Cixous, Julia Kristeva and Donna Haraway. Haraway's formulation of a cyborg identity[8] explicitly invokes science fictional imagery to construct a version of female identity not tied to existing religious, social and scientific models, and so Haraway's work is frequently cited by sf critics, but each of the other feminist theories interacts with science fiction in interesting ways as well. For instance, what if Woolf's 'room of one's own' becomes an entire planet of their own, as in Nicola Griffith's *Ammonite* (1993)? What if de Beauvoir's 'second sex' is the second of five gender options, rather than two, as Melissa Scott proposes in *Shadow Man* (1996)? Kristeva's idea of the *abject*, that is, that which must be cast out of consciousness in order to construct a (masculine) self,[9] can take concrete form in a piece of sf; an example might be the treatment of women in Suzette Haden Elgin's *Native Tongue* (1984). These interactions are not merely fortuitous, or the product of overly ingenious reading. Most women writers of sf since the 1970s are immersed in those very theories: they are in dialogue not only with the genre but also with the history of feminist thought. The acknowledged megatext for Gwyneth Jones's *White Queen* trilogy (1991–97), for instance, includes feminist reworkings of Jacques Lacan's psychological-semiotic theories. Jones's decision to construct fictional analogues of Lacan's ideas is discussed in her essay 'Aliens in the Fourth Dimension'.[10]

As I said above, parabolas are a particularly useful way to teach the complex history of sf's gender-coding, conscious and unconscious. Compiling a reading list for any sf course can be an exercise in frustration, since relevant stories are often available only in obscure collections and novels are likely at any time to go out of print. Yet because any given parabola is represented by a host of examples, there are always alternatives if one's first choice is unavailable. Nearly any parabola, including those mentioned above, can be investigated in terms of gender implications, but the following parabolas seem to me to be most useful in the classroom: the cyborg or artificial being, the shapeshifter, the androgyne, the single-sex utopia and the sexualized alien. Each has at least one core example. For the cyborg, C.L. Moore's 'No Woman Born' (1944) is still unsurpassed for its exploration of the implications of technological intervention into the human – and female – body. The shapeshifter or metamorphosis story is well represented by Octavia Butler's *Wild Seed* (1980), which contrasts two powerful ancestral figures: a protecting female shapeshifter and a body-stealing male spirit. Ursula K. Le Guin's *The Left Hand of Darkness* was not the first sf narrative to explore androgyny, but it established the parabola through its representation of undifferentiated, genderless beings. The same novel can also be read as a version of the single-sex utopia, but a more central instance of that parabola might be Suzy McKee Charnas's *Motherlines* (1978), in which, as Charnas says, she discovered that leaving the men out of the picture required the women characters to take on all the social and psychological roles. Finally, the parabola of the sexualized alien is summed up compactly and with devastating emotional impact in Alice Sheldon's 'And I Awoke and Found Me Here on the Cold Hill Side' (1972), set in a future in which humans respond to alien sexual signals so powerfully that they can no longer form attachments with other humans. The last of these examples has the additional virtue of being accessible in one of the most useful teaching anthologies for a gender-sf course, Justine Larbalestier's *Daughters of Earth* (2006),[11] which not only contains a number of relevant story selections but also a critical essay accompanying each.

How does one build a course around one of these parabolas? I recently taught an introduction to the literature of the fantastic (a broader category including not only sf but also many of its sources and analogues, such as classical myth, medieval romance, and the philosophical Gothic novel) organized around the theme of human-animal interfaces and transformations. It was not designed as a course in sf and gender, but it turned out that way, both because of the reading choices and because of the students' reactions to them. They discovered the gender implications early on, and without prompting from the instructor they alerted one another to many of the interactions between assigned texts. The required texts included Ovid's *Metamorphoses*, Apuleius's *The Golden Ass*, Marie de France's twelfth-century *Lais* of 'Bisclavret' and 'Yonec', Shakespeare's *The Tempest*, Coleridge's 'Christabel', and, for sf, H.G. Wells's *The Island of Doctor Moreau* (1896), Leslie F. Stone's 'The Conquest of Gola' (1931), Tiptree's 'And I Awoke' and 'The Women Men Don't See' (1972), Lisa Tuttle's 'Wives' (1976), Octavia Butler's *Clay's Ark* (1984), Pat Murphy's 'Rachel in Love' (1987), Molly Gloss's *Wild Life* (2000), and Karen Joy Fowler's 'What I Didn't See' (2002). All of the science fiction short stories except for the second Tiptree selection are found in Larbalestier's anthology.

Each text includes some sort of breaching of the boundary between human and animal. In the first half of the course, the transformations were magical or miraculous. Ovid, for instance, shows the gods turning human characters into stags, dolphins and spiders; Apuleius's protagonist spends much of the story in the form of an ass as a result of a spell gone awry; Marie's romances involve a werewolf and a knight who takes falcon form; Shakespeare's magician Prospero exerts his will through his two nonhuman slaves, birdlike Ariel and bestial Caliban; Coleridge's heroine is threatened by the shapeshifting, serpent-like Geraldine. With Wells, the course moved into sf proper, as magical transformations give way to biological processes and technological interventions. Doctor Moreau uses surgery and conditioning to turn a whole menagerie into quasi-people; Stone's 'Gola' presents a conflict between two races, each of which views the other as subhuman animals; Tiptree's 'The Women Men Don't See' involves not only an animal-like alien but also a pervasive metaphor that represents two of the characters as opossums living in secret niches in society; Tuttle shows aliens coerced into living as companions to human men; Butler's novel hinges on an alien plague that turns people into lean, wolflike predators; Murphy tells about a chimpanzee imprinted with the personality and memories of a teenage girl; Gloss's novel involves an interaction with anthropoids living in the dense forests of the Cascade Mountains; and Fowler's Nebula-Award-winning story uses a gorilla-hunting expedition in the 1920s to explore issues of racism, ageing, sexuality and both inter- and intra-species violence.

With this last story, the parabolic nature of the genre becomes explicit and is part of the meaning of the story, for both Fowler's title and the contents of her tale refer to the life and work of James Tiptree Jr. 'What I Didn't See' transforms Tiptree's 'The Women Men Don't See' into something simultaneously more personal and more universal: a first-person singular pronoun replaces the third-person plural noun, but the 'I' of the title can stand for both women and men who fail to see one another as well as the natural world around them. The gorilla hunt in the story is drawn from an incident in the life of Mary Bradley, mother of Alice Sheldon, creator of the masculine pen name and persona Tiptree.[12] Fowler's story is explicitly intertextual, but, again reading backward from recent to earlier works of sf, it alerts us to the degree of intertextuality that has always characterized the genre. It deals explicitly with gender, in the form of the expectations, constraints, poses and posturings that arise from the characters' positions as alpha male, desirable female, older and presumably desexualized female and so on. The narrator comments on these roles, which she has become aware of (and impatient with) through many intervening years and social upheavals. Reading other works from her perspective, we can see many of the same gendered assumptions operating in Tiptree's own story and on back through earlier works.

In teaching this interlocking set of readings, I first offered the students a stock of critical terms and strategies. One especially useful strategy for any study of gender, for example, is the structuralist trick of identifying binary oppositions in a story (human/animal, good/evil, masculine/feminine and so on) and looking for the way in which the events of the story rearrange those binaries. After demonstrating these techniques, I more or less stood back to see what would happen. Students were asked to read the stories, comment on them in an online forum, and then respond to someone else's forum posting, all before we talked about the stories together in class. Discussion of gender roles and identities began early on. The sexual content of Apuleius's bawdy tale led to heated debate over whether the story was sexist – for instance, was the wealthy woman who wanted to mate with the protagonist in donkey form any more ridiculous than the various male suitors and sinners? That led to the idea that species difference could stand in for sexual difference – that all heterosexual pairings could be read as versions of bestiality, an idea exploited in sf stories of the sexualized alien such as Tiptree's 'And I Awoke' or Tuttle's 'Wives'. By the time we got to Shakespeare, the class was ready to take Prospero to task for his assumption of control not only over his nonhuman slaves but also over the only female in the story, his daughter Miranda. Later on, one student proposed a quite compelling reading of Murphy's 'Rachel in Love' as a science fictional version of *The Tempest*, with the magician rewritten as a scientist, and the blended human/animal Rachel as both Miranda and Caliban.

In the above descriptions of some of the stories, I deliberately left out the gender content, since that was not the planned emphasis in the class. Yet, as students noted, every one of the stories is rife with gendered assumptions and challenges to those assumptions. The invading race in 'Conquest of Gola' is male; the defending Golans are matriarchal. Tuttle's 'Wives' are genderless aliens, but the role they are forced to play is that of playmates for the male explorers from earth – they must squeeze themselves into a painful and distorting femininity like feet into foot-binding shoes. Everywhere we looked in the stories we saw disguises and transformations, animals-as-humans and humans-as-animals, and the deeply disorienting effect of the Other looking back at oneself. Each of these elements, too, can function as a metaphor for sexual difference, and the more stories we read, the more they seemed to invite such readings. Stories began to converse with, even to rewrite other stories. Themes reinforced and complicated one another. All of this required almost no intervention from the instructor.

My main job was to keep reminding the class about historical contexts (though we allowed ourselves a bit of creative anachronism) and about the fact that theme is inseparable from form. I called attention to framing devices; fallible characters used as focalizers; narrative gaps; and the ways different voices might be heard directly, indirectly, or not at all in a given text. I asked students to look more closely at key scenes and even individual sentences to see how those contribute to the creation of a world unlike but related to our own and how they advance particular themes.

By the end of the course, we had discovered a specific and powerful story-form that might be called the Parabola of the Hidden Woman. Central examples were 'The Women Men Don't See', 'Rachel in Love', *Wild Life*, and 'What I Didn't See', although all the other readings from the course were related in some way, and one can detect hints of other cultural references, from *Tarzan* to *King Kong* to Hemingway's 'The Short

Happy Life of Francis McComber' (1936). This parabola is related to the sexualized alien, the shapeshifter and the single-sex utopia, but it is marked off from them by a particular setting, a cast of characters, a central action, and a number of thematic concerns, any of which can be brought forward at the author's discretion. The setting is somewhere exotic, outside of civilization. Tiptree's foundational text is set in the lowland coast of the Yucatan peninsula, Murphy's story takes place in the desert Southwest, Gloss's novel moves into the rain-drenched forests of western Washington, and Fowler's story unfolds in the Central African highlands. The reason for the exotic setting seems to be that in such a place many things might still be undiscovered: there are mysteries to be explored. In addition, the farther one moves from the centres of civilization, the more open to question social norms become.

Characters in the parabola include male scientists or explorers, female characters (often older women) who are outside the power structures of civilized society and who therefore see those structures at a critical remove, and a race of previously undiscovered intelligent aliens or nonhumans with whom the female characters come to identify. These roles can reduplicate or combine: Rachel, in 'Rachel in Love', is both the unconsidered woman and the alien. The action of each story involves sexual desire that is somehow frustrated or denied, a threatened or overt act of masculine violence, and an escape. The desire, the violence and the escape are all set in motion by a failure of perception: someone doesn't see someone or something else. In spite of these similarities between the stories, the mood and message of each is quite different. Tiptree's is characteristically bleak – the story implies that the only cure for gender difference is complete separation. Murphy's story, by contrast, strikes a positive note in spite of Rachel's potentially tragic situation: the mind of a young girl trapped in the body of a chimp. Rachel does find love, of a sort; she establishes communication through sign language; and even gains the legal right to her father/creator's ranch. Gloss's novel includes both loss and gain: it combines a Crusoe-esque story of survival in the wild and a voyage inward toward greater artistry. And Fowler implicates us all in the destruction of the gentle forest giants: her story, though feminist, doesn't let women take the moral high ground. This is a wide range of messages, and yet all tell something like the same story. Together, they form a much richer and more complex artistic pattern than any one of the stories in isolation, and they have more to say about our gendered ways of thinking and acting.

Similar groupings of readings could be developed for each of the parabolas mentioned above. For a course on the cyborg or artificial being, one might start with Mary Shelley's *Frankenstein* (1818), then move to del Rey's 'Helen O'Loy', Moore's 'No Woman Born', and Isaac Asimov's *I, Robot* (1950). (With regard to that last selection, nobody says that a story has to be feminist to have gender implications.) Next could come Tanith Lee's *The Silver Metal Lover* (1981), Piercy's *He, She, and It* and Emma Bull's *Bone Dance* (1991). There are many works in other media that could be incorporated as well, including the paired (but asymmetrical) TV series *The Six-Million Dollar Man* and *The Bionic Woman* and the films *Android* (1982) and *Making Mr. Right* (1987). Issues raised within this parabola include the relationship between body shape and identity, the implications of being able to choose one's gendered identity, the roles of mother and father and the possibilities of female paternity and male maternity; and the projection of sexual desire and therefore gender onto a machine.

Stories about shapeshifters go back to antiquity, but within the era of modern science fiction, one might include *Dracula* (1897), not really sf, but influential on the genre; John W. Campbell's 'Who Goes There?' (1938), the source of the Christian Nyby/Howard Hawks film *The Thing from Another World* (1951); Jack Williamson's *Darker Than You Think* (1948), a werewolf story with a strong dose of psychoanalysis and a lot of interesting gender construction; and Octavia Butler's *Wild Seed*. Always implicit in the shapeshifter scenario is the possibility of crossing gender lines, and this becomes the focus in several of John Varley's stories, especially his 'Options' (1980) and in Elisabeth Vonarburg's *La Silence de la Cité* (1981; translated as *The Silent City*, 1988). Virtual reality offers a new way of changing shape and gender, as explored in depth in Melissa Scott's *Trouble and Her Friends* (1994). When film and television take up the possibility of altering one's form, transformations between species are common but those across gender barriers are generally avoided, as with the shapeshifting Changeling race on *Star Trek: Deep Space Nine* (1993–99). Having male characters suddenly become female or vice versa evidently disturbs too many sexual taboos for the mainstream media, though *Star Trek: The Next Generation* (1987–94) did toy with the idea via its symbiotic species the Trill, which can inhabit male and female hosts over its long lifespan.

Androgynous beings appear in many myths, including a mock creation myth in Plato's *Symposium*. As mentioned above, the best known treatment of the theme, and the one that launched it as a parabola, is Le Guin's *The Left Hand of Darkness*, set on a planet whose inhabitants are hermaphroditic. Most of the time they are sexually neutral or latent, but in a phase of sexual receptivity called *kemmer*, they can take on the characteristics of either sex. The same individual can, at different times, both father and bear children. One strength of the novel is its exploration of the social implications of this arrangement: for instance, there is no rape, and no one is especially tied down by children because all are subject to childbearing. Le Guin has returned to the same imagined world in a short story called 'Coming of Age in Karhide' (1996), which explores some implications, especially regarding sexuality, that were left out of the novel.[13] An earlier work by Theodore Sturgeon, *Venus Plus X* (1960), imagines a similarly hermaphroditic race, which turns out to have been artificially created as a solution to many of humanity's deepest problems. David Gerrold's *Moonstar Odyssey* (1977) imagines a world in which individuals select a gender only upon reaching sexual maturity. Kelly Eskridge's story 'And Salome Danced' (1994) has a character of indeterminate sex who seems to be whatever the other characters desire her/him to be. Raphael Carter's 'Congenital Agenesis of Gender Ideation, by K.N. Sirsi and Sandra Botkin' (1998) is written in the form of a scientific paper on the inability of certain individuals to assign gender to others, though the problem turns out to be not blindness to gender but overly-acute awareness of it. The individuals affected perceive not two genders but twenty-two, which barely correspond with our conventional pair. In the absence of a clear binary system, everyone is potentially androgynous.

The idea of a single-sex utopia is that females or males can fully exhibit their gendered identities without interference or influence from the other sex. A closely related form of utopia includes both sexes, but puts one or the other in charge. That description is somewhat misleading: a work of fiction that imagines men in charge is not likely to be read as utopian or even science fictional – it comes too close to a zero degree of subjunctivity, or deviation from the historical world. Yet there are such works, and they include Elgin's *Native Tongue* as well as Katherine Burdekin's *Swastika Night* (1937), Margaret Atwood's *The Handmaid's Tale* (1985) and Suzy McKee Charnas's *Walk to the End of the World* (1974). These novels are utopian, in the larger sense of the word. Any rationally conceived ideal society contains potential flaws or abuses – the defects of its virtues. By emphasizing these, rather than improvements over current social systems, writers can turn the hopeful vision, sometimes called *eutopia* (or *utopia*), into its photographic negative, the social-experiment-gone-wrong or *dystopia*. Elgin's, Burdekin's, Atwood's and Charnas's novels are dystopian looks at patriarchy. They function simultaneously as warnings about future trends and as satires on existing society.

Utopias with women in charge, or with women entirely alone, fall into two main categories. There are dystopias written by men, emphasizing women's supposed inability to invent or adapt or organize – or their tendency to organize too well, forming a sort of hive society. These stories include William G. West's 'The Last Man' (1929), Edmund Cooper's *Gender Genocide* (1972) and a number of works in between, many of them explored in Joanna Russ's essay *'Amor Vincit Foeminam*: The Battle of the Sexes in Science Fiction' (1980).[14] A more recent work that hovers between positive utopia and anti-feminist dystopia is David Brin's *Glory Season* (1993). When women write about all-female or female-dominated societies, the result is much more likely to fall toward the positive, utopian side. After a handful of early works such as Gilman's *Herland* or Mary Bradley Lane's *Mizora* (1890), the form disappeared until the rise of second-wave feminism in the 1960s, which produced Charnas's *Motherlines* as well as Monique Wittig's *Les Guérillères* (1969), Dorothy Bryant's *The Kin of Ata Are Waiting for You* (1971), Sally Miller Gearhart's *The Wanderground* (1979), Alice Sheldon's 'Houston, Houston, Do You Read?' (1976; published as by James Tiptree Jr) and 'Your Faces, O My Sisters! Your Faces Filled of Light!' (1976; published as by Raccoona Sheldon) and Russ's *The Female Man*. More recently, a number of feminist works, while still more eu- than dys-topian, explore the difficulties of achieving a feminist paradise and even some of the darker ramifications of a society without gender balance. These include Joan Slonczewski's *A Door into Ocean* (1986), Nicola Griffith's *Ammonite* (1992) and Sheri S. Tepper's *The Gate to Women's Country* (1988).

One outgrowth of feminist critique has been the recognition that masculinity too is constructed and often constricting. Following on the all-female utopias, a few male separatist societies have appeared in sf – most of them, to date, written by women. The most fully developed are Lois McMaster Bujold's *Ethan of Athos* (1986), Ursula K. Le Guin's 'The Matter of Seggri' (1994) and Eleanor Arnason's *Ring of Swords* (1993). In the last two, the all-male society is paired, naturally enough, with a corresponding all-female society, though we don't see those close at hand. One additional work depicts not only sexually segregated societies but even the moment of division. In Philip Wylie's *The Disappearance* (1951), the separation is not a deliberate utopian venture but a mysterious occult event that pulls men and women into separate dimensions. Each group has to recreate the world with one half of its population missing. For women, the greatest challenge is stepping into leadership roles that have been denied them; for men, it is getting over masculine posturing and competitiveness. The women fare better.

Utopian fiction is relatively easy to teach. There are many fine critical and theoretical works to consult,[15] and the form lends itself naturally to classroom debate and writing assignments – design your own utopia, argue for your own society as a form of utopia, identify trends in today's world that could lead to dystopia. The parabola of the sexualized alien is considerably more difficult to turn into a teaching unit. Even if students have no problem reading about sexual matters, they are likely to balk at talking about them in class. It is possible to assemble a set of readings on sex or sexual desire between humans and aliens, though, and most of them are relatively tame with regard to erotic content, partly because the genre grew up with a strict code of censorship over such matters. Sex had to be snuck in, often disguised as something else. Many of the magazine stories of the 1930s are full of weirdly sexualized imagery, but that imagery is frequently attached to machines or bits of landscape. A good example (but unfortunately not an easy one to get hold of) is John Edwards's 'The Planet of Perpetual Night'. Edwards describes both a machine and a landscape apparently getting it on: 'Watching closely the blue beam, Dr. Davidson noted that it was slowly but surely pushing its sputtering way down to the surface below, moving and thrusting like a shaft of solid fire through the strange black shroud which obstructed its progress like a solid thing.'[16]

By the 1950s, however, sex could at least be considered, and Philip Jose Farmer was one of the first writers to take advantage of the change. His story 'The Lovers' (1953) started the parabola of human/alien sexuality, and a number of his later stories explore the possibilities, always from the point of view of a male human confronting female or feminized aliens. His aliens are genuinely weird, at least, and not just green-skinned dancing girls, as in the classic *Star Trek* episodes and a host of B-grade movies. Paul Park's *Coelestis* (1993) explores another side of the scenario of masculine desire, with an alien creature deliberately impersonating a female human. Park's novel is as much about colonization as sexuality, but in Lisa Tuttle's 'Wives', sexuality *is* colonization. The title of Tuttle's story is carefully chosen: it is about wives, not women, and about the process that warps the latter into the former. Tiptree's 'And I Awoke' is an essential work in this parabola; it is also included in a collection of such stories, *Alien Sex*, edited by Ellen Datlow.[17] The collection contains stories by Harlan Ellison, Pat Cadigan, Geoff Ryman, Pat Murphy and many other major sf writers.

Whichever parabola one teaches, the point is that science fiction is not only a collection of individual works of varying quality but also a collective enterprise. Reading masterworks such as *The Left Hand of*

Darkness not as isolated creations but as voices in a ongoing debate is the best way to let students discover that the genre is, above all, a way of thinking about things. One of the things it thinks about in particularly interesting ways is gender. Clustering together works related by form, theme, or the combination of form and theme that I am calling parabola allows individual texts to pose questions to which other texts may propose answers. Within any given parabola, the primary texts are also the best theoretical sources, offering the deepest insights into their own inner workings. Here I am in agreement with Carl Freedman, who proposes that science fiction is itself a form of critical theory.[18] The great theorists of sf – that is, Russ, Le Guin, Tiptree and so on – are the best teachers as well. They can teach students to ask questions where no questions are usually expected, where things 'go without saying'. Sf can teach us all to query the basic structures of thought and identity, including gender.

Notes

1. There are a number of useful studies of science fiction and gender, including Brian Attebery, *Decoding Gender in Science Fiction* (New York and London: Routledge, 2002); Marleen S. Barr, *Lost in Space: Probing Feminist Science Fiction and Beyond* (Chapel Hill and London: University of North Carolina Press, 1993); Jane Donawerth, *Frankenstein's Daughters: Women Writing Science Fiction* (Syracuse: Syracuse University Press, 1997); Justine Larbalestier, *The Battle of the Sexes in Science Fiction* (Middletown, CT: Wesleyan University Press, 2002); Sarah Lefanu, *In the Chinks of the World Machine: Feminism and Science Fiction* (London: Women's Press, 1988); Robin Roberts, *A New Species: Gender and Science in Science Fiction* (Urbana and Chicago: University of Chicago Press, 1993); Joanna Russ, *To Write Like a Woman: Essays in Feminism and Science Fiction* (Bloomington and Indianapolis: Indiana University Press, 1995); Lisa Yaszek, *Galactic Suburbia: Recovering Women's Science Fiction* (Columbus: Ohio State University Press, 2008).
2. Karen Joy Fowler, 'On James Tiptree, Alice Sheldon, and Bake Sales', 1996, http://www.scifi.com/sfw/issue22/tiptree.html (accessed 14 June 2008).
3. Brian Attebery, 'Science Fiction, Parable, and Parabolas', *Foundation: The International Review of Science Fiction*, 95 (2005): 7–22.
4. John G. Cawelti, *The Six-Gun Mystique* (Bowling Green, OH: Bowling Green University Popular Press, 1971); *Adventure, Mystery, and Romance: Formula Stories as Art and Popular Culture* (Chicago and London: University of Chicago Press, 1976).
5. Histories of the genre paying particular attention to the magazine era include Brian W. Aldiss with David Wingrove, *Trillion Year Spree: The History of Science Fiction* (New York: Avon, 1986); Mike Ashley, *The Time Machines: The Story of the Science-Fiction Pulp Magazines from the Beginning to 1950* (Liverpool: Liverpool University Press, 2000); Paul A. Carter, *The Creation of Tomorrow: Fifty Years of*

Magazine Science Fiction (New York: Columbia University Press, 1977); Edward James, *Science Fiction in the Twentieth Century* (Oxford and New York: Oxford University Press, 1994); and Brooks Landon, *Science Fiction after 1900: From the Steam Man to the Stars* (New York: Twayne, 1997).
6. The term *megatext* was borrowed from narratologist Philippe Hamon for use in science fiction criticism more or less simultaneously by Damien Broderick and Brian Attebery: see Broderick, 'Reading SF as a Mega-text', *New York Review of Science Fiction*, 47 (1992): 9; Attebery, *Strategies of Fantasy* (Bloomington and Indianapolis: Indiana University Press, 1992).
7. Darko Suvin, *Metamorphoses of Science Fiction: On the Poetics and History of a Literary Genre* (New Haven and London: Yale University Press, 1979); Gary K. Wolfe, *The Known and the Unknown: The Iconography of Science Fiction* (Kent, OH: Kent State University Press, 1979); Joanna Russ, 'Speculations: The Subjunctivity of Science Fiction', in *To Write Like a Woman*, 15–25.
8. Donna J. Haraway, 'A Cyborg Manifesto: Science, Technology, and Socialist-Feminism in the Late Twentieth Century', 1985; rpt. in *Simians, Cyborgs, and Women: The Reinvention of Nature* (New York and London: Routledge, 1991) 149–81.
9. Julia Kristeva, *Powers of Horror: An Essay on Abjection*, trans. Leon S. Roudiez (New York: Columbia University Press, 1982).
10. Gwyneth Jones, 'Aliens in the Fourth Dimension', in *Deconstructing the Starships: Science, Fiction and Reality* (Liverpool: Liverpool University Press, 1999) 108–19.
11. Justine Larbalestier, ed., *Daughters of Earth: Feminist Science Fiction in the Twentieth Century* (Middletown, CT: Wesleyan University Press, 2006).
12. Julie Philips, *James Tiptree, Jr.: The Double Life of Alice B. Sheldon* (New York: St Martin's Press, 2006).
13. Le Guin's version of androgyny has been attacked as implicitly privileging the masculine or assuming gender differences as natural or universal: see, for instance, Craig Barrow and Diana Barrow, '*The Left Hand of Darkness*: Feminism for Men', *Mosaic*, 20:1 (1987): 83–96. For Le Guin's own rethinking of the issue, see 'Is Gender Necessary? Redux', in *Dancing at the Edge of the World: Thoughts on Words, Women, Places* (New York: Grove, 1989) 7–16.
14. Joanna Russ, '*Amor Vincit Foeminam*: the Battle of the Sexes in Science Fiction', 1980; rpt. in *To Write Like a Woman*, 41–59.
15. See, for example, Tom Moylan, *Demand the Impossible: Science Fiction and the Utopian Imagination* (New York and London: Methuen, 1986) and Chris Ferns, *Narrating Utopia: Ideology, Gender, Form in Utopian Literature* (Liverpool: Liverpool University Press, 1999).
16. John Edwards, 'The Planet of Perpetual Night', *Amazing Stories*, 11:1 (1937): 15–57 at 52.
17. Ellen Datlow, ed., *Alien Sex* (New York: Dutton, 1990).
18. Carl Freedman, *Critical Theory and Science Fiction* (Hanover and London: Wesleyan University Press, 2000).

10
Teaching Postcolonial Science Fiction

Uppinder Mehan

Postcolonial science fiction is science fiction written by those who are the 'survivors – or descendants of survivors – of sustained, racial colonial processes; the members of cultures of resistance to colonial oppression; the members of minority cultures which are essentially colonized nations within a larger nation; and those of us who identify ourselves as having Aboriginal, African, South Asian, Asian ancestry, wherever we make our homes.' I shamelessly borrow from my afterword to the collection of short stories I was fortunate enough to co-edit with Nalo Hopkinson, *So Long Been Dreaming: Postcolonial Science Fiction and Fantasy*, because that polemical point brings up an important issue of identification.[1]

As is the case in studying and teaching postcolonial literature in general, so also is it the case in studying and teaching postcolonial science fiction that there is a broad distinction to be made between the literature of the colonizer and the literature of the colonized. This distinction lead to two different critical assumptions that guide analysis: the literature of the colonizer is examined in order to reveal its underlying racist and ethnocentric assumptions; the literature of the colonized is examined in order to understand how it responds to the colonizer, and how it imagines a future. While it is important to show the colonialist underpinnings of the literature of the colonizer, and I will address some of these issues below, I feel the greater focus should be on the literature of the (formerly) colonized. I should also point out a couple of caveats that anyone who has taught postcolonial literature for some length of time already knows: one, although colonialism formally ended around the second half of the twentieth century, imperialist nations are still structured by their colonial adventures and are still greatly conditioned by 'the rhetoric of empire' (as, of course, are the politically decolonized nations); two, much important literature of the colonizer is highly critical of colonialism and empire, and, conversely, not all literature of the colonized is automatically devoid of imperialist, racist and ethnocentric elements. The remainder of this chapter is divided into three connected sections: the first section, on postcolonial science fiction, examines the peculiar understanding postcolonial science fiction writers have of technology, history and the body; the second section, on colonial science fiction, examines racist and colonial/imperial assumptions in science fiction in general; and the third section introduces dissident science fiction which, although not written by postcolonial writers, is highly critical of colonialist/imperialist assumptions. When I teach postcolonial science fiction I find it useful to start by studying a couple of colonialist science fiction works. I have made use of H. Beam Piper's *The Fuzzy Papers* (coll. *Little Fuzzy*, 1962, and *Fuzzy Sapiens*, 1964) (and will make use of Mike Resnick's *Paradise*, 1989, the next time I teach the class) as an example of a novel that seems to me to be entirely unconscious of its racist and patronizing elements. It may appear so to inexperienced readers as well since its plot revolves around the question of sentience and the determination of sovereignty. For the purposes of this chapter with its focus on teaching postcolonial science fiction that is where I will begin.

Postcolonial science fiction

Although it is a truism that sf treats technology ambivalently (it is both the problem and the solution), postcolonial sf adds a further complication. The formerly colonized countries mistrust technology because it is seen as an 'alien' imposition by the colonizer – an imposition that shatters familiar cultural and social patterns (and in many cases the 'alien' technology destroys a native technology and supplants it) – but at the same time it is recognized that technology is the key to a more prosperous future. One fictional response to such a dilemma is to accept the technology but put it to the service of native goals, another response is to treat the technology as an inferior version of an earlier native practice, a third response explores the development of native technologies that had either been disrupted or ones that answer culture-specific concerns (see my article 'The Domestication of Technology...' for specific examples of Indian sf touching on these aspects[2]).

Surprisingly, the great anxiety and fear of technology enslaving humanity is not a strong feature of postcolonial sf partly because the survivors of colonialism realize that 'the degradation and dehumanisation caused by machines is nothing as compared to that imposed by poverty'.[3]

A remarkable postcolonial sf novel by Nalo Hopkinson presents an acceptance of technology that is more likely to be associated with the degrading surveillance of Big Brother in colonialist sf. In *Midnight Robber*, nanotechnology (one nanometer is 10^{-9} or one billionth of a meter) combined with AI (Artificial Intelligence) programs have enabled enterprising cultural groups to make entire planets inhabitable with a minimum of labour. The world in *Midnight Robber* is that of a Caribbean culture transported to its own planet. Caribbean traditions and holidays are maintained with an eye toward remembering and celebrating the past and present. Each member of the culture is born with nanomites already at work building an earbug that puts one in continuous communication with the main AI program, the beneficent Granny Nanny who helps maintain ease and social order.

Hopkinson could have given us a tale of the intrigues and predations of the Marryshow Corporation in the development of its Grande Nanotech Sentient Interface software that mimics the divine creative act in making the world ready for human habitation. She could have given us a tale of programming machines turning us into programmed beings. In other words, *Midnight Robber* could have been a story of the excesses of technological dependence and control (it is, but only in part) and it might even be appropriate for a writer from one of the victimized cultures of techno-imperialism to cast technology as only a negative. What we are offered instead is a tale of technology as a wise and beneficent god. The main AI program monitors and communicates through an aspect of itself affectionately called Granny Nanny. This humanly-perceptible reduced version of the main program that can see in all dimensions is individually attuned to every single person through sub-programs that are called Eshu. The Eshu are also AI programs that rest inside one's head and are primarily used to access information and to make life almost labour-free. Finally, technology has made it possible to labour authentically; no longer are workers trapped in the Marxian hell of sacrificing their art and labour in the production of an alienated object.[4] No one need work; those who do so select the crafts that satisfy some need. Or so it appears, for some of these workers are busy re-learning older technologies in order to produce goods that will allow Granny Nanny to gather only the most basic information about their physical health. As it turns out Granny Nanny gives them the illusion that they can create a system of goods and services outside her ken until she finds it necessary to punish those who harm others with their free will.

Granny Nanny is not simply a humanizing trope, translating the machine intelligence into a doting caretaker, it is also laden with a historical dimension of rebellion and protection. Granny Nanny was the *nom de guerre* of a slave woman in eighteenth-century Jamaica who escaped with members of her family into one of the Maroon communities and formed Nanny Town. Declared a national heroine in Jamaica in 1975, Granny Nanny helped free hundreds of slaves and repeatedly repelled the British over a period of some fifty years. Having knowledge of the historical Granny Nanny greatly affects the acceptance or rejection of technology in *Midnight Robber*, and postcolonial sf in general calls for a historical awareness in order to more fully comprehend and appreciate the plots and ideas of such novels.

Accordingly, Archie Weller's *Land of the Golden Clouds* assumes that the reader is aware of the historical nightmare of Australia's Aboriginal peoples. This dystopic novel is set some three thousand years after a nuclear holocaust in the second millennium. The plot revolves around the enmity between those who dwell on the surface and those who dwell underground. The hero's journey to the final battle site takes him through remnants of various deformed cultures from contemporary Australia as he gathers a band of fighters to face the Nightstalkers. The coda to the story shows how the two sides learn to work together and live in harmony. However, just before the big celebration that marks the end of the conflict, the major Aboriginal warriors leave with their leader. The surviving Aboriginals decline membership in the new multicultural Australia and go back to the land and their ancient ways.

An awareness of Australian history helps explain the refusal of Weerluk and Mungart (the twin warriors of The Keepers of The Trees) to join the new society. Contemporary Aborigines in Australia have already suffered an eco- and techno-catastrophe. In 1778 when Europeans started arriving in substantial numbers there were 300,000 Aborigines divided into over 500 tribes, each with their own distinct territory, history, dialect and culture. Just as in the US and Canada, so too in Australia; Dalaipi, a Queensland Aborigine, speaking in 1896 gives a tragic summary of European-Aboriginal interactions: 'We were hunted from our ground, shot, poisoned, and had our daughters, sisters and wives taken from us. They stole our ground where we used to get food, and when we got hungry and took a bit of flour or killed a bullock to eat, they shot us or poisoned us. All they give us now for our land is a blanket once a year.'[5]

Strongly connected to the issues of history and technology is the postcolonial body. Both postcolonial and sf writers have a rich literary history of complicating the notion of the body as an unmediated and sovereign entity: postcolonial writing examines the effects on identity when a profound distance is created between self and body by the histories of slavery and conquest which erase the lively and vibrant cultural context necessary for a fuller understanding of the native's body, and by the 'scientific' construction of the black or brown body as either inferior or superior to but definitely different from the 'normal' white body; while sf tales of robots, shape-shifting and humanoid aliens, androids, clones and cyberspace have all contributed to calling into question the 'natural' body far earlier than most commentators and critics. Although some sf writers have allegorically addressed the significance of bodies via alien versus human bodies or artificial versus human bodies, most have assumed when pressed that the constructs of race have disappeared in the far future. Unfortunately, the black or brown body is often the one that disappears in the new post-racial body. Both Samuel Delany and John Varley give us remarkable futures (Delany's *Triton*, 1976; and any fiction of Varley's set in Luna, *Steel Beach*, 1992, for example) where body and gender modification are considered the norm. None of Varley's characters are black and none consider becoming black whereas Delany's characters readily play with racial signifiers.

Perhaps the sf writer who has most consistently and most forcefully explored the territory of history, technology and body is Octavia E. Butler. The most significant discourse helping define the body and self in her Xenogenesis trilogy (*Dawn*, 1987; *Adulthood Rites*, 1988; and *Imago*, 1989; collected together in one volume as *Lilith's Brood*, 2000) is that of slavery. The trilogy focuses on a breeding programme, as did her Patternist series, but this time post-nuclear apocalypse humans are confronted by the alien oankali who make the humans an interbreeding offer they can't refuse. The oankali value biological diversity above all else, and they have come to an earth where those surviving humans are either sterile or give birth to horrific offspring. The trade the oankali offer is to make humans fertile and whole and physically far superior in return for the privilege of mating with us. The central character of the first novel and one of the main characters in the second and third is an African-American woman named Lilith who lost her husband and son in the nuclear catastrophe. She resists the offer of the oankali. Lilith's initial refusal is understandable but given that her only other option is, at best, to live out a sterile life in an isolated village, her reluctance makes less logical sense without an understanding of the lack of control over one's own body in slavery and the body under the oankali.

The opening scene of *Dawn* has almost nothing to do with aliens; Lilith could be in solitary confinement in any prison. She learns eventually that the prison is an organic part of a biological spaceship grown from a seed. The aliens travel from star to star, planet to planet, exchanging biological and cultural material and information with the many species they contact. The oankali are determined to offer Lilith a better life. They try to create human families for her, enhance her brain so that she can recall and learn with ridiculous ease, give her almost superhuman reflexes and healing abilities, but Lilith rejects them. She correctly sees that the more she lets them do for her, the less she remains herself. Although the oankali are not responsible for having separated Lilith from her family, they behave like slave owners who viewed the breeding of their slaves as their prerogative. By refusing to let her have paper and writing instruments, the oankali imitate slave owners who saw in education a threat to their control. In short, the oankali behave like the colonizers who seek to remake the savage into a more civilized being. Of course, by the end of the first part of the trilogy Lilith has been made pregnant by the aliens, and she spends the rest of her life trying to reconcile her conflicting feelings.

Colonial science fiction

The phrase I used earlier, 'the rhetoric of empire', is also the title of an insightful work by David Spurr which looks at the major tropes in colonial discourse.[6] Although Spurr's interest is in travel writing, journalism and imperial administration, the tropes of colonial discourse are in play throughout the field of postcolonial writing in general. After a brief discussion of the word 'alien' and the easy substitution of 'alien' for any number of minority groups (from Pacific Islanders to Native Americans to women to Easterners to Africans to African-Americans), I find it useful to begin by discussing briefly how Spurr's tropes are easily found in science fiction. A good trope for beginning a discussion of colonialism in science fiction is that of surveillance. There is little more powerful than a ship in orbit around one's planet to signal discovery and control. The distance of the ship from the planet is necessitated by physical laws of space travel but the orbiting also serves as a period of assessment and preparation for a safe, antiseptic entry into the alien biosphere. The fear of contamination in science fiction is rooted in biological safety rather than psychological unease, but it is often a short a step to viewing the alien native through the trope of debasement as the source of that contamination. If it is we humans who have come to the alien home world then, of course, we must be the more technologically advanced beings and therefore the natives are inferior to us (classification) and their real history starts with our arrival (negation). Spurr's discussion includes seven more tropes and I make use of them as occasion demands but those discussed above are a productive beginning. The main principle is that the tropes are a means of organizing either conscious justifications for eradicating others and taking over their land or subconscious attempts at reducing the cognitive dissonance that comes about from knowing that one is behaving abominably but wanting to believe that one is a good and moral being.

Rather than presenting a catalogue of the numerous thinly disguised colonialist science fiction novels, I'll mention two that allegorize settler colonization and occupation colonization (I take the terms from *The Empire Writes Back*, 1989, by Ashcroft, Griffiths and Tiffin as this is still the best introduction to the major issues of and approaches to postcolonial literature[7]). A settler colony takes over an area completely (Australia, for example) by eradicating or displacing any indigenes; indeed, the rhetoric of the settlers often figures the land as empty, awaiting development. The planet Zarathustra in *The Fuzzy Papers* by H. Beam Piper is valued for its mineral deposits and is seen to be devoid of any native life until a prospector, Jack Holloway, accidentally comes across a small furry biped. Holloway names this particular native Little Fuzzy and the rest of the story is a struggle between the rich, evil corporation that wants all rights to the planet and the Fuzzies. Much of the novel is taken up in establishing that the Fuzzies are sentient and that they have rights to the planet that supersede the rights of the corporation. This is certainly a step up from humans encountering BEMs (bug-eyed monsters) and just blowing them up, but it is a very small step. The Fuzzies apparently love Holloway and the 'good' humans and seek to re-make themselves over in their image. Piper inserts the occasional comment regarding the virtues of the simple life as practised by the Fuzzies but, on the whole, the natives are represented as innocent children in desperate need of protection and guidance. As it turns out, the economic justification for continued interaction between the Fuzzies and humanity is the presence of a euphoric bond between the two species somewhat like the affection between parents and children and pets. The Fuzzies are granted full sentience status and rights but the humans are clearly in control, and Piper makes it clear that the natives much prefer the joys of an idyllic existence to the burdens of administration and development.

Unlike the colonization of uninhabited new lands, the colonization of sovereign existing lands fully acknowledges a conflict between two populations over a territory. The rhetoric of discovery and the frontier gives way to the rhetoric of development. The occupiers willingly take on Kipling's 'white man's burden' in order to develop the land and to bring enlightenment and morality to the natives. All the civilizing weight falls on humans in Mike Resnick's novel *Paradise*. With his tongue firmly in his cheek Resnick informs the reader in the foreword that a parable Kenyans tell each other about the self-destructive nature of Africa 'obviously has nothing to do with this novel, which is about the mythical world of Peponi rather than the very real nation of Kenya'.[8] Anyone familiar with Kenya's history will recognize that Resnick has rewritten its colonialist past with a minimal patina of science fictionalization (instead of seagoing ships and aircraft there are spaceships, instead of the country of Kenya there is the planet of Peponi, instead of rhinos and elephants there are 'landships' which provide their version of ivory). Resnick has the narrator express admiration for the efforts of a particular native leader's attempts to develop his planet but nowhere in Resnick's universe has the educated native leader found a formerly undeveloped world become a developed country. A cursory examination of postcolonial countries in the real world would have shown Resnick a number of successes, and if not successes then certainly a variety of strategies that have contributed to the ongoing struggles in the postcolonial world. Although the narrator ends with a sentiment that the natives of Peponi (ill-suited as they are to modernity) will be the ones to decide the planet's future, the focus of the novel is on the nostalgia that a succession of human explorers, game-hunters, and farmers all have for the paradise they thought they had found.

Dissident science fiction

So much for colonizing science fiction, but not all science fiction that comes from the colonizer (or the beneficiaries of the colonizing process) is the simple translation of the colonizing process into space. A number of writers from within the centre (the Empire, the metropolitan – again, see *The Empire Writes Back*) offer important critiques of the process and effects of colonization. For the lack of a better word, I borrow a term from politics and call these writers 'dissidents'. Two such dissident writers who are fully aware of the various forms of violence that colonizing commits on all involved are Kim Stanley Robinson and C.J. Cherryh.

Robinson's Mars trilogy, *Red Mars* (1992), *Green Mars* (1994) and *Blue Mars* (1996), takes the reader from the original group of astronauts training in Antarctica to a terraformed Mars that is home to the second and third-generation descendants of those astronauts and millions of other immigrants who consider themselves Martians first. In outline, the trilogy follows the pattern of settler colonization but unlike Earth there are no sentient beings that need to be erased or managed out of any meaningful existence: the settlers arrive and under difficult circumstances spend the next few years creating inhabitable surroundings. As the years pass the colonists have less in common with the home country and begin to chafe at long-distance attempts to control them. The settlers eventually declare independence and create their own constitution. At first the constitution is closely modelled on the American constitution, but the Martians settle on a confederation with a mixed economy enshrining both free-market principles for non-essentials and not-for-profit status for social rights (housing, food, health-care, education). Robinson is historically astute enough to have one of the original settlers (importantly, the one who had stowed away on the original flight to Mars) sound a warning note about keeping a healthy distrust of regimes no matter how revolutionary their introduction. Whilst the Martians seek to create a global constitution they are fully aware that they are both Martians and inhabitants of more local places with each locality articulating its own mix of regional and global rights and responsibilities within the framework of the constitution. In the first few decades each region finds its place in the Martian political and economic landscape based on its technological strength and focus.

Although a few regions on Robinson's fictive Mars find an economic place due to tourism, the importance of technology to the development of a region or country cannot be understated. Countries that do not invest in technological and industrial development are doomed to be providers of either raw material or purveyors of tourism and manual labour (in a science fiction context the militarily contested planet Arrakis in Frank Herbert's *Dune*, 1965, exists solely as the source of 'spice' – a naturally occurring product necessary for space transportation). The technologies that come most readily to mind are related to weapons development and nuclear energy, with the arms race between the USA and the USSR each forcing the other to greater production of conventional and nuclear armaments. An important aspect of the arms race was an attempt to prevent the other side from acquiring the mechanical processes and theoretical knowledge that enabled the production of ICBMs and spy satellites. The fear of technology transfer is not new; countries have made various attempts to stop and/or direct that flow for centuries. The majority of patent, intellectual property and trademark laws were established over the course of the eighteenth and nineteenth centuries, and nations have also attempted to ban the sale and exportation of actual machines and the emigration of skilled workers (see Chang's *Bad Samaritans*, 2008, for an excellent discussion of the connections between protectionism, free trade, technology transfer and economic development[9]).

Although all of C.J. Cherryh's novels wrestle with the effect of technology on society, nowhere is it more pronounced and thorough than in the *Foreigner* series (to date ten volumes, commencing with *Foreigner*, 1994; *Invader*, 1995; *Inheritor*, 1996). Here, technologically superior humans find themselves far from home in an enclave on a planet with a sentient humanoid species. The atevi are about half as large again as the humans with jet black skin and hair and glowing eyes, have an intuitive grasp of higher-order mathematics, and structure their emotional lives and kinship patterns according to loyalty above all else. The humans are allowed one interpreter who must study the major sociological and linguistic intricacies of atevi culture before interacting with them in order to manage technology transfer without upsetting the balance of power among the atevi and between atevi and humans. Notably, Cherryh does *not* represent the less technologically developed atevi as primitive natives awaiting the boon of human technology. Neither does she represent the humans as gods deigning to bestow marvellous but harmless largesse on the benighted savages.

Rather than show the atevi as either for or against technology Cherryh portrays atevi divided into various groups that have a sophisticated understanding of the potential disruptions. There are those who desire to maintain the status quo, while others recognize the inevitability of technological and thus cultural change. There are those who chafe under the limitations of the carefully scheduled transfer of human technology, and those who actively pursue their own technology. The humans themselves are conflicted about the reasons and methods for technology transfer. The isolationists want nothing further to do with aliens who might break the treaty that established the enclave, while the interventionists seek to work with the particular government in power to pursue policies most favourable to the humans and a third faction seeks to manipulate the atevi into building a space programme only sufficient to help the humans get back to their two-hundred-year old orbiting platforms.

Given the richness and variety of the literature available, any course or seminar that addresses postcolonial sf or reads/reinterprets sf through postcolonial theory and contexts offers fertile pedagogic possibilities. The following notes are provided to indicate the approach I have taken in my teaching of the subject.

Course design

In structuring a course on postcolonial science fiction, I make use of material from the following lists of creative and critical works:

Science fiction

Isaac Asimov, *Foundation* (1951)
Tobias Buckell, *Ragamuffin* (2007)
Octavia E. Butler, *Lilith's Brood* (2000) (collects the *Xenogenesis* trilogy, *Dawn*, 1987; *Adulthood Rites*, 1988; and *Imago*, 1989)
Samuel R. Delany, *Trouble on Triton: An Ambiguous Heterotopia* (1976)
Amitav Ghosh, *The Calcutta Chromosome* (1995)
Robert E. Heinlein, *The Moon is a Harsh Mistress* (1966)
Nalo Hopkinson, *Midnight Robber* (2000)
H. Beam Piper, *The Fuzzy Papers* (1979)
Kim Stanley Robinson, *Blue Mars* (1995)
Archie Weller, *Land of the Golden Clouds* (1998)
Selected stories from Sheree R. Thomas (ed.), *Dark Matter: A Century of Speculative Fiction from the African Diaspora* (1998) and *So Long Been Dreaming*

Additional reading

The following list of postcolonial science fiction writers and works is only partial. Two extremely useful places to start are the Carl Brandon Society (http://www.carlbrandon.org/index.html) and Afrofuturism (http://www.afrofuturism.net). I have purposely kept my list here focused on science fiction – it would be greatly expanded with the addition of fantasy.

Steven Barnes (with Larry Niven), *The Descent of Anansi* (1982)
Rimi Chatterjee, *Signal Red* (2005)
Andrea Hairston, *Mindscape* (2006)
Nalo Hopkinson, *Brown Girl in the Ring* (1998)
Larissa Lai, *Salt Fish Girl* (2002)
Walter Mosley, *Futureland* (coll. 2001)
George Schuyler, *Black Empire*
Vandana Singh, *The Woman Who Thought She Was a Planet and Other Stories* (2009)

Critical works

Monographs

Barr, Marleen S., *Feminist Fabulation: Space/Postmodern Fiction* (Iowa City: University of Iowa Press, 1994).

Crosby, Janice C., *Cauldron of Changes: Feminist Spirituality in Fantastic Fiction* (Jefferson, NC: McFarland & Co. Inc., 2000).
Delaney, Samuel R., *The Jewel-Hinged Jaw: Notes on the Language of Science Fiction*, rev. edn. (Middletown, CT: Wesleyan University Press, 2009).
Haraway, Donna, *Simians, Cyborgs, and Women* (London: Routledge, 1991).
Hayles, Katherine, *How We Became Posthuman: Virtual Bodies in Cybernetics, Literature and Informatics* (Chicago, IL: Chicago University Press, 1999).
Hume, Kathryn, *Fantasy and Mimesis: Responses to Reality in Western Literature* (London: Methuen, 1985).
Huntington, John, *The Logic of Fantasy: H.G. Wells and Science Fiction* (New York: Columbia University Press, 1982).
Jameson, Fredric, *Archeologies of the Future: The Desire Called Utopia and Other Fictions* (New York: Verso Books, 2007).
Le Guin, Ursula K., *The Language of the Night: Essays on Fantasy and Science Fiction* (New York: Perennial, 1993).
Melzer, Patricia, *Alien Constructions: Science Fiction and Feminist Thought* (Austin, TX: Texas University Press, 2006).
Myers, Robert E., *The Intersection of Science Fiction and Philosophy* (Santa Barbara, CA: Greenwood Press, 1982).
Rabkin, Eric S., *The Fantastic in Literature* (Princeton, NJ: Princeton University Press, 1977).
Rieder, John, *Colonialism and the Emergence of Science Fiction* (Middletown, CT: Wesleyan University Press, 2008).
Rose, Mark, *Alien Encounters: Anatomy of Science Fiction* (Cambridge, MA: Harvard University Press, 1981).
Sisk, David, *Transformations of Language in Modern Dystopias* (Santa Barbara, CA: Greenwood Press, 1997).
Slusser, George and Eric S. Rabkin, *Styles of Creation: Aesthetic Technique and the Creation of Fictional Worlds* (Athens, GA: University of Georgia Press, 1993).
Todorov, Tzvetan, *The Fantastic: A Structural Approach to a Literary Genre* (Ithaca, NY: Cornell University Press, 1975).
Wagar, Warren W., *Terminal Visions: The Literature of Last Things* (Bloomington, IN: Indiana University Press, 1982).
Westfahl, Gary, *Cosmic Engineers: A Study of Hard Science Fiction* (Westport, CT: Greenwood, 1996).
Wolfe, Gary, *The Known and the Unknown: The Iconography of Science Fiction* (Kent, OH: Kent State University Press, 1979).

Articles

Ahmad, Aijaz, 'Jameson's Rhetoric of Otherness and the "National Allegory"', *Social Text*, 17 (1987): 3–25.

Bhabha, Homi, 'Of Mimicry and Man: The Ambivalence of Colonial Discourse', in *The Location of Culture* (New York: Routledge, 1994) 85–92.

Chambers, Claire, 'Postcolonial Science Fiction: Amitav Ghosh's *The Calcutta Chromosome*', *Journal of Commonwealth Literature*, 3:1 (2003): 57–72.

Chrisman, Laura, 'The Imperial Unconscious? Representations of Imperial Discourse', *Critical Quarterly*, 32:3 (2007): 38–58.

Dery, Mark, 'Black to the Future: Interviews with Samuel R. Delany, Greg Tate, and Tricia Rose', in *Flame Wars: The Discourse of Cyberculture* (Durham, NC: Duke University Press, 1994) 179–222.

Dillon, Grace L., 'Miindiwag and Indigenous Diaspora: Eden Robinson's and Celu Amberstone's Forays into "Postcolonial" Science Fiction and Fantasy', *Extrapolation*, 48:2 (2007): 219–43.

Fanon, Frantz, 'On National Culture', in *The Wretched of the Earth* (New York: Grove Press, 1965) 206–49.

Gilbert, Sandra, 'Costumes of the Mind: Transvestism as Metaphor in Modern Literature', *Critical Inquiry*, 7:2 (1980): 391–417.

Harlow, Barbara, 'Narratives of Resistance', in *Resistance Literature* (London: Methuen, 1987) 75–116.

hooks, bell, *Postmodern Blackness* (http:www.africa.upenn.edu/ Articles_Gen/Postmodern_Blackness_18270.html) (accessed 28 June 2010).

Said, Edward, 'Crisis', in *Orientalism* (New York: Vintage, 1979) 92–110.

Sharpe, Jenny, 'Figures of Colonial Resistance', *Modern Fiction Studies*, 35:1 (1989): 137–55.

Shklovsky, Victor, 'Art as Technique', in Lee T. Lemon and Marion J. Reiss, eds, *Russian Formalist Criticism: Four Essays* (Lincoln, NE: University of Nebraska Press, 1965) 3–24.

Showalter, Elaine, 'Feminist Criticism in the Wilderness', *Critical Enquiry*, 8:2 (1981): 179–205.

Sterling, Bruce, 'Preface', in *Mirror Shades* (London: Paladin, 1986) vii–xiv.

Students are provided with two introductory handouts: the first offering several definitions of science fiction; the second a list of imperial tropes from Spurr's *The Rhetoric of Empire* (1993).

Handout one: definitions of science fiction

- 'We do not expect romances to provide subtle psychological portraits of fully rendered images of the world as we know it. Rather, we

expect to hear of marvels and adventures in strange places populated by such preternatural creatures as giants and dragons. ...Call your magic a "space warp" or a "matter transformer," your enchanted island the planet Einstein ... call your giants and dragons "extraterrestrials," and what you have is merely the contemporary form of one of the most ancient literary kinds.'[10]
- 'From the beginning, characters in science fiction have tended to be types rather than personalities – the scientist, the ordinary man, the religious fanatic...'[11]
- 'Science fiction is the search for a definition of mankind and his status in the universe which will stand in our advanced but confused state of knowledge (science), and is characteristically cast in the Gothic or post-Gothic mode.'[12]
- 'Science fiction is a literary genre whose necessary and sufficient conditions are the presence and interaction of estrangement and cognition, and whose main formal device is an imaginative framework alternative to the author's empirical environment.'[13]
- 'Science fiction is romance fitted out with the trappings of technological futurism.' (Anonymous)
- 'Science fiction frequently tries to imagine what life would be like on a plane as far above us as we are above savagery; its setting is often of a kind that appears to us as technologically miraculous.'[14]

Handout two: imperial tropes from David Spurr's *The Rhetoric of Empire*

1 Aestheticization – objectification and containment leading to consumption
2 Surveillance – discovery and control
3 Classification – for example, Joseph-Arthur, Comte de Gobineau's hierarchy of races: White, Yellow, Black. Phillipe Rushton is a contemporary manifestation.[15]
4 Debasement – abjection and contamination
5 Negation – darkness, void, denial of history, for example, in *Stargate* (Roland Emmerich, 1994) the abducted Egyptians have a static society until the Americans arrive.
6 Eroticization – seduction, fear and loathing, for example, in *Stargate* Jaye Davidson as the homosexual and despotic, vampiric alien, Ra, dresses in metal and gossamer, surrounds himself with pretty semi-naked boys and muscle-bound guards: the sexually degenerate Oriental.
7 Appropriation – land – colonizer is rightful inheritor because he is civilization. Lord Lugard's *Dual Mandate* (1922): 'The tropics are the

heritage of mankind and neither, on the one hand has a suzerain power the right to their exclusive exploitation, nor, on the other hand, have the races which inhabit them a right to deny their bounties to those that need them. The merchant, the miner and the manufacturer do not enter the tropics on sufferance or employ their technical skills, their energy and their capital as interlopers or "greedy capitalists," but in the fulfillment of the mandate of civilization.'[16]

Appropriation – development – eighteenth-century international law – if land doesn't appear settled it can be taken over.
8 Affirmation – justification of moral and legal superiority
9 Idealization – 'Noble Savage'
10 Naturalization – closer to Nature, the assumption that the current state of affairs is the natural state of things.
11 Insubstantialization – the dreamlike alien land as backdrop to the play of the self.

After an introductory period of two to four weeks depending on the level of the class and their familiarity with science fiction, I pair up a creative work with a critical work each week of the semester. I have usually begun by screening *The Matrix* (Wachowski brothers, 1999) and *Blade Runner* (Ridley Scott, 1982). However, now *District 9* (Neill Blomkamp, 2009) and *Avatar* (James Cameron, 2009) are available I will begin with them in order to make apparent some of the issues around race, ethnicity, colonization, migration and so on considered on the course. The students create alter-avatars of themselves (that is, avatars that are visibly different from their 'normal' gendered, racial, ethnic selves) and then spend time each week of the course interacting with others in a virtual space such as Second Life to ascertain and reflect on reactions to their alternate selves. As a bridge between the films and the literature I show *The Last Angel of History* (John Akomfrah, 1995), a video that examines science fiction and pan-African culture.

Undergraduate assessment

The modes of assessment for the course depend on the level of delivery and vary in order to mobilize different learning styles. They include:

- a portfolio of weekly meditations on the students' experiences in Second Life as alter-avatars;
- a ten-minute presentation on the creative work scheduled for a particular seminar session;

- a 1000-word (or four-page paper) that reads at least one of the creative texts through one of the critical texts explored on the course;
- a 3000-word (or twelve-page paper) analysing either a creative work not covered in class or a different creative work from a writer discussed on the course. The topic must be negotiated with the tutor/instructor.

Graduate assessment

Two presentations:

- select a novel from the Additional Reading list and present your understanding of one aspect of the imagined world.
- locate the novel in a critical discussion centring on one of the critical works from the list provided.

Each presentation should be approximately 20 minutes, in order to leave sufficient time for questions and feedback.

- Final Paper – the final paper may be a development of one of your presentations or it may be a new topic but either way it must encompass more than one creative work. You may also decide to write a science fiction story as your final paper; however, it must be accompanied by a shorter critical paper in which you demonstrate your awareness of the major issues of the course as they pertain to your story.

Since I started by quoting myself from *So Long Been Dreaming* I'll come full circle and end by doing the same. In postcolonial science fiction, whether by postcolonial writers or dissident writers, the

> binaries of native/alien, technologist/pastoralist, colonizer/colonized are all brought into question by … thematic and linguistic strategies that subtly subvert received language and plots. One of the key strategies employed by these writers is to radically shift the perspective of the narrator from the supposed rightful heir of contemporary technologically advanced cultures to those whose cultures have had their technology destroyed and stunted. … [Postcolonial science fiction] is both a questioning of colonial/imperialist practices and conceptions of the native or the colonized, and an attempt to represent the complexities of identity that terms such as 'native' and 'colonized' tend to simplify.[17]

In the context of teaching science fiction, such literature is essential in challenging students' assumptions and preconceptions regarding history, culture, identity and ideology.

Notes

1. See Uppinder Mehan, 'Final Thoughts', in Nalo Hopkinson and Uppinder Mehan, eds, *So Long Been Dreaming: Postcolonial Science Fiction and Fantasy* (Vancouver, BC: Arsenal Pulp Press, 2004) 269–70.
2. Uppinder Mehan, 'The Domestication of Technology in Indian Science Fiction Short Stories', *Foundation: The International Review of Science Fiction*, 74 (1998): 54–66.
3. Baldev Raj Nayar, *India's Quest for Technological Independence: Policy Foundation and Policy Change*, 2 vols (New Delhi: Lansers Publishers, 1983) 1.
4. Karl Marx, *Early Writings*, trans. Rodney Livingstone and Gregory Benton (Harmondsworth: Penguin, 1975).
5. Dalaipi cited in Nigel Parbury, 'Terra Nullius: Invasion and Colonization', in Rhonda Craven, ed., *Teaching Aboriginal Studies* (Australia: Allen and Unwin, 2000) 101–28 at 104.
6. David Spurr, *The Rhetoric of Empire: Colonial Discourse in Journalism, Travel Writing, and Imperial Administration* (Durham: Duke University Press, 1993).
7. See Bill Ashcroft, Gareth Griffiths and Helen Tiffin, *The Empire Writes Back: Theory and Practice in Post-Colonial Literatures* (London and New York: Routledge, 1989).
8. Mike Resnick, *Paradise: A Chronicle of a Distant World* (New York: Tor Books, 1989) ix.
9. See Ha-Joon Chang, *Bad Samaritans: The Myth of Free Trade and the Secret History of Capitalism* (New York: Bloomsbury Press, 2007).
10. Mark Rose, *Alien Encounters: Anatomy of Science Fiction* (Cambridge, MA: Harvard University Press, 1981) 8.
11. Ibid., 8.
12. Brian Aldiss with David Wingrove. *Trillion Year Spree: The History of Science Fiction* (New York: Atheneum, 1986) 25.
13. Darko Suvin, *The Metamorphoses of Science Fiction: On the Poetics and History of a Genre* (New Haven: Yale University Press, 1979) 8–9.
14. Northrop Frye, *Anatomy of Criticism: Four Essays* (1957; Princeton: Princeton University Press, 1990) 49.
15. See Comte Joseph Arthur de Gobineau, *Essai sur l'inégalité des races humaines* (Essay on the Inequality of the Human Races, 1853–1855), trans. Adrian Collins (1915; New York: Fertig, 1999) and J. Phillipe Ruston, *Race, Evolution and Behaviour: A Life History Perspective* (New Brunswick, NJ: Transaction, 1995).
16. Frederick Lugard cited in Spurr, *The Rhetoric of Empire*, 28.
17. Mehan, *So Long Been Dreaming*, 269–70.

11
Teaching Latin American Science Fiction and Fantasy in English: A Case Study

M. Elizabeth Ginway

I am currently teaching a course, in English, entitled 'Latin America Science Fiction and Fantasy'. Although I have taught courses on Brazilian science fiction in Portuguese, this is the first time that I have taught texts from Spanish America and Brazil in English translation. Based on my experience so far, I hope to provide some suggestions in this chapter to help others put together a similar course. I begin with a list of possible films, and then discuss the general themes of the stories included in *Cosmos Latinos: An Anthology of Science Fiction from Latin America and Spain* (2003), edited by Andrea L. Bell and Yolanda Molina-Gavilán. Since these stories alone cannot fill an entire semester, I suggest other novels and stories available in translation, as well as the possibility of including novels written by Anglo-Americans about Brazil.

Incorporating a section or module on texts from Latin America into sf courses provides an opportunity to examine underlying assumptions about First World political and technological hegemony. In the countries of Latin America where First World and Third World realities coexist, the role of technology cannot be taken for granted. It may be imposed or misused by the authorities, or be unavailable to the majority of the population. Often, Latin American sf stories about space exploration re-interpret the conquest of the New World or examine political relations between the First and Third Worlds. I have found that the recasting of common sf icons, such as aliens, mutants, the Cold War, time travel, and even cyberspace, gives new resonances to these tropes in light of Latin America's distinct sociopolitical reality.

Science fiction and fantasy films from Latin America

The Brazilian comedy *Basic Sanitation: The Movie* (*Saneamento Básico, O Filme*, 2007), directed by Jorge Furtado, makes a clear reference to science fiction, although it is not an sf film per se. In fact, the film is about the making of an sf film and, as such, is a commentary on how the special-effects blockbusters that we associate with sf are out of reach for Third World filmmakers. As *Basic Sanitation* shows, however, directors like Furtado are able to use the genre to comment on First World/Third World economic, artistic and political realities.

Although some of my students thought *Basic Sanitation* had little to do with sf, I convinced them to be patient and to focus on the sf film within the film and its relevance to Latin American reality. Big budget special effects are out of the question for Third World countries, where the film industry is often concerned with portraying national reality instead of providing Hollywood escapism. Thus, to understand Latin-American science fiction, it is often necessary to consider the genre from a slightly different perspective, seeing its presence in seemingly unlikely places. In the frame story of *Basic Sanitation*, town leaders find out that although they need money to fix the sewer the only government funds available are for making a creative or fiction-based film. They arrive at the idea of making a low-budget sf film, with the intention of using the rest of the grant to fix the town's drainage problem. Unfortunately, their production – based loosely on Jack Arnold's 1954 *The Creature from the Black Lagoon* – is so deficient that they opt to hire a professional editor/director to 'fix' it. Ultimately the movie is a success, but they still have the sewer problem. Here we see the contradictions surrounding the Brazilian film industry, which uses government and private sector funds that are needed for basic necessities such as sanitation in order to promote filmmaking instead. The government itself engages in 'escapism' since, while priding itself on elevating national culture via cinematic prestige, it neglects problems of basic infrastructure. This is again mirrored in the behaviour of the characters themselves, who lose touch with reality by becoming so involved in movie-making that they forget about the money for the sewer. In the end, the sewer monster 'lurks' in the background, in the form of the unresolved sanitation problem, showing us how an 'escapist' genre can reflect the ongoing environmental and political concerns of the townsfolk.

Another film that could be used at the onset of the course is an Argentine short, 'Trip to Mars' ('Viaje al Marte', 2004), directed by Juan Pablo Zaramella.[1] In this claymation film, an Argentine boy dreams of space travel to Mars, only to be magically transported there in an old tow truck by his grandfather. In the final scene, when American astronauts land to find him already on Mars, they call Earth to say, 'Houston, we have a problem.' These comedies, which challenge our usual expectations about the language and culture of space travel and sf, may not seem like 'real' science fiction to American students and teachers, because they do not meet our conventional First World expectations. A course like this helps us rethink and recast our own conceptions about sf and its presence in cultures other than our own.

I included several additional films touching on themes such as the Cold War, dictatorship and issues of cultural and technological hegemony. The films are from Brazil, Argentina and Mexico, countries that produced, additionally, the highest number of science fiction texts.[2] Fortunately all of these have English subtitles.[3] The film *The Sputnik Man* (*O Homem do Sputnik*, 1959), directed by Carlos Manga, is a type of Brazilian comedy called a 'chanchada' that pits stereotyped agents from the US, the USSR and France against common-sense Brazilian locals, thereby shifting the discourse of the Cold War away from hegemonic powers and toward the Third World. Alberto Pieralisi's *The Fifth Power* (*O Quinto Poder*, 1962) is a Brazilian film about foreigners inciting unrest via subliminal messages in order to justify a right-wing takeover aimed at allowing foreign exploitation of Brazil's natural resources. Its suspenseful chase scenes, filmed in Rio de Janeiro are quite spectacular, despite the film's generally uneven timing and editing. *Macunaíma* (1969), directed by Joaquim Pedro de Andrade, long considered a Cinema Novo classic, has been re-issued recently, and could be considered a fantasy film. In *Macunaíma*, the eponymous hero, based on a trickster of indigenous lore, changes from black to white and encounters giants and other figures from Brazilian folklore and popular culture, thus showing how fantasy hides a critique of the fast-paced policies of development adopted by the military dictatorship. Eventually we see the hero devoured by the country's 'self-cannibalism', as he is caught in the struggle between leftist guerrillas, right-wing capitalists and the temptations of consumerism.[4]

In Argentina, science fiction films also explore the theme of military dictatorship during the period 1976–83, albeit in a more subdued way. Eliseo Subiela's films, *The Man Facing Southeast* (*Hombre mirando al sudeste*, 1986) and *Don't Die Without Telling Me Where You Are Going* (*No te mueras sin decirme adónde vas*, 1995), use science fiction and fantasy to question issues of power and collective imagination. The first film deals with an alien who suddenly appears in a mental hospital. Endowed with unusual powers, he represents a source of hope to the hospital patients and a threat to the establishment, both political and medical. Laden with imagery that recalls religious art and the Holocaust, the film poses many moral and political dilemmas in a country where thousands disappeared during the 'Dirty War' under the 1976–83 military dictatorship.[5] *Don't Die Without Telling Me Where You Are Going* involves a man who invents a machine to read dreams, and his wheelchair-bound friend, who invents a service robot that sings the songs of the legendary tango singer Carlos Gardel. Subiela entwines stories of invention and reincarnation, using technology for pursuits that are spiritual, personal or political rather than practical. For example, the robot Carlitos fails miserably as a service robot, dropping all the dishes on his first trial run, but succeeds as a singer and philosophical conversationalist. The dream machine allows the protagonist to converse with a friend, long dead, who disappeared during the military's Dirty War. The film thus combines the fantasy and icons of science fiction to fit Argentine reality. Another Argentine sf film is Gustavo Mosquera's *Moebius* (1996), about a mathematician/engineer hired to track a mysterious subway train that appears periodically as if caught in a dimensional trap like a Moebius strip. With its slow build up of suspense and its convincing if low-tech special effects capturing the sensation of the runaway subway car, the film recalls themes of the disappeared and of Jorge Luís Borges's preoccupation with the infinite.

Finally, low-budget Mexican films such as *The Aztec Mummy vs. the Human Robot* (*La momia azteca contra el robot humano*, 1957) directed by Rafael Portillo, and *Santo and Blue Demon vs. Doctor Frankenstein* (*Santo y Blue Demon contra el doctor Frankenstein*, 1974), directed by Miguel M. Delgado, can be used to discuss the struggle between the icons of Mexican culture (the Aztec mummy) or Mexican folk heroes (the masked wrestlers or 'luchadores')[6] and villains such as mad scientists Dr Krupp and Dr Frankenstein, who represent foreign technology and interests. In the historical context of post-revolutionary Mexico in the twentieth century, the country's cultural identity has centred on its indigenous heritage and the greatness of Aztec and Mayan cultures. The prevalent themes in these popular films are tradition vs. technology, or 'old' Mexico vs. 'new' Mexico. The theme of loss is reinforced by the scientists, who sell out national patrimony to imperialist or outside interests either by stealing the mummy's amulet and belt or by kidnapping women from the countryside. When the treasure and the women are rescued by the legitimate Mexican heroes, the educated archaeologist in the case of the Aztec mummy films and the wrestlers Santo and Blue

Demon in the other, we experience a cultural victory by Mexico. This is reinforced in *Santo and Blue Demon vs. Doctor Frankenstein*, when the scientist is foiled by the wrestlers, since Golem, Frankenstein's strong but slow-witted henchman, fails to kidnap one of the wrestlers for Golem's future brain transplant. The role of Golem is replayed by Ron Perlman's character in Guillermo del Toro's *Cronos* (1993), a film in which an ailing Mexican man seeks to prolong his life via the 'chronos' machine, enlisting the aid of his American nephew, Angel de la Guardia, played by Perlman. Sent to find the machine, which has fallen into the hands of an Argentine antique dealer exiled and living in Mexico, Perlman represents the violent, thieving, ignorant American. The fact that the antique dealer, Jesús Gris (Frederico Luppi), whose name recalls that of Jesus Christ, is now living in Mexico with his wife, a tango instructor, and their grandchild, suggests that the girl's parents were likely victims of Argentina's Dirty War. In *Cronos*, it is a machine that causes vampirism and provides eternal life, but at the price of a craving for blood, a circumstance that recalls both Latin America's bloody past and its ambivalence towards technology. The film provides the vampire myth with family ties through a Third World version of the typical vampire plot, and like the Santo and Aztec mummy movies, it again pits Latin-American culture against that of United States, since the hero, Jesús Gris, chooses tradition, family and sacrifice over progress, individualism and technology.[7]

While these films are not typically sf, most contain recognizable elements of the genre, such as Cold War scenarios, space ships, alien creatures, sinister technologies, robots, mad scientists and fantastic figures with super powers, all of which are familiar to students with a passing knowledge of the genre. In my experience, the screenings generated lively discussion, since most students feel confident about expressing their own feelings and interpretations.

Since many of the students in the class are majoring in Latin American Studies, Anthropology, Spanish or Portuguese, they are generally familiar with the region or the study of foreign cultures. I did have to offer some critical concepts to help them with the broad outlines of science fiction and fantasy, especially the idea of the social contract and the dialectic structure of utopias (for which I looked to Northrop Frye and Darko Suvin).[8] I also employed David Hartwell's 'sense of wonder',[9] Suvin's concepts of the novum and cognitive estrangement, as outlined in his *Metamorphosis of Science Fiction* (1979), and Gary K. Wolfe's exploration of the iconography of Golden Age sf from his *The Known and the Unknown* (1979). Many of these concepts are outlined in my own book *Brazilian Science Fiction* (2004), which may serve as a quick study guide. I gleaned material from Larry McCaffrey's introduction to *Storming the Reality Studio* (1991) for discussions of cyberpunk in general, and included summaries of Latin American theories of postmodernism, such as Beatriz Sarlo's *Scenes from a Postmodern Life* (1994) and Martin Hopenhayn's 1995 essay 'Postmodernism and Neoliberalism in Latin America'.[10] I also relied on introductions to alternate worlds (or alternate histories) and feminism in sf in Clute and Nicholl's *The Encyclopedia of Science Fiction* (1993).

In order to supplement and add variety to the readings, I included texts of the Latin American fantastic or 'magical realism' subgenre, since these are more commonly associated with Latin America. I believe it is important to characterize the Latin American subgenre as a variant of the fantastic, akin to what Farah Mendlesohn characterizes as 'liminal', or absurdist fantasy, in that their characters experience little or no surprise even when faced with strange situations.[11] I use Mendlesohn's taxonomy to distinguish Latin American fantasy from other more conventional types, such as *The Lord of the Rings*. In addition, the Todorovian concept of a reader's 'hesitation' between natural and supernatural explanations of a story's events is an essential concept for understanding the workings of a fantastic text. I cite these theoretical and critical sources on handouts, but find that lectures or outlines are most efficient in conveying this material, which students can explore further in assignments and exams. My general approach, however, has always been to compare texts from the Anglo-American science fiction and fantasy tradition to their Latin America counterparts. In this way, instructors, tutors and students can draw on their own knowledge to explore the genres productively from a new perspective.

Themes in *Cosmos Latinos*

The same problems that make film selection difficult are evident in the search for suitable texts, since many works, especially those from Brazil, are unavailable in translation. The foundational text for the course is the aforementioned *Cosmos Latinos: An Anthology of Science Fiction from Latin America and Spain*. It is an excellent anthology, with a solid introduction and short introductory notes on the authors, and it offers an overview of different periods and themes. It provides a useful starting point for teaching Latin American sf, since it is clearly annotated and concisely written, although instructors may wish to supplement their students' knowledge of the political history of specific countries.

The stories discussed below are all from *Cosmos Latinos*, which begins with early selections from the utopia and sf genres, in which authors view science as a means of overcoming the remnants of colonialism. These early stories also show that technology has not always been viewed in Latin America as a threat to the region, especially in the late nineteenth and early twentieth centuries. By the mid-twentieth century, we begin to see an appropriation of Golden Age sf's iconography, but not always its narrative trajectory. Many stories include astronauts, aliens and spaceships, but their conventional heroes are often defeated by the very aliens they set out to conquer. Clearly, such inversions can be seen as fantasies of reverse colonization. They are most clearly evidenced in stories coming from communist or socialist regimes, such as Cuban Ángel Arango's 'The Cosmonaut' (1966), or Chilean Hugo Correa's 'When Pilate Said No' (1971), in which outside threats to national sovereignty are strongest.

Latin American Cold War or post-Holocaust texts often convey the sense of individual and national powerlessness felt during the period. This can be observed in the figure of an astronaut lost in orbit in Salvadoran Álvaro Desleal's 'Cord of Nylon and Gold' (1965). It is also prominent in Brazilian Jerônimo Monteiro's 'The Crystal Goblet' (1964), where the disenchanted protagonist experiences both anti-communist imprisonment and visions of nuclear destruction. The theme of powerlessness is at its most acute in the lives of painfully under-educated protagonists who are trying to survive in a post-nuclear holocaust world in Argentine Alberto Vanasco's 'Post-Boom Boom' (1967).

Fears of mechanization, modernization and military governments are evident in stories in which technology fails to help protagonists escape from demeaning forms of existence. In Argentine Pablo Capanna's 'Anacronia' (1966), life in a utopian society becomes so routine as to fall into spiritual entropy, and humans appear more mechanized than the robots that serve them. Allusions to T.S. Eliot's poem 'The Hollow Men', pepper the text, capturing the sense of existential angst. Venezuelan Luís Britto García's three-page story 'The Future' (1970), structured as a series of theses, antitheses and syntheses, parodies a dialectical argument of progress: as technology advances to replace all organs of the body, these cease to function, until even the human brain becomes obsolete. In Argentine Eduardo Goligorsky's 'The Last Refuge' (1967), the protagonist finds himself living in a future where censorship and isolation from the rest of the world afford him few pleasures. When his son unwittingly shows his album of forbidden space travel photographs to his classmates, the man is immediately pursued by the authorities who have closed off their society from alien contact, technological progress and space travel. After running day and night, the man hopes to escape with the aliens, yet fails to gain entry to a departing alien ship. The first two stories portray disillusionment with the promises of technology for improving the human condition – both the mind and the body deteriorate in the presence of technology – while the third uses sf iconography as an allegory of escape from a repressive regime. Both prophetic and tragic, Goligorsky comments in the story's brief introduction that he wrote it to protest the violent, nationalistic, internecine fighting and military dictatorship that plagued Argentina from the late 1960s to the early 1980s.

The excesses of nationalist rhetoric are critiqued in time-travel narratives, while other stories, written under dictatorships, combine social criticism and the sexual revolution, although in Latin American terms. In the time-travel narratives of Argentine Magdalena Moujan Otaño, 'Gu Ta Guttarak' (1967), and Spaniards Ricard de la Casa and Pedro Jorge Romero, 'The Day It Changed' (1996), the travellers are not solitary heroes as in the Anglo-American tradition, but rather partners or families. Their experience is used to question nationalistic discourse and promote democratic values in Argentina and Spain.

Alternate sexualities and alien presence are examined in Argentine Angélica Gorodischer's 'The Violet Embryos' (1973), a brilliantly disturbing anti-sexist and anti-military text, in Brazilian André Carneiro's 'Brain Transplant' (1978), an exploration of polymorphous sexuality, and in Cuban Daína Chaviano's 'The Annunciation' (1983), a re-writing of the biblical scene between Mary and Gabriel, transformed by sexuality, aliens and eugenics. Chaviano's story is perilously close to heresy in its challenge to both communist and Catholic dogma. Gabriel criticizes Mary for her people's codifying moral teachings to establish a religion while also seducing her in a scene that mocks the Immaculate Conception. In these stories, sexuality subverts the hypocrisy and censorship of authoritarian regimes in Argentina, Brazil and Cuba.

Cyberpunk themes appear in stories from Mexico, such as Guillermo Lavín's 'Reaching the Shore' (1994), and Pepe Rojo's 'Gray Noise' (1996), and also from Brazil, in Braulio Tavares 'Stuntmind' (1989). As I have suggested,[12] with the advent of neo-liberalism in the late 1980s, technology and the global market 'invade' the Latin American region, leaving the population vulnerable to forces beyond their borders. Thus, these cyberpunk stories often represent the physical body as portraying a sense of crisis in the body politic, a sense of powerlessness in the face of new technologies, or of violation stemming from torture and disappearances during the periods of political dictatorship. The protagonists of these stories, unlike those of Anglo-American cyberpunk, have implants that they consider more as a violation of their identity than as an enhancement, showing technology's invasive threat to the body and, perhaps, the body politic. In Tavares's story, 'stuntminds' are humans capable of absorbing knowledge from aliens. In exchange, the aliens (known as 'Intrusos' or Intruders) gain access to human sensations, but the stuntminds' lifespans are greatly shortened. Even though very few humans benefit from the aliens' esoteric technological knowledge, the desire for prestige and hunger for novelty makes the stuntminds' sacrifice worthwhile to the governments of Earth. This represents the rapid influx of technoculture to the region, and the crisis of future shock, a sense of powerlessness and informational overload. Another story of violation is 'Exerion' (2000), by Chilean Pablo Castro, in which the protagonist's hacking skills allow him to recover the files regarding his father's disappearance. At the same time, however, a new interface in the computer allows the government to send viruses to mutilate his mind and body, eroding his memories of his father's disappearance and his own pain, until he finally dissolves into cyberspace. As he becomes an avatar of Exerion, the game he once played, his given name, Víctor Morales, or moral victory, suggests that the sacrifice has deeper significance.

Supplementing *Cosmos Latinos*

Despite the high quality and diversity of the stories it contains and the brief essays that introduce them, *Cosmos Latinos* does not provide enough material for an entire semester, though it would provide more than sufficient fiction for a focused seminar or two. Equally, in my biased view as a Brazilianist, it has far too little material from Brazil, a country that constitutes half of South America in population and territory. What I propose here is supplementing *Cosmos Latinos* with several Brazilian absurdist fantasy stories available in English. Among the first would be 'The Siamese Academies' (1884) by Machado de Assis, in which the two main characters, a king and his concubine, magically exchange 'souls' (that is, genders), then return to their original state after six months. As an early story about transgendered characters, it raises questions about gender roles, and how society maintains order, since the doctrine regarding transgendered souls is violently repressed. Machado often points out the hypocrisy of the Brazilian nineteenth-century elite, and as a self-educated mulatto who rose to the literary pinnacle of his day – founding the Brazilian Academy of Letters shortly before his death in 1908 – he criticizes the repression of Otherness and difference while appearing to endorse it. I read the story as a literary example of Jacques Derrida's 'Law of Genre'[13] in that just as 'genres are not to be mixed', the same could be said of genders. Machado de Assis uses the story to reveal the madness underlying the sense of order that governs gender relations, a madness repeated in his own society's defence of slavery.

Similarly, the fantastic stories of Murilo Rubião, which originally appeared in the 1940s and were later anthologized in *The Ex-Magician and Other Stories* (1979), are politically and culturally illuminating. The unending building of 'The Edifice' recalls stories by Jorge Luís Borges, because it uses the concept of the infinite, yet does not remain abstract or theoretical in the style of Borges's masterful 'Library of Babel' (1941), which shares a similar theme. Rubião's main character, the engineer João Gaspar, is at first enthusiastic but then horrified at the prospect of building an edifice with an infinite number of floors. By the end of the story, like an artist or a prophet, he begins to question the undertaking, as the physical weight of the project weighs on him psychologically, while the workers cheer him on as their hero. Similar ecological, economic and ideological questions arise regarding the wisdom of engineering projects undertaken by the Brazilian military government (1964–85), such as the failed transamazonian highway, the damming of rivers for the construction of the Itaipu hydroelectric power plant, and the construction of the lengthy bridge linking the cities of Rio de Janeiro and Niterói. The ideology of economic 'development' is also captured in Rubião's 'Barbara', a story that can be read as an absurdist allegory of colonization and late development. When her husband meets her desires for water from the ocean and a baobab tree, her desires, along with her body, grow ever larger. She ignores her own child while demanding an ocean liner, even though the couple live far from a port. Paralleling Brazil's destructive colonial past and irrational need to industrialize at all costs, Barbara ignores the needs of her stunted child while admiring the ship her husband brings in by rail.

Rubião's rural counterpart, José J. Veiga has published two stories along similar lines, 'The Misplaced Machine' and the 'Importunate Rooster', both appearing in *The Misplaced Machine and Other Stories* (1970). In the story 'The Misplaced Machine', a machine is assembled overnight in a small-town square, and while its use is unknown, it immediately becomes the centre of the town's cultural and political events, attracting the envy of other towns in the region. The innocence and enthusiasm of the narrator and the region's population are misdirected at the sinister machine, whose only action is to catch a drunkard's leg in one of its gears. Veiga's 'Importunate Rooster' recounts the building of a new, modern highway. When finally opened, the highway seems ideal, until a strange rooster begins to attack cars and passengers. While accounts of the attacks vary, the military is eventually sent in, but after a tank is reduced to molten metal by the beast, the highway is closed and abandoned. As allegories of modernization, both stories capture a naive admiration for technology, while linking it to the questionable development policies of the military regime.

Sf writer André Carneiro has three stories available in English translation: 'Darkness' (1963), about an unexplained phenomenon that impedes the functioning of the sun or any other light source on Earth, 'A Perfect Marriage' (1966), about the failure of a computer-based conjugal match, and 'Life as an Ant' (1986), a story about a man who earns success after an alien takes over his body. As I suggest in my analysis of these stories,[14] each offers a particularly Brazilian perspective on its topic. In 'Darkness' the protagonist experiences a type of temporary blindness, much like that of St Paul, as suggested by the story's setting in São Paulo, Brazil's largest city. After reaching out to a neighbouring family and allowing a community of the blind to lead them to a safe haven, the protagonist experiences an unexpected renewed faith in urban life. In the utopian society of 'A Perfect Marriage' a newly married couple, although maliciously mismatched by computer hackers, choose not to have their union annulled, preferring to live in a type of domestic anarchy that undermines the government's official ideology. Similarly, the female protagonist of 'Life as an Ant' begs the alien visitor who inhabits her boyfriend's body to stay, since she has come to enjoy the multifaceted nature of their relationship. None of the characters choose a clear-cut or obvious solution (urban flight, annulment or a break-up), selecting instead what anthropologist Roberto DaMatta characterizes as the 'in-between space' of the Brazilian social imaginary, consciously avoiding either-or choices.[15]

Additional textual possibilities beyond Brazil could include stories from Argentine Jorge Luís Borges's *Ficciones* (1944), such as 'Tlön, Uqbar, Orbis Tertius'. In this playful, ironically pretentious story in the guise of an essay, the narrator immerses the reader in the workings of an imaginary utopian world, only to jolt us when its objects suddenly appear in the narrator's world (and our own). Anthologies including Roberto González Echeverría's *The Oxford Book of Latin American Short Stories* (1997) and Cass Canfield Jr's *Masterworks of Latin American Short*

Fiction (1996) also provide canonical tales of the fantastic and magical realism from Spanish America and Brazil. In addition to the uncanny tale of pseudo-science by Argentine Juana Manuela Gorriti, 'He Who Listens May Hear' (1876), *The Oxford Book of Latin American Short Stories* contains more contemporary stories of the fantastic, including 'The Third Bank of the River' (1962) by Brazilian João Guimarães Rosa, 'The Garden of the Forking Paths' (1944) by Borges, 'Night Face Up' (1966) by Julio Cortázar, and 'Walk' (1965) by Chilean José Donoso. Another Guimarães Rosa story, 'My Uncle, the Jaguar' (1962) also appears in translation in *Masterworks of Latin American Short Fiction*. Other notable Argentine novels include Adolfo Bioy Casares's *The Invention of Morel* (1940), concerning a man trapped on an island with human holograms, and Manuel Puig's *Pubis Angelical* (1981), the third part of which refers to a grim, dystopian future. These are canonical texts and criticism on them is more readily available in English.

There are also several novels that could be used to supplement course readings. I recommend Ursula K. Le Guin's translation of Argentine author Angela Gorodischer's *Kalpa Imperial* (1983), a fantasy novel about the rise and fall of an imaginary empire, Bolivian writer Edmundo Paz Soldán's slipstream novel *Turing's Delirium* (2003), or Latino author Junot Díaz's *The Brief Wondrous Life of Oscar Wao* (2007). These novels represent different subgenres and distinct time periods. The first, *Kalpa Imperial*, is an idiosyncratic fantasy, filled with castles, empires, royalty and servants, which uses Gothic imagery while following a labyrinthine, repetitive logic that, in my mind, captures the suppression of trauma and the cycles of Argentina's experience with authoritarianism and political violence. The novel opens cautiously, in a time of repression and censorship, with a storyteller who begins a tale calculated to restore collective memory. The second novel, by Paz-Soldán, takes place in the imaginary city of Rio Fugitivo, Bolivia. The novel explores the internet as a place to construct an alternate reality, a type of momentary refuge to escape persecution and political trauma. Eventually, however, this sanctuary slips into the politicized world of anti-globalization hackers and government agents bent on hunting them down and killing them. The portrayal of the young, lower-class hacker Kadinsky, and the older characters, with their recurrent memories of past political crimes, offers a distinct view of the internet in a country that has been plagued by dictatorship and political trauma.[16] A third alternative, Junot Díaz's *The Brief Wondrous Life of Oscar Wao* (2007), is a work written in English about Oscar, whose family members flee the Dominican Republic after trauma suffered under the brutal Trujillo dictatorship (1930–61).

Although neither sf nor fantasy per se, the text likens the plight of Oscar, a gifted student and social misfit in his tough neighbourhood of Paterson, New Jersey, to that of a mutant or alien attempting to fit into human society: 'You really want to know what being an X-Man feels like? Just be a smart bookish boy of colour in a contemporary U.S. ghetto. Mamma mia! Like having bat wings or a pair of tentacles growing out of your chest.'[17] Although peppered with footnotes, references to comics, and sf and fantasy genres, the narrator also refers to spirits that are more typical of 'Macondo' (the setting of García Márquez's *One Hundred Years of Solitude*, 1967, the quintessential novel of magical realism), than 'McOndo', the gritty text of the novel itself.[18] 'McOndo' is a reference to a literary movement pioneered by Chilean Alberto Fuguet, who believes that Latin America's latest generation of authors needs to incorporate the violent urban underworld into their fiction, shunning the facile exoticism of magical realism.[19] In short, all three of these novels use fantasy, sf and variants of cyberpunk effectively to criticize their country's past, where political crimes continue to haunt the present, even in conventionally escapist scenarios of the fantasy realm and the internet.

Translated SF novels by Brazilian authors

In the case of Brazil, choices are more limited. Three Brazilian novels that have been translated into English are Herberto Sales's *The Fruit of Thy Womb* (1976), Ignacio de Loyola Brandão's *And Still the Earth* (1981) and Marcio Souza's *The Order of the Day* (1983). *The Fruit of Thy Womb* concerns a society where a technocratic government enforces a strict, zero-growth birth-control programme in order to save the population from starvation. The second, *And Still the Earth*, describes an eco-dystopia in which an everyman protagonist is faced with stifling heat, mutants and military officers as he travels through a nightmarish São Paulo toward a desert-like Amazon. The third novel, *The Order of the Day*, is about two aliens who control rival military officers in a type of good (democracy) vs. evil (dictatorship) scenario, as Brazil undergoes the transition to democracy. The reservation I have concerning these works is that they are written by mainstream authors who venture into the genre only to criticize the policies of Brazil's military government (1964–85), using the 'low-brow' genre of sf to make their point. As is evident in the brief plot summaries, the iconography and themes employed are somewhat hackneyed and unoriginal, with authors using sf tropes more to denigrate government than to use the genre to explore new ideas. I used

The Fruit of Thy Womb with some success, however, since it can be compared to similar dystopias, including Margaret Atwood's *A Handmaid's Tale* (1985) and P.D. James's *The Children of Men* (1992). Still, in the Brazilian novel, the constant oppression and silencing of women, who are allegorically supposed to represent the Brazilian people, is disturbing, and its messianic ending by a male saviour, clichéd.

Works of fantasy and science fiction about Brazil

In seeking alternative readings for the course, I decided to compare sf works written by Latin-American authors with similar works by Anglo-American writers who employ Latin America as their setting. I found several candidates for this comparison. What follows is a guide and a caveat to those who wish to explore this topic. Paralleling the works by Gorodischer, Paz-Soldán and Díaz outlined above are the fantasy novel *Through the Arc of the Rainforest* (1990) by Karen Tei Yamashita, and the hyperkinetic, high-tech, time-warp novel, *Brasyl* (2007) by Ian McDonald. I will also briefly discuss S.N. Lewitt's *Songs of Chaos* (1993), a work I find so stereotypical that it could be used to illustrate the pitfalls of 'tropicalization' or exoticism, outlined below. I conclude with a brief analysis of Samuel Delany's 'Driftglass' (1967), an earlier story whose cultural authenticity and postcolonial critique are lacking in some of the other texts.[20]

Accordingly, the concept of 'tropicalization' is useful in studying the literary representation of Latin America by outsiders. It is a term I borrowed from *Tropicalizations: Images of Latinad* (1997), a collection of essays edited by Frances R. Aparicio and Susana Chávez-Silverman. Tropicalization parallels Edward Said's concept of Orientalism, but applies to the stereotyping of the population of Latin America rather than that of the Middle East. I would note that, as the editors point out, the authors represented in this collection are of varied backgrounds: some are Latinos living in the US, while others are from Latin America. This allows for 'plural forms and multiple subject locations'. This circumstance differentiates 'tropicalization' from Orientalism, which is unilateral and refers to European discourse about the Orient.[21]

In general, as Said and others have noted, both tropicalization and Orientalism tend to reveal more about the anxieties of the colonizer (or global power) than about those of the colonized (or global underling), in that they invent, fantasize and take liberties with an exotic or unknown culture.[22] In Said's view, intellectuals in Europe and other developed nations create a discourse whose very construction naturalizes power over 'recalcitrant phenomena', that is, other cultures.[23] Two useful essays from *Tropicalizations*, the first by Debra Castillo and the second by Steven Benz, make it clear that while tropical lands may inspire Anglo-American writers, any insight derived from cultural 'contact' with the people living there is more of a projection than a reality.

Brazil poses a slightly different problem in that, along with its tropical exoticism, it also has a futuristic side symbolized by the modernist architecture of Brasília, its planned capital. As early as 1941, Stefan Zweig dubbed Brazil 'the land of the future', implying that it had the basis for cultural progress (because of its lack of overt racism) and that it was on the brink of an economic breakthrough (because he believed in the potential of its vast natural resources).[24] I have found that the 'tropicalization' in novels set in Brazil has more to do with authors 'going native' and believing that a basic familiarity with Brazil's cultural icons (the Amazon region, carnival and samba schools, Afro-Brazilian culture, soccer) gives them instant insight into Brazilian culture. Like Zweig, outsiders tend to be blind to racial and social divisions that lie below the surface, and to the deep historical roots of urban tensions or social problems stemming from modernization which are among the most difficult to resolve. Even in films such as Victor Meirelles and Katia Lund's urban drama *City of God* (*Cidade de Deus*, 2002), violence is glamorized, shot in MTV style, all quick cuts and bright topical colour. Rather than fearing the Brazilian Other, the outsider tends to be seduced by a facile exoticism, which is viewed from a position of naive wonder.

As an illustration of a reductive combination of Brazil's traditional and futuristic cultures, I offer a brief analysis of S.N. Lewitt's sf novel *Songs of Chaos* (1993). In my view, this novel is a lesson in how not to write about Brazil. Lewitt's novel is clearly sf, as it takes place on a space ship run by Afro-Brazilian deities, with a culture based on the samba schools of the *favelas* (slums) of Rio de Janeiro. Here the use of religion and carnival are the first evidence of a cultural misconception. Afro-Brazilian religions and carnival function within the structure of Brazil's markedly hierarchical society, and putting them to 'use' to run the ship breaks with their basic principles of subversion and self-expression. In the novel, the ship runs on a mystical biotechnology that operates on frequencies of samba rhythms that defy the purely scientific solutions of other 'rational' cultures. The protagonist, the freethinking cyberneticist Dante, escapes persecution by the repressive and conformist Eurostate, stowing away on the Brazilian space ship. After a period of adjustment, he is able to appreciate the ship's tropical wonders, with its exotic talking parrots and macaws, and its crew, who are obsessed with samba music and whose 'samba schools' prepare to compete in a carnival parade. In the end, Dante is able to use his creativity to help some recalcitrant crewmembers overcome the division between the rational and intuitive, helping their school win the samba competition. In my view, the novel reads like a tourist describing the marvels of Rio de Janeiro and carnival while on vacation – with some futuristic touches. While films like *City of God* exaggerate drug violence, this novel misrepresents *favela* culture by ridding it of all the unpleasant social realities of poverty, and related social or political problems.

Karen Tei Yamashita's fantasy novel, *Through the Arc of the Rainforest* (1990), is more subtle than Lewitt's, although it does not hesitate to emphasize the exoticism of Brazil. Yamashita has the advantage of being married to a Brazilian and having lived nine years in Brazil, which explains why her text has fewer linguistic and cultural errors. Her experience in Brazil allows her to examine the diverse classes and ethnicities that come together in São Paulo, where the Japanese have a marked presence, along with immigrants from the impoverished region of the Brazilian north-east. Her novel has a wide cast of characters who are incorporated into the kind of episodic plots and melodramatic situations associated with Brazilian telenovelas. She also captures the strength of popular religion, contrasting and mixing popular and elite classes, while including American characters, in an effort to highlight the assimilative nature of Brazilian culture. Two foreigners – a Japanese man who becomes inseparable from a ball that inexplicably gyrates in front of his forehead, and an American executive with an extra arm – feel at home in Brazil, but they represent antagonistic forces and their respective personal and corporate interests start to collide. The main plot hinges on a potential ecological disaster in the Amazon, where a giant plastic bubble with magnetic qualities appears to have come through the river's tributaries and broken through the forest floor. The curative power of the bubble or 'matacão', as it is known, attracts pilgrims and corporations, threatening to destroy the pristine rainforest and its surrounding area. While I find Yamashita's characterization of Brazilians and their culture to be accurate, I find her unexplained scientific phenomena (the man's gyrating ball, the third arm, the magnetic plastic of the matacão) more problematic. Yamashita's strength is that she offers a believable social panorama combined with ecological concerns. Her plotline is successful in drawing together myriad characters, and she manages to blend a sensitive concern with improving the lives of the Third World poor with First World ecological concerns about the Amazon.

Ian McDonald's *Brasyl* (2007) is by far the most ambitious of foreign sf or fantasy texts written about the country. Indeed, it was hailed as a 'masterpiece' by *Asimov's Science Fiction*, according to the novel's jacket, which also states that the novel takes a perspective that is neither European nor American, offering an original view of South America's 'largest and most vibrant country'. Paul Raven praises McDonald's novel in his 2008 review for *Foundation*, for its authentic and refreshing portrait of a 'Latino metropolis'.[25] Gary K. Wolfe also gave the novel a positive review in the February 2007 edition of *Locus*,[26] stating that it seemed to follow in the line of Brazilian cyberpunk – dubbed *tupinipunk* by Roberto de Sousa Causo – which I analyse in some detail in my book *Brazilian Science Fiction*.[27] I disagree with this assertion since *tupinipunk* tends to be highly allegorical, mystical, satirical and political, and a critique of First World powers impinging on Brazilian sovereignty. It is precisely this political critique that McDonald misses, replaying the flaw that Timothy Brennan points out in his essay about the novel of empire, 'The National Longing for Form', in which the Anglo-European '"novel of empire" in its classic modernist version ... has been blind to the impact of a world system largely directed by Anglo-American interests, however much it involved itself passionately, unevenly, and contradictorily in some of the human realities of world domination'.[28] In *Brasyl*, African deities and secret warriors from the past and present are collapsed into a multiverse, de-historicizing the central role played by slavery, monarchy and neo-colonial powers such as the United States and the British Empire during Brazil's period of national formation,[29] ultimately turning the country into a globalized pop-phenomenon for foreign consumption.

Although *Brasyl* takes place during widely separated years (2006, 2032 and 1732), interweaving three stories set in the three periods, there is no sense of history, only a cyberpunk façade of postmodernity, predicated on a sense of the commodification of art and the destruction of historical memory.[30] As the work takes us from contemporary Rio de Janeiro to a near-future São Paulo, then back to the eighteenth-century Amazon, we follow a cast of characters that runs the social gamut from slum dwellers to the social and cultural elite. One of these, Marcelina Hoffman, a producer of television reality shows and practitioner of *capoeira* (a type of Brazilian martial art), becomes a multiverse-jumping ninja, who rushes to the rescue of the other characters. Edson/Efrim, a bisexual, cross-dressing thief of high-end fashion attire, falls in love with the heroine from another line of the multiverse, whom he consults in order to free himself of a tracking device on a pilfered item. Luís Quinn, an eighteenth-century priest, finds himself going native after imbibing an indigenous potion that reveals the presence of the multiverse and the value of multicultural history. He takes up arms against a Portuguese Jesuit who navigates a large craft along the rivers of the Amazon region, forcibly recruiting and converting all those who fall under his domain. While all of these story lines are told with narrative suspense, they fall short of capturing more than a superficial understanding of Brazilian history, geography and culture.

While the shifting narratives allow McDonald to offer views of diverse regions, cultures and classes, the novel re-packages Brazil for consumption by non-Brazilians (hence his inclusion of a 'playlist' of Brazilian music for readers at the end of the novel). I found more allusions to Brazilian music, pop culture and current events in one chapter of *Brasyl* than in all the other novels combined. As a Brazilianist, I can generally follow these allusions, but one wonders whether this would be possible for average readers or, more specifically, students. References to supermodel Gisele Bundchen, the international hit film *The City of God*, and the Brazilian martial art of *capoeira* may be familiar to some readers, but the film *Bus 174*, acronyms like the PCC (Primeiro Comando da Capital, a powerful prison gang that organized massive bus stoppages and burning in São Paulo in 2006), MST (Movimento Sem Terra, the landless movement), and words like Skol (a brand of beer) and *ladeiras* (the word for steep streets, often rendered incorrectly by McDonald as 'ladeiros') are certainly much less widely known. While McDonald includes a glossary (which averages one to three Portuguese spelling or factual errors per page), I found that *Bus 174*, PCC, ladeira, and MST fail to appear in it. José Padilla's *Bus 174* (2002), for example, is a documentary portraying a dramatic hostage scenario, in which a black man holds a white female student hostage. The film examines his background and the motivations behind his crime. In every sense, McDonald's text displays a postmodern density that can be overwhelming, especially in light of the necessity of understanding a complex plot set in a foreign culture. While the fast pace of the novel appeals to students, they may complain about confusion when confronted with so much information.

In the end, I think the novel can be useful as a teaching tool, since few Brazilian cyberpunk texts are available in translation. Some web research by instructors or students on the history and practice of *capoeira*, historical figures like Padre Antônio Vieira (a seventeenth-century priest who defended the rights of Amerindians in the north), the eighteenth-century Jesuit missions in southern Brazil, and the social role of Brazilian soap operas in television viewing habits may offer some counterbalance to the cultural exoticism of the text.

Concluding observations

One American text about Brazil that I find rewarding is Samuel R. Delany's 1967 short story, 'Driftglass', which captures the grittiness of life in the Brazilian north-east. Despite its inaccurate Portuguese spellings (such as Juao for João), it conveys a remarkable cultural authenticity. Moreover, Delany's portrayal of teenagers who are willing to undergo surgery that allows them to do underwater mining, often risking life and limb, seems to fit the psychology of Brazil's regional poor. It also seems accurate in portraying a Brazilian fishing village that offers the expatriate protagonist Cal Svenson, a crippled former miner, a sense of community and belonging. As David Samuelson points out in the critical commentary following the story in *The Science Fiction Research Association Anthology*'s 1988 edition, Delany consciously and artfully alludes to characters from Shakespeare's *The Tempest*, a text about the colonization of the New World. The character of Cal, in particular, can be seen as a parallel to Shakespeare's Caliban, inverting the typical roles of the indigenous culture (represented by Caliban), and the foreign white colonizer (associated with Prospero), which recasts the story in a Latin American or postcolonial light.

I began investigating the topic of Brazil in fantasy and science fiction because I thought I might eventually want to teach more courses in English. Since only a few Brazilian sf novels are available in translation, I began looking for appropriate texts. Of all the works I have examined, I would recommend teaching those of Yamashita and Delany, though I have to admit that McDonald does bring a cybernetic edge to Brazil, a theme otherwise unavailable in translation. These authors convey a portrait of Brazil that I would share with students and non-Brazilianists, although other novels would also make for interesting discussion. These may include Patricia Anthony's *Cradle of Spendor* (1996), Orson Scott Card's *Speaker for the Dead* (1986), Amber Hayward's *The Healer* (2002), Richard Kadrey's *Kamikaze L'Amour: A Novel of the Future* (1995) and John Updike's *Brazil* (1994).[31]

As I draw to a conclusion, I ponder the verbal feedback of my students. They requested a change in classroom practice (that I send out questions and introductions before the readings), but liked the fact that they were able to choose their presentation topics freely. As I worked through the material, I found that *Cosmos Latinos* works very well, although students tend to over-generalize themes and interpretations based on only one story. They were also surprised that there were few women writers in translation. The best I could do was to refer to articles I wrote about recent sf

198 Teaching Science Fiction

written by Latin American women.[32] I was generally pleased with the film selection. Students who were unfamiliar with sf thanked me for showing them that the genre was something more than 'spaceships and aliens'. One student initially asked that more magical realism texts be included, but later told me that she realized that she had exposure to those texts in her Latin American literature classes. She also commented that she had never thought of linking Borges to science fiction. I invite you to read these texts, to try them out on a class of undergraduates and to judge for yourself how sf is enriched by the Latin American perspective.

Notes

1. The film is included on the DVD accompanying María Cinta Aparisi, José A. Blanco and Marcie D. Rinka, *Revista: Conversación sin barreras*, 2nd edn (Boston: Vista, 2007).
2. See Yolanda Molina-Gavilán, Andrea L. Bell, Miguel Ángel Fernández-Delgado, M. Elizabeth Ginway and Juan Carlos Toledano Redondo, 'A Chronology of Latin-American Science Fiction', *Science Fiction Studies*, 34:3 (2007): 369–431.
3. With the exception of *The Fifth Power*, supplied to me by Alfredo Suppia, a film specialist at the Universidade Federal de Juiz de Fora, the films are available at Brazilian bookstores and possibly online. Professor Suppia is most willing to help others in locating or suggesting Latin American sf films. He can be contacted at alsuppia@terra.com.br.
4. For an allegorical reading of the film, see Randal Johnson, 'Cinema Novo and Cannibalism: Macunaíma', in Randal Johnson and Robert Stam, eds, *Brazilian Cinema* (Irvington, NY: Columbia University Press, 1995) 176–90.
5. In its modern history, Argentina has experienced political strife among Peronists (supporters of populist leader General Juan Perón, who built his support among unions and the working classes in 1940s), and other military leaders, who first overthrew Perón in 1955. Another military dictatorship, headed by Juan Carlos Onganía, ruled the country after 1966 until Perón's takeover in 1973. Following Perón's death in 1975, a military junta led by Gen. Jorge Videla took power and began the 'Dirty War', in which thousands disappeared. The junta's rule ended after the Falklands War in 1983.
6. For a list of plot summaries of Santo films, see http://terpconnect.umd.edu/~dwilt/santo.html (accessed 23 July 2009). Santo has fought – among other villains – Martians, mummies, Frankenstein and mad scientists. As for secondary texts, Lourdes Grobet, *Lucha Libre: Masked Superstars of Mexican Wrestling* (Mexico: Trilce, 2005) is a pictorial history with an essay by Carlos Monsivais in Spanish, one of the few Spanish texts that addresses this phenomenon in a scholarly way. A more recent study is Heather Levi, *The World of Lucha Libre: Secrets, Revelations, and Mexican National Identity* (Durham, NC: Duke University Press, 2008).
7. Themes of Mexican migrant labourers, outsourcing and water rights are brought up in New York-based filmmaker Alex Rivera's *Sleep Dealer* (2007), which won the award for Best American Screenplay at the Sundance

Film Festival in 2008. See http://www.fest21.com/en/blog/sundance/sleep_dealer_wins_alfred_p_sloan_prize (accessed 23 July 2009). The film recalls several of the Mexican cyberpunk stories in Andrea L. Bell and Yolanda Molina-Gavilán, eds, *Cosmos Latinos* (Middletown, CT: Wesleyan University Press, 2003); see http://www.slashfilm.com/2008/09/16/sleep-dealer-movie-trailer/ (accessed 23 July 2009). Rivera's web page, http://www.alexrivera.com/, has his contact information. His five minute mockumentary short, 'Why Cybraceros', explores similar themes in a low-tech way. See http://www.invisibleamerica.com/movies.html (accessed 23 July 2009).
8. For definitions of utopia I use the traditional sources: Northrop Frye, 'Varieties of Literary Utopias', in Frank Manuel, ed., *Utopias and Utopian Thought* (Boston: Houghton Mifflin, 1966) 25–59 and Darko Suvin, 'Defining the Literary Genre of Utopia: Some Historical Semantics, Some Genealogy, a Proposal, and a Plea', *Studies in the Literary Imagination*, 6:2 (1973): 121–45.
9. As Hartwell notes, 'A sense of wonder, awe at the vastness of space and time, is at the root of excitement of science fiction.' See David Hartwell, 'Worshipping at the Church of Wonder', in *Age of Wonders* (New York: Walker, 1984) 40–58 at 41.
10. Larry McCaffery, *Storming the Reality Studio: A Casebook of Cyberpunk and Postmodern Science Fiction* (Durham, NC: Duke University Press, 1991); Beatriz Sarlo, *Scenes from Postmodern Life*, trans. Jon Beasley-Murray (Minneapolis: University of Minnesota Press, 2001). In Sarlo's view, postmodernity typically celebrates dispersion, the breakdown of traditional social ties and the loss of traditional communities. Once freed or 'de-territorialized', these new cultural nomads theoretically represent the new found autonomy of cultural minorities. However, in Argentina, she posits that this may not always be the case. New technologies blur class traditional differences, but economic opportunity and education remain highly unequal (88–95). Hopenhayn outlines the insidious implications of neo-liberalism and the myth of the market within postmodern celebration of diversity in Latin America. See 'Postmodernism and Neoliberalism in Latin America', in John Beverly, José Oviedo and Michael Aronna, eds, *The Postmodern Debate in Latin America* (Durham, NC: Duke University Press, 1995) 93–109.
11. See Farah Mendlesohn, *The Rhetorics of Fantasy* (Middletown, CT: Wesleyan University Press, 2008) 182–245.
12. See M. Elizabeth Ginway, 'The Body Politic in Brazilian Science Fiction: Implants and Cyborgs', in Donald M. Hassler and Clyde Wilcox, eds, *New Boundaries in Political Science Fiction* (Columbia, SC: University of South Carolina Press, 2008) 198–211.
13. Jacques Derrida, 'The Law of Genre', trans. Avital Ronell, in W.J.T. Mitchell, ed., *On Narrative* (Chicago: University of Chicago Press, 1981) 51–77.
14. See Ginway, *Brazilian Science Fiction: Cultural Myths and Nationhood in the Land of the Future* (Lewisburg, PA: Bucknell University Press, 2004) for a discussion of Carneiro's 'Darkness' (80–1) and of 'A Perfect Marriage' (78–80).
15. In his essay 'For an Anthropology of the Brazilian Tradition or "A Virtude está no Meio"'' DaMatta asks, 'Is it possible that Brazil is caught among one perspective that is truly Catholic, another that is authentically civic and modern, and still another that is fully popular and Carnivalesque', implying that Brazilians accommodate all three belief systems, avoiding the typical

either-or logic of Western thought. See DaMatta's essay in David J. Hess and Roberto DaMatta, eds, *The Brazilian Puzzle: Culture on the Borderlands of the Western World* (Irvington, NY: Columbia University Press) 270–91 at 281.
16. For more on the sf debate on this novel and its sf provenance, see J. Andrew Brown, 'Edmundo Paz-Soldán and his Precursors: Borges, Dick and the SF Canon', *Science Fiction Studies*, 34:3 (2007): 473–83.
17. Junot Díaz, *The Brief Wondrous Life of Oscar Wao* (New York: Riverhead Books, 2007) 22.
18. Ibid., 7.
19. See Mac Margolis, 'Is Magical Realism Dead?' *Newsweek*, 6 May 2002 at http://www.letras.s5.com/af0812047.htm (accessed 23 July 2009).
20. One might also include James Tiptree Jr's 'The Women Men Don't See' (1973), which takes place on Mexico's Yucatán Peninsula. After their light plane crashes in a remote area, the white male hero treats the women and the male Mexican pilot in the same chauvinistic way, hardly believing that they do not accept him as their 'natural' leader. Instead they prefer to leave with alien visitors rather than remaining with him. The story, told from the male narrator's point of view, explores gendered perspectives and literal and metaphorical alienation, it does not examine the Mexican culture of the 'other', a lacuna left for readers to ponder. Clearly, each of these works should be read with a certain wariness regarding cultural context, content and approach.
21. See Frances R. Aparicio and Susana Chávez-Silverman, eds, *Tropicalizations: Images of Latindad* (Durham, NH: Dartmouth College, 1997) 1–17 at 2.
22. See Edward Said, *Orientalism* (New York: Vintage, 1979) and John Storey, *Cultural Theory and Popular Culture* (Essex: Pearson, 2001) especially 79–80.
23. Said, *Orientalism*, 146.
24. Author and biographer Stefan Zweig (1881–1942) left his native Austria for fear of Nazi persecution. After becoming an English citizen in 1938, he travelled to South America in 1940, deciding to reside in Brazil. While in Rio de Janeiro he wrote *Brazil: A Land of the Future* (1941), in which he saw the future in the country's racial tolerance and in its natural resources. Pessimistic about the potential spread of Nazism, he committed suicide in Rio de Janeiro in 1942. Because of his importance in promoting Brazil, the populist president at the time, Getúlio Vargas, had his funeral paid for at state expense. See Stefan Zweig, *Brazil: A Land of the Future*, reprinted, with an afterword and translation by Lowell A. Bangerter (Riverside, CA: Ariadne Press, 2000).
25. Paul Raven praises McDonald's novel in his 2008 review for *Foundation*, for its authentic and refreshing portrait of a 'Latino metropolis'. See '*Brasyl* by Ian McDonald' *Foundation*, 102 (Spring 2008): 105–10 at 106. Latino seems to be used incorrectly here; 'Latin American' would have been a better choice. Also the novel includes a whole section that takes place in the Amazon, which is hardly a metropolis. 'Latino' more aptly refers to people of Spanish American descent living in the United States. Few Brazilians see themselves as 'latinos'.
26. Gary K. Wolfe, review of *Brasyl*, by Ian McDonald, *Locus*, February 2007, at http://www.locusmag.com/Features/2007/02/locus-reviews-ian-mcdonald.html (accessed 23 July 2009).

27. Combining issues of race, tribalism, technology, sex and an urban setting, its general feel is street-smart, yet it is analogue rather than digital in nature, since none of the action takes place in cyberspace. See Ginway, *Brazilian Science Fiction*, 155–7.
28. Timothy Brennan, 'The National Longing for Form', in Homi K. Bhabha, ed., *Nation and Narration* (New York, Routledge, 1990) 44–70 at 48.
29. The English were key in having the Portuguese court move to Brazil in 1808, allowing them to take advantage of a new open port policy to obtain new markets for their manufactured goods. See Nelson Piletti, *A história do Brasil* (São Paulo: Ática, 1991), 89. The War of Paraguay or the Triple Alliance of 1865–70 was also largely financed by the English to crush the fledgling economic independence of Paraguay, resulting in a near genocide of its male population, and in the indebtedness of the alliance (Brazil, Uruguay and Argentina) to England. During the same period, the United States began to buy more than half of Brazil's coffee crop (harvested by slave labour), becoming an important trading partner. This was also the beginning of America's long-term influence in the region in the twentieth century. See ibid., 112–15.
30. I am thinking here of Carl Freedman's *Critical Theory and Science Fiction* (Hanover, NH: Wesleyan University Press, 2000) 190–200.
31. I am indebted to Roberto Causo who told me about several of these novels and lent me copies of texts by Kadrey and Lewitt.
32. M. Elizabeth Ginway, 'Recent Science Fiction and Fantasy Written by Women', *Foundation*, 99 (2007): 49–62. Here I explore how women writers first appropriate male voices, then place women in male roles, and finally explore incipient feminist themes in the fantasy and horror genres. See also Mary Ginway, 'Interview with Argentine Author Liliana Bodoc', *Femspec*, 9:1 (2008): 20–8, about Bodoc's trilogy about the role of women in her re-writing of the conquest of the New World from the point of view of indigenous peoples.

12
Teaching Science and Science Fiction: A Case Study

Mark Brake and Neil Hook

This chapter describes a unique experiment: namely, the design and delivery of an undergraduate border study at the University of Glamorgan which explores the interrelationship of science and science fiction. We begin by looking at the context of the degree award: previous educational initiatives, the widening access agenda, and the award's avowed intent to address the issue of social inclusion in science education at university level. We go on to look at the structure of the award itself, including a curricular analysis of the degree's content. Finally, we consider the salient aspects of this unique experiment in terms of the broader outcomes after a decade of teaching the science and science fiction programme.

Introduction

As a theme for undergraduate study, science is a giant in the academic world. It has acquired a generic status through representing not only its own constituent and pure knowledge areas, such as physics and biology, but also as a methodological paradigm associated with the pursuit of truth. Through systematic attempts to publicly refute or verify hypotheses and theories, this paradigm has been adopted for the teaching of social sciences. But science also extends beyond the laboratory. It extends beyond the academic community, beyond the associated scientific professions. It positions itself within popular culture, and specifically within science fiction. The proliferation of science fiction in literature, cinema, television and gaming reflects its increasing impact. Science fiction has moved into the mainstream with the advent of the information age it helped realize. Of the fifty highest grossing movies of all time, science fiction films account for twenty-two entries as of 21 July 2009 (a further thirteen are fantasy).[1] Audiences of all ages will watch the latest science fiction blockbuster in the cinema. Millions of viewers regularly tune in to the BBC to watch *Doctor Who*, *Life on Mars* or *Ashes to Ashes*. Science fiction even has its own channels running back to back series and films. And in the ever-expanding field of computer gaming, science fiction titles dominate. The fastest selling media product in history was Microsoft's science fiction video-game *Halo 3*, with the game's sales generating US$170 million on its first day.

The use of a broad theme for the application of scientific ideas and methods is commonplace within higher education. At the most powerful levels it has led to the creation of new disciplines associated with, for example, the study of behaviour, psychology, and the study of society, sociology. Nonetheless, the exploration of science through science fiction was a new endeavour for our academic community, representing an important challenge to conventional curriculum design.

Traditions and perspectives within education question the positioning of scientific knowledge within society, and within popular culture. A common dialectic has often been used: science against art, and the conflict of paradigms associated with what at first seem to be such different traditions within academia. An effective technique for exploring this kind of academic debate involves a critical exploration of the boundaries and barriers that define what, at first glance, appear to be discrete subject areas and methodologies.

Our degree award is an attempt to explore one such boundary. It seeks a critical and multidisciplinary understanding of the relationship between science and science fiction. It examines the texts of genre fiction, whilst testing the validity and integrity of scientific theories and methods. The intention is to produce a unique, provocative and compelling account of science fiction as a touchstone of the dialectic of science and progress. The programme aims to explore the metamorphoses of science fiction and their rapport with science. And to encompass both the science fictional visions that have shaped science, politics and society, and conversely, the impetus given to science fiction by discovery and invention.

Science fiction narratives are well established as a mode of thinking. Their crucial field of discourse is the reducible gap between the new worlds uncovered by science and exploration, and the fantastic strange worlds of the imagination through which we come to see our own conditions of life from a new and potentially revolutionary perspective. With this in mind, it was our intention to present science fiction as a sustained, coherent and often subversive check on the oppositions and contradictions of science – the promises and pitfalls of progress through the ages. In this way we hoped to highlight the genre as a story of our hopes and fears for science, of the ongoing relationship between scientific materialism and the cultural scepticism of science fiction. Furthermore, there was clear potential that the programme would enable an evolving and unparalleled description of the way in which science fiction has influenced issues and dialogues in the communication of science. Science fiction is still the leading creative catalyst of scientific ideas into symbols and metaphors of the human condition; an often unconscious and therefore especially valuable reflection of the assumptions and attitudes held by society. By virtue of its ability to project and dramatize, science fiction is recognized as a particularly effective, and perhaps for many people the only, means for generating concern and thought about the social, philosophical and moral consequences of scientific progress.

Such an approach to the study of science had a good pedigree. In the late 1970s and early 1980s, the SISCON (*Science in a Social Context*) project was launched at a number of UK universities including Edinburgh, Manchester, Stirling and Sussex. SISCON was a joint programme whose aim was to introduce social aspects in the study of science, including the sociological, economic, technological and ecological effects of science on society. Another aim was to produce a different kind of science graduate. In the past, higher education in science had focused on educating highly skilled and specialized professional scientists, graduates proficient in the techniques of a particular scientific discipline. But the belief had grown that there was also scope to produce graduates with a unique mixture of skills, possessing flexible and practical abilities to respond to a dynamic and evolving cultural working environment where artistic creativity and science often meet. With this in mind, we began to realize that the study of science fiction may be a powerful factor in extending the franchise for science education, to perhaps draw in those excluded by science's apparent mathematical and technical exclusivity. Perhaps the border study of science and science fiction could promote a greater social inclusion for lifelong learners who may otherwise feel disenfranchised from such study.

Context

The BSc Science and Science Fiction emerged out of an initiative led by Higher Education institutions in South Wales in partnership with community groups. This has come to be known as the Community University of the Valleys, and was cited by the Dearing Report as an example of good practice in widening access and increasing participation in higher education in the UK.[2] Courses at accredited and non-accredited levels are offered within local learning centres located at community venues, and where possible new and innovative curricula are offered to a wide range of learners. They include disaffected youth, as well as those who have been redundant for a number of years.

One of the new community courses that proved a success was a module on the science and culture of astrobiology.[3] The module attracted much attention from local lifelong learners who proved very interested in this rather speculative and multidisciplinary aspect of astronomy. In many cases these individuals had no formal qualifications in science related subjects, yet they demonstrated understanding and pronounced interest in aspects of scientific enquiry. It became apparent that these community students had interpreted a wide range of science fiction texts. They had used knowledge sources that reach beyond the more conventional source literature, extending into the critical reading of magazines, role-play exercises, fanzines and video games.

The community experience led eventually to the creation of a degree award in astronomy, which is now contained within the University of Glamorgan's curriculum portfolio. Details of the early development of our programme were reported to the 162nd Colloquium of the International Astronomical Union at London and the 110th National Conference of the Astronomical Society of the Pacific at Albuquerque, New Mexico.[4] Subsequent developments, especially to the more science fictional and astrobiological aspects of the programme, were reported on the Great Barrier Reef, PCST-8 in Barcelona, NASA Ames, Seattle and Canterbury.[5]

The programme attracted much interest from students and staff, and it was soon realized that science fiction was a recurring and even dominant theme for discussion. The planning of the degree programme was approved in September 1998, and a grant awarded to engage in more detailed curriculum planning, involving the schools of science, humanities and art and design. One of the key initial considerations was the need to identify a demand for this new curriculum, and an indication that it would also appeal to a new kind of student, thereby achieving the objectives of increasing access and widening participation.

Aims and objectives of the degree

The degree award in science and science fiction that emerged focuses primarily on science, both historical and contemporary, as an integral part of culture. The vast majority of degree awards in science – and particularly 'pure science' – specialize exclusively in the science domain. They pay little regard to the context in which science is developed, practised and received. The science and science fiction degree is an award *about* science as much as it is an award *in* science, since it encompasses the multifarious influences brought to bear on the continuous creation and consumption of science. In particular, the award uses a number of contrasting methodologies to explore the relationship between science, culture and society. The science fiction modules provide, in one sense, an imaginative forum that focuses on this relationship.

Aims

The aims of the science and science fiction degree award are to produce graduates who have a dynamic and pluralistic understanding of the nature and evolution of science and who can also critically develop and communicate ideas about science and its cultural context. Science fiction is the vehicle for an exploration of the relationship between science and culture. The award provides the students with the conceptual and methodological frameworks necessary to achieve these aims. These frameworks include science: its methodology, philosophy and sociology. Critical theories from media and cultural studies are also explored. It is hoped that, in this way, the students gain a more dynamic and critical understanding of science, that they recognize that issues in science also require social and cultural analysis. Naturally, the award also specifically hopes to cultivate a critical analysis of science fiction, one that recognizes its scientific, philosophical, cultural and social influences. It is hoped that this exploration of the boundaries between disciplines will also have another benefit; and that ability is engendered in the students to imaginatively communicate the nature and evolution of science, and science fiction, and their interrelationship.

Objectives

The objectives of the award were manifold. The intention was to inculcate in students a critical understanding of the social development of science and science fiction, as well as examining the nature of science and its relationship with science fiction. The use of science fiction on the award should also lead to a greater understanding of issues related to the public understanding of science, particularly the social implications of science and technology, and the way in which they are represented within various forms of media and culture.

Degree structure and cognate strands

The award encompasses two cognate strands: the science strand, and the science fiction strand. In each strand students are provided with the necessary research tools, frameworks and methodologies to enable them to construct differing interpretations, paradigms and perspectives on the nature of the subjects under study. In many ways, the science fiction strand represents an open debate forum for the award. It is here that the convergence of the cognate strands is potentially the most dynamic, providing an opportunity for debate and contrasting the differing perspectives and frameworks encountered in the two strands. The award represents a unique mixture of skills since it brings together science and the humanities, challenging the 'two culture' myth. It is hoped that graduates develop flexible and practical abilities to respond to a dynamic and evolving working environment after graduation.

Science strand

The modules chosen for this strand are drawn from the physical sciences and astronomy. There is an appropriate rationale for this choice. As well as being a fascinating and challenging subject in its own right, astronomy can also be used to teach the principles of other sciences: in particular physics, earth science, chemistry and some important aspects of life science. Optics, thermodynamics and mechanics can be applied to astronomical objects – an effective way to make the learning process more dynamic and motivating.

Furthermore, our account of the physical sciences is pluralistic, and that is probably its most important innovation. We recognize that the scientific revolutions have influenced, or have been influenced by, conceptual changes in cosmology, chemistry, biology, physics, philosophy and religion. Specialized accounts are perhaps inhibited from analysing the nature of these links and their influence upon the growth of human knowledge and endeavour. Indeed, pursuit of this pluralism has led to a second innovation – our modules repeatedly cross the institutionalized boundaries which separate 'science' from 'history' or 'philosophy'.

Our science strand provides a cognate group of multidisciplinary modules. They are based on the physical sciences and astronomy, but use an innovative syllabus balanced between the scientific and historic/cultural aspects of each topic. The modules are also open to students of all other disciplines. The strand explores the development of scientific ideas and beliefs through the use of social and historical frameworks. This helps lend clarity to the nature and evolution of scientific concepts and methods, whilst also embracing the wider cultural influences and impact.

Each module is studied through lectures, tutorials and directed study. The tutorials are provided to enable all students to study the modules without the need of exempting prerequisites, whilst extending the opportunity to promote the understanding of science beyond the confines of normal undergraduate science programmes.

Science fiction strand

One of the key aims of the award is an exploration of the relationship between science, culture and society. As was mentioned earlier, the science fiction strand acts as an imaginative forum that focuses on this relationship. Consequently, our definition of science fiction, and our associated choice of key texts, had a great bearing on the content of this strand. Science fiction has been variously defined.[6] Even though students are discouraged from the naive notion of science fiction as simply reflecting science, our emphasis remains on the relationship between science, science fiction and society. Science fiction questions science, examines individuals and communities often in terms of technological systems, and those systems and technologies in terms of identity and consciousness. For example, Judith Merril defines the heart of science fiction as:

> the mode which makes use of the traditional 'scientific method' (observation, hypothesis, experimentation) to examine some postulated approximation of reality, by introducing a given set of changes – imaginary or inventive – into the common background of 'known facts', creating an environment in which the responses and perceptions of the characters will reveal something about the inventions, the characters, or both.[7]

Sam Moskowitz (1963) suggests a definition that is useful because of its catholic conception of science, a conception that was not always as broad nor as acceptable to practitioners and readers of science fiction as it is today:

> science fiction is . . . identifiable by the fact that it eases the 'willing suspension of disbelief' on the part of its (audience) by utilising an atmosphere of scientific credibility for its imaginative speculations in physical science, space, time, social science, and philosophy.[8]

Joanna Russ (1995) holds that science fiction, 'attempts to assimilate imaginatively scientific knowledge about reality and the scientific method, as distinct from the merely practical changes sciences has made in our lives'.[9] Patrick Parrinder suggests that, 'up to the present, SF has continued to be moulded and shaped by scientific thought, even in its moments of rebellion against it'.[10] In short, science fiction has been used as a way of imagining the relationship between technology, science and society. It is the conviction of the science fiction strand that in following this approach a student would find the extrapolations of science fiction more intriguing, rewarding and challenging, and would gain, as a result, a more rounded and informed criticism of science itself. As a consequence, the criteria for selecting works is not solely on literary merit, but also takes into account the ways in which works articulate the relationship between scientific thought and society.

Traditionally, works of, and courses in, science fiction have been legitimated within a literary tradition, that is, the creation of canonical works, and an evaluation of works in terms of their contribution to the development of a humanistic aesthetic. However, for all of its imagination and innovation, science fiction would have remained the province of a limited readership had it not been for the expansion of the genre to the visual media. Consequently, literature is not prioritized within the award; common materials also involve works from television, film and other media. Nor are literary techniques especially used to analyse these materials. As Joanna Russ points out:

> criticism of science fiction cannot possibly look like the criticism we are used to. It will – perforce – employ an aesthetic in which the elegance, rigorousness, and systematic coherence of explicit ideas is of great importance. It will therefore appear to stray into all sorts of extra-literary fields: metaphysics, politics, philosophy, physics, biology, psychology, topology, mathematics, history and so on.[11]

She also remarks that: '(medievalists) enjoy ... (sf) ... much more than do students of later literary periods. So, in fact do city planners, architects, archaeologists, engineers, rock musicians, anthropologists, and nearly everyone except most English professors.'[12] Therefore, our degree award focuses on the concept of fiction as an invented idea or statement or narrative, an imaginary thing; and as the act or process of inventing imaginary things, or a conventionally accepted falsehood. The notion of truth and falsehood has also been central to the evaluation of science fiction. The award addresses this issue in a number of ways: first, through the physical limits of realizing imagined scientific invention; second, through the connections between fact and fictional work, which leads to deeper questions about science's dependence on narrative to support and justify scientific thought and activity; and third, through the possibility of achieving a mimetic relationship between reality and representation.

The creation of science fiction is a social and cultural practice involving practitioners and audiences; a product of cultures of production and consumption. The science fiction strand therefore exploits the close links between science practitioners and the production of science fiction. It recognizes that science fiction has a particular appeal to scientists who evaluate it and write it in terms of their own cultural competencies. Science exists as a prestigious idea and commodity within particular cultural groups who have their own hierarchies of taste that run counter to the literary imagination. So, the science fiction strand also seeks to analyse the parameters and composition of these groups.

Award content and curricular analysis

Table 12.1 Award structure and cognate strands

Science strand	Science fiction strand
Level 4	
Space I: Planets and Philosophy	What is Science Fiction?
Space II: The Nature of the Universe	The Evolution of SF
Earth Story	Independent Study
Level 5	
Stars, Science and the Bomb	Utopias and Dystopias
Cosmology and Controversy	Exploring Space and Time
Exploring the Sky	Independent Study
Level 6	
Life in the Universe	CyberScience
Project/Dissertation	Quantum Worlds

Curricular analysis of Level 4

Science strand	Science fiction strand
Space I: Planets and Philosophy	What is Science Fiction?
Space II: The Nature of the Universe	The Evolution of SF
Earth Story	Independent Study

When we were faced with the curriculum challenge of representing the border study of science and science fiction, we considered the ways in which the genre could be pared down into six modules of study, two at each of levels four, five and six. Like most of the modules listed in the schema above, each science fiction module represented 20 credits of study.

How then should we present the genre alongside science? Rather than plumping for a linear, episodic or genre-oriented approach, our minds were made up for us by the fact that many of the modules in the science strand were already validated and running. So, the award was structured in order that each cognate strand presents at each level modules whose curriculum themes run concurrently with the other strand. In other words, the themes and sub-themes presented in the science fiction strand reflect the major themes of study in the science strand.

Consider Level 4 (Year One): the main themes in the science strand are critical analyses of the nature and evolution of science. For example, the module 'Space I: Planets and Philosophy' introduces the students to the evolutionary role of planetary astronomy in the development of Western thought. The students study a history and philosophy of scientific knowledge, which demonstrates the importance of culture and anthropology to a critical understanding of modern science. Thus, in 'Space I', the evolutionary development of science is studied in a cultural context, from the Greeks through the Renaissance and the determinism of the Newtonian synthesis, to the indeterminate models of the twentieth century.

In 'Space II', the critical method and sceptical tradition of science is presented by communicating not only the findings and products of science, but also the actual, tortuous history of its great discoveries, along with the frequent misapprehensions and occasional stubborn refusal by its practitioners to change course. Scientific development is characterized by parallel acceptance (development) and denial (dogma). The students are encouraged to realize that the popularizer and communicator of science may use its history to enable communicants to distinguish science from pseudoscience: the method of science is as important as the findings of science. In 'Earth Story', the study of the home planet enables the students to critically examine the various causes and processes, both proximate and ultimate, of globalization: human migration, cultural and socio-political. Case study material allows the students to understand the modern world's inequalities without reverting to Eurocentric or even racist stereotypes.

With the curriculum of the science strand in mind, the science fiction strand introduces its concurrent themes against a changing socio-scientific background. In 'What is Science Fiction?' we introduce the themes and sub-themes to be studied in the strand, and in 'Evolution of Science Fiction' present an examination of how science fiction has critically perceived developments in science throughout its 500-year history, particularly the last two centuries. The students are also introduced to the necessary theory to enable an understanding of the signification of science fiction work. The strand offers a critical approach to the question of science and culture, helping to promote the science fiction strand as a forum for the award, an imaginative meeting place where contrasting scientific and cultural theories converge.

In all modules students are expected to communicate clearly, both verbally and in writing, and take responsibility for their own learning. An 'Independent Study' module enables them to engage in an independent study of a focused topic in greater breadth and depth than in the main programme of taught modules. Use of tutorials and seminars throughout encourages students to act as critics and analysts rather than mere recipients of presented information, both scientific and cultural.

Curricular analysis of Level 5

Science strand	Science fiction strand
Stars, Science and the Bomb	Utopias and Dystopias
Cosmology and Controversy	Exploring Space and Time
Exploring the Sky	Independent Study

It is important to realize that science fiction is not ghettoized to the science fiction strand itself. Many of the core science strand modules, at all levels, use science fiction texts to complement, criticize and communicate the main science subjects under study.

For example, one of the main themes at Level 5 in the science strand is the social responsibility of science and scientists. The module 'Stars, Science and the Bomb' looks at the parallel development of stellar nucleosynthesis and the hydrogen bomb in the first half of the twentieth century. Many of the key players made major contributions to both stellar evolution and the Manhattan project. Essentially, a star is a bomb that goes off slowly. The role of Wells's 'The World Set Free' is examined in the module, as are the post-apocalyptic fictional commentaries of Pat Frank (*Alas, Babylon,* 1959), Walter Miller Jr (*A Canticle for Leibowitz,* 1959), Stanley Kubrick (*Dr Strangelove or, How I Learned to Stop Worrying and Love the Bomb,* 1964) and Kurt Vonnegut (*Slaughterhouse Five,* 1969).

Ominous trends in bomb theory and practice are also assessed in terms of their influence on the socio-political landscape of the Cold War epoch. These ideas sit very comfortably alongside the sister module, 'Utopias and Dystopias' which discusses, among other things, absolute power and totalitarianism in society, and the rise of post-apocalyptic fiction under McCarthyism and Stalinism.

The space race and subsequent space exploration are considered in this political light and greatly inform the curriculum agenda in the science fiction module, 'Exploring Space and Time'. The module evaluates the mechanics of spacetime travel, technically informed by the 'Cosmology and Controversy' module in the science strand, which looks at the postwar emergence of cosmology as a science, and the changing nature of the concept of spacetime itself. 'Exploring Space and Time' also explores the notion of space as an allegory of imperialist venture and the causal relationships of spacetime travel as theorized within science and fiction.

Curricular analysis of Level 6

Science strand	Science fiction strand
Life in the Universe	CyberScience
Project/Dissertation	Quantum Worlds

A major part of Level 6 study is the concept of life, both natural and artificial. The astrobiology double module, 'Life in the Universe', is placed in the science strand, but is a heady mix of the science and culture on the questions of life. How has the concept of life changed? How will life evolve in the future? Is there life on other planets? Indeed, what is the future for life in the cosmos?

In recognition of the growing academic research status of astrobiology, NASA established its Astrobiology Institute (NAI) in 1998 as one element of its research programme. The NAI Roadmap outlines a network of pathways for development among academic researchers worldwide. The Roadmap includes a crucial societal and cultural dynamic, recognizing the intrinsic public interest in astrobiology that offers an opportunity to educate and inspire the next generation of citizens.

In a paper presented to the Astrobiology Science Conference at NASA Ames in 2004, Sam Abrams and David Morrison surveyed 1364 science departments in North American universities, yielding data on around 50 undergraduate courses on 'life in the universe'. From the posted curricula for these standard astrobiology courses, it was clear that the question of alien life in philosophy, fiction and the imagination plays an important part in these programmes. Furthermore, two members of our teaching team, Mark Brake and Martin Griffiths, served for three years as co-founders of the NAI science communication group. Through the example of our own 'Life in the Universe' module, an Astrobiology Communication Roadmap was developed, which explicitly recognizes the innovative use of popular literature and film as a bridge to public consciousness on the more reflective questions of astrobiology.

So, our 'Life in the Universe' module uses a blend of the science and culture of astrobiology to look at the history and development of the 'plurality of worlds' tradition, informed and critical speculation on the question of alien life, and visions of the future of human evolution. Key cultural commentators are used, including Stapledon, Lem, Clarke and Kubrick, and the Strugatsky brothers.

In light of these thoughts on life, the 'CyberScience' module critically assesses the science and culture of intelligence, identity and consciousness. Fictional speculation on the question of artificial intelligence is considered alongside emergence, the way in which complex systems and patterns arise out of a multiplicity of relatively simple interactions. This philosophical, systems theory approach is used to examine the question of human intelligence and evolution.

'Quantum Worlds' looks at the relationship between quantum mechanics and relativity theory and narrative structure within the genre. Specifically, the module critically examines the influence of quantum indeterminacy and the many worlds interpretation, and its use in science fiction. A distinction is drawn between quantum-influenced alternate timelines and the alternative history sub-genre, which firmly locates a counterfactual history in a single past to create long-term social speculations. Counterfactual works are examined as an instance of an alternate timeline where only one such timeline is portrayed. Parallels are drawn between historical sciences, such as astronomy, cosmology and evolutionary biology, and this sense of past and future history in science fiction. Life's pathway on planet Earth is considered as a single actualized history among millions of possibilities. The students are encouraged to critically consider science fiction as a serious creator of plausible futures, to examine the genre's sense of history and deliberations on the question of free will. Science fiction is critically considered for the way in which it presents a different sense of history to its readers.

The classroom experience

Amit and Maggie Goswami remind us that:

> Science Fiction is that class of fiction which contains the currents of change in science and society. It concerns itself with the critique, extension, revision, and conspiracy of revolution, all directed against static scientific paradigms. Its goal is to prompt a paradigm shift to a new view that will be more responsive and true to nature.[13]

The traditional classroom experience has been based around a deficit model of communication. The deficit model is focused on the idea that teaching and communication in science seeks to overcome problems caused primarily by a lack of adequate knowledge. Associated with this idea is the contention that by providing ample information about science we can surmount this 'knowledge deficit'. In essence the model of teaching associated with the deficit model is a linear model in which information flows from the lecturer to the student whose comprehension is measured through the repetition of that information. The deficit model of teaching (involving lectures, essays and exams) has been with the formal Western model of education since its inception. Although undergraduate teaching at Glamorgan had its origin within this system we moved away from this in favour of a dialogue model of science communication.

In this dialogue model (sometimes referred to as 'the public opinion' model), the key is democracy. The pivotal concept within a democracy is public participation in all facets of discussion. The dialogue model of science communication highlights the need to create venues and opportunities for discussion. It emphasizes the need for seminar-based work. As part of the development of the teaching practice associated with the undergraduate course in science and science fiction we responded to this new model with a set of modules designed around the concept of democracy. Students respond to the material being presented in a wide variety of ways, with significant portions of their assessed work being in the public realm (presentations and seminar discussions) as opposed to private linear communication between teacher and student (essays).

Following from the success of this approach it was decided to take things a stage further and adopt the deference model of science communication as it can be applied to the teaching and classroom experience. We found that a paradigm shift to a new view that was more responsive and true to nature was required. This third approach is 'a model of communication according to which scientists acknowledge the value of, or "defer" to, the insights of other intellectual disciplines and cultural activities on their own'.[14] We found ourselves increasingly moving towards this nexial approach in which we draw upon the experience and approaches of other academic fields. In particular science fiction is ideally suited to this approach as the deference model 'relates to the possible contribution of arts, humanities, and social sciences to the better understanding of science's place within contemporary culture'.[15]

This deference model emphasized extending the communication of science through the deficit model (of linear communication) and past the dialogue model (in which student response is integrated into the teaching) to a context in which students draw down their own experiences to cascade an integrated and holistic synthesis into the learning experience. The results were very encouraging. We found there was an increase in cohort cohesion, the cross-pollination of ideas and mutual support was developed, and a peer-enriched learning environment was created.

Outcomes

The science and science fiction degree has now been taught for the best part of a decade. We hope that the award has provided students with a more dynamic and critical understanding of science than is normally achieved in typical undergraduate programmes. A common feature of the modules has been a multidisciplinary approach. The science fiction modules, in particular, are delivered through the use of staff teaching teams, giving students an experience of a variety of viewpoints from contributing fields personified by informed experts from those fields. The use of such staff teams has helped present the broadest possible selection from the genre, producing intellectual versatility in graduates and encouraging them to approach science from a range of different theoretical viewpoints.

The exploration of the boundary study of science and science fiction has engendered in the students an imaginative ability to communicate the nature and evolution of science and science fiction, and their interrelationship. Witness to this observation are a number of graduates who have proceeded to postgraduate study in communicating science. Such graduates have a clear tendency for better imagination, articulacy and comprehension of issues in science than their 'lab rat' counterparts who have been educated through the more traditional route of science undergraduate training.

On the eve of the millennium *The Times* asked a number of prominent scientists to identify major issues in science leading into the twenty-first century. Professor Susan Greenfield of Oxford University, the first female head of the Royal Institution, suggested *the* scientific breakthrough of the twenty-first century would be 'The engagement of the public in science and the expression of scientific ideas in a way they can understand and contribute to.'

Our development of a border study in science and science fiction has led to a number of further broad and positive outcomes in public outreach. The award team acted as educational consultants to the Science

Fiction Museum in Seattle on its launch in 2004. This is the world's first museum devoted to the ideas and experiences of the genre, carrying exhibitions to promote appreciation and education of science fiction media, while encouraging visitors to envision new futures for science and humanity.

As was mentioned earlier, members of our teaching team were among the co-founders of the NAI science communication group. This cross-disciplinary service to the academic and wider communities has provided an Astrobiology Communication Roadmap which clearly identifies and encourages the use of science fiction for an effective and broad communication of astrobiology across diverse audiences including citizens, policymakers, administrators and sponsors.

The unusual nature and subsequent prominence of our programme has also attracted the interest of a number of publishers, most notably Macmillan and the Science Museum in London. Consequently, a number of book projects are planned which seek to further explore the symbiosis of science and science fiction. The first of these, Brake and Hook's *Different Engines: How Science Drives Fiction and Fiction Drives Science* (2007) and *FutureWorld: Where Science Fiction Becomes Science* (2008), have already been completed.

Finally, it is our contention that the border study of science and science fiction can help demystify science, highlight its social and cultural context, and act as a bridge to public consciousness on controversial issues in the communication and control of science. In short, science fiction can help to play an important part in bringing science out of the laboratory and into the culture.

Notes

1. See www.imdb.com/boxoffice/alltimegross?region=world-wide (accessed 21 July 2009).
2. See Sir Ron Dearing, 'Higher Education in the Learning Society', National Committee of Inquiry into Higher Education (London: HMSO, 1997). An electronic copy is available at www.leeds.ac.uk/educol/ncihe/ (accessed 21 July 2009).
3. See Mark Brake, Martin Griffiths, Neil Hook and Steve Harris, 'Alien Worlds: Astrobiology and Public Outreach', *International Journal of Astrobiology*, 5:4 (2006): 319–24.
4. Mark Brake's relevant papers were 'An Integrated, Interdisciplinary Astronomy Teaching Programme', presented at New Trends in Astronomy Teaching, 162nd Colloquium of the International Astronomical Union, London, 8–12 July 1996; and 'An Interdisciplinary Approach at the University of Glamorgan, UK', presented at the Educational Symposium on Teaching

218 *Teaching Science Fiction*

     Astronomy to Non-Science Majors, at the 110th Annual Meeting of the Astronomical Society of the Pacific, Albuquerque, New Mexico, 25 June–1 July 1998.
5. The relevant papers and publications are: Mark Brake and Martin Griffiths, 'Broad Horizons: SETI, Science Fiction, and Education', proceedings of the Bioastronomy and Fulbright Education Conference, Hamilton Island, Great Barrier Reef, Australia, 8–12 July, 2002, later published in *International Journal of Astrobiology*, 3:2 (2004): 175–81; Mark Brake, Rosi Thornton and Naomi Turnbull, '"What if . . . ?": Science Fiction and PCST', paper presented at the 8th International Conference on Public Communication of Science and Technology, Scientific Knowledge & Cultural Diversity, Barcelona, Spain, 3–6 June 2004; Mark Brake and Martin Griffiths, 'Alien Worlds – Astrobiology & Public Outreach', NASA Astrobiology Institute Conference, University of Colorado, Boulder, 10–14 April 2005; Mark Brake, Neil Hook, Rosi Thornton, Naomi Turnbull and Kathryn Williams, 'The Counterfactual Classroom', paper presented at the 26th Eaton Conference 'Inventing the 21st Century: Many Worlds, Many Histories', Seattle, 5–7 May 2005; Mark Brake, Martin Griffiths and Neil Hook, 'Astrobiology and the Curriculum', paper presented at UKAC06 'Life Here, There and Everywhere' Conference, University of Kent, 18–21 April 2006.
6. See, for examples, Brian Aldiss and David Wingrove, *Trillion Year Spree: The History of Science Fiction* (London: Gollancz, 1986) and Darko Suvin, *Positions and Presuppositions in Science Fiction* (Basingstoke: Macmillan, 1988).
7. Judith Merril, 'What Do You Mean: Science? Fiction?', in Thomas D. Clareson, ed., *SF: The Other Side of Realism* (Bowling Green, OH: Bowling Green University Press, 1971) 53–95 at 60.
8. Sam Moskowitz, *Explorers of the Infinite: Shapers of Science Fiction* (New York: Hyperion, 1963) 11.
9. Joanna Russ, *To Write Like A Woman: Essays in Feminism and Science Fiction* (Bloomington: Indiana University Press, 1995) 7.
10. Patrick Parrinder, *Science Fiction: A Critical Guide* (London: Longman, 1979) 67.
11. Russ, *To Write Like A Woman*, 12.
12. Ibid., 6.
13. Amit Goswami and Maggie Goswami, *The Cosmic Dancers: The Science in Science Fiction* (Columbus, OH: McGraw-Hill, 1985) 2.
14. Brian Trench and Kirk W. Junker, 'Scientists' View of Public Communication', proceedings of the 6th International Conference on Public Communication of Science and Technology, Trends in Science Communication Today: Bridging the Gap Between Theory and Practice, Geneva, 1–3 February 2001. Available at www.cern.ch/pcst2001/programme.html (accessed 21 July 2009).
15. See ibid.

13
Design, Delivery and Evaluation
Andy Sawyer and Peter Wright

Developing and delivering a course in science fiction poses opportunities and challenges, particularly to the lecturer or instructor undertaking such a venture for the first time. Accordingly, this chapter addresses some of the factors relevant to the construction of a science fiction course whilst offering practical guidance on syllabus structure, modes of teaching and possible forms of assessment. It is not, in any way, intended to be prescriptive. Rather, it highlights a number of approaches and strategies valued by the contributors to the current volume.

Designing a science fiction module

Given the wealth of primary material available, one of the key challenges for lecturers and instructors developing a course in science fiction is shaping an appropriate curriculum. The selection of primary texts depends, of course, on one's *purpose* in teaching a science fiction course in the first place. Curriculum content will necessarily reflect the lecturer's or instructor's *intention*. The fecundity of science fiction will satisfy a variety of academic objectives; whether the lecturer's or instructor's aim is to familiarize students with the historical development of sf, to undertake a genre-based or modal approach, to adopt a specific ideological stance to the literature (a feminist or postcolonial position, for example), or to employ an intertextual or megatextual study tracing a particular science fictional concept through its various historical and/or formal manifestations.

In *Inside Science Fiction* (2nd edn, 2006) James Gunn, almost certainly the person with the greatest experience of teaching sf still engaged in the practice, notes that when he began offering sf courses in 1969 he identified four ways of tackling the task.[1] The first was a 'great books' approach, wherein attention was given to significant novels or stories and to analysing what made them 'great'. This method is not only selective but subjective. Nevertheless, the debates that are likely to arise from the presentation of a particular text as a 'great' work of science fiction will provide considerable learning opportunities. The themes of the course could encompass the literary canon, alternative canonization, the classification of, and tensions existing between, literature and paraliterature within the academy and popular culture, the historic/generic/modal/thematic qualities of sf, and literary and cultural marginalization both within and outside science fiction itself.

Gunn's second approach was a focus upon the ideas in sf: 'How SF stories can be used to dramatise contemporary problems or to encourage critical thought.'[2] Here, Gunn's strategy inevitably leads to an exploration of the ideology both in and of science fiction. In any discussion of the representation of possible futures, new technologies or alien encounters, there is the understanding that such representations are ideologically inflected. Why, scholars and students might feel entitled to ask, are the futures envisaged in so much science fiction the apparent property of one particular version of human culture? If there is, as many have claimed, a megatext or 'default future' in science fiction, has this made it more difficult, rather than easier, for dissenting voices to be heard? In *Critical Theory and Science Fiction* (2000) Carl Freedman argues that critical theory and sf share a similar 'project' of *explaining* or at least demystifying the world. How that demystification or explanation is achieved inevitably requires an interrogation of the assumptions, prejudices and alternate voices of science fiction.

Gunn's third method acknowledged the possibility of teaching another subject – physics, biology, history, sociology, politics, religion – by considering how these subjects had been treated in science fiction. This is not uncommon, particularly in the United States. Leroy Dubeck, for example, was a pioneer in the early 1990s in using sf films to teach science, a practice that resulted in Dubeck, Moshier and Boss's *Fantastic Voyages: Learning Science through Science Fiction Films* (1994).[3] In *Teaching Science Fact with Science Fiction* (2004), R. Gary Raham offers resources and lesson plans for American High School teachers intent on the same strategy.[4] Gregory Benford, in Gunn, Barr and Candelaria's *Reading Science Fiction* (2008) describes how physics can be examined effectively through the employment of science fiction.[5] A representative example of this use of science fiction is outlined in Chapter 12 of the current volume. In the majority of cases, however, science fiction courses are provided within English departments with a largely literary focus.

Gunn's fourth approach returned critical attention to the literature itself by first analysing the nature of contemporary sf and then considering how it reached that point; it is, in effect, a historical course structured using a reverse chronology. It is a method not uncommon in some first-year literature survey courses which begin with contemporary literature and work back through Modernism, Victorian literature and so forth. Gunn's own teaching, as he describes it, drew upon the first, second and fourth categories; that is, on using 'great' books to explore sf historically and ideologically.

Gunn's influence can be readily observed in a number of undergraduate sf courses delivered by contributors to this volume. Chris Ferns, for example, adopts an approach comparable to Gunn's in the sf course he teaches at Mount Saint Vincent University in Halifax, Nova Scotia. In the introductory material he provides for his students, he identifies four central topics:

1 The emergence of science fiction as a distinct genre, and its relation to the fears and anxieties aroused by social and technological change. Does science fiction offer a critique, or a celebration of the notion of progress?
2 The implications of new technologies – genetic engineering, biotechnology, artificial intelligence – for our understanding of what constitutes the human. How is our concept of 'humanity' in fact constructed?
3 Issues of gender and its representation in a genre which has historically been dominated by male authors. In what ways does science fiction either challenge, or reinscribe conventional gender stereotypes?
4 The ideological implications of narrative. What sorts of *stories* do writers choose to tell about the worlds they imagine? What ideological assumptions do these stories imply?

In order to address these questions, Ferns constructs a syllabus according to the 'great' book criteria identified by Gunn:

Mary Shelley	*Frankenstein* (rev. edn, 1831)
H.G. Wells	*The Time Machine* (1895)
H.G. Wells	*The War of the Worlds* (1898)
Aldous Huxley	*Brave New World* (1932)
Stanislaw Lem	*Solaris* (1961)
Philip K. Dick	*Do Androids Dream of Electric Sheep?* (1968)

Ursula K. Le Guin   *The Left Hand of Darkness* (1969)
William Gibson   *Neuromancer* (1984)
Michael Crichton   *Jurassic Park* (1990)
Marge Piercy   *He, She and It* (1991)

Rob Latham at the University of California, Riverside, teaches two sf courses: 'The History of SF' and the more focused 'Topics in SF', the thematic content of which varies from semester to semester. As Latham points out,

> My 'History of SF' class is a large class (around 100 students), conducted in lecture format and ... assumes the students have no previous acquaintance with the genre. I do use the first day's session, however, getting them to volunteer – or just call out – their own ideas about what the characteristics of a genre called 'science fiction' might be, and it is clear they know some basics (at least from media culture): it's about future societies, alien beings, new technologies, space travel, etc. My selection of texts covers the field from Wells to roughly the present, with units on the early pulps, the Golden Age, the 1950s, the New Wave, feminist SF, and cyberpunk. I do try and pursue thematic threads: sometimes, I only use texts that deal with the theme of 'artificial persons' broadly construed, starting with Wells's *The Island of Doctor Moreau* (1896) and running through Asimov's *I, Robot* (coll. 1950) to the cyborgs of Gibson's *Neuromancer* (1984). We read novels and stories, and I try to make them representative of major authors.

More specialized is Latham's 'Topics in SF' class, which 'is designed for English majors only. It also assumes no prior knowledge of the field, though having taken my "History of SF" class helps. Its content varies by thematic emphasis or historical focus: I have taught a class on the New Wave under this rubric, for example, and hope to teach a class on "Gender and Sexuality in SF" soon.'

M. Elizabeth Ginway's course is also historical, running from

> Wells to Gibson, broadly speaking, which assumes no previous knowledge and which, in its selection of texts, provides students with at least two texts from different periods that are thematically, conceptually and/or historically related; e.g. for time travel we consider Wells' *The Time Machine* (1895) and Moorcock's 'Behold the Man' (1966); for gender Lester Del Rey's 'Helen O'Loy' (1938) and James Tiptree Jr's 'The Women Men Don't See' (1973).

Such a preponderance of historically structured courses does not reflect a lack of imagination amongst teachers, but the recognition of the benefits of a coherent historical structure to students new to the subject. Of course, the historical approach to curriculum design presupposes that there is a coherent and consistent literature that can be termed 'science fiction', that it can easily be identified, and that it has a recognizable history that can be traced from one historical period to the next. Such assumptions are not necessarily to be trusted and are certainly the basis of academic debate – as the chapters in this book have indicated. Nevertheless, for undergraduates often unfamiliar with science fiction beyond its cinematic and televisual manifestations, the historically structured course provides a convenient framework that leaves open the possibility of contesting its assumptions which, by postgraduate level, students should certainly be invited to do.

Of course, the essential decision in formulating any course is the choice of an appropriate (depending on purpose) starting point. For sf, Shelley's *Frankenstein* (1818), Wells's *The Time Machine* (1895), Gernsback's first *Amazing Stories* (1926) or even More's *Utopia* (1516) can all be claimed as seminal texts, but the courses that evolved from each could be significantly different in content and nuance as a consequence of that initial discriminatory selection. Whatever starting point is chosen, the judicious selection of subsequent texts can render a historically-structured course a rich learning experience capable of familiarizing students with the themes, concerns and concepts pertinent to a broader understanding of the subject. The following table sets out a course, based on a twelve-week semester, that attempts to ensure such a learning experience.

The first week of the module is designed to introduce students to the discourse of science fiction by identifying it in the context of the fantastic (Vance's 'Turjan of Miir' and Weis and Hickman's appendix to *Dragon Wing*). The extracts from Wolfe's *Shadow of the Torturer* and *The Claw of the Conciliator* facilitate students' understanding of sf by exploring the discourse of science fantasy or rationalized fantasy. Finally, 'The Woman Who Loved the Centaur Pholus' assists the students' comprehension of sf's rationalist perspective and the ways in which language is employed to construct its sense of rational speculation. Brian Attebery's *Strategies of Fantasy* (1992), Damien Broderick's 'SF as Generic Engineering'[6] and Mendlesohn's 'Introduction' to *The Cambridge Companion to Science Fiction* (2003) provide useful critical starting points for undergraduates.

Wells's *The Time Machine* is an ideal text for offering students additional contextual material relating to utopian and anti-utopian fiction

Table 13.1 Proposal for a 12-week semester sf course

Week	Topic	Text(s)
1.	What is 'Science Fiction'?	Jack Vance, 'Turjan of Miir', from *The Dying Earth* (1950) Margaret Weis and Tracy Hickman, 'Magic from the Sundered Realms: Excerpt from a Sartan's Musings', appendix to *Dragon Wing* (1990) Gene Wolfe, extracts from *The Shadow of the Torturer* (1980) and *The Claw of the Conciliator* (1981) and 'The Woman Who Loved the Centaur Pholus' (1979)
2.	The Strange and the Familiar: Cognitive Estrangement and Utopianism	H.G. Wells, *The Time Machine* (1895)
3.	Pulp Science Fiction	E.R. Burroughs, *A Princess of Mars* (1912/1917) Hugo Gernsback, extracts from *Ralph 124C 41+* (1925) L. Taylor Hansen, 'The Undersea Tube' (1929) John W. Campbell, 'Twilight' (1934)
4.	The Golden Age	Lester del Rey, 'Helen O'Loy' (1938) Robert A. Heinlein, 'The Roads Must Roll' (1940) Isaac Asimov, 'Liar' (1941) A.E. Van Vogt, 'The Weapon Shop' (1942)
5.	The Iconography of SF	Arthur C. Clarke, *The City and the Stars* (1956)
6.	British SF 1: Science Fiction and the Catastrophe	John Wyndham, *The Day of the Triffids* (1951) J.G. Ballard, 'The Terminal Beach' (1964) Charles Platt, 'The Disaster Story' (1966)

7.	British SF 2: The New Wave	Langdon Jones, 'I Remember Anita' (1964) Michael Moorcock, 'Symbols for the Sixties' (1965) and 'Behold the Man' (1966) J.G. Ballard, 'You and Me and the Continuum' (1966) Pamela Zoline, 'The Heat Death of the Universe' (1967)
8.	Divine Madness: Philip K. Dick	Philip K. Dick, *Do Androids Dream of Electric Sheep?* (1968)
9.	Encountering the Alien: Colonialism, Postcolonialism and Science Fiction	Harry Harrison, 'The Streets of Ashkelon' (1965) Gene Wolfe, *The Fifth Head of Cerberus: Three Novellas* (1972) Carole McDonnell, 'Lingua Franca' (2004)
10.	Feminism and SF	C.L. Moore, 'No Woman Born' (1944) Judith Merril, 'That Only a Mother' (1948) Joanna Russ, 'When It Changed' (1972) James Tiptree Jr, 'The Women Men Don't See' (1973)
11.	Cyberpunk and Postmodern SF	Bruce Sterling, 'Introduction' to *Mirrorshades: The Cyberpunk Anthology* (1986) William Gibson, 'Johnny Mnemonic' (1981), 'The Gernsback Continuum' (1981) and 'Burning Chrome' (1985)
12.	Contemporary SF	Variable

while introducing them to Suvin's concepts of the novum and of science fiction as cognitive estrangement. Freed from Suvin's rather limiting Marxist application, cognitive estrangement – and the forms of estranging effect found in sf – affords students a key critical framework from which to read science fiction. Equally, the idea of the novum focuses attention on how sf texts can be interpreted as thought experiments dramatizing social, political and historic concerns. Additionally, Wells's Time Traveller's efforts to comprehend the social structure and socio-political history of the year 802,701 dramatize the reading strategies and protocols, so often based upon contingency, that individuals employ when reading sf. Teaching *The Time Machine* – in part – as a metafiction can be useful in alerting students to how they read, or are learning to read, sf.

In weeks 3–4, the course introduces students to the origins of American sf, stressing the importance of the pulp and magazine years. The stories and extracts selected introduce pulp sensationalism and the influence of the 'Machine Age' (*Ralph 124C 41+*), the separation and gradual reconciliation of scientific and literary discourses (notably through 'The Undersea Tube' and 'The Roads Must Roll'), the influence of Wells (Campbell's 'Twilight'), the significance to American sf of two key editors: Hugo Gernsback and John W. Campbell, and the political possibilities and limitations of the genre in its masculine North American context (Heinlein, Asimov and van Vogt). Readings from Westfahl's *The Mechanics of Wonder* (1999) and Ashley's *The Time Machines: The Story of the Science Fiction Pulp Magazines from the Beginning to 1950* (2000) make available reliable historical material. Westfahl's *Hugo Gernsback and the Century of Science Fiction* (2007) and Albert Berger's *The Magic That Works: John W. Campbell and the American Response to Technology* (1993) give additional insights into these two seminal figures while Thomas D. Clareson's *Understanding Contemporary American Science Fiction: The Formative Period 1926–1970* (1990) presents a good assessment of the nature of pulp and Golden Age sf.

Week 5, which takes its critical approach from Gary K. Wolfe's *The Known and the Unknown: The Icons of Science Fiction* (1979), allows students to reflect back on their learning at this mid-point whilst acquiring an additional mode of (structuralist) interpretation readily applicable to Clarke's *The City and the Stars*. Clarke's novel provides a series of resonant and multivalent icons (the spaceship, the city, the wasteland, the robot, the monster) all of which are discussed by Wolfe. Extracts from *The Known and the Unknown* draw attention not only to the strategies available for interpreting these resonant icons but also to each icon's dynamic and ideologically rich potential. As a consequence the stories considered in weeks 3–4 obtain new interpretative possibilities as students can reassess, for example, the robot ('Helen O'Loy', 'Liar'), the city ('Twilight', 'The Roads Must Roll') and the monster (*A Princess of Mars*).

Clarke's novel also represents a turning point in the course as attention shifts from American to British sf. Although *The City and the Stars* borrows much of its iconography from American sf and, indeed, its narrative structure adheres to the expansive nature common to the American context, its initial tone – often melancholic and elegiac – is distinctly British. As such, it prepares students for the more pessimistic nature of much British sf of the 1950s–1970s. Week 6 addresses a key theme in British sf: catastrophe. Antecedents for the disaster fiction of Wyndham and Ballard include Defoe's *Journal of the Plague Year* (1722), Shelley's *The Last Man* (1826) and Shiel's *The Purple Cloud* (1901). The selection of texts above (possibly supplemented with extracts from Defoe, Shelley and Shiel where appropriate) make available a compressed history of the form in the last half of the twentieth century which ranges from the comparatively straightforward recovery narrative of *The Day of the Triffids* to the physical and psychical catastrophes of Ballard's nuclear-inspired story to Platt's satiric treatment of the form, which exposes the tradition's conventions with stark and often bitter brevity.

Ballard's story and Platt's critical metafiction prepare students for a week considering New Wave science fiction and its self-conscious opposition to the characteristics – thematic, conceptual, ideological – of American sf. Following Moorcock's manifesto, 'Symbols for the Sixties', each story selected draws attention to at least one of the New Wave's principle preoccupations. American writer Pamela Zoline's 'The Heat Death of the Universe' brings the New Wave's fascination with entropic dissolution into the domestic sphere to explore in a strongly feminist narrative the meaningless routine, expectations and pressures placed on a wife and mother. Moorcock's irreverent retelling of the crucifixion in 'Behold the Man' draws attention to the New Wave's preoccupation with psychology or 'inner space'. The novella is likely to provoke considerable debate amongst students surprised by its treatment of faith, myth, self-delusion and sacrifice. It is also a useful contextualizing exercise to trace the controversy that followed this story and Jones's soft-core, post-apocalyptic tale, 'I Remember Anita', in *New Worlds*' letters pages and editorials. The responses therein highlight the contemporary conservatism of sf and its readership and frame distinctly the conventions and attitudes Moorcock was prepared to challenge. For investigating the stylistic experimentation of the New Wave, Ballard's 'You and Me and the Continuum' is an instructive example. Ballard's 'condensed novel' provides an elegant puzzle in the form of twenty-seven paragraphs, each subtitled with a heading that begins with the successive letter of the alphabet following an 'Author's Note'. It is 'A.N. A–Z' in which the reader has the opportunity to reconstruct the deconstructed, 'condensed' narrative in a variety of possible ways. As such, it is a valuable text for assisting students in reflecting on the activity of reading in both sf and wider contexts, in highlighting how meaning is, and can be structured, and in underlining the writerly – in the Barthesian sense – aspects of sf.

Such an awareness is vital for the consideration of the demanding fiction of Philip K. Dick and Gene Wolfe. Dick's writing again allows students to reflect on their learning, particularly their understanding of the icon of the robot and the role of entropy, while drawing attention to the possible importance of a writer's philosophical beliefs and other autobiographical details. The questions underpinning Dick's work – what is real? And what makes us human? – can generate significant debate, particularly through *Do Androids Dream of Electric Sheep?* Studying Dick, however briefly, also encourages students to explore the extensive critical literature available on him, and to observe how a single author can sustain a considerable critical industry and assist in the acceptance of sf as a serious literature within the academy.

Weeks 9–11 read sf through three key critical discourses: postcolonial theory, Anglo-American feminism and postmodernism. In Week 9, students are introduced to three narratives dramatizing the consequences of human colonization on indigenous alien populations. All address and/or problematize key colonial and postcolonial concepts, including the notion of aboriginal peoples, primitivism, the binary logic of imperialism, the concept of colonial discourse, mimicry and hybridity. In Mehan's taxonomy as presented in Chapter 10, Harrison's 'The Streets of Ashkelon' is an excellent example of colonial science fiction and Wolfe's *The Fifth Head of Cerberus: Three Novellas* an equally valuable instance of dissident sf. Together, they provide a fruitful contrast. Harrison sees the commercial exploitation of an indigenous people as acceptable – even excusable – and religious conversion as culturally, spiritually and psychically damaging. The story reinforces the binarism underpinning colonial discourse whilst implicitly defending capitalist exploitation. Wolfe's novellas, on the other hand, deconstruct the binarism of colonial discourse to raise broader philosophical and political questions regarding identity, memory, culture and miscegenation.

Carole McDonnell's distinctly postcolonial 'Lingua Franca' (2004) is much more direct in its critique of colonialism and cultural imperialism than Wolfe's elliptical, writerly text. On an obliquely described alien world, 'Earthers' surgically alter the silent, indigenous population to encourage them to communicate verbally in English rather than through the sophisticated system of sign language they have traditionally employed. The Earthers' motivation is purely commercial; their objectives typical of any imperial enterprise: assimilation and exploitation. Recounted through an alien perspective, McDonnell's story illustrates, by paradoxical inversion, how the Earthers steal the population's authentic 'voice'. They alienate the younger generation from their elders – here represented elegiacally through a mother-child relationship – and instigate an irrevocable change to their culture. As such 'Lingua Franca' forms a stark contrast with Harrison's naive representation of capitalism as comparatively benign.

Additional pertinent primary material can be found in Sheree Thomas's edited collections, *Dark Matter: A Century of Speculative Fiction from the African Diaspora* (2000) and *Dark Matter: Reading the Bones* (2004). In terms of relevant texts, Patricia Kerslake's *Science Fiction and Empire* (2007) and John Rieder's *Colonialism and the Emergence of Science Fiction* (2008) provide genre-specific starting points, but the wealth of theoretical writing available on colonialism and postcolonial theory provides students with the opportunity to apply a non-sf related critical discourse to science fiction in new and intellectually stimulating ways. Introductory texts include John McLeod's *Beginning Postcolonialism* (2000), Bill Ashcroft, Gareth Griffiths and Helen Tiffin's *Postcolonial Studies: The Key Concepts* (2nd edn, 2007) and Barbara Bush's *Imperialism and Postcolonialism* (2006). These are all helpful starting points, but students should also be encouraged to engage with Franz Fanon's *Black Skin, White Masks* (1952) (which is particularly relevant to *The Fifth Head of Cerberus*), Edward Said's *Orientalism: Western Conceptions of the Orient* (1978) and *Culture and Imperialism* (1993), and, more specifically, Philip D. Morgan and Sean Hawkins's edited volume, *Black Experience and the Empire* (2004).

Similarly, the week dedicated to feminist sf enables students to use critical frameworks and concepts drawn from cultural and literary studies in the study of science fiction. Most importantly, it encourages students to recognize the potential of sf for envisioning and advocating feminist objectives. From around 1970 (when Joanna Russ published her influential essay 'The Image of Women in Science Fiction') feminist critics have continued to explore the role of women as readers and writers of science fiction, the influence of feminist theory on writers and their works, and the way sf, especially in its utopian form, could address matters of concern to women.

James Tiptree Jr's 'The Women Men Don't See', with its incisive, sophisticated treatment of women's objectification and alienation, forms a valuable link between postcolonial sf and feminist sf, focusing as it does on othering and otherness. With its male/female persona-slippage reverberating between the author's pseudonym, her real identity as Alice B. Sheldon, her authorship of genuinely feminist stories within her 'male' perspective, the ineluctably masculine tone of her writing, her bisexuality, and the stark viewpoints expressed within the story, 'The Women Men Don't See' remains highly pertinent and is capable of sparking off heated debates. A useful teaching strategy is to ask, after discussing the story, how many of the group are aware that the author was in fact a woman. (With a following supplementary question about whether this actually *matters*.) Similar questions could be applied to L. Taylor Hansen's 'The Undersea Tube', if the tutor has not already disclosed Hansen's identity.

Tiptree's critique of male attitudes toward women and to female alienation can be developed through Moore's earlier 'No Woman Born', which addresses themes including the construction of women under patriarchy, female identity and the nature of humanness. It can be read productively in the context of Donna Haraway's 'Manifesto for Cyborgs: Science, Technology, and Socialist-Feminism in the Late Twentieth Century' (1985) and in response to Del Rey's 'Helen O'Loy'. Both stories focus on the social construction of gender through the metaphor of the robot/cyborg yet approach their topic from very different perspectives. Merril's 'That Only a Mother' and Russ's 'When It Changed' are both important texts for considering gender roles, subjectivities and the impact of male perspectives on female–child relations. Key critical reading for the week could include selections from Justine Larbalestier's *The Battle of the Sexes in Science Fiction* (2007), Lisa Yaszek's *Galactic Suburbia: Recovering Women's Science Fiction* (2008) and Brian Attebery's *Decoding Gender in Science Fiction* (2002).

In Week 11, the course turns its attention to cyberpunk, perhaps the latest re-invigoration science fiction has experienced, a new New Wave equally preoccupied with contemporary relevance and literary style, although it rejected the more extreme experimentations of the 1960s. Sterling's 'Introduction' to *Mirrorshades* provides a useful starting point and, although it documents contemporary changes in sf rather than setting out a manifesto in the manner of Moorcock's 'Symbols of the Sixties', it points to the association between the two phenomena and the debt owed by cyberpunk writers to the New Wave and Philip K. Dick. Although Gibson's *Neuromancer* is the most perceptible cyberpunk text, his stories are condensed treatments of cyberpunk's key preoccupations: artificial intelligence, bodily invasion and physical augmentation by technology, the interface of the human brain with digital information systems, the effects of global capitalism, street culture and criminality, all conveyed on a jetstream of hardboiled prose and punk aesthetics. Gibson's stories permit sufficient space for a discussion of these concepts and cyberpunk's ambivalence towards the interface between human and machine. Given Western humanity's growing reliance upon information technology, a fact readily apparent to students who understand the benefits and hazards of the internet, cyberpunk generally fosters considerable discussion and debate regarding the growing intimacy in the relationship between the human and the machine. Scott Bukatman's *Terminal Identity: The Virtual Subject in Postmodern Science Fiction* (1993), Dani Cavallaro's *Cyberpunk and Cyberculture* (2000) and McCaffery's *Storming the Reality Studio: A Casebook of Cyberpunk and Postmodern Science Fiction* (1991) all provide possibilities for key critical reading.

The topic of the final week of any science fiction module is likely to undergo annual or biannual revision to accommodate discernible shifts in the literature. Possible candidates include 'mundane sf', a form founded by Geoff Ryman which eschews scientific improbabilities (interstellar travel, particularly) in favour of credible technological speculation. Ryman's *Air* (2005) or *When It Changed: Science into Fiction* (2009), a collection of mundane sf stories edited by Ryman, are appropriate texts. *When It Changed* is of particular interest given that each story is written following advice from a scientist who then explains the plausibility of the story in an accompanying endnote. As a concept, mundane sf is valuable for encouraging students to reflect back on the course and consider the representation of technology, technological speculation and technological change throughout twentieth century science fiction. Such (re-)contextualization also reinvigorates debates regarding the relationship between science fiction and the fantastic and the role of technological rationalization within sf.

The discrete borders implied by generic classification can also be questioned in a final session on the 'New Weird', an often stylistically and conceptually sophisticated literature displaying a synthesis of tropes and conventions from sf, the fantastic and horror fiction. Jeff and Ann Vandermeer's anthology *The New Weird* (2008) provides a range of representative texts from Michael Moorcock, China Miéville, Clive Barker and Hal Duncan. Alternatively, Jeff Vandermeer's *City of Saints and Madmen* (2004) or Miéville's *Iron Council* (2005) are accomplished and instructive examples of the form, although these lengthy novels may increase a students' workload unnecessarily. In either case, the New Weird highlights the fluidity of the conventions of popular fiction and reminds students that literature is a dynamic medium, shifting, synthesizing and engaging in aesthetic and conceptual dialogue.

Accordingly, a thoughtfully structured historical survey course can avoid the compartmentalizing effects of concentrating on historical periods by drawing out connections across the semester using themes, icons, approaches to representation (of gender, of the alien, of political systems and so forth), and the contextual and megatextual qualities of individual narratives. With sufficient primary reading, lecturers and instructors can direct students to reflect back on the course to reconsider sf modally; that is, to readdress what can be encompassed within the term 'science fiction' or 'speculative fiction'. Through the judicious selection of primary material, the historical course can equally draw attention to the many different voices that 'speak' science fiction. A year-long course would obviously provide greater opportunity for listening to these voices more intently. Feminist sf could be explored to a greater depth through selections from Pamela Sargeant's *Women of Wonder* anthologies (most recently *Women of Wonder, the Classic Years: Science Fiction by Women from the 1940s to the 1970s* and *Women of Wonder, the Contemporary Years: Science Fiction by Women from the 1970s to the 1990s*, both 1995). Equally, European sf could be incorporated more readily to balance the largely Anglo-American bias of the course outlined above. James Morrow and Kathryn Morrow's anthology, *The SFWA European Hall of Fame: Sixteen Contemporary Masterpieces of Science Fiction from the Continent* (2008), provides a useful source that can be supplemented with fiction by Jules Verne, Stanislaw Lem and others. Andrea L. Bell and Yolanda Molina-Gavilán's *Cosmos Latinos: An Anthology of Science Fiction from Latin America and Spain* (2003) is equally important, collecting stories that range historically from the 1860s to 2001 from countries including Mexico, Brazil, Argentina and Spain. In selecting from these anthologies, the tutor can expose certain assumptions, the most common (and dangerous) being that there is a single coherent narrative of science fiction.

Delivering a science fiction module

Clearly, any historical course must acknowledge that while sf is, as a branch of literature, subject to exactly the same theoretical approaches (Marxism, feminism, postcolonialism, and so forth) as other literary texts, its criticism – to a greater degree than that of other popular fictional forms – has engaged in a distinct argument with traditional literary studies. This argument is primarily against the idea of the canon and the liberal-humanist approach of studying the 'best' and arguably most appropriate texts. Sf criticism might argue that the most central texts are not necessarily the 'best' in conventional literary terms. For example, in *The Mechanics of Wonder* Gary Westfahl argues strongly that the 'tawdry illiterate'[7] *Ralph 124C 41+* by Hugo Gernsback is one of modern sf's most important documents. Inevitably, the historical sf course – and most courses that purport to explore science fiction representatively – will engage with such fiction. In some cases literature students more familiar with Austen, Dickens, Eliot and Joyce – or Melville, Whitman, Dickinson and Wharton – will take considerable persuasion to accept that it is perfectly appropriate to study *Ralph* since they often view it with the condescension usually reserved for comic books or soap operas. Alternatively, they may feel that they ought to value (and treat) it as a 'literary text' because it is on an academic syllabus. When they discover that it does not conform to any literary standards with which they are familiar, they have little idea how to approach it.

Overcoming any student's dismissal, distaste or confusion when encountering sf for the first time, or when first experiencing sf's historical, literary and/or cultural diversity, can be challenging. Many students, schooled in the reading protocols appropriate to the literary canon, simply do not comprehend how to read science fiction. Recognizing this fact is the first step in engaging students and diffusing any resistance or cynicism one might encounter in seminars. In his excellent *Science Fiction in the Twentieth Century* (1994), Edward James draws a distinction between the 'mainstream', which he takes to be 'synonymous with "the modern novel", "the contemporary novel", the novel as taken seriously by the *Times Literary Supplement* and the *New York Review of Books*' and science fiction.[8] Acknowledging that his observations reflect 'generalities', James provides a series of contrasts between the mainstream and science fiction.[9] These are summarized in Table 13.2.

As a consequence of these differences, readers new to sf often require assistance in developing reading protocols appropriate to an understanding of the formal qualities of the subject. As James points out, 'One of the problems for the non-sf reader approaching an sf book is that a different style of reading is involved from that encountered in most "mainstream" fiction.'[10]

The delivery of any sf course needs to take this observation into account. An early introduction to Darko Suvin's conception of science

Table 13.2 Contrasting 'mainstream' and science fiction

'Mainstream' fiction	Science fiction
The subject matter of mainstream fiction focuses on human personalities and human relationships. Provides perceptions of, or perspectives on, the human psyche.	The subject matter of science fiction concentrates on the created environment and the interaction of characters with that environment. Speculates about human potential and humanity's position within the cosmos 'either with serious extrapolative intent or playfully'.[a]
Traditionally set in the world as experienced.	Usually set in or on worlds that have been altered in either minor or significant ways.
Usually located in the writer's present in a recognizable geographical location.	Often set in the future and/or on other worlds or on Earths rendered radically different by time, technology and so on.
The readers of mainstream fiction can assume that they know how the world works, that they 'share a knowledge of the background to the narrative with the author'.[b]	Science fiction readers can make no such assumption. They must construct and revise their conception of the fictional world as they glean more information from the events of the narrative.
Mainstream fiction generally concentrates on individual characters and their personal development.	Frequently science fiction is 'more concerned with the individual as a representative of humanity as a whole than with the individual's particular quirks'.[c] Sf is often more interested in the fate of groups, populations or species than of individuals.

Notes: (a) James, *Science Fiction in the Twentieth Century*, 96; (b) ibid.; (c) ibid., 97.

fiction as 'cognitive estrangement' is therefore essential. Admittedly, the totality of Suvin's *The Metamorphoses of Science Fiction* (1979) might be somewhat indigestible to many undergraduates. Nevertheless, it is possible to extract two key statements. The first, that 'SF is a literary genre whose necessary and sufficient conditions are the presence and interaction of estrangement and cognition and whose main formal device is an imaginative alternative to the author's empirical experience'[11] reassures the unfamiliar reader that the often dizzying sense of defamiliarization found in sf is a formal quality of the material. Sf's various estranging effects can form a coherent series of seminar exercises, where students could be encouraged to identify and critique an author's use of historical estrangement (through alternative histories or extrapolated futures), unfamiliar environments, defamiliarizing language, technological innovations, evolutionary changes and so forth, all of which are available for decoding.

Estrangement is something to be expected and it underpins sf's cognitive dimension. Indeed, as James indicates, sf's 'main subject' is cognition, 'the process of acquiring knowledge and of reason'.[12] Recognizing these qualities, and experiencing their effects through an appropriate text situated early in the course – Wells's *The Time Machine* is extremely useful in this instance – prepares the reader for the more extreme estrangement found in subsequent narratives (Wolfe's *The Fifth Head of Cerberus: Three Novellas*, for example, or Gibson's cyberpunk stories). Suvin's second observation, that 'SF is distinguished by the narrative dominance or hegemony of a fictional "novum" (novelty, innovation) validated cognitive logic'[13] alerts the reader to the centrality of ideas – speculations, innovations, subjunctivity – in science fiction. The notion of 'the idea as hero' in science fiction, a concept advanced by Kingsley Amis in *New Maps of Hell: A Survey of Science Fiction* (1960), one of the earliest scholarly treatments of sf, remains pertinent. Although a proportion of science fiction has increasingly reflected literary aspirations regarding character development and style (particularly after the New Wave and the emergence of feminist sf), the novum remains central to sf's formal qualities. Again, Wells's *The Time Machine* provides an accessible example, with the eponymous craft and the denuded world of 802,701 providing hegemonic innovations requiring cognitive consideration. It is important, however, to consider sceptically Suvin's Marxist tendency to reject the majority of what is commonly considered science fiction because it lacks a critical/ideological agenda. As James remarks, 'Suvin's formula ... has much to offer us ... particularly if we regard it as a definition of the *core* of what is sf and do not use it over rigidly to include or exclude.'[14] From Tom Shippey's perspective, '"Estrangement"... means recognising the novum; "cognition" means evaluating it, trying to make sense of it. You need both to read science fiction.'[15]

Encountering a literature with unfamiliar formal properties, acquiring a fresh set of reading protocols and learning to discuss fiction though a range of theoretical frameworks and methodologies both old and new can be an anxious time for students. To compensate for such anxiety, it is often valuable to deploy material likely to be familiar to students in particular teaching scenarios. Most students are familiar with sf in its cinematic and televisual forms and, whilst the analysis of sf film and television often requires its own set of critical approaches, such material can be beneficial in assisting the sf student's development from novice to practised reader. With this in mind, it goes without saying that lectures and seminars could be illuminated by a creative use of visual materials. Indeed, the lecture – whose value as a learning and teaching strategy has often been questioned, yet which remains a mode of delivery both economically and pragmatically viable – can be greatly enhanced by the incorporation of visual sources that facilitate a range of learning styles, particularly amongst increasingly visually-oriented student populations.

Rather than merely supplementing literary studies, film or television extracts – or even examples of author interviews found on the web or available commercially – can be employed more productively. Visual material can introduce and expose, often dramatically, the qualities, tensions, ambiguities and ideology of specific science fictional concepts. For example, Gary Wolfe's account of the *iconography* of science fiction described above is telling, because the 'icon' is a visual image, expressing an object or idea by presenting in sometimes striking visual form its qualities for interrogation.

An 'icon', as Wolfe uses the term for science fiction, is a fundamental image. It is *known* and understood far beyond its context. As such, it shares similarities with the concept of the 'emblem' as used to describe the spectrum of late-medieval and Renaissance public and occult symbolism, including heraldic devices, pageants, masques, hieroglyphs, hermetic magic and alchemical writings. In this sense, an emblem is both a rhetorical and a moral device consisting of an image, a motto and a verse gloss. In science fiction, symbols or emblems often appear in visual form, in films, on television, in graphic works and on the covers of pulp magazines and paperbacks. These appearances range from general images (the spaceship, the robot) to more specific representations, such as the 'Star Child' in the Kubrick/Clarke film *2001: A Space Odyssey* (1968). Sometimes they constitute a visual shorthand somewhere between the two, such as the cityscapes of 1920s and 1930s print science fiction, which owe a considerable debt to Lang's *Metropolis* (1927) (inspired by Lang's first view of New York as he and his wife arrived in the harbour), David Butler's *Just Imagine* (1930) and William Cameron Menzies's *H.G. Wells's Things to Come* (1936). In other instances, resonant images are generated specifically through text: Clarke's unforgettable 'Overhead, without any fuss, the stars were going out' from 'The Nine Billion Names of God' (1953) or the confusions of identity in Philip K. Dick's 'Colony' (1953) where the protagonist, Hall, is attacked first by a microscope and then by a towel and a belt. Dick glosses, 'the ultimate in paranoia is not when everyone is against you but when every*thing* is against you'.[16]

Clearly, the emblematic resonance of an icon depends upon its specific treatment in a particular narrative. By focusing upon the complex and often contradictory nature of an icon's visualization in a lecture before embarking upon textual analysis during the seminar, the intricacies of meaning in an sf story – and more broadly within sf itself – can be rendered more vividly. Magazine covers – many readily available on the internet – offer both implicit and explicit visual renderings of different forms of sf. The pulp covers from the 1930s often emphasize sf's sensationalist adventure story possibilities (and often bore little resemblance to the stories they purported to illustrate); in contrast the space vistas of 1960s *Analogs* and the baroque machines of early *Astoundings* speak of a more austere sense of wonder. On rare occasions, cover images constitute a 'device' reminiscent of the Renaissance use of the term, providing an explicit pictorialization of a particular conception of sf. The celebrated cover of *Amazing* from September 1928, for instance, is a crude but effective use of symbolism designed specifically to define Gernsback's concept of 'scientifiction':[17]

> Science is represented by the gear wheel, while the pen represents the fiction part. Here, then, we have Fact and Theory ... the frame of the design, representing structural steel, suggests more machinery. The flashes in the central wheel represent Electricity. The top of the fountain pen is a test tube, which stands for Chemistry, while the background, with the moon and stars and planet, gives us the science of Astronomy.[18]

The rest of the cover evokes a sense of movement through the title lettering, the star to the left of the giant 'A' and the respectable letters (PhD) after the name of contributing author David H. Keller.

A more complex and subtle example of the visual conceptualization of sf was Frank R. Paul's 'eye' cover of the April 1928 issue of *Amazing*.[19] The eye, surrounded by 'lashes' of forked lightning/electric bolts, contains within it a 'march of human progress' from primitive club-wielding 'cave-men' to futuristic machines. The cover perhaps alludes to, or symbolizes, the 'mind's eye' within which the inventions of Gernsback's 'scientifiction' are visualized, and can be examined in a number of ways. Students may well notice the clunky gear-wheels and other simplistic signs of 'science' which constitute the September cover, but will they notice that the signs of 'progress' in the April cover are concerned with weapons of war? Such visual material can also be used to initiate seminar activities. Once attention is drawn to these 'emblems of science fiction', discussions can focus upon what these images might *mean*, with students encouraged, individually or in groups, to analyse the images and/or design their own symbols for science fiction. Asking students to produce emblems they deem representative of feminist or postcolonial or New Wave sf can expose initial preconceptions and, following critical analysis and debate, lead to iconic aide-memoirs. Additional semiotic analyses of cover art during seminars can explore the ways in which different magazines over various periods of time reflect contrasting assumptions regarding technological change, for example, or how particular 'icons' – a space scene, a mechanical creature, a cityscape or alien life – are used and reused in simple combinations to attract changing audiences.

Considering the ways in which particular magazines (*Astounding* or *New Worlds*, perhaps) experimented at different times with different images or visual styles is also a productive exercise, providing an opportunity for locating science fiction in broader cultural contexts (the 'Machine Age' or the 'Atomic Age', for example). A simple but revealing activity is to take a cover illustrating a short story and, before students read that story, ask them to write notes about what they are expecting from the narrative given the 'evidence' of the cover. Then, once the story is read, the students may note how these expectations have, or have not, been fulfilled. As a consequence, their sensitivity to how sf has been marketed through cover art becomes more acute. Their awareness of factors including sensationalization, emphasis and distortion inform their understanding of mediation and reception.

A lengthier – and often more instructive – version of this exercise involves considering how a particular novel has been marketed through the cover art of its first edition and its subsequent reprints. One could ask how these covers reflect changes in attitudes to the novel, its author and/or science fiction in general, since it was first published. Such changes could include different emphases upon the book's subject-matter by its publishers and markets (foreign-language translations can be rewarding here), and different cultural evaluations of the book and its author (Philip K. Dick's movement from minor 'sci-fi' writer to a cult figure in the 'literary post-modern', for instance). Both exercises can lead the student to a greater understanding of sf in its various cultural contexts.

Design, Delivery and Evaluation 239

Whilst such activities certainly assist students in thinking critically about science fiction, it is equally important for the tutor or instructor to encourage learners to think 'science fictionally', to develop further the reading protocols necessary for a deeper comprehension of sf's formal qualities. Given that science fiction is a speculative literature, students should be encouraged to think speculatively – about technology, society, gender and so forth. An initial task might require them to reflect on how one piece of technology has impacted upon human behaviour (the mobile phone, which most of them carry habitually, is often the most useful example). Relevant questions might include: how has such technology changed their society over the last decade? How has it changed their personal and social behaviour or the behaviour of those they know? How would their lives be changed if they did not have access to such technology? Following this discussion, it is then possible to move students from thinking reflectively to thinking speculatively. One might ask, what piece of so-far uninvented technology might they find particularly valuable (or threatening)? From here, it is only a small step to introducing the key subjunctive question, What if…? Students could be asked to imagine their own speculative scenarios. The tutor might provide a familiar or plausible example: what if a volcanic eruption grounded all air traffic – not for a few days (as over Europe following the eruption of the Eyjafjallajökull volcano in Iceland), but for months? As students work through the process of speculation and implication, it generally becomes clearer to them how science fiction writers undertake the same activity.

From this sort of exercise, the kind of mental processes involved in literary speculation can be explored, and the students' own imaginings of how a technology may create difference could be read alongside essays such as Judith Merril's 'What Do You Mean? Science? Fiction?'[20] in which she discusses the use of the scientific method and its tradition of hypothesizing imaginary changes into the common background of 'known facts'. It is always worth engaging the students in reflecting on the unintended consequences of any technological development, exploring, as William Gibson puts it, how 'the street has its own use for things'.[21]

More exploratory learning designed to investigate science fiction's use of language could centre around the nomenclature/neologisms of sf. How language shapes fictional reality (and, by extension, the quotidian world) may be examined by engaging with the different linguistic registers of science fiction – the difference, for instance, between language that is 'opaque' (the recontextualized archaisms of Gene Wolfe's *The*

Shadow of the Torturer, 1980, for example) and that which is awkward or unsophisticated (the 'telephots' and 'detectophones' of Gernsback's *Ralph 124C 41+*). Samuel R. Delany's *The Jewel Hinged Jaw* (1979) or Peter Stockwell's *The Poetics of Science Fiction* (2000) provide useful possible directions here. In this instance, students might be asked to explore how authors construct an alternate, estranging reality through language. Similarly, they might critically assess how a story is recounted from the viewpoint of an alien. Creative as well as critical exercises can be productive for enabling students to think in science fictional terms. Students could be asked to write a paragraph describing a narrative event from a sense not possessed by humans, for example. Alternatively, they can engage in describing an object familiar to human beings from the perspective of an alien to whom the item is completely unfamiliar (Craig Raine's 'A Martian Sends a Postcard Home', 1979, makes an engaging starting point for this approach to estrangement). More critically, close-reading approaches can focus upon the lexical sets pertinent to the information communicated in specific science fiction texts. Greg Egan's *Diaspora* (1997), for instance, contains language which is heavily science- or mathematically-centred. The novel also features passages which absolutely reflect mundane life – apart from the fact that the viewpoint character is actually sentient software sharing none of the biological senses familiar to humans. When words like 'see', 'heard', 'said' are used as metaphors rather than descriptors, or the language of sexual attraction is being employed, the reader needs to reflect on how far he or she has understood the events and experiences recounted.

Further means of access into sf for students can be found in the multimedia nature of sf's textuality. One of this book's editors recalls a colleague fulminating at length about a student who wrote a commendable essay on John Wyndham's *The Midwich Cuckoos* (1957) – except that it was quite clear from the student's description of events that they were drawn from Wolf Rilla's 1960 film adaptation, *Village of the Damned*. Such an occurrence can, of course, be attributed to laziness, to a refusal to read a book when a film is more accessible. Nevertheless, the fact that sf texts exist in multiple media forms provides an opportunity for employing one version to illuminate another. For example, a short film extract can be used to open up the discussion of a short story or novel with stark immediacy. A key scene in Steve Sekeley's 1963 version of Wyndham's *The Day of the Triffids* (1951) is a case in point. Struck blind, the crew of an airliner instil a very British 'stiff-upper-lip' calm into their passengers by preparing for landing in a professional way until a young child asks whether the pilot 'is blind too' and all-out panic ensues.

Such events – absent from the source novel – provide a means of recognizing Wyndham's quiet reserve and the extended metaphor of blindness intrinsic to the novel. Similarly, contemporary radio adaptations of classic short stories such as Murray Leinster's 'First Contact' (1945) or Katherine MacLean's 'The Snowball Effect' (1952) offer opportunities to explore the ways in which such stories were interpreted and which sub-texts were emphasized or decentred in the process of adaptation at a given time. Indeed, even a film as flawed and ideologically unsound as *Avatar* (James Cameron, 2009) can, when considered within the context of other relevant sf texts (Ursula K. Le Guin's *The Word for World is Forest*, 1976, for example), highlight sf's intertextual nature and the idea of the science fiction megatext with a directness lacking from many textbooks.

Perhaps more than any other literary subject, sf challenges the traditional authority of the seminar discussion itself, where students tend to look to the tutor/instructor as the authoritative source of knowledge and wisdom. Indeed, sf is exactly the kind of subject where the tutor-student relationship can be at its most ambiguous. Most tutors and instructors working with sf will have encountered the student who knows more about aspects of the subject than they do, who has read authors unfamiliar to them, or who will be more closely involved in the fannish aspects of the field than they. Inevitably, tutors will admit their ignorance of various aspects of the topic (a particular author or text, for example). The revelation that the 'teacher' does not have all the answers (or at least does not have all the facts) should not be a surprise to either tutor or student. In discussing a field which has partaken of the nature of 'cult fiction', it is hardly remarkable that some (albeit a small minority) of the students will have been attracted to the academic study of sf by having been heavily involved in some aspect of the subject. They will have read, perhaps, the entire oeuvre of an author who is represented on the course by one story.

It may be uncomfortable for those students new to sf to observe their tutor as being less knowledgeable in certain subject matter than one of their peers. It may also be an uncomfortable experience for the tutor/instructor. Nevertheless, such circumstances provide valuable learning opportunities for all concerned. The tutor is alerted to additional – and hopefully pertinent – material; those students familiar with particular aspects of sf are encouraged to re-evaluate their knowledge from various academic and critical standpoints; and the students who are less familiar with the topic benefit not only from the exchange between the tutor and their peers but from being reminded of the nature of the enterprise in which they are engaged. Seminars are intended to facilitate a flow of knowledge, an exchange rather than a one-way presentation. Having an informed peer or peers within the group highlights the fact that science fiction is a literature discussed *outside* the academy. It may be the subject of debate by enthusiasts and experts who may not be enthusiasts and experts in other forms of literature (though they sometimes are), who may not be academics (but occasionally are, although not necessarily in literary studies), and who are, in on-line discussion groups and conventions and other collective modes, engaged in a subject for pure pleasure rather than the instrumental learning that can often define student engagement with undergraduate courses and evaluation. The recognition of this fact can help students transcend the institutionalized objectives of a course by alerting them to the 'pleasures of the text' that lie outside the narrow delineations of set reading, learning outcomes and assessment.

Assessment strategies

Evaluation for most courses is something bound by the practices of the providing institution and, in the UK at least, by learning outcome-oriented assessment strategies and national benchmark statements. Nevertheless, there is usually sufficient flexibility within such strictures to allow for varied and subject-specific assessment. Of course, like any other means of evaluation, sound assessment strategies for sf modules will encourage students to interpret and critique what they are reading. Students should be directed to move beyond the text itself to theoretical interpretation, incorporating literary and, if necessary, scientific theory, and considering the importance of historical, literary, scientific and generic contexts in the understanding of texts. However, a student's understanding of sf can be most productively evaluated with assessment strategies that test their acquisition of sf's reading protocols. Both M. Elizabeth Ginway and Peter Wright partly assess their undergraduate sf courses with 1500-word assignments that require students to analyse a key sf text using Suvin's concept of cognitive estrangement. Although almost all sf texts are amenable to this form of analysis, Wells's *The Time Machine*, with its aforementioned potential for metafictional interpretation, is often a useful text to set.

Given the varied nature of science fiction, with its contrasting literary and paraliterary styles, its diverse subject matter and its megatextual and/or transmedial nature, students often discover a particular interest in specific authors, themes or concepts. As most tutors and instructors recognize, assessment strategies often elicit the students' best work when they are enabled to explore those new interests. Clearly, this can be achieved through the conventional academic essay, written in response to either set questions or to assignment titles/subjects negotiated with the tutor. However, one of the key shortcomings of the academic essay is that its content – the texts, interpretations and conclusions – is barely disseminated. An end-of-module 'student conference' provides a solution, where students deliver the results of their research as conference papers in a conference environment (with moderators, panels and questions to follow). This not only allows students to share the results of their research with staff and peers but also assists them in developing key communication skills valuable for graduate interviews, professional presentations and/or postgraduate conferences. If the archiving of assessment is a requirement – as it is in many UK universities – the presentation can be recorded and the script submitted together with any multimedia elements (Powerpoint slides and the like).

Where the application of cognitive estrangement to a particular text and the organization of a student conference provide possible examples of formative and summative assessment, the fanzine or blog allows the tutor or instructor to ensure continuous engagement from the students. Student critical responses to texts may be evaluated by asking them to produce and/or post book reviews modelled on various sf-related publications (for example, a popular magazine, an online resource and an academic journal). Here, the intention is also to draw the student's attention to the similarities and differences between the discourse used within each publication and its implications for style, structure and content. These reviews – and longer work – can be presented as a printed fanzine or as a live blog. Such activity draws attention to the differing contexts within which sf is read, mediated and consumed.

Ancillary material can easily be added into the fanzine or blog, providing further opportunities for varied assessment. Exercises set early in a science fiction course might include a simple bibliographical activity, for example. A select bibliography of novels addressing the theme of invasion or alien contact, with a critical commentary comparing the anxieties to be found within them, is a useful means of broadening the students' knowledge and preparing them for possible extended pieces of work set later in the semester.

In contexts where creative–critical assignments are encouraged (or permissible), assessing students' capacity to think 'science fictionally' can become a much more stimulating process. This is evident from the variety of responses to papers set by Chris Ferns at Mount Saint Vincent

University. By uniting the creative with the critical, Ferns is able to engage his students directly (and at times wittily) in the processes of cognitive estrangement, critical analysis and scholarly reflection. For example:

Topic 1: The Martians invade Nova Scotia (H.G. Wells, *The War of the Worlds*, 1898)

Imagine you are H.G. Wells. Having travelled forward in time, you are now writing an alien invasion narrative set in early twenty-first century Nova Scotia. Your response paper is a part of that narrative. Bear in mind that Wells's invasion story is a fantasy about jolting people out of their complacent assumptions, about undoing the effects of urban expansion, and about showing Western society on the receiving end of what it does to other species, and indeed other races. See if your narrative can touch on one or more of these themes.

Alternatively, imagine you are one of the Martians, landing in Nova Scotia. What is *your* perspective on the chaos you create?

Topic 2: *Brave New World*

You are an Alpha from Brave New World, and as part of a research project, you have visited *our* world for a month. What is wrong with it? How do you answer justifications like 'at least we're free'?

or

You have been visiting Brave New World, and have decided to stay. What made you decide to do so? Why do you find it preferable to our world?

or

Write some copy for a tourist brochure advertising Brave New World as a holiday destination. Try using an actual travel brochure as a model – or else a travel piece from one of the daily papers – and see how far you can make Brave New World appeal to the same kind of audience that such writing assumes.

Topic 3: Ursula K. Le Guin's *The Dispossessed* (1974)

> FROM: The Stabiles on Hain   DATE: Cycle 93 E.Y. 1508
> TO: Members of the Terra/Gethen
> Education Exchange Programme
> RE: End of Year Report
>
> You are Gethenian students taking part in an education exchange programme which involves spending three years at a Terran university. To minimize culture shock, you have been assigned to a region where the climate and speed of traffic most closely resemble those on Gethen – Nova Scotia, which is a small province of a large, sparsely inhabited country in the Terran northern hemisphere.
>
> You have now spent one year at Mount Saint Vincent University, an institution where roughly 85% of the students are female,* and while you received a thorough briefing from Genly Ai and his colleagues before your departure, you will doubtless have encountered much that is strange and unfamiliar. For the benefit of students taking part in future exchanges, you should try to answer the following questions:
>
> - What aspects of Terran society have you found most problematic?
> - What kinds of behaviour should you at all costs avoid?
> - What differences have you noticed between the behaviour patterns of female and male* Terrans? Do you believe these differences to be cultural, or biological in origin?
> - What have you learned during your stay?
>
> * There being no words for female/male in Gethenian, the above represents a translation of the Gethenian word for persons in the culminant phase of kemmer.

Fern's assessments demonstrate the creativity that science fiction tutors and instructors can employ in both assessing and enhancing their students' reading and understanding. They epitomize the opportunities offered by science fiction, its teaching and learning, for fostering intelligent and critical reflection not only upon a salient popular cultural phenomenon, but also on the nature of human speculation, aspiration and anxiety. More than any other literature, sf has the capability for exposing and challenging the assumptions and prejudices that continue to define contemporary societies and international relations. It has the potential to awaken politically lethargic students to the possibility of cultural change beyond the technological. Accordingly, it is never a question of *if* science fiction should be taught and always a matter of *when*.

Notes

1. James Gunn, *Inside Science Fiction*, 2nd edn (Lanham, MD: Scarecrow Press, 2006) 82.
2. Ibid.
3. Leroy Lubeck, Suzanne E. Moshier and Judith E. Boss, *Fantastic Voyages: Learning Science through Science Fiction Films* (Melville, NY: AIP Press, 1994).
4. See R. Gary Raham, *Teaching Science Fact with Science Fiction* (Portsmouth, NH: Teacher Ideas Press, 2004) 57–104.
5. See Gregory Benford, 'Physics Through Science Fiction', in James Gunn, Marleen S. Barr and Matthew Candelaria, eds, *Reading Science Fiction* (Basingstoke: Palgrave Macmillan, 2008), 212–18.
6. Damien Broderick, 'Sf as Generic Engineering', *Foundation*, 59 (Autumn 1993): 16–28.
7. Gary Westfahl, *The Mechanics of Wonder* (Liverpool: Liverpool University Press, 1998) 92.
8. Edward James, *Science Fiction in the Twentieth Century* (Oxford: Oxford University Press, 1994) 95–6.
9. Ibid., 96.
10. Ibid., 107.
11. Darko Suvin, *The Metamorphoses of Science Fiction* (Yale: Yale University Press, 1979) 7–8.
12. James, *Science Fiction in the Twentieth Century*, 108.
13. Darko Suvin, *Victorian Science Fiction in the UK: Discourses of Knowledge and of Power* (Boston, MA: G.K. Hall, 1983) 63.
14. James, *Science Fiction in the Twentieth Century*, 111.
15. Tom Shippey cited in ibid., 112.
16. Philip K. Dick, *The Collected Stories of Philip K. Dick Volume One: Beyond Lies the Wub* (London: Millennium, 1999) 404.
17. The cover is viewable, at http:www.philsp.com/mags/amazing_stories.html (accessed 24 June 2010).
18. Hugo Gernsback in *Amazing*, September 1928: 519.
19. Frank R. Paul's cover is also viewable, at http:www.philsp.com/mags/amazing_stories.html (accessed 24 June 2010).
20. Judith Merril's 'What Do You Mean? Science? Fiction?', in Thomas D. Clareson, ed., *SF: The Other Side of Realism* (Bowling Green, OH: Bowling Green University Press, 1971) 53–95.
21. For a more detailed discussion of this concept see Gibson's article 'Rocket Radio' in *Rolling Stone*, 15 June 1989. The essay is also available online, at http://www.voidspace.org.uk/cyberpunk/gibson/rocketradio.shtml (accessed 25 June 2010).

References, Resources and Further Reading

Useful organizations/websites

The British Science Fiction Association, http://www.bsfa.co.uk/.
Center for the Study of Science Fiction, http://www2.ku.edu/~sfcenter/index.html.
International Association for the Fantastic in the Arts, http://www.iafa.org/.
Locus magazine, http://locusmag.com/.
The Science Fiction Foundation, http://www.sf-foundation.org/.
The Science Fiction Hub, http://www.sfhub.ac.uk/.
Science Fiction Research Association, http://www.sfra.org/.
Science Fiction Writers of America, http://www.sfwa.org/.

Further Reading

Key Journals

Extrapolation: A Journal of Science Fiction and Fantasy, http://extrapolation.utb.edu/.
Femspec, http://www.femspec.org/.
Foundation: The International Review of Science Fiction, http://www.sf-foundation.org/publications/foundation.html.
Journal of the Fantastic in the Arts, http://ebbs.english.vt.edu/iafa/jfa/jfa.html.
New York Review of Science Fiction, http://www.nyrsf.com/.
Science Fiction Studies, http://www.depauw.edu/SFs/.

General

Aldiss, Brian W. *Science Fiction Art*. New York: Bounty Books, 1975.
Aldiss, Brian. *The Detached Retina: Aspects of Science Fiction and Fantasy*. Liverpool: Liverpool University Press, 1995.
Amis, Kingsley. *New Maps of Hell: A Survey of Science Fiction*. London: Victor Gollancz, 1961.
Atheling, William, Jr [James Blish]. *The Issue at Hand*. Chicago: Advent, 1964.
Atheling, William, Jr [James Blish]. *More Issues at Hand*. Chicago: Advent, 1970.
Ben-Tov, Sharona, *The Artificial Paradise: Science Fiction and American Reality*. Ann Arbor: University of Michigan Press, 1995.
Booker, M. Keith and Anne-Marie Thomas. *The Science Fiction Handbook*. London: Wiley-Blackwell, 2009.
Bould, Mark, Andrew M. Butler, Adam Roberts and Sherryl Vint, eds. *Fifty Key Figures in Science Fiction*. London: Routledge, 2009.
Bould, Mark, Andrew M. Butler, Adam Roberts and Sherryl Vint, eds. *The Routledge Companion to Science Fiction*. London: Routledge, 2009.
Brake, Mark and Neil Hook. *Different Engines: How Science Drives Fiction and Fiction Drives Science*. Basingstoke: Macmillan Science, 2007.

248 References, Resources and Further Reading

Brake, Mark and Neil Hook, *FutureWorld: Where Science Fiction becomes Science*. Basingstoke: Macmillan Science, 2008.

Clareson, Thomas D. *SF: The Other Side of Realism*. Bowling Green, OH: Bowling Green University Popular Press, 1971.

Clarke, Stephen R. *How to Live Forever: Science Fiction and Philosophy*. London: Routledge, 1995.

Clute, John. *Look at the Evidence: Essays and Reviews*. Liverpool: Liverpool University Press, 1995.

Clute, John. *Canary Fever: Reviews*. Romford, Essex: Beccon, 2009.

Clute, John. *Scores: Reviews 1993–2003*. Romford, Essex: Beccon, 2009.

Clute, John and Peter Nicholls, eds. *The Encyclopedia of Science Fiction*. London: Orbit, 1993.

Disch, Thomas M. *The Dreams Our Stuff is Made of: How Science Fiction Conquered the World*. New York: Simon and Schuster, 2000.

Gunn, James, Marleen Barr and Matthew Candelaria, eds. *Reading Science Fiction*. Basingstoke: Palgrave Macmillan, 2008.

Hartwell, David. *Age of Wonders: Exploring the World of Science Fiction*. New York: Tor, 1996.

Hassler, Donald and Guy De Wilcox, eds. *Political Science Fiction*. Columbia: University of South Carolina Press, 1997.

Hassler, Donald and Clyde Wilcox, eds. *New Boundaries in Political Science Fiction*. Columbia: University of South Carolina Press, 2008.

Hollinger, Veronica and Joan Gordon, eds. *Edging into the Future: Science Fiction and Contemporary Cultural Transformation*. Philadelphia: University of Pennsylvania Press, 2002.

James, Edward and Farah Mendlesohn, eds. *The Cambridge Companion to Science Fiction*. Cambridge: Cambridge University Press, 2003.

Kincaid, Paul. *What Is It We Do When We Read Science Fiction*. Essex: Beccon Publications, 2008.

Knight, Damon. *In Search of Wonder: Essays on Modern Science Fiction*. Chicago: Advent Publishers, 1956. Second Edition, Chicago: University of Chicago Press, 1967.

Manlove, Colin N. *Science Fiction: Ten Explorations*. Ohio: Kent State University Press, 1986.

Mendlesohn, Farah. *The Rhetorics of Fantasy*. Middletown, CT: Wesleyan University Press, 2008.

Moskowitz, Sam. *Seekers of Tomorrow: Masters of Science Fiction*. Cleveland: World, 1966.

Moskowitz, Sam. *Strange Horizons: The Spectrum of Science Fiction*. New York: Scribner's, 1976.

Pierce, John J. *Odd Genre: A Study in Imagination and Evolution*. Westport, CT: Greenwood, 1994.

Prucher, Jeff. *Brave New Words: The Oxford Dictionary of Science Fiction*. Oxford: Oxford University Press, 2007.

Rieder, John. *Colonialism and the Emergence of Science Fiction*. Middletown, CT: Wesleyan University Press, 2008.

Roberts, Adam. *Science Fiction*. London: Routledge, 2000. Second Edition, London: Routledge, 2005.

Sawyer, Andy and David Seed, eds. *Speaking Science Fiction: Dialogues and Interpretations*. Liverpool: Liverpool University Press, 2000.
Schneider, Susan. *Science Fiction and Philosophy: From Time Travel to Superintelligence*. London: Wiley-Blackwell, 2009.
Scholes, Robert and Eric Rabkin. *Science Fiction: History – Science – Vision*. Oxford: Oxford University Press, 1977.
Seed, David, ed. *A Companion to Science Fiction*. London: Wiley-Blackwell, 2005.
Stableford, Brian. *Science Fiction and Science Fact: An Encyclopedia*. London: Routledge, 2006.
Stableford, Brian. *Heterocosms: Science Fiction in Context and Practice*. Rockville, MD: Borgo Press, 2007.
Telotte, J.P. *Replications: A Robotic History of the Science Fiction Film*. Champaign, IL: University of Illinois Press, 1995.
Wagar, Warren W. *Terminal Visions: The Literature of Last Things*. Bloomington: Indiana University Press, 1982.
Warrick, Patricia S. *The Cybernetic Imagination in Science Fiction*. Cambridge, MA: MIT Press, 1982.
Weiner, Norbert. *The Human Use of Human Beings: Cybernetics and Society*. New York: Doubleday, 1950.
Westfahl, Gary. *Cosmic Engineers: A Study of Hard Science Fiction*. Santa Barbara, CA: Greenwood Press, 1996.
Westfahl, Gary. *Space and Beyond: The Frontier Theme in Science Fiction*. Santa Barbara, CA.: Greenwood Press, 2000.
Westfahl, Gary and George Slusser, eds. *Science Fiction, Canonization, Marginalization and the Academy*. Santa Barbara, CA: Greenwood Press, 2002.
Westfahl, Gary and George Slusser, eds. *Science Fiction and the Two Cultures: Essays on Bridging the Gap between the Sciences and the Humanities*. Jefferson, NC: McFarland and Co. Inc., 2009.

Bibliographical guides

Barron, Neil. *Anatomy of Wonder: A Critical Guide to Science Fiction*. London: Elek/Pemberton, 1975.
Bleiler, Everett F. *Science Fiction: The Early Years*. Ohio: Kent State University Press, 1992.
Bleiler, Everett F. and Richard J. Bleiler. *Science Fiction: The Gernsback Years*. Ohio: Kent State University Press, 1998.
Clarke, I.F. *The Tale of the Future*, 3rd edn. London, Library Association, 1978.
Ruddick, Nicholas. *British Science Fiction, 1478–1990: A Chronology*. Santa Barbara, CA: Greenwood Press, 1992.
Watson, Noelle. *Twentieth Century Science-Fiction Writers*. Farmington Hills, MI: St James Press, 1991.

History

Aldiss, Brian, W. and David Wingrove. *Trillion Year Spree*. London: Gollancz, 1986.
Alkon, Paul. *Science Fiction before 1900: Imagination Discovers Technology*. Woodbridge, CT: Twayne Publishers, 1994.

250 References, Resources and Further Reading

Ashley, Michael. *The Time Machines: The Story of the Science Fiction Pulp Magazines from the Beginning to 1950*. Liverpool: Liverpool University Press, 2000.

Ashley, Michael. *Transformations: The Story of the Science-Fiction Magazines 1950–1970*. Liverpool: Liverpool University Press, 2005.

Ashley, Michael. *Gateways to Forever: The Story of the Science Fiction Magazines, 1970–1980* Liverpool: Liverpool University Press, 2007.

Bartter, Martha. *The Way to Ground Zero: The Atomic Bomb in American Science Fiction*. Santa Barbara, CA: Greenwood Press, 1988.

Carter, Paul A. *The Creation of Tomorrow: Fifty Years of Magazine Science Fiction*. New York: Columbia University Press, 1977.

Clareson, Thomas D. *Some Kind of Paradise: The Emergence of American Science Fiction*. Westport, CT: Greenwood, 1985.

Clareson, Thomas D. *Understanding Contemporary American Science Fiction: The Formative Period 1926–1970*. Columbia: University of South Carolina Press, 1990.

Davin, Eric Leif, ed. *Pioneers of Wonder: Conversations with the Founders of Science Fiction*. New York: Prometheus Books, 1999.

Harris-Fain, Darren. *Understanding Contemporary American Science Fiction: The Age of Maturity, 1970–2000*. Columbia: University of South Carolina Press, 2005.

James, Edward. *Science Fiction in the Twentieth Century*. Oxford: Oxford University Press, 1994.

Landon, Brooks. *Science Fiction after 1900: From the Steam Man to the Stars*. Woodbridge, CT: Twayne Publishers, 1997.

Luckhurst, Roger. *Science Fiction*. Cambridge: Polity Press, 2005.

Philmus, Robert. *Into the Unknown: The Evolution of Science Fiction from Francis Godwin to H.G. Wells*. Berkeley: University of California Press, 1970.

Roberts, Adam. *The History of Science Fiction*. Basingstoke: Palgrave, 2007.

Seed, David, ed. *Anticipations: Essays on Early Science Fiction and its Precursors*. Liverpool: Liverpool University Press, 1995.

Seed, David. *American Science Fiction and the Cold War: Literature and Film*. Edinburgh: Edinburgh University Press, 1999.

Stover, Leon. *Science Fiction from Wells to Heinlein*. Jefferson, NC: McFarland and Co., 2008.

Theory

Attebery, Brian. *Strategies of Fantasy*. Bloomington and Indianapolis: Indiana University Press, 1992.

Csicsery-Ronay, Istvan. *The Seven Beauties of Science Fiction*. Middletown, CT: Wesleyan University Press, 2008.

Delany, Samuel R. *The Jewel-Hinged Jaw: Notes on the Language of Science Fiction*. Middletown, CT: Wesleyan University Press, 2009.

Freedman, Carl. *Critical Theory and Science Fiction*. Middletown, CT: Wesleyan University Press, 2000.

Gunn, James. *Speculations on Speculation: Theories of Science Fiction*. Lanham, MD: Scarecrow Press, 2004.

Huntingdon, John. *Rationalising Genius: Ideological Strategies in the Classic American Science Fiction Short Story*. Piscataway, NJ: Rutgers University Press, 1989.

Malmgren, Carl D. *Worlds Apart: Narratology of Science Fiction.* Bloomington: Indiana University Press, 1991.
Parrinder, Patrick. *Science Fiction: A Critical Guide.* London: Longman, 1979.
Scholes, Robert. *Structural Fabulation: Essays on Fiction of the Future.* Indiana: University of Notre Dame Press, 1975.
Stockwell, Peter. *The Poetics of Science Fiction.* Essex: Longman, 2000.
Suvin, Darko. *The Metamorphoses of Science Fiction: On the Poetics and History of a Genre.* New Haven: Yale University Press, 1979.
Suvin, Darko. *Positions and Presuppositions in Science Fiction.* London: Macmillan, 1988.
Wolfe, Gary K. *Critical Terms for Science Fiction and Fantasy: A Glossary and Guide to Scholarship.* Santa Barbara, CA: Greenwood Press, 1986.
Wolfe, Gary K. *The Known and the Unknown: The Iconography of Science Fiction.* Ohio: Kent State University Press, 1979.

Utopia and anti-utopia

Bailey, J.O. *Pilgrims through Time and Space: Trends and Patterns in Scientific and Utopian Fiction.* New York: Argus Books, 1947.
Bammer, Angelika. *Partial Visions: Feminism and Utopianism in the 1970s.* London: Routledge, 1992.
Ferns, Chris. *Narrating Utopia: Ideology, Gender, Form in Utopian Literature.* Liverpool: Liverpool University Press, 1999.
Jameson, Fredric. *Archaeologies of the Future: The Desire Called Utopia and Other Science Fictions.* London: Verso Books, 2007.
Katerberg, William. *Frontier West: Utopia and Apocalypse in Frontier Science Fiction.* Lawrence: University of Kansas Press, 2008.
Kilgore, De Witt Douglas. *Astrofuturism: Science, Race, and Visions of Utopia in Space.* Philadelphia: University of Pennsylvania Press, 2003.
Kumar, Krishan. *Utopia and Anti-Utopia in Modern Times.* London: Wiley-Blackwell, 1987.
Kumar, Krishan. *Utopianism.* Milton Keynes: Open University Press, 1991.
Kumar, Krishan and Stephen Bann, eds. *Utopias and the Millennium.* London: Reaktion Books, 1993.
Little, Judith A. *Feminist Philosophy and Science: Utopias and Dystopias.* New York: Prometheus Books, 2007.
Mohr, Dunja M. *Worlds Apart? Dualism and Transgression in Contemporary Female Dystopias.* Jefferson, NC: McFarland & Co., 2005.
Morton, Arthur Leslie. *The English Utopia.* London: Lawrence and Wishart, 1952.
Moylan, Tom. *Demand the Impossible.* London: Methuen, 1986.
Moylan, Tom. *Scraps of the Untainted Sky: Science Fiction, Utopia, Dystopia.* Boulder, CO: Westview Press, 2000.
Moylan, Tom and Raffaella Baccolini, eds. *Dark Horizons: Science Fiction and the Dystopian Imagination.* London: Routledge, 2003.
Parrinder, Patrick. *Learning from Other Worlds: Estrangement, Cognition and the Politics of Science Fiction and Utopia.* Liverpool: Liverpool University Press, 1999.
Sargisson, Lucy. *Contemporary Feminist Utopianism.* London: Routledge, 1996.

Scientific romance

Bergonzi, Bernard. *The Early H.G. Wells: A Study of the Scientific Romances.* Manchester: Manchester University Press, 1961.

Clarke, I.F. *Voices Prophesying War: Future Wars, 1763–3749.* Oxford: Oxford University Press, 1992.

Parrinder, Patrick. *Shadows of the Future: H.G. Wells, Science Fiction and Prophecy.* Liverpool: Liverpool University Press, 1995.

Ruddick, Nicholas. *The Ultimate Island: On the Nature of British Science Fiction.* Santa Barbara, CA: Greenwood Press, 1993.

Stableford, Brian. *The Scientific Romance in Britain 1890–1950.* New York: St Martin's Press, 1985.

Pulp science fiction

Ashley, Michael and Robert A.W. Lowndes. *The Gernsback Days.* Rockville, MD: Wildside Press, 2004.

Asimov, Isaac. *In Memory Yet Green: The Autobiography of Isaac Asimov, 1920–1954.* Garden City: Doubleday, 1979.

Attebery, Brian. 'The Magazine Era: 1926–1960', in *The Cambridge Companion to Science Fiction*, eds Edward James and Farah Mendlesohn. Cambridge: Cambridge University Press, 2003, 32–47.

Bleiler, Everett F., with Richard Bleiler. *Science-Fiction: The Gernsback Years.* Kent, Ohio: Kent State University Press, 1998.

Westfahl, Gary. *The Mechanics of Wonder: The Creation of the Idea of Science Fiction.* Liverpool: Liverpool University Press, 1999.

Westfahl, Gary. *Hugo Gernsback and the Century of Science Fiction.* Jefferson, NC: McFarland & Co., 2007.

Golden Age science fiction

Berger, Albert I. *The Magic That Works: John W. Campbell and the American Response to Technology.* San Bernardino, CA: Borgo Press, 1993.

Campbell, John W., Jr. *The John W. Campbell Letters, Volume I*, ed. Perry A. Chapdelaine, Tony Chapdelaine and George Hay. Franklin, Tennessee: AC Projects, 1985.

Clarke, Arthur C. *Astounding Days: A Science Fictional Autobiography.* New York: Bantam, 1990.

Pohl, Frederik. *The Way the Future Was: A Memoir.* New York: Ballantine, 1978.

Williamson, Jack. *Wonder's Child: My Life in Science Fiction.* New York: Bluejay, 1984.

New Wave

Greenland, Colin. *The Entropy Exhibition: Michael Moorcock and the British New Wave in Science Fiction.* London: Routledge and Kegan Paul, 1983.

Latham, Rob. 'The New Wave', in *A Companion to Science Fiction*, ed. David Seed. London: Blackwell Publishing 2005, 202–16.

Luckhurst, Roger. *The Angle between Two Walls: The Fiction of J.G. Ballard.* Liverpool: Liverpool University Press, 1997.

Postmodern science fiction

Baudrillard, Jean. *Simulacra and Simulation*, trans. Sheila Glaser. Ann Arbor: The University of Michigan Press, 1994.
Broderick, Damien. *Reading by Starlight: Postmodern Science Fiction*. London: Routledge, 1994.
Bukatman, Scott. *Terminal Identity: The Virtual Subject in Postmodern Science Fiction*. North Carolina: Duke University Press, 1993.
Cavallaro, Dani. *Cyberpunk and Cyberculture: Science Fiction and the Work of William Gibson*. London: Continuum, 2000.
Dinello, Daniel. *Technophobia! Science Fiction Visions of Posthuman Technology*. Austin: University of Texas Press, 2006.
Docherty, Thomas. *Postmodernism: A Reader*. London: Longman, 1992.
Featherstone, Mike and Roger Burrows, eds. *Cyberspace/Cyberbodies/Cyberpunk: Cultures of Technological Embodiment*. London: Sage Publications, 1996.
Graham, Elaine. *Representations of the Post/Human*. Piscataway, NJ: Rutgers University Press, 2003.
Gray, Chris Hables. *The Cyborg Handbook*. London: Routledge, 1995.
Gray, Chris Hables. *Cyborg Citizen: Politics in the Posthuman Age*. London: Routledge, 2000.
Haney, William S. *Cybercultures, Cyborgs and Science Fiction: Consciousness and the Posthuman*. New York: Editions Rodopi, 2006.
Haraway, Donna. 'Manifesto for Cyborgs: Science, Technology, and Socialist-Feminism in the Late Twentieth Century'. *Socialist Review* 80 (1985): 65–108.
Harvey, David. *The Condition of Postmodernity: An Enquiry into the Origins of Cultural Change*. London: Wiley-Blackwell, 1991.
Hayles, N.K. *How We Became Posthuman: Virtual Bodies in Cybernetics, Literature and Informatics*. Chicago: University of Chicago Press, 1999.
Heuser, Sabine. *Virtual Geographies: Cyberpunk at the Intersection of the Postmodern and Science Fiction*. New York: Editions Rodopi, 2003.
Hollinger, Veronica. 'Science Fiction and Postmodernism', in *A Companion to Science Fiction*, ed. David Seed. London: Blackwell, 2005, 232–47.
Jameson, Fredric. *Postmodernism: Or, the Cultural Logic of Late Capitalism*. London: Verso, 1992.
Lyotard, Jean-François. *The Postmodern Condition: A Report on Knowledge*, trans. Geoff Bennington and Brian Massumi. Manchester: Manchester University Press, 1984.
McCaffery, Larry, ed. *Storming the Reality Studio: Casebook of Cyberpunk and Postmodern Science Fiction*. North Carolina: Duke University Press, 1992.
Palmer, Christopher. *Philip K. Dick: Exhilaration and Terror of the Postmodern*. Liverpool: Liverpool University Press, 2003.
Slusser, George and Tom Shippey. *Fiction 2000: Cyberpunk and the Future of Narrative*. Athens GA: University of Georgia Press, 1992.
Vest, Jason P. *The Postmodern Humanism of Philip K. Dick*. Lanham, MD: Scarecrow Press, 2009.
Yoke, Carl B. and Carol L. Robinson. *The Cultural Influences of William Gibson, the 'Father' of Cyberpunk Science Fiction*. Ceredigion: Edwin Mellen Press, 2007.

Gender and science fiction

Armitt, Lucie, ed. *Where No Man Has Gone Before: Essays on Women and Science Fiction*. London: Routledge, 1991.

Attebery, Brian. *Decoding Gender in Science Fiction*. London: Routledge, 2002.

Barr, Marlene, ed. *Future Females*. Ohio: Bowling Green University Press, 1981.

Barr, Marlene. *Feminist Fabulation: Space/Postmodern Fiction*. Iowa City: University of Iowa Press, 1992.

Barr, Marlene. *Lost in Space: Probing Feminist SF and Beyond*. Chapel Hill: University of North Carolina Press, 1993.

Cortiel, Jeanne. *Demand My Writing: Joanna Russ, Feminism, Science Fiction*. Liverpool: Liverpool University Press, 1999.

Davin, Eric Leif. *Partners in Wonder: Women and the Birth of Science Fiction, 1926–1965*. Lanham, MD: Lexington Books, 2005.

Delany, Samuel R. *The Motion of Light on Water: Sex and Science Fiction Writing in the East Village*. Minneapolis: University of Minnesota Press, 2004.

Donawerth, Jane. *Frankenstein's Daughters: Women Writing SF*. New York: Syracuse University Press, 1996.

Donawerth, Jane and Carol Kolmerten, eds. *Worlds of Difference: Utopian and Science Fiction by Women*. Liverpool: Liverpool University Press, 1994.

Larbalestier, Justine. *The Battle of the Sexes in Science Fiction*. Middletown, CT: Wesleyan University Press, 2002.

Larbalestier, Justine, ed. *Daughters of Earth: Feminist Science Fiction in the Twentieth Century*. Middletown, CT: Wesleyan University Press, 2006.

LeFanu, Sarah. *In the Chinks of the World Machine: Feminism and Science Fiction*. London: The Women's Press, 1988.

Melzer, Patricia. *Alien Constructions: Science Fiction and Feminist Thought*. Austin: University of Texas Press, 2006.

Merrick, Helen and Tess Williams. *Women of Other Worlds: Excursions through Science Fiction and Feminism*. Perth: University of Western Australia Press, 1999.

Noonan, Bonnie. *Women Scientists in Fifties Science Fiction Films*. Jefferson, NC: McFarland, 2005.

Roberts, Robin. *A New Species: Gender and Science in Science Fiction*. Urbana: University of Illinois Press, 1993.

Russ, Joanna. *To Write Like a Woman*. Bloomington: Indiana University Press, 1995.

Wolmark, Jenny. *Aliens and Others: Science Fiction, Feminism and Postmodernism*. Iowa City: University of Iowa Press, 1994.

Yaszek, Lisa. *Galactic Suburbia: Recovering Women's Science Fiction*. Columbus, OH: Ohio State University Press, 2008.

Postcolonial science fiction

Ashcroft, Bill, Gareth Griffiths and Helen Tiffin. *The Empire Writes Back: Theory and Practice in Post-Colonial Literatures*. London: Routledge, 1989.

Ashcroft, Bill, Gareth Griffiths and Helen Tiffin. *Postcolonial Studies: The Key Concepts*. 2nd edn. London: Routledge, 2007.

Bhabha, Homi K, ed. *Nation and Narration*. New York, Routledge, 1990.

Bush, Barbara. *Imperialism and Postcolonialism*. London: Longman, 2006.

Eakin, Marshall C. *Brazil: The Once and Future Country*. New York: St Martin's Press, 1997.
Fanon, Franz. *Black Skin, White Masks*. New edition. London: Pluto Press, 2008.
Grayson, Sandra M. *Visions of the Third Millennium: Black Science Fiction Novelists Write the Future*. Trenton, NJ: Africa World Press, 2003.
Hopkinson, Nalo and Uppinder Mehan, eds. *So Long Been Dreaming: Postcolonial Visions of the Future*. Vancouver: Arsenal Pulp Press, 2004.
Kerslake, Patricia. *Science Fiction and Empire*. Liverpool: Liverpool University Press, 2007.
McLeod, John. *Beginning Postcolonialism*. Manchester: Manchester University Press, 2000.
Morgan, Philip D. and Sean Hawkins, eds. *Black Experience and the Empire*. Oxford: Oxford University Press, 2004.
Rieder, John. *Colonialism and the Emergence of Science Fiction*. Middletown, CT: Wesleyan University Press, 2008.
Said, Edward. *Orientalism*. New York: Vintage, 1979.

Latin American science fiction and fantasy

Aparicio, Frances R. and Susana Chávez-Silverman, eds. *Tropicalizations: Transcultural Representations of Latinidad*. Durham, NH: Dartmouth College Press, 1997.
Bell, Andrea and Yolanda Molina-Gavilán, eds. *Cosmo Latinos: An Anthology of Science Fiction from Latin America and Spain*. Middletown, CT: Wesleyan University Press, 2003.
Beverly, John, José Oviedo and Michael Aronna, eds. *The Postmodern Debate in Latin America*. Durham, NC: Duke University Press, 1995.
Causo, Roberto de Sousa, *Ficção Científica, Fantasia e Horror no Brasil, 1875 a 1950*. Belo Horizonte, Brazil: Editora UFMG, 2003.
Ginway, M. Elizabeth. *Brazilian Science Fiction: Cultural Myths and Nationhood in the Land of the Future*. Lewisburg, PA: Bucknell University Press, 2004.
Grobet, Lourdes. *Lucha Libre: Masked Superstars of Mexican Wrestling*. Mexico: Trilce, 2005.
Hess, David J. and Roberto DaMatta, eds. *The Brazilian Puzzle. Culture of the Borderlands of the Western World*. New York: Columbia University Press, 1995.
Johnson, Randal and Robert Stam, eds. *Brazilian Cinema*. New York: Columbia University Press, 1995.
Levi, Heather. *The World of Lucha Libre: Secrets, Revelations, and Mexican National Identity*. Durham, NC: Duke University Press, 2008.
Piletti, Nelson. *A história do Brasil*. São Paulo: Ática, 1991.
Puig, Manuel. *Pubis Angelical*, trans. Elena Brunet. Minneapolis: University of Minnesota Press, 2000.
Sarlo, Beatriz. *Scenes from Postmodern Life*, trans. Jon Beasley-Murray. Minneapolis: University of Minnesota Press, 2001.

Index

Abrams, Sam, 213
Adam Adamant Lives! 82
Aldiss, Brian W., 5, 30–1, 40, 44, 74, 100, 105, 122, 126
  Barefoot in the Head, 32
  definition of science fiction, 49
  Greybeard, 32
  Report on Probability A, 126
  Space Opera, 47
  Trillion Year Spree (with David Wingrove), 11, 49
alternate history, 41, 47, 48, 83, 139
Amazing Stories, 6, 12, 25–8, 43, 98, 223, 237
Amis, Kingsley, *New Maps of Hell*, 11, 235
Analog, see *Astounding Stories*
Anderson, Kevin J., *Slan Hunter*, 87
Anderson, Poul, 30
Android, 156
Anthony, Patricia, *Cradle of Spendor*, 197
Apulius, *The Golden Ass*, 152–4
Arango, Ángel, 'The Cosmonaut', 185
Arnason, Eleanor, *Ring of Swords*, 158
Arnold, Jack, *The Creature from the Black Lagoon*, 180
Asimov, Isaac, 8, 11, 15, 19, 28–9, 31, 39, 87, 94–6
  Before the Golden Age, 87
  'Bicentennial Man', 29
  Foundation trilogy, 29
  The Gods Themselves, 139
  I, Robot, 28, 94–6, 101, 106, 156
  'Little Lost Robot', 95
  'Nightfall', 28
  'Robot Dreams', 29
  three laws of robotics, 28–9, 94–6, 102
Astounding Science Fiction, see *Astounding Stories*
Astounding Stories, 14, 28, 43, 88, 90, 91, 97, 105, 238

as *Analog*, 120, 237
Attebery, Brian, 16, 45, 86, 109, 111, 146, 223, 230
Atwood, Margaret, 7
  The Handmaid's Tale, 56, 65, 157, 192

Bacon, Francis, *The New Atlantis*, 23, 55
Bailey, Hilary, 'Fall of Frenchy Steiner', 27
Bailey, J.O., 4
  Pilgrims Through Space and Time, 10–11, 44, 224–5, 227–8
Ballard, J.G., 2, 16, 34, 37, 117, 119–22, 125–7, 132
  The Atrocity Exhibition, 32, 84, 132
  Crash, 142
  The Crystal World, 32
  'You and Me and the Continuum', 225, 228
Bammer, Angelika, 56–7
Banks, Iain M., 126
  Consider Phlebas, 35
Barnes, Steven, *The Descent of Anansi*, 172
Barron, Neil, 42, 46
Baudrillard, Jean, 15–16, 130, 140–3
Baxter, Stephen, 21
  Coalescent, 35
  The Time Ships, 26
Bear, Elizabeth, *Hammered*, 36
Bell, Andrea L. (with Yolanda Molina-Galiván), *Cosmos Latinos*, 17, 179, 184–7, 197, 232
Bell, Neil, 72
Bellamy, Edward, *Looking Backward*, 55, 58–60, 63, 65–6
Bellow, Saul, 132
Benford, Gregory, 220
  Beyond the Fall of Night, 89
  Beyond Infinity, 89
  In the Ocean of Night, 33

Timescape, 33, 139
Berdiaeff, Nicholas, 60, 61, 65
Beresford, J.D., 72, 74
Bernal, J.D., 61
Bester, Alfred, *Tiger! Tiger!*, 30
Biggle, Lloyd Jr, 38
Binder, Eando, 'I, Robot', 106–7
Bionic Woman, The, 156
Bleiler, Everett F., 38, 46
Blish, James, 30
Bloch, Ernst, 63, 69
Bogdanov, Alexander, *Red Star*, 56
Borges, Jorge Luis, 198
  Ficciones, 189
  'The Garden of the Forking Paths', 190
  'The Library of Babel', 188
  'On Rigor in Science', 138, 182, 188
Boulle, Pierre, 36
Bova, Ben, 38, 120
Brackett, Leigh, 98–100
Bradbury, Ray, 44, 99
  The Martian Chronicles, 30, 86
Bradley, Marion Zimmer, 'The Wind People', 109–10
Brake, Mark, 18
Brigg, Peter, 42
Brijs, Stefan, *The Angel Maker*, 36
Brin, David
  Glory Season, 158
  Sundiver, 33
Broderick, Damien, 19, 45, 161, 223
Brunner, John, 132
  The Sheep Look Up, 122
  Stand on Zanzibar, 32
Bruno, Giordano, 22
Bryant, Dorothy, *The Kin of Ata Are Waiting for You*, 158
Buck, Doris Pitkin, 'Birth of a Gardener', 110
Buckell, Tobias, *Ragamuffin*, 36
Budrys, Algis, 30, 38, 39, 41, 52
Bujold, Lois McMaster
  Ethan of Athos, 158
  The Warrior's Apprentice, 33
Bulgarin, F.V., *Plausible Fantasies*, 25
Bull, Emma, *Bone Dance*, 156
Burdekin, Katherine, *Swastika Night*, 26, 157

Burke, Edmund, and the sublime, 24, 136
Burroughs, Edgar Rice
  Llana of Gathol, 98
  Pellucidar, 23
  Princess of Mars, 98
Burroughs, William S., 117, 121, 132, 224
Butler, Andrew M., 5, 15–16
Butler, Octavia, 166
  Clay's Ark, 152
  Wild Seed, 151, 156

Cadigan, Pat, 2, 159
  Synners, 34
Cameron, James, *Avatar*, 241
Campanella, Thomas, *City of the Sun*, 22, 55, 65
Campbell, John W., 14, 28, 43, 87, 91–2, 96–7, 100, 105–6, 120, 224
  'The Black Star Passes', 28
  definition of science fiction, 43
  'Night', 28
  'Twilight', 28, 226
  'Who Goes There?', 156
Canfield, Cass Jr., *Masterworks of Latin American Short Stories*, 189–90
Capanna, Pablo, 'Anacronia', 185
Capek, Karel, *R.U.R. (Rossum's Universal Robots)*, 10, 28–9
Card, Orson Scott, *Speaker for the Dead*, 197
Carneiro, André
  'Brain Transplant', 186
  'Darkness', 189
  'Life as an Ant', 189
  'A Perfect Marriage', 189
Carter, Raphael, 'Congenital Agenesis of Gender Ideation, by K.N. Sirsi and Sandra Botkin', 157
Casanova, Jacques, *Icosameron*, 23
Casares, Adolfo Bioy, *The Invention of Morel*, 190
Castro, Pablo, 'Exerion', 187
Cavendish, Margaret, *The Blazing World*, 23

Charnas, Suzy McKee, 2
  Motherlines, 151, 158
  Walk to the End of the World, 157
Chatterjee, Rimi, *Signal Red*, 172
Chaviano, Daína, 'The Annunciation', 186
Cherryh, C.J., 17, 169
  Foreigner series, 171
Chesney, George T., *The Battle of Dorking*, 26, 73, 79–80
Cixous, Hélène, 131, 150
Clareson, Thomas D., 4, 50, 226
Clarke, Arthur C., 8, 15, 21, 35, 49, 98, 119, 147, 214, 224
  2001: A Space Odyssey, 31, 89, 236
  Against the Fall of Night, 88
  Astounding Days, 87
  Childhood's End, 31, 86
  The City and the Stars, 31, 226–7
  'The Nine Billion Names of God', 236
  Rendezvous with Rama, 121
Clarke, I.F., 79
  Voices Prophesying War, 47
Clement, Hal, 51
  Mission of Gravity, 28
Clute, John, 4, 6, 8–9, 42, 184
cognitive estrangement, 7, 42, 45, 150, 183, 224, 226, 234, 242, 243–4
Coleridge, Samuel Taylor, 'Cristabel', 152
colonial science fiction, 167–9, 228
  see also postcolonial science fiction
Conklin, Groff, 46
Conquest, Robert, 1, 19
Conroy, Robert, 48
Constantine, Murray, *see* Burdekin, Katherine
Cooper, Edmund, *Gender Genocide*, 158
Correa, Hugo, 'When Pilate Said No', 185
cosy catastrophe, 31, 37
critical utopia, 56, 67–9
Cronenberg, David, *Videodrome*, 134
Crowley, John, 11
curriculum design, 205–17, 219–23

cyberpunk, 2, 6, 15, 30, 34, 46–7, 52, 83, 107, 116, 118, 119, 126, 134, 144, 184, 186–7, 191, 195–6, 199, 222, 225, 230–1

Dann, Jack, *The Memory Cathedral*, 48
Dante, Joe, *Gremlins II*, 135
Darwin, Charles, 25–6, 72, 78, 131
  On the Origin of Species, 25
Davenport, Basil, 50
De Andrade, Joachim Pedro, *Macunaíma*, 181
De Assis, Machado, 'The Siamese Academies', 187–8
De Beauvoir, Simone, 150
De Camp, L. Sprague, 28
De la Casa, Ricard (with Pedro Jorge Romero), 'The Day It Changed', 186
De France, Marie
  'Bisclavret', 152
  'Yonec', 152
De Loyola Brandão, Ignacio, *And Still the Earth*, 191
Defoe, Daniel, *Journal of the Plague Year*, 227
Del Rey, Lester, 28, 38, 127–8
  'Helen O'Loy', 147–8, 156, 222, 224, 230
Del Toro, Guillermo, *Cronos*, 183
Delany, Samuel R., 2, 40, 45, 51, 56, 70, 121, 149, 166, 172
  The Ballad of Beta, 2, 149–50
  Dhalgren, 33
  'Driftglass', 17, 192, 197
  The Jewel-Hinged Jaw, 240
  Nova, 33
  Triton, 58, 122
Delgado, Miguel M., *Santo y Blue Demon contra el doctor Frankenstein (Santo and Blue Demon vs. Doctor Frankenstein)*, 182–3
Desleal, Álvaro, 'Cord of Nylon and Gold', 185
Díaz, Junot, *Brief Wondrous Life of Oscar Wao*, 190–1
Dick, Philip K., 2, 5, 6, 16, 96, 101, 121, 134, 225, 228, 231, 238
  'Colony', 236

Do Androids Dream of Electric Sheep?, 30, 91, 221, 225, 228
Dr Bloodmoney, 134
Eye in the Sky, 48
The Man in the High Castle, 30, 139
Now Wait For Last Year, 135
The Three Stigmata of Palmer Eldritch, 30
Time Out of Joint, 10, 125, 135, 142
Disch, Thomas M., *Camp Concentration*, 122–3, 125
Doctor Who, 19n, 82, 203
Doni, Anton Francesco, *I Mondi*, 22
Dos Passos, John, *USA*, 32, 132
Doyle, Arthur Conan, 72
The Lost World, 73, 81
Duchamp, Marcel, 131
Dumas, Alexandre, *The Count of Monte Cristo*, 30
dystopia, 7, 26, 46, 47, 56, 60–2, 67, 89, 91, 99, 127, 131, 127, 140, 157–9, 190–2, 210, 212

Echeverría, Roberto González, *The Oxford Book of Latin American Short Stories*, 189–90
Edison, Thomas Alva, 25
Edisonades, 25
Edwards, John, 'The Planet of Perpetual Night', 159
Egan, Greg, 34–5, 139
Diaspora, 34, 240
Electrical Experimenter, 25
Eliot, T.S., 131, 185, 233
Elgin, Suzette Haden, *Native Tongue*, 151, 157
Ellis, Edward S., 25
Ellison, Harlan, 2, 47, 122, 127, 159
'A Boy and His Dog', 32
Dangerous Visions, 32, 119
I, Robot: The Illustrated Screenplay, 95
'"Repent, Harlequin!" said the Ticktockman', 32
Eskridge, Kelly, 'And Salome Danced', 157
Evans, Arthur, 76
Evans, Christopher, 35

extrapolation, 41, 50–1, 61, 116, 150, 209
Extrapolation, 4

fandom, 6, 12, 27, 40–1
Farmer, Philip José, 'The Lovers', 159
feminist science fiction, 16, 33, 46, 108, 109, 123–4, 146–9, 222, 229–30, 232, 235
Ferns, Chris, 13, 55, 221, 243–4
Forster, E.M., 'The Machine Stops', 137
Foundation: The International Journal of Science Fiction, 4, 9, 11, 195
Fowler, Karen Joy
Sarah Canary, 33
'What I Didn't See', 152–5
Fowler Wright, Sydney, 72, 74, 147
Deluge, 24
Frank, Pat, *Alas, Babylon*, 212
Franklin, H. Bruce, 50, 180
Freud, Sigmund, 105, 125, 132
Furtado, Jorge, *Basic Sanitation: The Movie*, 8, 180
future war, 40, 47, 49, 79

Galaxy, 29, 86, 105
García, Luís Britto, 'The Future', 185
Gearheart, Sally Miller, *The Wanderground*, 158
gender, 146–61
genetic modification, 24, 221
genres, 21–2, 40–52, 56, 59, 73, 81, 84, 86, 149
Gernsback, Hugo, 6, 8, 13–14, 25, 27–8, 223, 237
definition of science fiction, 43
Ralph 124C 41+, 11, 27, 224, 226, 233, 240
Gerrold, David, *Moonstart Odyssey*, 157
Ghosh, Amitav, *The Calcutta Chromosome*, 172
Gibson, William, 2, 69, 144, 225, 235, 239
Neuromancer, 15, 19, 34, 83, 135–6, 222, 231
Gilbert, Sandra, 150
Gilman, Charlotte Perkins, 5
Herland, 56, 146, 158, 179
Ginway, M. Elizabeth, 8, 17, 222, 242

Glass, Philip, 132
Gloag, John, 72
Gloss, Molly, *Wild Life*, 152, 153
Godwin, Francis, *The Man in the Moone*, 22–3
Godwin, Tom, 'The Cold Equations', 28, 148–9
Goligorsky, Eduardo, 'The Last Refuge', 185–6
Golden Age, *see under* science fiction
Gorodischer, Angelica
  Kalpa Imperial, 190, 192
  'The Violet Embryos', 186
Gott, Samuel, *Nova Solyma*, 23
Greenland, Colin, 127
  The Entropy Exhibition, 118
  Take Back Plenty, 35
Greg, Percy, *Across the Zodiac*, 73, 81–2
Griffith, George, 72
Griffith, Nicola, *Ammonite*, 150, 158
Griffiths, Martin, 213
Grimwood, Jon Courtenay, *Pashazade*, 35
Gubar, Susan, 150
Gunn, James, 4, 219–21

Hairston, Andrea, *Mindscape*, 172
Haldane, J.B.S., 61
Haldeman, Joe, *The Forever War*, 122, 125–6
Hamilton, Edmond
  'Captain Future' series, 27
  'The Man Who Evolved' , 149
  The Star of Life, 100
Hansen, L. Taylor, 'The Undersea Tube', 224, 226
Haraway, Donna, 131, 150, 230
hard sf, 28–9, 31, 33, 35, 46, 126
Harris, Robert, *Fatherland*, 139
Harrison, Harry, 'The Streets of Ashkelon', 225, 228
Harrison, M. John, 51, 126
  Centauri Device, 32
  Light, 32
Hartwell, David G., 43, 183, 199
Hawks, Howard, *The Thing From Another World*, 156
Hawthorne, Nathaniel, 'Rappaccini's Daughter', 24

Haywood, Amber, *The Healer*, 197
Heard, Gerald, 72, 74
Heinlein, Robert A., 11, 15, 28, 31, 39, 44, 52, 95–8, 119, 125, 147, 149, 226
  'Coventry', 94
  definition of science fiction, 44, 50
  For Us, the Living, 94
  'If This Goes On –', 91–3
  The Man Who Sold the Moon, 29
  Methuselah's Children, 94, 97
  The Moon is a Harsh Mistress, 29
  The Number of the Beast, 9
  Revolt in 2100, 29, 91, 93
  'The Roads Must Roll', 19, 29, 224
  Sixth Column, 92
  Starship Troopers, 86
  Stranger in a Strange Land, 29
  Time Enough For Love, 94
  'Universe', 149
Herbert, Frank, *Dune*, 30, 170
Hickman, Tracy (With Margaret Weiss), *Dragon Wing*, 223
Hillegas, Mark, 3
Hodgson, William Hope, 72
Holberg, Ludvig, *Niels Klim in the Underworld*, 23
Holdstock, Robert, 35
Hook, Neil, 18, 202, 217
Hopkinson, Nalo, 17
  Brown Girl in the Ring, 172
  Midnight Robber, 164, 172
  So Long Been Dreaming, 162
Huxley, Aldous
  Brave New World, 3, 27, 39, 56, 60–6, 221, 244
  Brave New World Revisited, 65
  Island, 56
Huxley, T.H., 78

icons of science fiction, 4, 10, 150, 179, 182, 183, 185–6, 191, 224, 226–8, 232, 236–8
If, 29
Interzone, 35
Ishiguro, Kazuo, 7

James, Edward, 5, 44–5, 105, 233
James, P.D., *Children of Men*, 192

James Tiptree Jr. Award, 147
Jameson, Fredric, 15, 59–60, 131, 134–6, 143
Jeffries, Richard, *After London*, 24, 80
'jonbar point', 48
Jones, D.F, *Colossus*, 139
Jones, Gwyneth, 5
  Spirit, 30
  White Queen, 35, 151
Jones, Langdon, 'I Remember Anita', 225, 227
Jonson, Ben, 11
  Newes from the New World Discovered in the Moone, 22
Joyce, James, 131, 233

Kadrey, Richard, *Kamikaze L'Amour: A Novel of the Future*, 197
Kant, Immanuel, 24
Kelly, James Patrick, 'Think Like a Dinosaur', 148
Kepler, Johannes, *Somnium*, 22
Kerslake, Patricia, *Science Fiction and Empire*, 229
Keyes, Daniel, 30
Kincaid, Paul, 12, 21
Kingsley, Charles, *The Water Babies*, 26
Knight, Damon, 42–4
  definition of science fiction, 44
  Orbit, 119
Kornbluth, C.M. (with Frederik Pohl), *The Space Merchants*, 30
Kristeva, Julia, 131, 150
Kubrick, Stanley, 214
  2001: A Space Odyssey, 136, 236
  Dr Strangelove or, How I Learned to Stop Worrying and Love the Bomb, 212
Kuttner, Henry, 100
  'The Piper's Son', 149

Lacan, Jacques, 151
Lai, Larissa, *Salt Fish*, 172
Lake, Jay, *Mainspring*, 36
Lang, Fritz
  Frau Im Mond, 90
  Metropolis, 131, 236
Larbalestier, Justin, 11
  Daughters of Earth, 151

Latham, Rob, 15, 58, 116, 222
Latin American science fiction, *see under* science fiction
Lavín, Guillermo, 'Reaching the Shore', 186
Le Corbusier, 131
Le Guin, Ursula K., 6, 56, 86, 147, 160, 190, 222
  'Coming of Age in Karhide', 156
  The Dispossessed, 33, 58, 60, 66–9, 245
  The Left Hand of Darkness, 33, 51, 146, 151, 156–7
  'The Matter of Seggri', 158
learning outcomes, 130, 216–17, 242
Lee, Tanith, *The Silver Metal Lover*, 156
Leiber, Fritz, 30
Leinster, Murray, 100
  'First Contact', 241
  'Proxima Centauri', 149
Lem, Stanislaw, 36, 232
  Solaris, 68, 221
Lewis, C.S., 10, 72
Lewis, Wyndham, 131
Lewitt, S.N., *Songs of Chaos*, 192–4
Link, Kelly, *Stranger Things Happen*, 33
lost world stories, 80–1, 82
Lucian of Samosata, *True History*, 8, 22
Luckhurst, Roger, 43, 45
Lyotard, Jean-François, 15, 130, 133–4, 136–40, 143–4

Maclean, Katherine
  'And Be Merry . . .', 109–10
  'The Snowball Effect', 241
MacLeod, Ian, *The Light Ages*, 84
MacLeod, Ken, *The Star Fraction*, 35
Magazine of Fantasy and Science Fiction, 29, 38, 86, 105
Mailer, Norman, 132
Making Mr. Right, 156
Malmgren, Carl, 45
Manga, Carlos, *O Homem do Sputnik (The Sputnik Man)*, 181
Manning, Lawrence, 149
Marxism, 130, 134, 140–1, 232
McAuley, Paul
  Cowboy Angels, 35, 48
  Fairyland, 35

McDonald, Ian
  Brasyl, 17, 192, 195–7, 200
  River of Gods, 35
McDonnell, Carole, 'Lingua Franca', 225, 229
McIntyre, Vonda, *Superluminal*, 148–9
megatext, 14, 19n, 150–1, 161n, 219, 220, 232, 241, 242
Mehan, Uppinder, 16–17, 162, 228
  So Long Been Dreaming (with Nalo Hopkinson), 162
Méliès, Georges, *Le voyage dans la Lune*, 131
Melville, Herman, 233
  Moby Dick, 133
Mendlesohn Farah, 5, 9–10, 184, 223
Menzies, William Cameron, *Things to Come*, 90, 236
Merrick, Helen, 11
Merril, Judith, 208, 225, 239
  definition of science fiction, 208
  England Swings sf, 32
  'That Only a Mother', 230
metafiction, 120, 133, 226, 242
Miéville, China, 231
  Iron Council, 231
  Perdido Street Station, 35, 84
military sf, 33, 36, 47, 50
Miller, Walter M., *A Canticle for Leibowitz*, 30, 86, 212
Modern Electronics, 25
modernism, 131–3
Molina-Galiván, Yolanda (with Andrea L. Bell), *Cosmos Latinos*, 17, 179, 184–7, 197, 232
Monteiro, Jerônimo, 'The Crystal Goblet', 185
Moorcock, Michael, 31–2, 118–22, 126, 225, 227, 230–1
  'Behold the Man', 222, 227
  Jerry Cornelius novels, 132
  The Land Leviathan, 83
  The Steel Tsar, 83
  The Warlord of the Air, 83
Moore, Alan
  The League of Extraordinary Gentlemen, 84
  Watchmen, 144
Moore, C.L., 100

'No Woman Born', 106–7, 151, 156, 225, 230
Moore, Ward, *Bring the Jubilee*, 139
More, Thomas, *Utopia*, 22, 55
Morris, William, 78
  News From Nowhere, 55–6, 59, 63, 65
Morrison, David, 213
Moskowitz, Sam, 93
  definition of science fiction, 49, 208
  first college sf course, 3
Mosley, Walter, *Futureland*, 172
Mosquera, Gustavo, *Moebius*, 182
Moylan, Tom, 56–8
Mullen, R.D., 3, 38
mundane sf, 35, 126, 231
Murphy, Pat, 147, 159
'Rachel in Love', 152–5

Neville, Henry, *The Isle of Pines*, 23
New Wave sf, 6, 7, 15, 31–3, 47, 52, 116–28, 132, 137, 222, 225, 227–8, 230–1, 235, 238, 252–3, 255
New Weird, 25, 35, 84, 231–2
New Worlds, 31–2, 35
Noon, Jeff, *Vurt*, 136
Nordau, Max, 78
Nowlan, Philip Francis, *Armageddon 2419 A.D.*, 100
Nyman, Michael, 132

Odoevsky, V.F., *The Year 4338*, 25
Orientalism, 192
Orwell, George, 26
  Nineteen Eighty-Four, 3, 26, 59–60, 63–4
Otaño, Magdalena Mouján, 'Gu Ta Guttarak', 186
Ovid, *Metamorphoses*, 152

Paltock, Robert, *The Life and Adventures of Peter Wilkins*, 23
Panshin, Alexei and Cory Panshin, definition of science fiction, 49
'parabola' formula, 16, 149–60
Park, Paul, *Coelestis*, 159
Parrinder, Patrick, definition of science fiction, 208

Paul, Frank R., 237
Paz Soldán, Edmundo, *Turing's Delirium*, 190–1
'Perry Rhodan' series, 36
Picasso, Pablo, 131
Pieralisi, Alberto, *O Quinto Poder (The Fifth Power)*, 181
Pierce, John J., 50
Piercy, Marge, 56
  He, She and It, 149, 156, 222
  Woman on the Edge of Time, 67
Piper, H. Beam, 17
  The Fuzzy Papers, 168, 172
  Little Fuzzy, 163
  Fuzzy Sapiens, 163
Plato, *Symposium*, 156
Poe, Edgar Allan, 6
  The Narrative of Arthur Gordon Pym of Nantucket, 24
Pohl, Frederik, 121
  The Space Merchants (with C. M. Kornbluth), 30
  The Way the Future Was, 87
Pollock, Jackson, 132
Portillo, Rafael, *La momia azteca contra el robot humano (The Aztec Mummy vs. The Human Robot)*, 182–3
postcolonial science fiction, 16, 162–77
  see also colonial science fiction
postmodernism, 2, 5, 15–16, 34, 36, 40–1, 75, 84, 118, 120–1, 126, 129–45, 184, 195, 196, 225, 228, 253
  and science, 138–9
Pound, Ezra, 131
Priest, Christopher
  The Affirmation, 32
  The Inverted World, 32
  The Separation, 27
  The Space Machine, 26
Priestley, J.B., *I Have Been Here Before*, 27
Proyas, Alex, *I, Robot*, 95
Prucher, Jeff, 42
Puig, Manuel, *Pubis Angelical*, 190
pulp science fiction, 2, 3, 8, 14, 27, 40–1, 43–6, 49, 72, 86–101, 116–19, 125, 222, 224, 226, 237–7, 252

Pynchon, Thomas, 133
  Gravity's Rainbow, 121

quantum mechanics, 14, 48, 138–9, 210, 213–14

Rabkin, Eric, 45
Raine, Craig, 'A Martian Sends a Postcard Home', 240
reading protocols, 6, 40, 233–5, 239, 242
Reed, Ishmael, 233
Resnick, Mike, *Paradise*, 163
resources, 5, 247–55
Rilla, Wolf, *Village of the Damned*, 240
Robbins, Tom, 7
  Even Cowgirls Get the Blues, 133
  Still Life With Woodpecker, 133
Roberts, Adam, 5, 13–14, 43, 45, 72
  The History of Science Fiction, 7
  Splinter, 75
Roberts, Keith
  The Chalk Giants, 32
  Pavane, 32
  'Weinachtsabend', 27
Robinson, Kim Stanley, 17, 56
  'Mars Trilogy', 34, 169–70
robots, 10, 24, 28–9, 46–7, 88, 94–5, 98, 102, 106, 150, 166, 182–3, 185, 226–8, 230, 236
Rojo, Pepe, 'Gray Noise', 186
Romero, Pedro Jorge (with Ricard De La Casa), 'The Day It Changed', 186
Roth, Philip, 132
Rothko, Mark, 132
Rubião, Murilo, *The Ex-Magician and Other Stories*, 188
Russ, Joanna, 2, 5, 45, 56
  definition of sf, 208–9, 225
  The Female Man, 33, 120, 136, 158
  'The Image of Women in Science Fiction', 229
Russell, Bertrand, 66
Ryman, Geoff, 34–5, 128n, 159, 231
  Air, 34, 35, 231

Said, Edward, 192
Sakers, Don, 'The Cold Solution', 148

Sales, Herberto, *The Fruit of Thy Womb*, 191–2
Sarban (John W. Wall), *The Sound of His Horn*, 26
Sawyer, Andy, 18, 219
Saxton, Josephine, *Queen of the States*, 33
Scalzi, John, *Old Man's War*, 36
Schoenberg, Arnold, 131
Scholes, Robert, 4, 45
Schuyler, George, *Black Empire*, 172
science and science fiction, 18, 202–17
science fiction
  'academic invasion', 41
  assessment of courses, 176–7, 242–3
  British science fiction, 35
  challenges to the canon, 10–11
  classification, 42, 45–7, 220, 231
  conceptions of the future, 8–9
  critical terms, 39, 41–2, 153
  definitions, 21, 38–52, 86, 103–5, 174–5, 208–9, 235
  editors, 27–8, 31–2, 38, 43, 105, 118, 149, 226
  first college courses, 3–4
  'First SF', 6–7, 9, 12–14, 16–17
  genre categories, 52
  Golden Age, 14–16, 28, 41, 102–15, 117–20, 137, 183, 185, 222, 224, 226, 252
  Gothic mode, 24–5, 36n, 49, 175
  growing literary sensibility of, 2–3
  history of, 7, 12, 21–37, 116
  imperial tropes in, 175–6
  language of, 9–10
  Latin American science fiction, 179–98
  literalizing the metaphor, 10, 51
  magazines, 27–30, 35, 43
  pedagogical value, 5–6, 13, 16, 18, 77–8, 104, 118, 147, 171
  preconceptions of, 11
  race and ethnicity, 9
  reference books, 5
  themes, 46–8
Science Fiction Research Association, 4, 38, 49
Science Fiction Studies, 4, 38, 134
scientific romance, 7, 13, 13–14, 49, 69, 71–85

scientifiction, 25, 27, 37n, 237
Scott, Melissa
  Shadow Man, 150
  Trouble and Her Friends, 156
Scott, Ridley, *Blade Runner*, 135, 136, 144, 176
Serviss, Garrett P., *Edison's Conquest of Mars*, 25
Shakespeare, William, 11, 144, 154
  The Tempest, 101, 152–4, 197
Sheckley, Robert, 121
  Options, 133
Sheers, Owen, *Resistance*, 27
Sheldon, Alice (James Tiptree Jr), 2, 122, 153, 160, 230, 255
  'And I Awoke and Found Me Here on the Cold Hill Side', 151–4, 159
  'Houston, Houston, Do You Read?', 125, 156
  James Tiptree Jr. Award, 147
  'The Women Men Don't See, 10, 33, 124, 152, 155, 200n, 222, 225, 230
  'Your Faces, O My Sisters! Your Faces Filled of Light', 158
Sheldon, Raccoona, *see* Sheldon, Alice
Shelley, Mary
  Frankenstein, 24, 40, 55, 74, 137, 156, 221
  The Last Man, 24
Shiel, M.P., 72
  The Purple Cloud, 227
Shippey, Tom, 42, 235
Silverberg, Robert
  Dying Inside, 32
  New Dimensions, 119–20
  Son of Man, 32, 122
Simak, Clifford D., *City*, 100
Singh, Vandana, *The Woman Who Thought She was a Planet, and Other Stories*, 172
Sinisalo, Johanna, *Not Before Sundown*, 36
Sisk, David, 60
Six Million Dollar Man, The, 156
Skinner, B.F., *Walden Two*, 56
Sladek, John, *The Steam Driven Boy*, 132
Sleight, Graham, 6
Slonczewski, Joan, *A Door into Ocean*, 158
Smith, Cordwainer, 29

'Alpha Ralpha Boulevard', 122
'The Ballad of Lost C'Mell', 29
'The Dead Lady of Clown Town', 29
Smith, E.E.
  'Lensman' series, 27, 90, 91
  'Skylark' series, 27
Souza, Marcel, *The Order of the Day*, 191
space opera, 27–8, 30, 33, 35–40, 42, 46–7, 88, 90, 96, 100, 126
Spinrad, Norman
  Bug Jack Barron, 122, 124–5
  definition of science fiction, 44
Stableford, Brian, 4, 11, 49, 72–4, 77
Stapledon, Olaf, 21, 72, 214
  Last and First Men, 27, 73, 82, 131
  Star Maker, 82, 131
Star Trek, 2, 14, 33, 90–1, 159
Star Trek: Deep Space Nine, 156
Star Trek: The Next Generation, 156
Star Wars, 2, 14, 33, 69, 90–1, 100
steampunk, 13, 36, 42, 46, 73, 83–4, 144
Stephenson, Neal, *Snow Crash*, 34
Sterling, Bruce, 2
  The Difference Engine (with William Gibson), 83
  Islands in the Net, 34
  Mirrorshades, 34, 225, 230
Stevenson, Robert Louis, *The Strange Case of Dr Jekyll and Mr Hyde*, 25
Stoker, Bram, *Dracula*, 76, 156
Stone, Leslie F., 12
'The Conquest of Gola', 152, 154
Stravinsky, Igor, 131
Stross, Charles, 34–5
  Accelerando, 34
Strugatsky, Arkady and Boris, 214
Stuart, Don A., *see* John W. Campbell
Sturgeon, Theodore, 15, 28, 44
  definition of science fiction, 44
  More Than Human, 86
  Venus Plus X, 157
Subiela, Eliseo
  Hombre mirando alsudeste (*The Man Facing Southeast*), 181–2
  No te mueras sin decirme adónde vas (*Don't Die Without Telling Me Where You Are Going*), 181–2
subjunctivity, 45, 150, 157, 235, 239

Suvin, Darko, 4, 7, 10, 40, 42, 45, 56–7, 104, 150, 183, 226, 233–5, 242
Swift, Jonathan, 40
  Gulliver's Travels, 23, 74
  'A Modest Proposal', 142

Taine, John, *The Time Stream*, 100
Tavares, Braulio, 'Stuntmind', 186–7
Tenn, William, 38
Tepper, Sheri S.
  The Gate to Women's Country, 158
  Gibbon's Decline and Fall, 33
Thomas, Sheree, *Dark Matter*, 172, 229
Tiptree, James Jr, *see* Sheldon, Alice
Tolkien, J.R.R., *The Lord of the Rings*, 183
tropicalization, 17, 192
Tsukamoto, Shinya, *Tetsuo*, 134
Turtledove, Harry, 48
Tuttle, Lisa, 'Wives', 152–4, 159
Twain, Mark, *A Connecticut Yankee in King Arthur's Court*, 26

Updike, John, *Brazil*, 197
utopias, 25, 49, 50, 55–71, 146, 158, 183, 210, 212

Vanasco, Alberto, 'Post-Boom Boom', 185
Vance, Jack, 'Turjan of Miir', 223
Van der Rohe, Mies, 131
Van Vogt, A.E., 96–7, 226
  Slan, 96–7, 149
  The Voyage of the Space Beagle, 28
  The Weapon Shops of Isher, 28, 224
  The World of Null-A, 97
Varley, John
  The Ophiuchi Hotline, 33
  'Options', 156
  Steel Beach, 166
Veiga, José J., *Misplaced Machine and Other Stories*, 188–9
Verne, Jules, 6, 13, 27, 40, 73–7, 232
  Around the Moon, 77, 81
  Around the World in Eighty Days, 77
  From the Earth to the Moon, 25, 77
  Hector Servadac, 75–7, 81
  Journey to the Centre of the Earth, 23
  Robur the Conqueror, 25
  Twenty Thousand Leagues under the Sea, 25, 76–7

Vinge, Vernor, 48
Voltaire (François-Marie Arouet)
  Contes, 74
  Micromègas, 23
Vonarburg, Elisabeth, *Silent City*, 156
Vonnegut, Kurt, 30, 121, 132–3
  Breakfast of Champions, 133
  Cat's Cradle, 122, 133
  Slaughterhouse, 5, 133, 212

Wachowski brothers, *The Matrix*, 144, 176
Walpole, Horace, *The Castle of Otranto*, 24
Watson, Ian, 35
Weinbaum, Batya, 11
Weinbaum, Stanley, *The New Adam*, 100, 149
Weir, Peter, *The Truman Show*, 142
Weiss, Margaret (with Tracy Hickman), *Dragon Wing*, 223
Weller, Archie, *Land of the Golden Clouds*, 165
Wells, H.G., 2, 6, 11, 26, 28, 30, 40, 58, 60, 62–3, 68–9, 72–4, 77–83, 131, 222
  The First Men in the Moon, 26, 81
  The Invisible Man, 26
  The Island of Doctor Moreau, 26, 78–9, 152
  Men Like Gods, 56
  A Modern Utopia, 56
  The New Adam, 100
  The Sleeper Awakes, 26
  The Time Machine, 26, 61, 68, 83, 78, 221–4, 226, 235, 241
  Things to Come, 236
  The War of the Worlds, 25, 79–80, 221, 244
  The World Set Free, 212
West, William, 'The Last Man', 158
Westfahl, Gary, 14, 40, 86
  The Mechanics of Wonder, 11, 105, 226, 233
White, T.H., *Earth Stopped*, 27
Wilcox, Don, 149
Wilcox, Fred McLeod, *Forbidden Planet*, 100–1, 104–5, 108–9

Wilkins, John, *The Discovery of a World in the Moone*, 23
Williamson, Jack, 48, 113
  After World's End, 88
  Darker Than You Think, 156
  The Legion of Time, 89
  Wonder's Child, 187
Wingrove, David, 49
  Trillion Year Spree (with Brian W. Aldiss), 11, 49
Wittig, Monique, *Les Guérillères*, 158
Wolfe, Gary K., 4, 12–13, 38, 150, 183, 195, 226, 236
Wolfe, Gene, 5, 6, 228–9
  Book of the New Sun, 34, 223–4, 239–40
  The Fifth Head of Cerberus, 225, 228, 235
  'The Woman Who Loved the Centaur Pholus', 223
Wollheim, Donald, 124
  definition of science fiction, 49
Woolf, Virginia, 131, 150
  The Waves, 131
world-building, 51–2, 121
Wright, Peter, 18, 242
Wright, Ronald, *A Scientific Romance*, 13, 26
Wylie, Philip, *The Disappearance*, 158
Wyndham, John, 7, 227
  The Chrysalids, 31
  The Day of the Triffids, 31, 224, 227, 240
  The Midwich Cuckoos, 240

Yamashita, Karen Tei, *Through the Arc of the Rainforest*, 17, 192, 194, 197
Yazek, Lisa, 11, 14–15, 102, 230

Zamyatin, Yevgeny, *We*, 26, 55, 60, 62, 63–4
Zaramella, Juan Pablo, 'Viaje al Marte' ('Trip to Mars'), 180–1
Zelazny, Roger, 'A Rose for Ecclesiastes', 122
Zoline, Pamela, 122
  'The Heat Death of the Universe', 32, 119, 125, 132, 136, 225, 227